TWISTED TIDES

Are they fated to love
or drown in their secrets?

STEPHANIE GIDRON

"The heart of man is very much like the sea. It has its storms, it has its tides, and in its depths, it has its pearls too."

-Vincent Van Gogh

"And now that you don't have to be perfect, you can be good."
                                        -John Steinbeck

ISBN: 979-8-9991525-0-3

Cover design by: Miblart
Library of Congress Control Number: 2018675309
Printed in the United States of America

To my mother, who always keeps me from drowning.

CONTENTS

TWISTED TIDES PLAYLIST

I Can't Help Myself - Nobody's Angel

Part Of Your World - Jodi Benson

Pocketful Of Sunshine - Natasha Bedingfield

Beautiful Girls - Sean Kingston

Feels Like Tonight - Daughtry

Don't Trust Me - 3OH!3

With You - Chris Brown

Shadow Of The Day - LINKIN PARK

Take A Bow - Rihanna

4 Minutes - Madonna ft. Justin Timberlake & Timberland

Lollipop - Lil Wayne

No Air - Jordin Sparks & Chris Brown

Say - John Mayer

Viva La Vida - Coldplay

Bleeding Love - Leona Lewis

Dog Days Are Over - Florence & The Machine

PROLOGUE

The First Swim

Neera

Eleven feet beneath the surface of her primary school's pool, the pressure weighed down on her from all sides as the blue, liquid blanket almost smothered her hearing. The chlorine water that managed to enter her nose singed her nostrils, her chest burning as she fought against her human instinct to breathe. *Burning...*

Just one minute...Maybe two.

Sure, a minute seemed like plenty of time...but she could go longer.

Pushing the ache in her chest aside and the usual alarm bells to the back of her head, ten-year-old Neera let her mind wander.

Her mountain of homework.

Her annoying teacher, Mrs. Burke, who always picked on her despite never raising her hand.

Her best friend since she was five, Elayne Ukiyo, who just couldn't get that studying did not mean watching the newest episode of Buffy the Vampire Slayer.

Her overbearing dad who cut his hours at work to watch over her every move, especially after what happened to her mum.

Her mum who died two weeks ago.

Two weeks, three days, and twelve hours ago, to be exact.

Burning...

Her dad had told her it was a car accident, which so happened to be Neera's birthday and the day they were supposed to have their first swim together. Neera learned to swim as soon as she hit the water as a baby. She was a natural.

"My Little Guppy" was what her mum would always say.

Although her mum never physically swam with her, Neera always counted on her to shower her in encouragement from the shore.

One day–the night before Neera's 10th birthday–they threw a girls' night while her dad worked late at the office. Colorful blankets and sheets were draped over their table and chairs, creating a tiny castle in their dining room.

Inside was everything a sleepover needed: nail polish, chocolate chip cookies, pizza, and primary school gossip. Her mum might not have been as hands-on as she would've wanted because of her fear of water, but she supported Neera through everything while being the coolest mum ever.

She is her best friend. Was.

While braiding her hair, her mum planned a very special gift to give Neera for her birthday. Not only was she giving her a physical gift, she was going to face her fear and finally swim with her. That she was ready to do it, and she wouldn't be able to do it with anyone else but her daughter.

Neera was ecstatic to experience something so monumental yet sort of nervous at the same time. She couldn't even sleep that night because of the anticipation.

What if her mum accidentally got a cramp while swimming? What if she almost drowned? Those thoughts had invaded her mind, but she immediately swept them away.

Neera would find a way to keep her safe, that was what.

The next day, her mum handed her a stack of fluffy pancakes stuffed with chocolate chips and slathered in maple syrup. She beautifully sang Neera a birthday song while her dad clapped along. He wasn't much of a singer, but Neera felt the same enthusiasm emanating from him as well.

Neera and her mum danced while singing to Neera's new favorite song, "I Can't Help Myself", in their dark green SUV on her way to school. She knew the entire dance routine by heart at that point. She must've inherited her dad's singing abilities, yet her mum jammed along as if she was the next tween pop star.

They ended their impromptu concert with her mum kissing her forehead right before dropping Neera off at school.

"Always remember how special you are, my Little Guppy! Love you!"

That was the last time she would see her.

When Neera's dad picked her up from school in his black two-seater, her dad's red eyes and dark, puffy face looked ominous. The car ride was sickeningly silent as dark clouds loomed over them. The low hum of the engine added an overly inflated sense of dread the longer the ride went on.

He didn't even try to hide it or sugar-coat it. After what felt like forever, he admitted that the last time he heard from her mum, she was going out to finish some errands. He kept emphasizing that he should've been the one to take the SUV.

Then he received a phone call from the police saying she was in a car accident. Her SUV was found crumpled and burnt at the bottom of a cliff overlooking the Pacific Ocean. She didn't make it.

Neera couldn't think. Couldn't breathe.

Burning...Fire...

When her dad tried to comfort her, something broke. Guilt flooded her mind.

Did she get hurt trying to do something for her birthday?

Was it because she was nervous about the swim?

Did fear drive her to destruction? Did the pressure distract her into an accident?

So many questions, yet they all led to one conclusion. It was the one that would stick with Neera forever: Her mum's demise was all Neera's fault.

Some birthday.

For the next two weeks, Neera mentally withdrew from her studies and then physically withdrew from her classmates and friends. That was when her classmates started to call her all sorts of names, like *weirdo* and *freak*.

Those incidents didn't hurt as much as the look of pity from her teachers, who knew what had happened. Elayne, the only person Neera directly told, tried to distract her with sleepovers and after-school study sessions, but Neera could sense the underlying *pity*. Her world was no longer full of color and optimism, but lonely and bleak. A world of possibilities and music was now hollow with unbearable silence and unwarranted fear.

Her dad became overbearing. Always making her call him when she hung out at Elayne's house and always hovering, when all Neera wanted to do was hide. It strained their relationship more—a constant reminder of what happened.

Everything came at her from all sides, and she felt trapped. Confined in a pitiful cage. The only way she ever felt the walls slacken was when she swam...

Her lungs were on fire, pleading for release. Her body was immersed in only the sound of her heart beating in her ears.

Just one more minute. Her vision darkened as her eyelids slid closed.

An image of her mum's long, wavy dark hair tickling her cheeks while watching *The Sea Princess* for the fifth time appeared. Her slender, olive-skinned fingers gently twisted Neera's curly, dark strands to make an intricate French braid. Her perfect, Grecian nose crinkled as she accidentally snagged a stubborn curl. Her jade green eyes beamed with unconditional love at her child.

Her warm smile always made Neera feel safe...

Neera thought she heard a voice above her. A pocket of air escaped her lips, her lungs reaching capacity. Annoyed at her body's betrayal, yet relieved some of the pressure in her chest lessened, she ignored the interruption and returned to her memory.

Her mum sang along with the Sea Princess in "Part of Your World." She might be biased, but Neera had never heard anyone sing as enchantingly as her mum. Her mum nudged her to join in despite Neera's initial protests, but she sang anyway. Only because no matter how she sounded, she was loved beyond comparison.

Singing will never be the same. And she hadn't sung a song since...

Neera felt a hand grip her wrist and tug upwards before she could get to the climax of the song.

NO! I wasn't finished. I was almost there!

Her eyes shot open in exasperation, and it took her a second to adjust to the chlorine.

The hand was attached to...a boy?

She tried to yank her arm away, but the boy held firmer. He continued swimming upwards, pulling her along until they broke the surface. Probably too preoccupied playing hero to notice her eyes were open and her mouth had released the trapped air. He impressively launched his body over the edge, then dragged Neera along, rolling her on her back.

He freaking believed she was DROWNING!

She internally cringed.

With no other reasonable choice, Neera snapped her eyelids shut, held her breath again, and relaxed her face. Hopefully, he'd retrieve an adult and she could sneak away before he even noticed.

After two quick pumps to her chest, which was absolutely painful, Neera realized she couldn't take it anymore. What if he tried to give her mouth-to-mouth like in those romance movies she "accidentally" stumbled upon?

Her eyelids shot open and were greeted by warm hazel

eyes, a slightly tan face with short brown hair plastered to his head, and a tiny cut over his thick eyebrow. Her heart thumped feverishly in...nervousness? Attraction? Shame?

Yeah, it had to be shame.

He was kind of cute and a bit familiar, but she couldn't put her finger on a name. Maybe someone she passed by in the hallway. It didn't matter since the wrongdoer rudely interrupted her alone time, and properly bruised her chest.

Besides, Neera was not interested in anyone, especially after losing the one person she loved the most. Well, possibly her poster of Prince Eric from *The Sea Princess* movies.

It was just something about this boy in particular that seemed...intriguing.

Panic weighed down on her chest in the absence of his arm pumps.

Neera really liked his face...unfortunately, it just so happened to be an inch away from hers.

LIAM

So, saving a life wasn't on the agenda today...

Liam Dern was technically classified as a new kid. Although he was so used to moving back and forth between Virginia and California, being "new" was really getting old. The beauty of being the "new kid" meant people were always drawn to him.

They usually found him mysterious when he sat alone at lunch, but his style and "picture-perfect" smile tended to ease other students' discomfort. Thus, meeting new people and making acquaintances came effortlessly–whether he liked it or not. It didn't take long for him to become popular at his latest elementary school.

Consequently, his unpredictable lifestyle meant he never had a best friend or developed long-term relationships he could grow up with...

But none of that mattered to Liam. The only things that mattered were his family, playing football for fun, and impressing his dad, *The* Dan Dern.

His dad, a famous microbiologist and genetic researcher, came from a long line of scientists. Eventually, it would be Liam's turn. Despite their constant traveling, his dad had consistently instilled in Liam the importance of STEM, obedience, and–most importantly–loyalty to family above everything else. Liam and his baby brother, Danny, were his legacy, and that was something Liam would always hold dear. That meant Liam had to maintain good grades, listen to his parents, and try not to get in trouble.

Be their perfect son.

Their perfect heir to the Dern's Research legacy.

He could play football in his free time. No big deal.

Right after school, Liam beelined straight to the football field behind the school and scrimmaged with some boys he met at lunch. There was nothing like the rush he got from the earthy scent of the grass, his teammates shouting plays, and the opposing team chasing him down. He could mess up, get dirty, and get hurt. He could laugh out loud and howl at the unforgiving sun. Liam felt like he could do anything.

Like he could breathe.

The pressure of expectations from his dad would disappear.

Noticing the time on his sports watch, he realized he had to go home to do his homework and, once again, adorn his mask of perfection.

After Liam showered in the locker room, retouched his short hair, and changed into his spare clothes that he kept on him, he paused his movements at the sound of *The Sea Princess*, or whatever, blasting from the indoor pool. He didn't expect anyone, other than his football buds, to be at school that late in the day. Usually, it wouldn't bother him and he would just hurry home, but something just didn't feel right. The future researcher in him felt compelled to check it out.

So he pushed the swing door open and entered the pool area. The chlorine smell smacked him in the nose, causing it to twitch. His sneakers squeaked against the tile floor as he shuffled closer to the large pool. It looked pretty empty as if no one had occupied it for a while. The only things present were a small, pink CD player emitting the music from a bottom bleacher seat, small wire-rimmed glasses, and a green, tribal-patterned backpack that he may have seen before but couldn't recall.

Did someone just leave their stuff here?

"Hello?" Liam called out, fixing the collar of his Polo shirt. "Anyone here?"

No response.

Wait, there was a response. He noticed a few bubbles emerge from the left side of the pool. The deep end where the adults always tell them to avoid. He cautiously stepped closer to the edge and noticed a body at the very bottom.

A kid-sized body.

Liam's initial reaction was to run and grab an adult, but he didn't know how long that person was underwater. He had to act quickly. Liam might not be the best swimmer in the world, but he knew the basics. It shouldn't be that difficult.

Wasting enough time, he took a huge breath. His chest expanded like a balloon before he dove into the forbidden deep end. Pushing through the pressure in his ears and the chlorine burning his eyes, Liam pushed further down towards the... girl?

Long, black hair fanned out behind her. A long-sleeved, light-green swimsuit complemented her light brown skin perfectly as her arms were spread wide. Liam refocused when he noticed her eyes were closed and she wasn't moving, like a statue.

He grabbed her floating wrist and started tugging upwards. Pure adrenaline fueled his already sore legs to propel him towards the surface. She was heavy for a small girl. Despite the use of one arm, he concentrated on the surface with no other thought but inhaling precious air.

Was it always this difficult to rescue someone? Those episodes of Baywatch made it seem so easy.

As she laid flat on the tile floor, unmoving and eyes closed, Liam started to panic a little. Should he go get help? He remembered that in one of the episodes, the lifeguard would dramatically push on the person's chest and then blow in their mouth...*or was it the other way around?*

She was kind of pretty, so the idea of touching her made him extremely nervous; however...her life was at stake!

So Liam positioned his hands on a spot in the center of her chest and pumped his straight arms as hard as he could. After a couple of pumps, her eyebrows furrowed. *Was it supposed to hurt?*

Here was the part he dreaded.

He turned towards the door, hoping actual help would show up, and then turned back to her. Filling his lungs, Liam hovered over her partially open lips. So close he could see tiny, brown dots sprinkled across her nose.

Focus, Liam! You're trying to save a life here!

Her eyes bulged open. *Oh crap.*

She braced her palms against his chest and PUSHED Liam on his butt. Momentarily stunned, he blinked a few times, then gave a reassuring smile.

"I saved your life!" Liam beamed, pride inflating his chest.

The girl rolled her eyes. *Rolled them!*

She sat up unharmed and retorted with annoyance, "I wasn't drowning, genius. How did you even see me?"

Liam's smile twitched. He couldn't believe what he was hearing. Maybe there was still water in his ears. He shook his head, trying to clear the imaginary water. "I saw you...with my own eyes! You weren't even moving!"

"Yeah, that was on purpose," she huffed with her chin tilted up and arms crossed over her chest. "And I almost set a new record until you ruined it!"

What the heck?!

Exasperation heated his face. Maybe a little embarrassment. He roughly ran a hand through his soaked hair as a frown pulled down the edges of his mouth. She looked frozen underwater, yet she had the NERVE to be angry at him for saving her life. *Ungrateful!*

Liam was starting to regret ruining his clothes. How was he supposed to explain his wet clothes to his parents?

"Sorry, Mom and Dad, I got soaked from saving someone who wasn't even in danger."

After closer inspection of her sea-green eyes and heart-shaped face, recognition slapped him in the face. One of his football buddies mentioned a girl in this school with light brown skin and green eyes who was weird and quiet. They heard some dark things happened to her family, and she had to go into witness protection, like in those crime shows. Liam wasn't sure, and he usually didn't care about gossip, but with the way she reacted to him, he started to believe it.

Guilt churned in his stomach, so instead of arguing further, he stood up and offered a hand. Hesitantly, she took it, and his heart overreacted. He pulled her up, but for some reason, he didn't let go.

"Sorry for ruining your world record," Liam muttered with a smirk, attempting to distract from how the cells of her palm naturally fit into the cells of his hand. The mysterious girl was making him feel strange, and he couldn't logically explain it. The longer she looked at him, the longer he wanted to hold her hand; and that in itself, was too freaky. He had to get out of there.

Fortunately for him, she was equally freaked out enough to snap her hand away, before he could do something stupid like *ask to hang out* or something.

"It's okay," she muttered nervously while rubbing her arm with that same hand. "My name is–HEY!"

That was all Liam heard as he hustled out of the pool area, out of the doors of the locker room, and outside, where he could finally breathe.

THE DREAM

Chapter 1

Neera

8 YEARS LATER...

It was dark. Neera was surrounded by a cool body of water. The chasmic blue body wrapped around her like a blanket, like a long-awaited hug. Although something was different about this one. Not because the water was devoid of any other life despite its immense size. Not because she was wearing her baggy denim overalls underwater instead of her usual green swimsuit.

It was the fact that she was breathing as if she was on land.

Her body floated, and her hair fanned around her, but she was breathing effortlessly. The longer she remained there, the more sinister it felt—like something was lurking and watching from the shadows. Her heart increased its pace as apprehension kicked in. The pressure only increased with the anticipation.

Neera was uncomfortable, almost itching to leave. The absence of water sloshing in her ears was the last straw. She screamed and yelled to get anyone's attention, her voice cut off by the water weighing down on her chest.

She needed to get out. Fast.

Her body kicked into swimmer mode as she tried to swim upwards, quickening her movements until a chilling feeling swept over her.

There was no surface.

Only more water.

The pressure only amplified the longer she was in there, and her panic turned into full-blown terror.

Nowhere to escape. Nowhere to run.

But she had to try.

Neera pushed and pushed until her arms cramped from the effort, and her legs couldn't move, but she kept going. It was natural. It was right to keep moving up because up meant freedom.

When her motivation waned, a green light appeared above her. It glowed brightly despite the darkness surrounding it. Its glow was so otherworldly that it beckoned Neera towards it. Maybe it was the sun. Either way, she had to take the chance. She mustered all her strength and reached towards the green anomaly, stretching her fingers to freedom. So close...

When she reached it, she burst through the surface of her school's indoor pool with a sudden desire to breathe fresh air. The large windows that encased the pool allowed ample sunlight to brighten the space, a stark contrast to the darkness of the water below.

Neera looked around, noticing the usual empty pool, standard bleachers, and on-site emergency safety equipment. She looked down at the distorted image of her body, suddenly adorning a green one-piece swimsuit. She must've been submerged a little too long and started to hallucinate.

"Deep breaths, Neera," she coached herself as she tried to calm down. Maybe there was such a thing as "too much swimming."

As Neera placed her hands on the edge of the pool, she felt something clasp her ankle and tug her down. Shocked by the sudden movement, she wasn't able to grip the edge and plunged back into the water. The thing, never letting up, continued to drag her deeper into the dark depths below. She silently screamed and flailed her arms, trying to fight against it.

Chancing a glance down at the culprit, there was a wrinkled, pale, but surprisingly strong hand attached to her ankle like a chain. No face or other body parts were visible.

As she attempted to kick the hand with her other foot, more hands of different varieties sprouted out of the darkness and attached themselves to both of her ankles. With the added weight, Neera had no choice but to uselessly sink into the abyss.

Feeling helpless, she looked up for any succor, and all that greeted her was the taunting, green light.

Neera awakened in her bed. The sunlight pouring from her bedroom window caused her eyes to squint. Still frightened and a bit sweaty, she felt around for her wire-rimmed glasses on the bedside table. After putting them on, she scanned her room.

Everything looked normal. Her CD player was still on her dresser. Posters of Avril Lavine, Michael Phelps, and the one and only Bajan princess, RiRi, adorned her beige walls. The "always-slightly-ajar" door, the earth-toned decor, and lastly, the picture of her mum smiling brightly as she hugged her daughter, with the words "My Girls" etched on the bottom of the ceramic frame, were all in their usual positions.

She sighed in relief that this was her reality and not another dumb dream. They had become more frequent in the past few days. Instead of worrying about them, she chalked them up to hormones, suppressed emotions from eight years ago, or just too much of her dad's hot chocolate. None of those things could be changed.

Her dad poked his dark brown head into her room with his eyes closed. He cheerfully asked in his thick British accent, "Ready for school, love?"

"Uh...I'm working on it," Neera responded as she shot out of her bed and ran to the door, hiding her body behind it. Sure, she was used to her dad being a "Papa Bear," but she was almost eighteen for crying out loud! He shouldn't monitor her every bloody move. Hiding in her seashell onesie and fuzzy blue socks also didn't help, hence why she had to preserve the rest of her dignity behind the door.

With his eyes closed, he urged, "Well, hurry before your

breakfast gets chilly."

Neera rolled her eyes, but she agreed to finish getting dressed.

Once he left, Neera took a shower and put on her outfit that Elayne thought was "freakin' lame": a pink miniskirt over her denim bell bottoms, a green cami over a white blouse, and brown buckle sandals. She also didn't forget the mandatory bikini that she wore underneath. Neera had no idea what Elayne was talking about. Her style was original and, more importantly, she could blend in with her classmates. No one bothered her or pitied her...at least not to her face. It worked so far in the steel jungles of high school, and with it being her last year, she intended to keep this anonymity going until she walked out those front doors for the last time.

Neera met her dad in the kitchen, scrunching her nose at the Full English breakfast that he unfailingly prepared because it was "healthy": toast, baked beans, eggs, and some black tea with a bit of milk. Sometimes yams with egg stew. Why he couldn't just throw some sugary cereal and milk in a bowl was beyond her comprehension.

He greeted her again with a big smile and a kiss on her forehead, his thick glasses grazing her hairline. Then they fell into their usual morning routine of eating, conversation filled with dad jokes and genuine chuckles, and then him dropping her off at school with a rib-crushing hug.

Neera never once mentioned the dreams, and she didn't plan to. A small part of her guessed the dreams were trying to warn her of something, like impending danger, but she would immediately disregard it as one of her anxious thoughts, or whatever her primary school counselor called it.

The frequency of the dreams did seem somewhat alarming to Neera for them to mean anything, but in order to move on–to be normal–she HAD to believe they were just one of the perks of growing up.

LIAM

When the lunch bell rang, Liam was ready to catch up on some much-deserved sleep. Today's lunch consisted of baked spaghetti with a side of peas and a carton of apple juice, which he didn't mind skipping out on.

He discovered an empty table on the far end of the large cafeteria, perfect for his impromptu nap. He sat with folded arms on the table and buried his head in the gap between them. Despite the cacophony of laughter and gossip, he immediately passed out. Between maintaining his 4.0 GPA, his after-school football scrimmages, and attempting to have a social life, Liam hadn't been getting much sleep. The recent dreams didn't exactly help, either.

His mind conjured up the images that had been haunting him for the past two nights.

Instead of sweet darkness, his mind placed him at the edge of a cliff overlooking sharp boulders and destructive waves crashing into each other. The air was thick with foreboding. He looked behind him at an inky forest with mysterious beings lurking within it. Shifting shadows and hissing noises made the hair on the back of his neck stand.

He was trapped.

Every time he tried to choose the forest, he couldn't move. He unwaveringly remained in the same position as anxiety crawled over his body like fire ants. Usually, he woke up when the pressure became unbearable, but this time, fate decided to nudge him towards the obvious death-sentence of the waves. As much as Liam wanted to turn around, his legs disobeyed him as he shambled to the very edge of the cliff.

The slippery dirt underneath him gave way before he tumbled down.

He could physically feel his stomach drop while his heart stopped for just a second. This was it. He was a goner. The world rapidly bled together in terrifying blues and browns until it suddenly stopped, the water taunting him from below. He was suspended from something.

Liam looked up and noticed a light brown hand gripping his forearm. He chanced a look up...and it was Neera. Her sea-green eyes held him in a trance as her lips thinned in struggle. She used another hand to clutch his arm and pull him up. All Liam could do was stare.

Why was she helping him? What did any of it mean?

Not a single word was exchanged, but her intentions were clear. She was trying to save him. An uncomfortable feeling washed over him...like he didn't deserve to be saved.

He gazed at her face again as if trying to find some semblance of regret. Of defeat. Nothing.

She was every bit determined.

With no control over his body, Liam suddenly grabbed her wrist with his other hand. She looked almost relieved in Liam's unanticipated efforts. Unfortunately, her pretty face immediately soured as he shifted his weight downwards, pulling her down with him as they plunged into the rocky waves below...

"Liam, wake up!" An annoying yet familiar voice yelled next to his ear.

He startled awake and noticed his previously deserted table filled with his peers. It didn't go unnoticed that the popular kids tend to gravitate towards Liam despite his nonchalance toward the whole "high school popularity hierarchy."

Jessica, the head cheerleader, and her triad of "besties" stared pointedly at him from across the table. Next to him was Nate, captain of the Pasa Verde Panthers football team. His chestnut brown hand was on Liam's shoulder as he raised an eyebrow at him, no doubt the perpetrator who woke him up. The guy was annoying as hell, but an impressive football player, so Liam let his antics slide most of the time.

Liam shook him off, stretched his arms overhead, and squinted as he adjusted to the fluorescent lights.

"What's up?" He asked no one in particular.

Jessica leaned in. "Who are you taking to prom?"

Typical Jessica. Instead of being concerned about his sleep schedule, she refused to pass up a chance to be nosy and gain something from it. Everyone nodded in anticipation.

"Uh..." Liam ran a hand through his hair as he tried to think of an excuse.

That was definitely none of her business, but people couldn't just tell her that. Not because she was scary...okay, maybe a little.

Just as he was about to respond, Neera and another girl walked by their table with lunch trays. The other girl was giggling about something, and Neera was listening intently with a soft smile. Her wire-framed eyes ended up locking with his, and that smile faltered a little.

Damn. Liam could look away or pretend he wasn't staring at her like a creep, but he didn't. Couldn't. That tightening feeling in his chest returned full-throttle, like his heart wanted to be somewhere else besides his chest.

Neera broke the contact, and they continued on their way as the tightening feeling finally released its grip on him.

His attention returned to Jessica, who rolled her eyes into oblivion at his obvious staring.

"Hope it's not that weirdo," Jessica nodded in Neera's direction, which unintentionally caused Liam to bristle visibly. "I mean, look at her clothes. She looks like a Sesame Street reject. And those dorky glasses? She must be blind or a total geek."

Everyone laughed except Liam, who remained silent. Okay, her fashion choices were a bit...eccentric, but she definitely didn't deserve this kind of hate. He thought it was cute at times. Besides, she openly expressed herself in her own way, and he admired her for that. These guys would rather die than be their true selves.

Now you're defending her like a boyfriend, genius!

"You know what I heard?" One of Jessica's minions added. Everyone leaned in as she continued. "Someone murdered her mom or something, and, like, she had to go into witness protection. They forced her to dress like a Special Ed kid to throw off the killer."

Liam seethed in his seat at what she was insinuating about Neera. That chick, who he couldn't care less what her name was, was the type that never had to use her brain to get what she wanted, but she had the nerve to disrespect Neera and kids with special needs. At that moment, his silence unintentionally conveyed acceptance of their disrespect and was only escalating things.

So he countered flatly, "That was the dumbest shit I've ever heard, even from you."

Everyone–especially the chick–was shocked by his response and fell silent. They weren't used to others challenging them. After a moment of awkwardness and the minion's face blushing a deeper pink, Nate and the other guys laughed to ease the tension.

"Hey, it's 2008," Nate said between chuckles. "We're about to have our first black president. Anything is possible."

Jessica flipped her blonde hair over her shoulder and scoffed. "I know for sure that she's bad news. Just stay away from her. I've known her since, like, the seventh grade and she gives everyone the creeps. Literally, go to prom with anyone else."

Liam's temple ached, maybe from the lack of sleep, because his tolerance for their bull was at zero. Instead of going back and forth with her, he snatched his bag and left the table. Class was going to start in ten minutes. Maybe he could get there early and finish napping before the bell rang.

He couldn't help but ruminate over what they said. There was no way their rattling was true, but his dream had definitely confused him. Almost like a bad omen.

Liam had only seen Neera in between classes and maybe asked her for a pencil or something insignificant like that, but that was it. Since the first time they met, he moved back to Virginia after fifth grade and didn't return to Pasa Verde until his sophomore year. He never got the chance to know her, and it wasn't like it was by choice. It was just that every time he strummed up the courage to, he would get lost in her enchanting eyes or her sweet smile, and that uncomfortable feeling would plague his chest.

Luckily, they never ran in the same circles, so avoiding her was easy. If that strange feeling in his chest, the demented dreams, and his peers' incessant teasing constituted anything, being around Neera would only lead to pain for the both of them.

All he knew was that no matter how he felt about her, for his sake, he had to stay away from Neera Ran.

THE DIVE

Chapter 2

Neera

"Did you see that Liam dude staring at you at lunch?"

Elayne squealed as she bobbed her head to RiRi's latest album while lying upside-down on Neera's bed, her black bangs splayed awkwardly. She had completely abandoned her history book during their "study session" and was currently absorbed in a family-sized pack of Oreos and gossip—more pertinent things.

Neera tried to ignore her BFF as she attempted to immerse herself in her history textbook. As usual, Elayne had a knack for compelling Neera to abandon her responsibilities–well, redirect her priorities, as she would so nicely put it.

So Neera started contemplating about the guy who constantly popped in and out of her life. Again.

But she wasn't going to admit that outright to Lay-Lay. She gave a one-sided shrug.

"Not really. I don't think it's that big of a deal."

"Oh, come on," Elayne countered in feigned annoyance. "You two totally had a moment. And he's stupid hot, like if Zac Efron and Jesse Metcalph had a hotter younger brother." She pointed an upside-down finger at Neera. "You better ask him to prom."

Neera's mouth gaped in disbelief. Maybe Lay-Lay had been upside-down for too long because that was the most ridiculous idea she had ever heard.

Neera and Liam have barely spoken to each other, and she thought that merited Neera to ask him out? It didn't matter that he was super smart, hot, and loaded...

Or that his warm, hazel eyes could drag anyone from a gloomy darkness like sunshine after a cloudy day.

Or that his square jawline was chiseled to perfection.

Or how perfectly styled and maintained his brown hair and preppy clothes were...

It didn't mean he was a good person, mainly since he hung out with that *witch*, Jessica, and her followers. Good people didn't hang out with awful people. That, in itself, gave him points on the "Jerk-hole Board." Not to mention, he was entirely out of her league.

So many signs pointed to untouchable. Why would she even bother?

Another part of her–the obviously insane part–imagined the first time they met. At her lowest, he could've passed the responsibility onto an adult, but he decided to help her. To save her without hesitation. He was the first person, other than Elayne, to treat her like a normal person and not some pitiful freak. The only one, actually.

Whenever they passed each other, his eyes always seemed to find hers. As if they were ships drifting towards a lighthouse or the roots of a tree soaking in rainwater. Every time she was around him, her stomach transformed into a butterfly pavilion, and yet, at the same time, her body felt tranquil, like a small wave caressing the shoreline.

Oh crap, she had a bigger crush on him than she thought. Familiar gloom accumulated and took over her mind.

Maybe I should ask him out. Then he'll reject me, and I'll never have to think about him ever again.

Neera pursed her lips and slapped her book closed, startling Elayne into a sitting position on the edge of the bed.

Her face was lined with concern.

"You're right," she smirked at Elayne's rightfully shocked expression at her words. "I'll ask Liam to prom...I still think he'll say no."

"But he might say yes!" Elayne exclaimed excitedly. She elicited enthusiasm as if she was the one taking the most significant risk of her life. A mischievous smile crossed her face, almost making Neera take back her decree. "BTW, if he says no, you still have me as your backup plan. Win-win situation."

Yeah, what could possibly go wrong? Neera snorted at herself.

The next day, Neera's nerves were working overtime. The prom was in just two days. Most people had their proposals and their gowns picked out by now. The school had posters plastered all over the blue lockers and white walls about the details on prom for a week. Announcements sounded over the speakers so the Senior class could remember that their exams were still happening after prom, while those same Seniors blatantly ignored them. Neera wasn't worried about the last-minute-ness since she was just going to borrow one of Elayne's outfits anyway.

After her last period, she texted Elayne to meet her by the AP Biology class lockers because Liam's locker was there. How she found his exact locker was classified. Like the supportive BFF she was, Elayne showed up in a minute flat, huffing and puffing. Neera kept her eyes trained on Liam's locker, like a hawk, while she fixed her two braids, and Elayne showered her in encouraging "Girl-boss" words.

A familiar face rounded the corner and opened his locker. His gray Polo suited his sun-kissed tan and athletic build, and his khaki shorts showed off his fit legs. On anyone else, Neera wouldn't have noticed since fashion wasn't her thing, but on him, it became a fascinating subject. Even his gray boat shoes looked regal on him. Liam looked every bit like a prince. Posh and unattainable.

Neera shook her head. *Let's just get this over with.*

After a few breaths, she plastered on what she hoped was a seductive smile and strutted towards Liam. From her peripheral, she could see the Sanderson sisters staring daggers at her from the other side of the lockers, but she ignored them. Confidence was key, and she couldn't let them deter her from diving in head first.

Liam's hazel eyes widened in shock when they landed on hers. That usual feeling in her stomach returned and almost caused Neera to run for the hills. This was a bad idea. The slap to reality will hurt like heck, but it was necessary. She smiled brighter to distract herself from the nervousness.

"Hey! Liam, right?" She could feel her glasses sliding off her nose bridge. He simply nodded slowly, with his jaw visibly tense. Not a good sign, but she pressed on regardless. "I don't think we've officially met, but my name is Neera."

Still silent.

Is this a good sign, or am I forking this up?

Neera bit her lower lip. She braced herself for the inevitable rejection. "I know it's pretty late, but prom is coming up...and I was wondering if you wanted to–"

SLAM!

Liam shut his locker door with just enough force to stop her speech. Neera's body jumped slightly. He closed his eyes and gritted his teeth.

"No." Just like that. *There it is.*

"Wha-what?" Neera spluttered.

He faced her fully, eyes open and filled with...Anger? Pain? Embarrassment?

"I know what you're going to ask, and I'm not interested." He ran a hand through the longer hair on top of his head. When Neera swallowed her words with a gulp, Liam's eyes roamed everywhere but her. He lowered his voice to barely a whisper. "I'm not even going."

With that, he turned on his heels with his backpack over his shoulder and scurried away, leaving Neera's carcass to be picked at by the bratty vultures.

The group swarmed her before she could escape and looked down on Neera. The pack leader, Jessica, shook her head as she held her books in her arms.

"You really thought he liked you, huh? You look like a stretched-out toddler."

The other girls surrounding her tsked. Those pitiful looks that Neera despised were their default expressions and the reason she disliked attention.

Neera glanced down at her outfit, which had been picked explicitly for Liam. It was her best stuff: rainbow-striped thigh-high socks with a pair of white sneakers, a green tank top to match her eyes, and denim overall shorts that displayed her "sensual side."

Guess not.

She started to consider their claims since Liam rejected her, and he failed to compliment her in any way or at least mention *nice-to-forking-meet-you.*

Neera's hands fisted briefly before relaxing. Violence only led to more violence; at least, that's what her parents taught her. Her parents didn't have a violent bone in their bodies. They only instilled that words work, and if she was ever in trouble, resolve it or get another adult to help. Even if Neera wanted to karate-chop them, she had no idea how. She had no choice but to verbally express her discontent...and hope the witches weren't feeling blood-thirsty.

As she was about to retaliate, Elayne shoved her way inside the sacrificial circle and tried to look all of them in the eyes with her long, straight hair swishing around.

"Unless you want your clip-ins to find a home in your throat, I suggest you guys leave. Now." Elayne glared at them with steel in her voice. Something about Lay-Lay, she was willing to attack anything. No matter how big, despite her 5'2 stature. That was what Neera adored about her spunky friend.

The vultures gave one last stink-eye and then scampered away, fortunately preserving their extensions for another day. Elayne hooked an arm around Neera and gave her a squeeze.

"Forget about him, Nee-Nee." She must've picked up on their body language during the failed conversation. "He's not worth it. And you still have me."

"Elayne," Neera began, still a bit overwhelmed about what happened. The Liam situation aside, she was tired of the bullying. Tired of the pitiful looks. Neera hoped she'd never have an encounter with Jessica, but it finally happened when she decided to come out of her shell. A reality slap would've been fine, but no, it had to be a gut punch.

This led to a wretched revelation: Her laid-back approach wasn't going to work after she graduated. People were always looking down on her, always keeping her under their feet. It would go on for the rest of her life if she didn't pick her head up and start doing whatever the heck she wanted. If she continued to avoid the spotlight.

Well, not anymore. "I need you to do something important for me."

Elayne eyed her best friend like a ticking time bomb.

"Sure, what is it? You need me to uppercut Jessica?" She asked as her fist punched upwards in a mock altercation.

"No..." It wasn't a bad idea, so she would table it for now. "Can you give me a makeover? I want to know what life is like in the sun for once."

Elayne stared as if she was processing what to say. A friend would say, *"You're perfect the way you are,"* but Lay-Lay was never one to pretend. Elayne moved in front of Neera with her ringed-covered fingers gripping her shoulders. A sneaky smile graced her fair-skinned face.

"Oh yeah. Let's step on some freaking necks."

LIAM

I'm literally the dumbest guy on the planet.

After getting sacked about four times by the opposing team, Liam discerned he needed a "Time-Out."

Literally.

They called Time, and his six teammates gathered around the metal bench, chugging their water or wiping their faces. Liam plopped down on a bench as he tried to catch his breath...and his thoughts. This was his time to let out his frustrations and forget about the day, but he couldn't when his "not-crush" was constantly haunting his mind.

Liam usually prided himself in his intelligence, but after what he said to Neera...he was seriously debating relocating again. The first real conversation he'd ever had with her almost made her cry, which was a bit excessive. All Liam wanted to do was keep her at a distance. He just wanted to say "no" and then move on to creepily watching her from afar.

His mind immediately conjured images of Neera's outfit, which was a bit zany but showed off her golden, slender legs for the first time. Her tank top complemented her eyes and hugged her torso like a glove. And yes, he'd been keeping tabs on her or whatever. He could go on for hours on just her eyes alone, especially how her glasses magnified them.

What was happening to him?

Cody, his football buddy, nudged Liam's shoulder, snapping him out of his perverted thoughts.

"What's up with you?" Cody asked, then took a sip of water from his water bottle. "If I knew you were gonna suck this bad, I would've chosen Clumsy Marvin instead."

Liam chuckled, scratching the back of his neck.

Was I that bad?

"Are you thinking about that Neera chick asking you out?"

Liam cut his eyes to Cody, then back to the field.

News must travel fast here.

He chose not to respond because, frankly, it was none of his business.

"I mean, she's definitely cute but kind of awkward. I don't really see you two together," Cody chuckled as he adjusted his shorts.

"No, I think he should take her," a husky guy chimed in, but Liam didn't know his name. "It might be one of those 'opposites attract'-kind of shit."

"You're right," Cody pointed at the guy. "Even better, she might even give it up faster."

The two guys cackled, despite Liam's scowl. It seemed Liam found some energy to take those two out in the next few downs.

He shook his head. "Let's just play another round."

Dinner time was the germane part of the day for Liam's family to cosplay the perfect nuclear family for two hours.

Dinner used to be an enjoyable time for Liam as a kid. From the surface, it looked normal. However, as young Liam grew up, he saw the underlining sham burrowed underneath. His mom was a housewife and stood by her husband through all the constant moving, and raising two sons. Just for his father, his role model at the time, to cheat on their mom while he was working "late". This shredded their perfect family facade to tatters, only from Liam's perception. To the rest of the world, they were still a happily married couple living in the ideal mansion. They said it was for their children, but he knew, truly, it was for their image.

Image was most important. Whether they liked it or not.

After his little brother set the table, everyone sat at their coordinated seats at the long Victorian-style oak table. Parents at the heads of the table, and the sons seated together on either side. The setting sun poured through the floor-to-ceiling windows onto their large spread of assorted foods. The caterer did a pretty good job.

His dad was served his plate first, then his mom served her kids, and served herself last. His dad boasted about how great the food looked to his wife. She smiled weakly at the attempt and promptly told them to bow their heads in grace.

After their prayer, his dad droned on about work and the latest discoveries on microorganisms. His mom pretended to care. Liam noticed that her frequent glances at her kids were a sign that she wasn't listening.

Danny pushed his green beans around his plate, silently eating his mashed potatoes and listening intently. Liam remembered when he was his age—so impressionable. He could be told anything and believe it as truth, not knowing that the truth was never told but discovered. Liam stared at his own plate of steak, mashed potatoes, and green beans. Uninterested in his rambling, he ate in silence.

"So..." His mom began, and Liam looked up in her direction, her brown eyes piercing him with interest. "I heard prom is coming up."

Liam inwardly cringed. *How many fucking times am I going to hear that this week?*

"Are you going? Do you have a date in mind?" His mom pressed. Her eyes brightened for the first time this whole evening.

"Honey, please," his dad scolded. Then he turned his scrutinizing eyes on his son. "You should be focusing on your AP Biology exam coming up. You don't have time to attend some ridiculous dance."

Before Liam could respond, his mom cut in. "That so-called dance was also when we had our first dance together."

"Hence why," his dad continued without his eyes leaving Liam. "Focusing on your studies is more important since you'll be inheriting the family's legacy soon. It'll actually benefit you in the long run."

His mom slammed her fork on the table, causing everyone to look in her direction. The bright excitement that saturated her eyes earlier transformed into pure fire. Even Danny shrunk from the tension.

"He's right, Liam," his mom plastered a smile on her face, which looked more like a grimace. "Your studies are important...but so is being young. You're eighteen years old, and it's the only prom you'll ever have. A wedding, however, is dispensable."

Liam was used to their opposing views on things. He learned, years ago, how to navigate between their bickering while simultaneously trying to keep them pleased. To be very honest, dating wasn't really something he was interested in. Technically he was no blushing virgin. He had hooked up with a few girls, even Jessica. However, they were never serious or past three dates since he was always busy. Prom was never on the table...

Until Neera almost asked him.

Maybe you should reconsider.

The thought of being stuffed in a penguin suit and pathetically asking a date's father to take her to a dance almost seemed tolerable if it was with Neera by his side.

You were supposed to stay away from Neera, or did you forget?

That small interaction was the most they'd ever spoken to each other, and he internally desired nothing more than to speak with her again. To be that close to her again. Liam wanted to know more about her without the judging eyes of his peers and without the pressure from his dad. Do what HE wanted for once.

Dangerous mindset.

It didn't help that his mom also encouraged Liam to live his life on his terms. Practically zealous at the idea of Liam straying away from his father's path. But his dad was right about focusing on his studies. His career. His...dream?

And that meant no distractions, no prom, and no Neera.

His dad grunted and glared at his wife.

His mom remained cool, taking a sip of her red wine.

I think dinner is officially over.

THE MAKEOVER

Chapter 3

Neera

"Damn all these beautiful girrrrrls~" Elayne's car speakers blasted as they cruised down to Fair Shore Mall after school.

When Neera decided to get a makeover, she wasn't expecting Lay-Lay to be so overzealous. She had to admit that her enthusiasm was a tiny bit offensive. Although, all her teen magazine reading was finally being put to good use.

The girls went from store to boutique, cringing at the overpriced items, and finally ended up at Charlotte Russe. Elayne greedily rummaged through every rack while Neera followed her around like a puppy, exploring the exciting world of teen fashion. Elayne came across a table of multi-colored, off-shoulder shirts, picked up a hot pink one, and held it in front of Neera.

"Let's get a couple of these shirts," Elayne demanded excitedly. She pointed to a stack of inappropriately deep V-neck, slim t-shirts. "And this shirt." She spun around to a table of assorted miniskirts. "You're so going to wear these from now on."

Neera scrunched her nose at everything. *Were these pieces even allowed in school?* "I don't know about this. I've never worn anything that showed off my body like this..."

Elayne dropped the pile of clothes into her shopping

cart. She looked Neera in the eyes and glared. "I thought you wanted to step on necks."

"I do, but–"

"But nothing," Elayne interrupted, then gripped both of Neera's shoulders. "You need clothes that are soft but tight, loose in the right places, but sexy. You won't turn heads the way you look NOW!"

Some customers glanced in their direction as Elayne shouted over the blaring, pop music. Neera's mouth gaped, completely mortified.

Elayne removed her hands and straightened Neera's straps. With a wince, she muttered. "Sorry, Nee-Nee."

Neera ran a hand across the offending cart's handle. After a moment she softened. "I did want this makeover. Still do. And despite your rudeness," she jokingly narrowed her eyes, then grinned. "I trust you."

Elayne returned the grin and took the cart handle.

"Okay. We'll buy these, then I'll pick the outfit for you to wear for your big debut and keep it at my house. Before school, you'll come over and we'll start the official makeover then. How does that sound?"

Absolutely absurd.

Neera nodded her head to shake off the negative thoughts, subsequently having to push her glasses back up her nose.

"Let's do it."

The morning before school started, Neera sorted through the pile of clothes Lay-Lay had forced upon her. They might've been more scantily clad than she was used to, but they weren't, somehow, too intimidating.

Her eyes roamed over the plain oversized tee and olive-green capris she would've worn to school if she wasn't on a mission. *Operation Neck-Stomp* would go into effect once she left her front door. Her dad didn't need to know her fashion transformation just yet.

Since Elayne lived a few blocks down from her, walking to her house was no trouble. It gave Neera some time to think about what she was actually getting herself into. It wasn't just the clothes that needed change, but her whole demeanor. She had to be comfortable with the attention, or even worse...they might just treat her exactly the same.

Neera greeted Elayne's parents with a curt bow as she hastily kicked her shoes off and left them by the door. She ran upstairs to Lay-Lay's room and locked the door with a startled Lay-Lay at her vanity mirror.

She practically dragged Neera to sit on her stool in front of the purple vanity. The table in front of her had multiple hair combs and accessories, hair ties, make-up kits, and a flat iron. It looked like a mad scientist's lab, if that mad scientist was an eccentric, teen girl.

Now I'm officially scared.

Elayne tapped a finger to her chin as she surveyed Neera's face. "Let's see what we can do first."

She removed Neera's wire-framed glasses, and cooed. "You have such pretty eyes. How dare you confine them like this."

Neera snorted and rubbed her own shoulder. "I never really paid attention. I guess I need them to see."

Elayne tucked them in her pocket and grinned with an eyebrow wiggle. "Seeing is not part of the mission today. You can grab some contacts later." She obnoxiously squeezed Neera's cheeks, her lips puckering. "Today, I want them so shocked to see you, they choke on their food."

Lay-Lay may be way too enthusiastic about this...

Neera chuckled, but actually contemplated how she was going to see throughout the rest of the school year. She wasn't blind, per say, but anything more than twenty-feet away could basically identify as a blur. Good thing she started at the end of the year when it didn't matter.

"Now that we got that out of the way, let's see your

face." Elayne leaned in closely, scanning every inch of her face. "Much better."

Now she's just being rude.

After a moment, Elayne came to a conclusion. "You must've been a model in your past life because there's literally nothing to change to make you look better. Even your freckles are cute."

Neera blushed.

Elayne picked up some lip gloss and applied it to Neera's lips. "That's better. Now onto your hair."

She carefully pulled out her Neera's hairbands, her long and curly tresses rolling down her back. She gently ran her fingers through the curls, parting small sections before running a flat iron through them. With each sizzle of the iron against her curls, Neera's anxiety climbed. She was really doing this. The old-her was receding, and...she kind of liked it.

After what felt like an hour, Elayne exhaled and nodded in approval at her work.

"Now," Elayne clapped her hands once. "You get changed, and let's rock and roll."

Neera took another look at the girl in the mirror. She was pretty, otherworldly. Nothing like herself, and everything like the other popular girls.

Can I ever be a part of their world?

LIAM

The nightmares hadn't reappeared, allowing him to get some sleep for once...only for him to be preoccupied with thoughts of Neera. Liam debated whether he should ask her to prom, even after that travesty of a proposal.

Suck it up and ask her to prom.

Maybe the nightmares will stop if you keep hanging out with her.

Maybe the nightmares were manifestations of being a wimp

and never asking her out.

He could forget about her and not go to prom like he initially planned, spending the night studying while everyone partied.

Or, he could finally be a teenager for once.

Screw it. He was going to ask Neera Ran to prom. *Hopefully, she doesn't hate you.*

Liam inconspicuously stalked Neera's locker while pretending to listen to Nate's predicament of choosing between two prom dates. *Tragic.* The last bell just rang, and still no Neera.

"...but Lexi is more likely to put out if I take her, so– whoa!" Nate's jaw dropped as he stared behind Liam.

Curious, Liam turned around, and the air was instantly knocked out of his lungs.

Neera. At least someone who resembled her.

Instead of being greeted by rainbow socks and oversized overalls, his eyes roamed over a short denim miniskirt flaunting her thighs, a low-cut, olive-green tank top, and a brown fringed vest. Her usual pigtails were released into loose waves, and her lips shined under the artificial lights. The usual glasses that clung to her nose bridge were gone, revealing the infamous gang of freckles.

Did you take too many hits to the head yesterday?

Liam wasn't the only one that was dumbstruck. All the guys in the hallway ogled her and, somehow, triggered Liam to head her way.

Not because he was jealous or anything.

Neera was taking her bag out of her locker before Liam stood on the other side of the door. He plastered on a flirtatious smile and dialed up the charm; unfortunately, the side effects included completely shutting down his reasoning.

"I think I've seen you before. Aren't you the girl with rainbow socks?" He immediately cringed as soon as the words left his mouth.

"Hmm," she hummed, biting back a smile. She closed her

locker and then pinned her enchanting eyes on him. "Aren't you the guy who knew exactly who I was and still rejected me?"

Liam swallowed hard. *Fair.*

Not what he expected, but definitely what he deserved. His heart was beating too quickly.

What was he trying to say again?

"Uh...sorry..." *Smooth.*

Neera clutched the strap of her tribal-patterned backpack and looked expectantly at Liam, her eyes holding him captive. Her presence clenched his chest. He was too busy trying to get rid of her yesterday to notice her disarming tropical perfume. That, plus her natural slight sea scent, felt like he was idling on a beach. Peaceful and serene.

All he had to do was ask her to prom. If she declined, then he knew where he was supposed to be. Where he belonged.

This is why you should never take chances!

No pressure.

He ran a hand through his hair and went for it. "I-I realized I was wrong yesterday, but I do want to go to prom with you...Are you still interested?"

The way he hung onto her next words was, personally, degrading.

She searched his face as if she noticed his breath being detained. A hint of a smile appeared as she replied coolly. "I'll go to Prom...with myself."

Liam's smile fell, then she added, "...But if we happen to see each other there, I wouldn't mind dancing with you."

With that, she turned on her heeled boots and strutted away, almost tripping a few times in the process. Liam shamelessly watched her until he felt a presence next to him, yet he couldn't bring himself to move.

"What was that all about?" Nate nudged Liam's side.

Liam finally released a breath in the form of a snort and cough.

"Looks like I'm going to prom."

BLAME IT ON THE BOOZE

Chapter 4

Neera

Neera replayed the interaction between Liam and her for the hundredth time in her head as she tried on another prom gown in the fitting room.

The school day was better than she expected. Different, but better. Neera could've done without the intense stares and the creepy ones from some of the guys, but thankfully no one touched her. Even Jessica and her witch coven kept their mouths closed for once.

Operation Neck-Stomp was working.

She waited all day for someone to belittle her, to call her an imposter, but no one tried her.

Well, no one except Liam. She had to admit, initially, it was disturbing that he took interest in her AFTER she changed her entire look. A small part of her believed he wasn't genuine. A large part of her, however, internally reveled in how nervous he was to ask her out.

What if it's some bet he made with his friends to embarrass me or sleep with me, like in that one movie?

Neera shook the anxious theory away. Whatever his

intentions were, she would be careful before giving her heart away. Besides, she was no prude or afraid of sex in the slightest. She didn't covet it as something only between *one-true-loves*. If he asked her out to only sleep with her, he wouldn't be the only one to gain something from it.

As long as she kept her heart close to her chest. As long as they were on the same page, they could move on, graduate, and never have to deal with each other ever again.

Yeah, never see each other again...

Without missing a beat, Neera relayed everything to Lay-Lay, which led to her dragging Neera to the nearest dress shop after school. The whole "world domination" plan was still in effect, so it was pertinent to find the perfect–most revealing–dress.

After the fourth gown, thoughts of Liam reappeared. How her heart couldn't stop beating quickly. How his hair fell over his face and how he shoved it back, revealing his toned bicep. How soft and pink his lips looked...

"Let me see how it looks!" Elayne yelled from the other side of the fitting room door, always ruining a moment.

Neera peered out of the room, then nervously stepped out into the circular space enclosed by mirrors that judged her every move. As if they saw right through her facade.

She nervously struck a pose like those models she'd seen in mags to ease some of her nerves, but it made her feel even more pathetic. The neck of the emerald, floor-length, silk-like gown was square and exposed her clavicle. Her back was open and only covered the very tip of her bottom, with a thin gold chain keeping the material together. That meant she had to forgo a bra. She bit her bottom lip.

The gown was *high-fashion*. For a high school prom, *almost criminal*.

"Oh, this is so the dress," Elayne drawled as she circled Neera. "I wish I had a body like yours. We would take over the world."

Neera snorted.

"Only if I don't get suspended over this gown."

Elayne stood next to Neera and gazed into the mirror.

"Those bozos will be wearing way worse and not even look half as good," she alleged. "And I know Liam will lose his freakin' mind."

Ugh, Liam. Her heart began to beat expeditiously for all the wrong reasons. She shouldn't be excited to see this guy, but every mention of his name gave her butterflies. She had his attention and played hard to get during their last conversation to portray confidence; however, she didn't really consider her next steps.

That nagging part of her brain taunted her, insisting she didn't deserve his attention and that this whole ploy was a waste of time. How her evening should be spent at home in her mermaid onesie, drinking hot cocoa, and studying for her exams. No mask, no scheme, no scrutiny. Safe.

"Sometimes pursuing what you want isn't the easiest route." Her mum would say while they watched The Sea Princess blissfully wave from the boat next to her prince.

"What are you thinking, Nee-Nee?" Elayne asked as she studied Neera's face in the mirror, sneaking another mirror picture.

Neera pushed her glasses back up her nose and half-heartedly smiled at Elayne.

"How amazeballs it would be to show up in matching dresses."

The hotel's event room had transformed into a fancy gala, adorned in black-and-gold decorations to commemorate the Senior class's "Last Dance". They really went all out with the school budget. An unknown band on stage decently played alternative rock covers. Near the entrance, a long table stood crowded with snacks, hors d'oeuvres, and red punch. Chaperones loitered near the food and surveyed the "troublesome" students as those students cheerfully danced.

Others gathered around the standing tables, waiting for friends or someone to ask them to dance.

After being dropped off by her dad and letting him know her plans for the evening, Neera and Elayne strutted into the space and took in the environment. More like Elayne. Neera focused more on not falling in her three-inch heels.

"They really did it up for us!" Elayne beamed as she scanned the room, her sleek high ponytail swishing with each movement. Her black, fitted pants suit reflected off the glittering lights around them. Her makeup was just as sharp and dramatic as her personality. She returned her gaze to Neera and wiggled her eyebrows. "Looks like everyone is more interested in you instead of the dance..."

Neera tore her eyes from the band and looked around the room, noticing several eyes on her. Heat crept up her neck, and she wished she knew what to do with her hands. At least forgoing her glasses made their stares less intimidating.

Lay-Lay nudged her side and whispered, "Here comes Mr. Hottie. Good luck!" She winked before scurrying over to the center of the dance floor to dance by herself, but Neera doubted she'd be by herself for long. She always admired Lay-Lay's confidence and carefree attitude. Maybe opposites did attract.

Neera widened her eyes and bit her lip as if it would compel her best friend to return, but realized she just looked ridiculous and ended up looking at the ceiling.

"You look beautiful."

Her head snapped in the direction of the flattery and found Liam two feet in front of her, fisting two clear cups of punch.

Here comes the butterflies.

However, they felt more like bees with how ferociously they swarmed.

He was right there. Right in front of her in all his hotness. His chocolate hair was slicked back into a wavy pattern on top, like a gentleman. His tuxedo looked expensive and classically black with a white button-up underneath.

Usually, suits looked oversized, but Liam's suit was perfectly molded to fit his athletic build. The thing that captured her attention the most was the small cluster of blue forget-me-nots pinned to his lapel.

Her favorite flower. *How did he know that?*

Liam held the cup out to her, wanting her to take it. Relieved to have a reason to respond to his compliment, she took the drink, thanked him, and took a sip. The cool liquid was bitter and produced a warm feeling in her body. Properly disgusting. Liam's grimace indicated he felt the same.

"Oh, they definitely spiked this punch," he chuckled.

It was actually the first time Neera drank alcohol since she had never been to a party, and Elayne had never pressured her into drinking for some reason. So she never had the desire to drink, but she knew it smelled toxic.

No one, however, told her about the tingly feeling that ensued or the lightness of her body. The chip she always kept on her shoulder momentarily disappeared. The eyes on her faded away. She was too enraptured by the drink to notice that Liam spoke.

"Can I have the rest of yours?" Neera asked, keeping her eyes on his cup and not on his intruding stare.

"Sure..." He offered her the cup, and she downed it like the lady she was. She took a deep breath, her body relaxed and her mind liberated, and gave him a more secure "thanks". He lowered his shoulders.

The music changed into a slower melody as the drums faded, the guitar center-stage. Liam asked, "You wanna dance?" His voice harmonized with the melody of the music.

Still floating, Neera nodded, and they moved past the other students to get to the center of the dance floor, where they could blend in. Other students politely swayed to the music while others were grinding to the sound of their raging hormones. She tried to ignore the people surrounding them and focused on Liam.

With newfound confidence, she slipped her hand in his

and snaked her other hand to his shoulder. He stiffened but timidly placed his other hand on her mid-back, which caused electricity to spark along her spine. She waited for him to move his feet first, but he remained planted like a tree. Neera glanced back up at his face. He looked serious. His entire face and neck were rouge.

Liam lowered his lips next to her ear and whispered, "I actually don't know how to dance."

Why would he ask me to dance if he doesn't know how? Also, why was that the cutest thing I've ever heard?

Neera snickered, then sucked in her lips to stop. She whispered back.

"Don't worry, just follow my lead."

Despite her less-than-optimal eyesight and obvious tipsiness, she instructed Liam on which foot went where, and gradually, they moved into a semblance of a waltz. She may have sacrificed a few toes in the process, but his bumbling around made it all worth it. He never gave up and humbly followed along, which was shocking for a guy who didn't dance.

The moment conjured memories of Neera's little six-year-old feet standing on top of her dad's shoes as they waltzed in the living room, swaying to *The Sea Princess* soundtrack. Her heart was filled with joy and love. Her mum would cut in, dancing with her dad, and his face beamed with admiration. It was beautiful and unconditional like they were the only three people in the entire world. A moment frozen in eternity.

When Neera gazed at Liam's face, she almost swore she could see the same look. Or it was just the punch. Whatever it was, she didn't want the feeling to end.

What happened to protecting your heart?

She could only hope that he felt the same, or this would be super awkward.

Still riding the love train of emotions, she leaned close to his lips–almost a breath's distance away–and admitted, "I don't want this night to end."

She internally slapped herself at the immense level of cringe. That move only worked in romantic comedies, and the fact that she thought anything but awkwardness would emerge from it demonstrated that alcohol was not her friend.

Liam pierced her eyes with a holding gaze, his hazel eyes darkening into a creamy brown, and closed the space between them. She was caught off-guard at first but liked the tiny spark from the initial touch.

Did he feel it, too, or is it the punch? The kiss was short and sweet before he jerked back, breaking the kiss.

Neera froze in shock.

Was it something I did? Was I that awful?

Right when she mentally drummed up an escape plan, Liam closed his eyes and dove in, his lips finding every way to mesh with hers.

The kiss was no longer soft and sweet, but hungry and full of desire. The swarm of butterflies burst out and fluttered every inch of her skin. Like something that was supposed to happen long ago, something repressed, and finally opening the gates to something more potent. More passionate.

It was the best kiss she ever had, even topping the sloppy one she received in middle school because of a dare.

Neera sighed when his hands slid down her bare back, then rested on her hips gently. The desire to be closer to him grew deeper the longer his fingers traced her skin. If there were other people near them, they were a figment of her imagination because all she could see was Liam, all she could feel was his tuxedo, and all she could hear were fireworks exploding with each beat of her heart.

He broke the kiss and placed his forehead to hers, like he ran to the ends of the Earth just to cross the finish line with her. Or maybe he was tipsy too, and needed some leverage.

"I don't want to leave you tonight," Liam whispered so softly she could barely hear it. His eyes remained shut as if frightened to see her reaction. Neera cradled his face with her hands, his jaw smooth against her palms.

He opened his eyes, finally dropping back to reality. His head looked at the stage for a moment, then back to Neera. The intensity in his gaze made her feel like making mistakes, and her mouth proved why alcohol should only be for fully-grown adults.

"Let's get a room."

LIAM

What the hell are you actually doing? It's not too late to back out!

After a curt lecture with his dad about responsibilities and avoiding anything that could negatively impact his future, Liam's mom kissed her son's cheek. She admired how handsome he was in his new tux while pinning some flowers to his lapel. How she convinced his dad to let him go was beyond him. The tux fit a bit tighter than he'd like, but apparently, it fit him like a glove, according to his mom.

Fifty pictures later, Liam headed to the hotel in his hunter-green All-American jeep. Since there were no windows, the wind wrapped around him in flowing blasts and hopefully knocked some sense into him. His knee trembled from the breeze the closer he got to dance. Yeah, definitely the wind.

Upon entering the event hall, Liam immediately surveyed the room for a particular curly-haired girl but only recognized a bunch of his peers dancing and grinding on each other. He spotted Nate and–maybe Lisa–dancing on the dance floor to alternative rock, and Nate gave him a slight nod while waving him over. Liam's nerves were already in a bunch; the last thing he needed was unsolicited advice from the captain of the football team.

Liam shook his head and pointed to the punch table while simultaneously walking over to it. He tried not to look suspicious as he grabbed a few crackers and observed the crowd. He wasn't the only wallflower present; nevertheless, his particular stance exuded desperation.

He noticed Jessica and some poor jock dancing close. Her sharp eyes captured his and clamped their jaws on them. He gave her an acknowledgment nod so she could release him, but her blue eyes had already found their next target. Not just her eyes, but almost everyone's eyes fell on her.

Neera Ran.

He was sure of it since this girl looked different again. She ambled distractedly toward the center of the room while looking at the ceiling and the band. It wasn't difficult getting to the center with the way the students dispersed and left a traveling bubble around her. He couldn't blame them. She radiated an ethereal glow and beauty that shirked the shadiness away.

Like the Belle of the fuckin' ball.

Her hair was long, pushed to one side, straight down to the center of her torso, instead of its usual waterfall of curls. No glasses again, showcasing her mesmerizing eyes and thick eyebrows. Very minimal makeup. Just a nice maroon with a tempting gloss over plump, Cupid's bow lips. Her dress had him contemplating life, pure shock that she was allowed entrance with it on. It was emerald green, like a football field.

Like his favorite color.

If he didn't move that second, he never would.

Liam filled up two cups of punch and headed over to Neera, trying his hardest not to spill them with all his shaking. He blurted out whatever thought that happened to betray him since she had that effect on him.

When she finally faced him, she avoided all eye contact with him. For some reason, that annoyed him the most, but he still offered her the drink. He tried to drink at the same time, but the strong bourbon taste hit him like a wave, and he tried not to gag whilst drinking.

If the chaperones didn't notice the smell, they're definitely in on it.

Liam attempted to make light of it so it didn't seem he was trying to drug her. Her body language started to relax visibly, and she finally bestowed eye contact. Her face blushed around her nose, causing her cute freckles to stand out. Her reaction indicated that this was her first time drinking.

Oh, this is not good. Great job, genius.

The band played a cover of a slow song, and more students started coupling up in the middle of the dance floor.

"And it feels like tonight..."

Going with the theme of verbal vomit, he asked her to dance, knowing he had never danced before and didn't know how. Instead of rightfully rejecting him, like he secretly hoped, she nodded, and they headed closer to the stage. In the middle of the packed dance floor, maybe people were less likely to see his epic fail at dancing. She positioned her hands on him like those dancers on *Dancing with The Stars*.

He froze. He wasn't going to screw this up more than he already had.

Until he admitted the truth, like a scared boy.

Instead of laughing and pointing a mocking finger at him, she demonstrated the correct hand positioning and steps. Naturally, Liam stepped on her toes, but she didn't chide him. Neera chuckled amusingly and encouraged him to try it again.

It might have been a minuscule moment to her, but to him, it was the only moment in his life that he didn't feel any pressure to be perfect. He could be average, or he could suck entirely, yet it didn't seem to matter to her. He felt...lighter, almost light-headed, from the pure giddiness and genuineness.

He knew the others were staring at him, and he probably looked like a clobbering dope, but for the first time, he couldn't care less what they thought. For all he knew, they were the only two people on the dance floor.

Liam took his eyes off her poor feet and gazed at her radiant face, but she was already gazing back. Was she looking the whole time? In this bubble, his heart was ready to burst from the rapid beating, and the old him would've taken this time to create distance. The feelings were intense, too much, and his head kept screaming to run.

To keep her as far away from him as possible.

Like a surfer at the first sign of a hurricane, he blatantly ignored the warnings and swam closer to the wild unknown.

What happened to keeping a distance?

"I don't want this night to end." *This can't be real.*

His lips brushed over hers before he quickly pulled away. Liam had no intention of going that far with her. Only a dance, and maybe her number. Not to KISS her.

They call it liquid courage for a reason.

Neera's eyes went wide, yet her lips were still puckered. *She must have felt it too.* That spark when their lips touched. Liam hoped she would push him away and run...because, in his haze, that was the only way he could ever let her go.

Liam closed his eyes. *Oh, you're in so much trouble now.*

He leaned in again and captured her lips, this time with the intent of never letting go.

"*You're the one thing that remains...I could stay like this forever.*"

The tightness in his chest ceased and burst into a tidal wave that engulfed his body, like something that needed to happen. Nothing felt forced. It was natural, part of nature. The calming waves started to transform into rip currents as his hormones kicked into overdrive, his more logical head no longer in control.

The kiss was no longer soft but devouring, as her sighs made it worse. Her back was as silky as her dress; the alcohol on her breath mixed with the cherry-flavored lip tint.

Dangerous.

Liam pulled away and placed his forehead against hers to calm himself, debating whether to run away to the nearest bathroom to take care of himself or to take her to his jeep and run away together. He chose to be honest and let her know that no matter what they do, whether it was hooking up or talking about the latest Bengals stats, he wasn't ready to separate from her.

"I don't want to leave you tonight."

Liam looked around, suddenly brought back to reality. There were people around them staring at the stage. The band cleared out, and in their place was the principal with a bouquet of flowers and two crowns on a silk, black pillow. They're about to announce the Prom King and Queen. Jessica and two other girls stood on stage with pageant smiles. Liam presumed he was nominated and should also go up on stage with the other guys who were lined up near the stage's steps.

However, when he looked over at his date, he'd rather be anywhere else with her. Preferably just the two of them. She must've had the same idea because her hooded eyes bore into his own.

"Let's get a room." *There goes being a gentleman...*

He wasn't expecting her to agree and it, for sure, wasn't to talk about the QB's latest rank. He cursed himself and grabbed Neera's hand, leading her towards the exit. She seemed addled at first but let him lead her out the door, like two runaway teens about to get hitched. He so wished he could blame it on the booze.

"...And it feels like tonight..."

CHANGING TIDES

Chapter 5

Neera

Being 18 makes life so much easier.

Without much fuss, Liam booked a single room in the hotel, three floors above the prom venue. The room simply contained a queen-sized bed, a large window on the opposite side with the curtains drawn shut, a telly in front of the bed, and a glass snack cabinet next to the telly. The decor was sleek and contemporary, perfect for a one-night rendezvous. Not the most scenic or spacious, but it was better than a car.

Most of the buzz she felt from the punch dissipated, but she oddly still felt relaxed. They both stood across the bed from one another, unsure what to do. Well, mainly Neera, since this was her first time doing anything in a hotel room, let alone being in a hotel room with a boy.

She was a "virgin". *So what?* She knew about "The Birds and the Bees" and had seen adult videos, but when it came to the actual act of doing it, she never ventured past first base. Honestly, it was viewed as a lack of experience rather than a part of her identity. Being timid and avoided like the plague didn't give a girl many options either.

Now, Neera had a hot guy who was actually interested in her. Who actually saw her as a person and not some broken doll. Someone who found her physically attractive. So even if his intention wasn't longevity, she wasn't going to let an opportunity like this slip by.

Life is short and never promised...

For the first time in years, negativity took the back seat, and the present was front and center.

Neera's body tensed in anticipation as she settled onto the bed with her strappy heels on. Her elbow propped her up while facing Liam with her entire leg exposed. Like in those sexy spy movies where the femme fatale seduced the spy to spill the organization's secrets, she gave Liam the "come-hither" eyes.

Instead of ravishing her as she expected, Liam remained standing with his hand rubbing the back of his neck and his eyes on everything but her. Then, he stalked over to the complimentary snacks and picked up a can of peanuts, showcasing it to Neera.

"I didn't know they had snacks. How convenient!" He exclaimed inappropriately.

Oh snap, he's nervous. Am I reading this all wrong? The negativity returned to its designated seat in the front.

Inwardly cringing, Neera got up and reached for the can he offered. Not even a second after her hand clutched the can, Liam moved to the other side of the bed again, not even "accidentally" grazing a shoulder. She furrowed her eyebrows in confusion.

This is a joke. He really isn't into me. Maybe this was some kind of dare to prove he could bag me, but he found the idea of sleeping with me repulsive. Do I seem that desperate? Ugh, I'm so stupid.

The negative thoughts bombarded her like an ambush until he sighed heavily, stealing her attention.

"Sorry for being so lame," Liam blurted on his next sigh as he loosened his bowtie. He ran a hand through his hair, inadvertently releasing his waves from their gel confinement. One of the locks hovered over his thick eyebrow, giving him a rugged look. "You make me nervous. I just wanted to hook up at first, but then I realized I'd rather just lay next to you and... talk. Is that weird?"

Neera was bemused, but she remained silent.

So he is nervous?

He stared for a moment, then removed his jacket, tossing it on the carpet.

"It's okay if you're not interested. I can get them to call you a cab or something."

Neera snorted and quickly admitted before she could stop the words from coming out.

"Talking sounds better, actually." A hint of a smile crossed his face. "And we have ten more minutes until the night is over."

She sauntered over to the bed with the nut can and laid down on her back. Liam rewarded her with a grin before following her and sitting next to her. His natural scent made her head spin, so she focused on his eyes. The same hazel ones that gazed at her like she was the only girl in the world, and she couldn't believe she almost talked herself into leaving.

Stop overthinking and live in the moment!

"Other than awkward chat, what do you do for fun?" Neera opened the nut can, risking her life as she popped a few into her mouth. *Not bad.*

Liam looked up at the ceiling, possibly pondering before he shrugged. "Going to parties, football games, and other events. Also, learning new things."

Neera internally gasped. Social events were a whole different universe to her, and she barely survived prom. Just the thought of pretending to be happy and energetic all the time was tiring.

"Sounds...exhausting."

His eyes seemed to peer into her very soul as if SHE was the one spilling the organization's secrets. Instead of countering her or defending his party-animal lifestyle, the tension in his body seemed to lighten as a teeny smile graced his lips.

What is he thinking?

"So...how'd you learn how to dance?" Liam asked, grabbing a handful of mixed nuts from the can between them. He tossed them in his mouth and then settled on his back, close enough to brush her shoulder.

Neera, perplexed by the direction of the conversation, answered anyway. "My dad and I would dance together, and he would let me stand on his toes while we waltzed. It's probably the only dance I know, by the way." She noticed his chortle seemed distant. "Does anyone in your family know how to dance?"

He shrugged. "If they do, I wouldn't know. We're not close."

A beat passed, and she realized the situation was breaching serious territory and that he wasn't going to elaborate. She tried to lighten the mood. "Well, I wish my dad would give me some space since I'm basically an adult now. Well, I'm used to the hovering since..."

She almost mentioned her mum.

He must've noticed it too, but acted like it didn't happen. "At least you got to learn fun skills and bond with your family."

"And I appreciate the time I have with them...well, had. As you should." Neera nudged his shoulder with hers, the brief contact warming her body. "My family is broken. All I have is my father, but I guess I appreciate how close we are. Hovering and all."

"You're not alone. Most families are broken. Some are just better at hiding it..." He trailed off, causing Neera to turn her head to him. His jaw was tense, and his eyes looked hard, like brittle soil. She must've struck a nerve, or he was thinking something fierce. Instead of going down that route, he returned to a more neutral expression. "I was debating whether to ask you or not about this since we technically just met..."

Neera braced herself for some reason.

"...Are you part of the witness protection program

because of what happened to your mom? The reason you're always so...discreet?"

Neera blinked once. Twice. Then laughed a bit longer than she could control.

"What...what in the world...Liam?" She managed between laughs.

Liam, probably startled by her laugh, looked nervous, only causing her to laugh harder. "W-was I not supposed to mention it?"

Tears. There were literal tears streaming down her cheeks. Her mascara was definitely smeared.

After a while, she finally calmed down as Liam waited patiently for an answer. Apparently too long because he reached over her body, grabbed her right wrist, and pulled her to him. The momentum caused her to roll on top of him. Her arm with their limbs tangled was tucked between their chests, and her other forearm was on his chest, holding her up.

Neera was speechless, yet impressed by the smoothness. Whatever humor she had left evaporated.

Liam stared intently into her eyes, then her lips, then her eyes again. Her body temperature officially skyrocketed, idly waiting to land anywhere. He pulled her closer. She leaned in, her face hot with anticipation and ready to hit the target; however, he stopped an inch away and muttered.

"Are you really in trouble? Is there any way I can help?"

Neera would laugh again if his sincerity weren't so palpable.

He wants to help me?

She could be "in danger," and Liam was willing to help, even if it meant getting into legal trouble. So, he was not like the other popular kids. He was intense, caring, awkward, and most importantly...real.

Her heart screamed for her to trust him and tell him everything. Her brain screamed to protect her heart because she still didn't know him. Neera had no choice but to hope she made the right decision.

"I'm not in the witness protection program. I swear," Neera bit back her smile when his face looked unconvinced. "Seriously, I'm not. I was just depressed for a long time after... my mother died. I ended up having bad panic attacks and diagnosed with anxiety ever since. At least that's what my therapist said."

Before he could ask, she added, "My mother died in a car accident. On my birthday. Nothing malicious, just messed up." She shuddered at the release of her repressed emotions. She hadn't confided in anyone else except Lay-Lay, so it felt like a scab being picked at. She took a deep breath, then another. "That's it."

Liam nodded, mulling over what she confessed.

"When is your birthday?"

She hesitated at first, aware of what his response would be when she admitted it. "Tomorrow," she finally choked out.

Liam craned his neck towards the alarm clock on the nightstand and noticed the time was 12:01 am. He turned back to her, and she cringed, waiting for the congratulations.

Instead, he pulled her in for a gentle kiss, taking her breath away at the tenderness. He broke away, only to hold her in an embrace as he rubbed her back.

Nothing else, no "Happy Birthday" or pitiful sorrows, just tenderness and compassion. Tears pooled in her eyes, and she didn't mind letting them fall.

For the next two hours, they talked about anything and everything, learning more about each other than she's ever had with anyone else. How she was a Gemini and he was a Scorpio. How she was going to UCLA and he was going to USC. How he enjoyed playing football, and she enjoyed swimming, yet they both felt free when doing them. How they both longed to be their authentic selves one day.

The negativity that was in the front seat of her mind left the vehicle and was replaced by someone she had only reserved for her Michael Phelps posters...Adoration.

Happy birthday, Neera.

After explaining to her dad that she found a ride home with Elayne, Neera rode in Liam's window-less jeep to her house. The wind blowing electrified her skin, giving her goosebumps. Liam glanced over at her and smiled a winning smile.

"Feels good, huh?" He asked a little louder over the wind.

Neera nodded cheerfully.

"Woo-hoo!" He shouted out to the darkness. "You try!"

Neera giggled at the ridiculousness of it but let out her own "woo-hoo."

"That's the spirit! Let go!" He shouted again.

They shouted the whole time, barely noticing the stares from other drivers. Neera's throat hurt from all the laughing, but she didn't care. She never felt so free in her life, even while swimming. This was a different kind of living. A different kind of breathing.

She looked over at Liam's excited face, his hair tousled by the draft, and realized her feelings for him flew faster than their trip down the highway.

Parked in front of her modest home, Neera saw the lights were still on, indicating her dad was still awake. There was no surprise there.

Liam detached his seatbelt as if he was about to walk her to her door. She quickly halted his hand movements and gave him an incredulous look.

"I think this is where we should part," Neera blurted.

Liam scoffed. "Okay, Shakespeare. You don't want me to meet your dad after such a wonderful night?"

It was Neera's turn to scoff. "Unless you want him to exercise his 2nd amendment right." Her dad would never, but he didn't know that.

Liam chuckled, then paused when her face remained serious. His mouth formed a straight line, and he offered her a hearty high-five.

Neera laughed, grabbed his outstretched hand, and turned it over to kiss his knuckles. "And I bid you a good morn'," she joked.

Liam chortled and mockingly shook his hand away.

"Get out of my car, Ran," he laughed, but he was flushed from his neck to his ears.

After entering her home, she detected her dad sitting idly on the gray sofa, watching the news. However, Neera knew her dad, and he was paying attention to her movements from his peripherals. His hearing was probably the same as a dog. He turned his head "nonchalantly" to greet his daughter with a smile.

"How was your night? Did it live up to your expectations?" Her dad made use of his Ph.D. in Psychology in any way possible.

Neera held her opposite shoulder and smirked. "It was a bit overrated, but definitely something I'll never forget."

Her mind instantly went to Liam, and she inconspicuously dug her nails into her shoulder to prevent herself from blushing. Her dad's observant eyes studied her for a minute too long, but apparently, it worked because he smiled back.

"Well, sorry it wasn't the best night ever, love. It's been a long day. Get some sleep."

Neera rounded the corner and hugged her dad a loving goodnight. It had been eight years since he lost his wife, the love of his life, and it was also the day the second love of his life was born. Neera could only imagine how tormented he felt when she stayed later than she should've, but he didn't yell or reprimand her for it. He rarely yelled at her.

He showed her love at all times, and she was grateful to have him. She may have lost her mother and best friend, but he didn't hesitate to show her she would always have a best friend.

Liam was right about not being broken.

With her dress hung up and hair pulled into a bun on

top of her head, she prepared to take a shower in her personal bathroom. It paid to be an only child sometimes. Just like any other night, she brushed her teeth and let the water run until it was scolding hot.

She stepped into the inferno and embraced the burn like an intimate hug, making sure her whole body was submerged...

Why do I feel tingly?

Her legs were tingling, like pins-and-needles, except this tingling intensified and spread all over her body. It felt like she was having an allergic reaction, but all within seconds.

All of a sudden, her legs gave out from under her, the world tilting. Her bottom hit the tiled floor next to her toilet bowl. Strangely, it didn't hurt that bad, like an extra cushion was added to her bottom. She looked down at her legs–wait...

That's a tail. That's a bloody fishtail!

She inspected her body. Her skin shimmered like a bucket of glitter had been dumped on her. Her chest, which should have been bare, now sported a green, scaly bra–if it even counted as a bra–that blended into her skin around the edges like a pastie gone wrong.

Back to the tail, the green, shimmering scales caught the bathroom light, causing it to look iridescent. The surface felt exactly like salmon scales, smooth and cool, as she slid her fingers across it. Her nerves construed it as her touching her normal thigh. It justifiably freaked her out. A scream climbed up her throat before she hastily slapped a hand to her mouth to keep it at bay, only emitting a muffled scream.

This has to be a dream! What the heck was in that punch?!

Neera was way too exhausted to make a fuss as her eyelids fought to stay open...Or she was passing out from shock.

Yeah, more likely the latter.

As her mind raced almost as fast as her heart, her brain made the executive decision to chalk this up as a dream and knocked her out to worry about it later.

THE MORNING AFTER

Chapter 6

Liam

Where is she? Liam mused as he passed by Neera's locker for the last time.

The last bell had rung for the end of the school day, and students shuffled out of their classes to go home. Many of the Seniors departed from their classrooms in sluggish lumber, clearly hungover from the night before. This amused him since he had always been the type to babysit the "drunks" instead of falling victim to the headaches.

Liam continued his search for the culprit who captured his heart and held his sleep captive. It would've been better if he had gotten drunk that night; then he would've, at least, gotten an ounce of sleep.

Her faint ocean smell, delicate light brown skin, adorable freckles, and toned yet soft body had haunted his thoughts since their kiss in the hotel. Her mirrored humor, compassion that she hid under her ambiguity, quirks, and story have ushered her into a position of someone he'd never thought of having so soon.

A girlfriend. Only if she consented.

However, she wouldn't be able to respond if she wasn't present.

You should've gotten her number.

He pushed a hand through his hair and cursed. As if he accidentally casted a spell, Neera's friend, Elayne, appeared and opened a locker. *Neera's* locker. Either they shared a locker, or something happened to Neera. His gears whirled. They talked about very personal things. Maybe he unlocked some sort of trauma.

Maybe the government removed her from school because she revealed her identity.

He took two steps toward her until a bleach blonde side-ponytail with a sparkly tiara swished inches in front of him. Liam backed up slightly, Jessica's mask of confidence staring directly at him.

"You missed your coronation, Liam," she smirked. "We were supposed to have our first dance, but you didn't even show up. They gave it to Nate instead, if you were wondering."

Liam's eyes remained on the straight-haired girl with a purple streak as he replied, "I'm happy for you two. You guys deserve it. Now, I actually have to go–"

"I saw you and Neera," she cut in with a slight edge. "Even after everything we told you, you're still interested in that weirdo."

Liam's jaw tensed, shoving his hands in his pockets to keep from pushing her out of the way. Jessica was rude and shallow, yet she always had the best intentions, even after their short-term fling. Nevertheless, her disrespect for Neera was crossing a line, and after last night, he couldn't stay silent.

"I suggest you watch your mouth about Neera, Jess," he warned when his eyes cut to hers, heat blazing. Her mask of confidence slipped, her lips thinning.

Purple Streak was on the move, her arms full of textbooks. He had to go.

Before Jessica could respond to his unexpected threat, probably to ramble a bunch of obscenities at him, Liam gave a quick smile and maneuvered around her.

"Congrats on the win, Queen," he threw over his shoulder as he hustled to the retreating girl.

Liam caught up to Purple Streak–Elayne. He cut right in front of her on the staircase descending to the front doors, ignoring the other students that had to swerve around them. He gave her his picture-perfect smile and tried not to sound like he wasn't stalking and chasing her for the past two minutes.

"Hey, it's Elayne, right?" *Smooth as always, Dern.*

"Yeah…" Elayne hissed, slightly annoyed. "What do you want?"

Momentarily taken aback but refusing to show it, he got straight to it. "I know you and Neera are best friends, and I haven't seen her all day today. I'm just wondering if she's okay." His heart flitted in suspense.

Elayne's eyes narrowed as she quipped, "Well, you should ask her yourself if you're that worried."

She tried to move around him, then huffed when he blocked her way again.

He was not usually this pushy, but her rudeness began to irritate him. He was usually nonchalant about his social life, but since his feelings developed for Neera, letting potentially concerning things slide seemed ridiculous.

"Listen," Liam slid a rogue wave back into place. "I don't understand your problem with me since we never spoke before, but–"

"No, YOU listen!" Her black eyes could melt a hole through the plaster walls. "What I know about YOU is that Neera left with you. Then the next day, she calls me, all upset, saying she can't come to school." Liam braced himself at the piercing assertion. Then prepared himself for more. "It doesn't help that I saw you and Jessica all buddy-buddy in the hallway earlier, too. I don't know if you two have some sort of bet going on, but if I find out you're using my BFF, I swear I'll stomp BOTH of your faces in."

Liam was dumbstruck. So Neera wasn't coming back to school, and it was all his fault?

He thought their night was perfect…Albeit she did cry in his arms, he assumed she was emotional and enjoyed their intimacy.

He must've read everything wrong. He must've put her in danger. He should've gone straight home and studied for his exams. He shouldn't have listened to his mom. His dad was right.

The urge to hit the football field irritated his skin.

No. There has to be another reason. You want her. You have to get her.

His mind spun, and he didn't even notice Elayne walking past him. He pushed past another student and blocked her way again, right before she touched the bottom of the staircase.

"There's no bet or whatever you're thinking," he countered, but she looked uninterested. "If I did anything harmful to her last night, I need her to tell me because I thought we had an amazing night. I really like Neera. Enough to call Jessica out on her bull and enough to beg someone I don't know for her number."

Elayne's gaze grew less murderous, but she was still wary. He continued calmly. "Tomorrow after school, I'll have the house to myself. I want you both to come over to figure this out. It'll be two-on-one, so you don't have to worry about any funny shit. Even though I'm sure you can take me on by yourself."

Elayne turned her head, obviously trying to hide her smile. She gave him another surveying look from top to bottom. Liam held his authentic gaze—no faux smile or arrogant grin. He wanted to be as transparent as possible.

Anything to be able to talk to Neera again.

"Since you put it that way," she curtly nodded. "I'll try talking to her."

Liam sighed and rubbed the back of his neck. She stared

at the movement observantly and then looked expectantly at him. "Don't you want her number?"

He totally forgot about the number, too excited about his chance to speak with her again—a small win. He was going to get to the bottom of this situation, federal government or not. He needed to know if she was okay like he needed his next breath.

"Uh…yeah, of course," he murmured as he pulled his cellphone out.

NEERA

It's a dream. It's a dream. It's a dream. It's a dream.

Her mind was drowning. Negativity flooded her chest, leaving her breathless. She tried to take several deep breaths, like her old therapist recommended, but they came out feeble.

Neera reached for the door, although she was at least ten feet away from it. Her heart pounded in her ears from the sheer force of her efforts. She tried to handle her panic attack on her own for the past five minutes, only for it to worsen.

She needed her dad.

As if summoning him, a dark head appeared between the crack in the door, like the dad from that horror movie. As usual, his eyes were closed as he knocked.

"Hey, love, ready for school?" He sang.

Neera wheezed.

With that, his eyes shot open, and he pounced, almost breaking the door as he slammed it open. He was not the most athletic man in the world, but when it came to protecting his loved ones, he would find all the strength in the universe to help them.

He kneeled next to his daughter and scanned her body, looking for the issue. She slapped her t-shirt-covered chest three times with a trembling hand and circled the center of her chest. Her non-verbal way of saying she was having a panic attack that they used when she was a child.

He immediately grabbed her face firmly and pulled her up into a sitting position. Neera hadn't noticed she was lying down. Her dad's hands held her face, breathing in a "four-in, six-out" sequence. Neera stared into her dad's kind eyes and tried to mimic his breathing.

Then came the series of questions. "What color is the room?"

Neera answered carefully. Then, "What color are my eyes?"

She answered easier while breathing. Then, "What else do you see?"

She would describe the things in her proximity, her heart rate evening out.

"You're present. You're here. I'm here. You're okay. Everything's okay," he repeated on each exhale. They stayed like that for a while, Neera was unsure, but soon the pounding in her ears died down. Her shaky breaths became more stable. The world wasn't spinning at the speed of light anymore.

She was in her bedroom. On the floor with her dad. It was Thursday. Everything was ok.

Except it's not. You have a tail.

She moved her head out of his hands to examine her legs–her normal, regular legs–and sighed in relief.

"What happened? Are you alright?" Her dad searched; she could feel his lingering fear even though he didn't show it.

She forced her eyes away from her legs and gave him a tight smile.

"Yeah. Must've been a bad dream. Thank you for helping me."

Neera really wanted to tell him what she saw, but her fear of ending up in an asylum was stronger.

What would he think if I told him I had a fishtail?

"Today is your...birthday, so I understand. Do we need... do we need to get you back on the medication?" He stammered, his glasses sliding down his wide nose and not bothering to fix it.

Her eyes widened as she shook her head vigorously. She remembered the day the therapist, Dr. Coney, prescribed her the anxiety medication three days after her mum's funeral. Neera suffered from panic attacks after her death, especially on her birthdays. The medication did negate some of her severe symptoms but had side effects that were a nuisance.

So, when her panic attacks subsided for a year, she took Neera off the meds and focused on therapy sessions and swimming.

"I'm alright. I just-I just don't feel well enough to go to school today. My exams don't start until tomorrow. Can I please stay home?" She was in no condition to face normal society, especially Liam, who knew all about her history of anxiety. The past twenty-four hours had been eventful enough, and she would surely benefit from a rest day.

A moment of observant staring later, he nodded, "Yes, of course. If you need anything, just call, and I'll be here immediately." He kissed her forehead, then helped her to her bed to tuck her in.

She sighed as he patted her head lovingly. He eventually left the room, the door always slightly ajar. Neera closed her eyes, and images of this morning filled her head:

Her alarm clock blared at 6 am, and she had awakened on the bathroom floor, completely nude and lacking a green tail. Confused and slightly dazed, she determined her brain hallucinated the tail. Probably from the alcohol, for some reason. She shook it off, got up to deactivate her alarm, and prepared for her shower. Being already naked helped speed things up.

With the water at the perfect temp of blazing, she stepped in and immersed herself in the water. Forebodingly, her body started tingling, and five seconds later, she was out of the shower and back on the tiled floor.

Still delusional, she shook her head and closed her eyes, hoping she would wake up from this nightmare...only to discover the same shimmery tail and "bra" from earlier. It wasn't a dream, no matter how many times she smacked herself or pinched herself. She had a tail. She had a tail!

She was a freak. More than they already saw her as.

Her world tilted again. More like flipped upside-down. She dragged her legless body to her bed, then registered that she couldn't get in bed. Defeated, she threw an old t-shirt on and laid curled up in a ball next to the bed while wallowing in the one thing she hated the most: pity. More than anything, she wanted her mum to come into the room, take one look at her, and tell her she could fix it and that everything would be all right.

More than anything.

When her mum didn't appear, a panic attack kicked in instead, stealing her last bit of breath and her last bit of hope.

Neera was unsure how long it had been since she laid in bed. The change in room color showed it had been several hours, at least. Her appetite was nonexistent. She mourned her sanity, even after stepping on necks at prom and becoming indoctrinated into "Hot Chick" status. Instead of laughing maniacally with Lay-Lay and gossiping about last night, all she could do was wallow in pity and hide herself from society.

Back to square one.

She mourned her new-found "relationship" with Liam. She couldn't even discuss it with him since she wasn't at school. To top it off, she forgot his number. He was probably bored of her by now and moved on with life. Her head buried further into the cool pillow, hopefully enough to suffocate her.

Worst of all, she mourned a proper shower.

Neera called Lay-Lay, hoping she could bring all her stuff from her locker because she wasn't feeling well. She rightfully freaked.

"What the hell happened?!" Her friend burst her eardrums. "Are you hurt? Did that Liam dude do something to you last night? I swear if he hurt you–"

Neera's eyes rolled to oblivion. Her friend was dramatic but the most trustworthy person she knew, aside from her dad, although she was pretty sure Lay-Lay was scrappier.

Neera tried to sound more reassuring, but her groggy voice was clearly not helping. "Hey, can you just bring my stuff, Lay-Lay? Please? I'll explain everything when you get here."

After several profanities, Elayne agreed and hung up. That caused Neera to smile.

Oh yeah, Elayne is definitely the scrappy one.

A knock on the door interrupted Neera's nap. A rapid session, then three slow ones. Elayne's secret knock they developed as kids. Instead of waiting for an answer, she just bulldozed herself inside and dropped her books–and Neera's– on her carpet. Her hidden eyebrows fused together in worry as her arms crossed over her chest.

"What's going on, Nee-Nee?" She inquired, stalking closer and scanning Neera's body. Neera could only assume that she looked a mess. "You look a mess."

Knew it.

Neera clutched her brown comforter, deciding if she should tell her the truth.

"And tell me the truth," she pressed.

Dang, she's good.

"Thanks for bringing my books, Lay-Lay," Neera croaked.

Elayne waited. She was at her scariest when that quiet.

Neera cleared her throat and confessed. "I've gone mad."

Her English is really channeling her dad's today.

Elayne visibly relaxed, then scoffed, "Yeah, what else is new?"

Neera balked, then bit her bottom lip. "Seriously! I think my mind has tricked me into thinking I'm a mermaid. Or a fish. I'm probably more of a fish."

Elayne closed the space between them and yanked the comforter off of Neera. She squealed at her exposed bare legs since she was only wearing an oversized t-shirt. "Looking very non-fishy to me." Elayne sniffed around her pelvis because she lacked boundaries. "You don't smell fishy either."

Neera sprang out of bed and shook Elayne's shoulders like the world was ending. "I'm dead serious, Lay-Lay! I can't even take a shower without turning into some...freak!"

Elayne's smirk dropped as her eyes searched Neera's face, probably looking for any indication of sarcasm. "Ok, show me." Neera dropped her hands, but her eyes were still wide. "If I see it too, then we'll know it's not just you."

Neera nodded lightly, believing the simple solution, but having it confirmed only made her more anxious. Elayne was already shuffling in her tights to the bathroom and turning on the shower. Water rained down on her arm, causing her to wince.

"Why the hell is your water so hot? Geez..." Elayne exclaimed, rubbing her forearm.

Neera ignored her and watched the shower in silent horror. This was the moment of truth. She discarded her t-shirt and stepped into the shower, enjoying the seconds of normalcy until the tingling engulfed her entire body. She started to tumble, but Elayne caught her under her arms with an astonished look.

Elayne lowered her onto the tiled floor and then backed up slightly, processing the situation. At least Neera wasn't mad. She was just a monster. Now, Elayne knew. Again, her silence and staring unnerved Neera, but she waited timidly for the disgusted jeers.

She'll never want to talk to me again.

"You..." Elayne gasped, then smiled, "Look so freakin' dope, Nee-Nee!" Her excitement climbing. "You're a mermaid! My best friend is a mermaid!"

She patted Neera's damp head like a champion show pony. "Look at the bright side. You get to cut your shaving time in, like, half."

Neera glared at her unexpectedly chipper friend.

"Get out of my house."

HOT TUB CONFESSIONS

Chapter 7

Neera

    LIAM: HEY. DIDNT C U TODAY. R U OK?
    NEERA: YUP. JUST A LIL SICK
    LIAM: SORRY. CALL ME? NEED 2 ASK U SMTH

Neera stared at the screen quizzically while Elayne "studied" her Calculus textbook on her bed.

After revealing her transformation, Elayne couldn't stop rambling about mermaid lore and asking Neera questions she had no clue of. Her body reverted back to normal as easily as subconsciously flexing a muscle. While her dad had an emergency client, she called to inform him that she was fine, so they decided to study as a distraction.

Then Liam texted her. She hated to admit how much she missed him.

So Neera retreated to her bathroom, closed the door, and dialed the number that texted him.

How did he get my number anyway?

It rang twice, and then she heard a smoky voice on the other end. "Neera." It wasn't a question.

She could feel her face heat, but she replied breathily,

"Liam...hey."

Smooth.

The silence between them didn't silence the electricity flowing through her.

He cleared his throat. "Did Elayne mention anything to you?"

Elayne? How does he know Elayne?

"No," she shook her head as if he could see, like a dork. "Why?"

"Uh..." She could picture him running his rough hand through his brown tresses. "I wanted to know if you and Elayne wanted to come over to my house tomorrow. Not like that, but I just wanted to see you in person. And your friend demanded it to be a supervised visit." He chuckled nervously.

Now it was Neera's turn to say, "Uh..."

"I'm not going to lie. I want to make sure you're actually okay and you're not hurt or anything from last night. I did get a little touchy, so I'm hoping you didn't feel pressured. Or, you know, taken away by the government."

Neera chuckled and rolled her eyes. He still believed she was in witness protection, although she did admit that her disappearance after confessing everything to him wasn't helping her case.

As for their physical interaction in the hotel, she never felt any pressure from him. It was more of the other way around. They ended up leaving the hotel because he didn't want to go further, no matter how persistent and reassuring she was of him to take it to the next level. He claimed the alcohol turned him off. He'd rather wait for the right time. Another reason why she liked him.

The other reason was how he managed to make Neera feel safe, comfortable, and secure enough for her to tell him everything. A guy she just officially met felt like someone she had known for a lifetime. She was not entirely sure how to deal with these intense feelings.

Should I keep him at bay since I'm experiencing some sort of metamorphosis? Or should I tell him and give into them…give into him?

"If you don't want to, I completely–"

"No, I want to," Neera squeaked, then cleared her throat and lowered her pitch. "We'll be there."

She could hear him smile. "Awesome. See ya then."

Neera hugged her arms, feeling her blush reach its peak. She opened her bathroom door, almost colliding with Elayne. Her best friend wiggled her eyebrows.

"We'll be there," she mocked in a lower voice. Neera pushed her friend out of the way. "We'll be there, Liam baby!"

Liam's mansion could house two of Neera's. His nearest neighbor had to be at least a hundred feet away, leaving them virtually alone. The Spanish-style architecture gave it an ancient feel, but the large windows, garage, and small dock modernized it. The tan house was textured, almost like clay on the outside, and the brown-tiled roof had different levels depending on the different parts of the house. Palm trees were sporadically perched around the entrance with a long and winding pebble driveway, while more palm trees were clustered some feet away. It looked old yet beautiful.

Antique.

Elayne parked her purple buggy in the driveway. The girls marveled at the monument of a house as they got out. They ambled up a few steps to the front door with Neera struggling a bit in her strappy, white wedges that Elayne insisted she wore.

Thinking her school look wasn't enough, Elayne insisted Neera wear something "sexy." This included a white cropped halter top that left nothing to the imagination, her curly hair pulled back into a ponytail with a green, triangle-folded bandana wrapped around it, and dark-washed, low-rise bootcut jeans that showed off her tummy.

Why Neera even listened to her was a mystery.

Elayne knocked on the dark oak door until Liam answered, looking slightly annoyed by the persistent knocking but instantly captivated by Neera.

"Hey," he smiled. He looked lush in his cream long-sleeve under a black tee, his hair slightly tousled, and his dark wash jeans. It was all hot, but his smile took the cake.

"Hey," Neera breathily replied. His warm eyes roamed her from top-to-bottom, then settled on her eyes.

She had no idea how long they'd been standing there until Elayne huffed, "Where do you keep the snacks?" And pushed past him, entering his home.

His eyes narrowed. "Well, isn't she a sweet pea?" A slight southern accent rolled off his tongue. He offered his hand, which she gladly took as he led her inside.

The entire floor was covered in dark hardwood, which gave it a modern feel. Compared to the exterior, the inside looked more Old English than she expected. Large golden curtains draped the large windows that spanned the rear of the house. The furniture looked like a king and queen had a yard sale, but it was kind of comfy. The kitchen was coated in marble, creams, and stainless-steel appliances. He lived like those celebrities on *Cribs*.

He's way out of my league.

Shoving negativity down, Neera let him lead her to the kitchen, where Lay-Lay was tearing into a family-sized bag of Hot Fries. She offered them some because her best friend was nothing but courteous. Liam just cringed and declined. If he was willing to put up with her hot mess of a friend, she would simply marry him on the spot.

"Actually," Liam turned to Neera. "I was hoping we could speak in private in the backyard." He turned his stare to Elayne, giving her an expectant look.

She took the hint, carrying the crinkled bag with her up the winding staircase. Liam called out to her. "Just stay out of the rooms with closed doors. They're forbidden."

"Well, then those are my first stops. Thanks," she threw

over her shoulder as she stomped her combat boots up the steps.

Liam tensed, probably about to scold her, but that was everyone's natural response to her. Neera gripped his hand and led him to the sliding doors of the backyard.

The outside was as equally beautiful as the inside. A patio set up off to one side, and then a decent-sized in-ground pool next to it. What really captured her attention was the island that looked around a few miles away. Well, what she assumed without her glasses, but it was like he had a beach in his backyard.

His own little paradise.

"...this was my granddad's place until my dad inherited it. Then, eventually, this place will be all mine." Neera didn't notice he was talking. She nodded and smiled anyway.

Liam grabbed her hand again and led her to a corner next to the patio, except more secluded. He led her to this circular object and released her hand to discard the green cover, revealing a hot tub with water in it.

"I filled it in case you two wanted to swim," he beamed, sweat beading on his forehead.

Neera's nerves went haywire but remained cool. She had to avoid getting wet, especially in front of him. At least not now. "I don't even have a swimsuit," she joked.

"You don't need one..." His face glowed bright red, and then he raised his hands in innocence. "I mean, like, my mom may have something..." Then he rubbed the hot tub as if it would release a genie to help stop him from the verbal throw-up.

"I actually wanted to see if you were okay," he redirected, eyes searching hers. "I know we talked about some hard topics, and I hoped it didn't affect you badly."

"I'm fine, really," she lied but tried to ease the tension. "It's not like I was relocated or something." She chuckled nervously.

He stepped closer to her and rummaged in his pocket. He

pulled out a small green heart on a keychain and handed it to her. She took it, feeling its soft exterior, and then squeezed. The heart bloated around her fingers, its material stretching and then returning to its original form when she released it.

"I heard that when people have panic attacks, they need something to ground them and things that release some of the tension help."

She gazed back into his eyes, his hazel ones more golden than brown. "If no one is around and things get hard, just squeeze it, and know that you're okay... And-and that you have me." He had the nerve to blush.

Thinking was useless as her stomach fluttered with butterflies. Thanking him didn't feel like enough. She wasn't enough. *Why does he care about me this much?* "Why? Why are you doing all this?"

He caressed her arms and shrugged. "I meant what I said at prom. I like you, Neera. You're the only person I can truly be myself with. Someone I can trust with everything in my life. I've never...never met someone who matches me like you do."

"I...I feel the same, but didn't know how to say it," she nervously giggled.

"Yeah?" His face couldn't get any redder, then she felt his breath as he sighed as if he had been holding it this entire time. "Do you wanna be my girlfriend?"

Before the negativity could yell from the back seat, Neera nodded eagerly. She was willing to take this chance with him. She hadn't done much of that since...since her world shattered over eight years ago. If there was one thing that would make sense in her messed-up mermaid life, it was being with Liam Dern.

Liam leaned down, and she immediately closed her eyes, remembering the first time they kissed and the—ahem—many kisses in the hotel room. She basked in it: his lips, his hands around her waist, his full heart that he left exposed on his sleeve. The butterflies in her stomach sounded bubblier.

Weird. I can actually hear them.

Neera broke the kiss and opened her eyes, noticing Liam looking dumbfounded at the pool. She turned and saw bubbles along the surface. Even the hot tub was bubbling.

"How'd you do that?" She asked, fascinated.

Liam shook his head, mouth slacked. "I didn't."

Her heart stopped, just for a second. She had a strong feeling it was her doing because why not? She was a mermaid, after all. She might as well add *water-bender* to the roster.

It died down, and they both visibly relaxed. She made a note to tell Elayne about it, secretly hoping he would let it go.

He backed up a little and rubbed the back of his neck. "So…anything else you want to tell me?"

I'm a mermaid, and I have no clue why. I hope you won't hate me after seeing it.

The feeling of a rope sliding across her foot snapped her out of her spiral. Glancing down, a dark tri-colored, medium-sized snake slithered across her bare toes. Neera froze. Her fear devoured her as her heartbeat thumped in her throat, threatening to scream.

Except she didn't because she was terrified of snakes. Something about its smoothness reminded her of her tail. Then that reminded her of the fear people have with scaly things, the very same fear she possessed. How misunderstood they were. This connection inhibited her scream and snuffed out her terror of reptiles but replaced it with trepidation for people discovering her secret.

Liam's hand snatched up the tail end of the snake as he ran towards the beach connected to his yard, blurting over his shoulder, "Don't worry, I got it! We get these all the time!"

He chucked the poor snake towards the shore, its body wriggling and landing in the sand. Neera smiled at Liam's attempt to be a hero but cringed at the snake's fate.

And hers.

LIAM

"Yo, Jess is having a party at her place. You coming?" Nate asked excitedly on the other end of Liam's cell. "Think of all the hotties that will be there."

Liam chuckled, but not at what Nate said. His thoughts were corrupted by his...*girlfriend*. Not to sound lame, but he'd never had a girlfriend for a good reason. All the constant moving made people, that weren't his family, temporary in his life. There was no point in getting attached. But now that he had a *girlfriend*, he was a bit scared to mess it up.

And you will.

No. You don't have to be perfect with her.

"Yeah, about that..." he grinned to himself as he flicked his yellow highlighter between his fingers. "I'm actually bringing someone with me, and don't make it a big deal—."

"Ooo..." Nate started. "It's not who I think it is?"

Liam tensed, preparing to defend Neera's honor if this went south. "You'll see when we show up."

At the sound of his door opening, he hung up and hid his phone underneath his textbook. His dad strolled into his bedroom and stood over his son, leaning slightly on the desk where Liam was seated. Liam wasn't the only one studying something as his blue eyes surveyed him.

"Anything new going on? Something you want to tell me?" His dad asked–more like interrogated.

He swallowed a knot in his throat. His mind filtered between possible admissions: new girlfriend, inviting strangers to their house without permission, and one of them leaving behind Hot Fry-dust stains. Liam's secret desire to attend a D1 university. His plan to sneak out to a party tomorrow night.

"I, uh," Liam cleared his throat. "I aced my Bio exam."

After what felt like minutes, his dad softened, and his mouth curled up a little. He was not a man of affection or warm smiles unless he was in front of the camera or strangers.

Liam stopped expecting them in private when he was younger, so he took this as a win.

"Great. I never expect anything less," he boasted as he clapped his hand on Liam's shoulder, exuding pride. Liam just wasn't sure if it was pride for him or for himself. Yet Liam grinned because his dad's respect would always mean something to him.

When he left, shutting the door behind him, Liam exhaled a breath he didn't know he was holding and called Neera.

Neera. His heart already surged just thinking about her.

Thinking about how she reacted to his gift, his grin widened. *Like a goof.* He'd researched anxiety and asked the school counselor for some advice on grounding methods during lunch. Anything to make her feel a little less alone in the world, and maybe to think of him during those times too.

Liam waited for her to pick up. Rang once. Twice.

"Hey," her breathy voice caressed his ears, giving him goosebumps.

"How are you feeling?" Liam asked, scooting his textbook to the side. Not because of her anxiety but because he genuinely desired to know everything about her. If he could, he wanted her to be okay. Always.

"Peachy. Just convinced the FBI to let me remain in the country," she quipped.

She will never let it go.

She might not be much of a talker, but when she did, it was always something worth listening to. She never failed to make him laugh, and he wasn't the humorous type.

"What are you doing tomorrow night?" He laughed.

She was silent, maybe thinking, until he realized what he could be implicating and felt his face getting hot, bringing him back to the night in the hotel room.

It's not the right time...yet.

"Nothing," she answered, her voice soft.

"You wanna go to a party? It's at Jessica's," he paused,

waiting for a huff-fest, but she remained quiet. "I want to show you off."

Stillness. *Did she hang up?*

"Can Elayne come?"

He blinked. He could barely sneak in his girlfriend; sneaking in Elayne would be a bigger challenge. "Uh...I only have the plus one."

Liam felt icky telling her this. He didn't hate Elayne; he just knew Jessica did. He felt even more horrible that Neera would be vulnerable.

No. Because she has him. She would get used to the attention.

Just like him.

Liam ran a hand through his hair. "Um, don't worry. You'll have me."

The silence stretched into minutes. His nerves bunched. He shouldn't be this nervous about inviting a date to a party. However, he genuinely wanted her to trust him.

"Hell—"

"Let's go. Call me when you get here."

The call ended just like that.

Liam studied the phone like some undiscovered artifact. She never said she trusted him. Even after everything they shared with each other. Even after he offered his heart to her. There was something about him she wasn't comfortable with.

Liam groaned and plunked his head on his desk.

It hasn't been twenty-four hours since she became your girlfriend, and you're already fucking this up.

Jessica's front yard was already packed with fellow classmates when Neera and Liam arrived at the entrance to her chateau. The all-white structure almost rivaled Liam's house in size, but it was more pristine. The large columns in the front made it seem presidential, or maybe it was the large Star-Spangled flag waving diagonally in front of the entrance.

Liam couldn't care less about that since a certain someone had stolen all his attention.

Neera looked amazing, as usual. Her curls were slicked up into a high ponytail, showcasing her cheekbones and gold hoop earrings. Her lips were glossy and subtly pink. The hot pink tube top showcased her chest while complementing her camouflage capris, which hugged her hips. He almost forgot that they had a party to attend.

Liam did, however, notice her uneasiness. As if he could telepathically tell her to trust him, he squeezed her hand and winked at her. Neera gave a hint of a smile yet mirrored his squeeze.

With that, they walked over to the side of the house and opened the white gate, entering a stereotypical, tiki-torched teen bash. 3OH!3 blasted from the outdoor speakers. People were dancing, some grinding, and others were playing beer pong on the grass-covered fold-out table. He recognized a few peers from his advanced classes there. Luckily the host was off somewhere else.

Nate strutted up to them with a red plastic cup in his hand and greeted Liam with their customary handshake. He gave Neera a nod of acknowledgment. She tried to smile but exuded timidity. *Cute.*

"Hello," she extended a hand like a job interview. "I'm Ne-"

"Yeah, I know who you are," he dismissed as he took a sip out of his cup.

He better be drunk or I'm decking the hell out of him.

Neera's hand clutched her other arm, and her freckles brightened, causing Liam's blood to boil, ready to shield her like a cocoon.

"You never know someone until you actually talk to them," Liam gritted out, his chest puffed like Neera's personal bodyguard. "Not about them."

Nate's jaw slacked, then he bristled and took a longer swig. "Ok, Dern."

He turned his attention to Neera, his eyes ogling her chest and back to her face. "Nice to meet you, Neera. I'm Nate, your boy's best friend-"

"I know who you are," she muttered. She looked around uncomfortably, and it broke Liam's heart a little. He said he would protect her, and he basically threw her into the ocean without a life vest. Her skin wasn't as thick as his.

Before he could sweep her away and apologize for putting her in this position, a bleach-blonde with a pink bikini and wrap skirt appeared next to Nate. Her pageant smile caused his adrenaline to spike, and not in a good way.

"Why would you bring HER?" Jessica sneered as if Neera wasn't literally in front of her. "I told you before prom to leave that weirdo alone."

Jessica had taken his softness as a weakness, and it was going to end now.

Neera pinched his elbow, forcing his attention on her. She gave him a half-hearted smile. "It's fine. I'm used to it. I'll let you hang out with your friends. I-I want to be alone anyways."

She strode away from him, struggling in her platforms, towards the other end of the yard with Liam frozen in anger and disappointment in himself. All he had to do was stop her and run off into the night, but his anger wouldn't allow it. He had to set things straight with his "friends" –and he used that term very loosely.

Their disrespect was unwelcomed when it came to his girlfriend. She was off-limits, and if Jessica went out of bounds one more time, he would have to embarrass her on her own property.

"Hey, man," Nate clapped a hand on his shoulder, his dimples appearing as he tried to diffuse the tension. "When I said you should take her to prom, I meant to hit it and quit it. Not cuff yourself."

"That weirdo is going to ruin your reputation," Jessica gibed.

"I'm getting tired of your shit," Liam addressed Jessica. "If you don't think getting chlamydia from a dude with chronic bad breath doesn't ruin your rep, then I think I'll be just fine."

Her jaw dropped, her head swiveling as she noticed many eyes gathering around. Some of them were jeering and applauding, and some were frozen in shock. Nate pulled him closer and hissed, "Chill, man, she's a girl and our friend."

Liam scoffed, clearly losing his mind. He grabbed whatever was left of Nate's drink and chugged it. The cool liquid warmed his entire body, loosening some of his agitation.

He smirked at Nate. "Says the elite jock who's faster in bed than on the field."

His personal audience snickered.

Nate's fist abruptly slammed into his jaw. Liam stumbled back but didn't fall. He could jump him right now, but he would rather let their revealed secrets fester.

"You're right. I have no idea what I'm talking about," Liam smirked while wiping the bit of blood from the corner of his mouth with his thumb. The audience dispersed at his "fake" confessions, relaxing the targets but not too much. He wanted them to know that he could and would ruin their lives with the secrets he never asked for. He could do it whenever he wanted, and one look at their insecure faces disclosed they knew it too.

"Get the fuck out of my party," Jessica shrieked.

"I will. After I get my girl."

Liam, jaw aching and a bit tipsy, jogged over to the hot tub in the far corner of the yard because it was the perfect spot to hide. Neera sat in the bubbly tub, steam rising into the night, except she looked different.

Really different...

"With You" played softly in the background the closer he approached the tub. As he approached, she stiffened, and their eyes met. He froze for some reason, suffocating in nervousness.

Neera's hair was down and wet, but it looked full and

wavy. Her eyes seemed greener, almost fluorescent. Almost as shiny as her bra. At least he thought it was a bra. They looked like pasties. At closer inspection, her skin sparkled like she was tattooed by the galaxy.

Silence must've been their love language. He stripped down to his boxers and carefully slid into the scolding tub. *What did she set it to? Hell?*

Liam ignored how red his skin was from the blazing water. Too preoccupied with her appearance and curious how she was able to change in such a short time, he stared at her in silent awe.

You should probably say something.

He cleared his throat. "I'm sorry for what they said. It's not true...what they said."

She stiffened. Maybe the apology wasn't specific enough.

He added, "I'm sorry for not protecting you. You're someone special. Someone who should always be protected. And I didn't...I'm genuinely sorry."

He was really close to her now and didn't remember scooting towards her. The scales on her top blended into her skin as if a special effects team was working overtime to make it.

She sighed. "There seems to be some truth in it." She eyed him carefully, scrutinizing. "You rejected me the second I asked you. Then you couldn't wait to see me the second I changed. You only care about appearances, just like them." She sharply nodded her head towards the party.

It was Liam's turn to be silent. He let them get to him in the beginning, that she was potentially dangerous. And then he let his "boy brain" forget that danger when she started dressing like the girls who usually hooked up with him.

She was right...to an extent.

Except he did like her quirky style and glasses that emphasized her beautiful eyes. He liked her freckles, her smile, which wasn't always there but always appreciated when shown, and her sarcasm, which never failed to make him laugh.

Most importantly, her heart, which was torn to pieces when her mom died, but she continued to open it anyway when the world repeatedly stomped on it.

Neera never needed to change for him to notice her. It was Liam that needed to change, to be braver and more open. He didn't think she would take their interaction as disdain.

He wanted to tell her all this, but his words tackled him like a defensive lineman.

Liam placed his hand on her arm and caressed it reverently.

"I was a wimp for not being brave enough to talk to you. It's true…The things you said. But I've always liked you, Neera."

Is my tongue always this thick?

Liam swallowed the knot in his throat. He moved closer to her. Only three inches away from her nose.

"I've always liked you the way you are. I just wasn't genuine enough to admit it."

His lips brushed her momentarily. Pure electricity shot through his body, hotter than the water they were wading in.

"Liam," she breathed, and his body shivered.

"I really like you, Neera," he held her chin between his thumb and pointer. "Whether it's overalls or miniskirts."

Neera closed her eyes and touched foreheads. She breathed in and out as if preparing herself and had finally come to a solution.

"What about a tail?"

Liam moved his head away, confused. It was not the time for a dark joke, so he didn't laugh. "What?"

She guided his hand underneath the water, and he almost shrunk back from the unusual texture, but her hand kept it there. It was textured yet smooth, almost like the snake he had caught yesterday, but this one was warm.

When her hand stopped moving, she looked to the other side of the hot tub, biting her bottom lip. Liam, still confused and a little scared, followed her line of sight…a shimmering

green fishtail waved seductively at him.
Did Nate punch you that hard?

FAMILY HISTORY

Chapter 8

Neera

What did I just do?

All Neera wanted to do was relax her nerves after the verbal ambush Liam's friends released on her. She wanted to fight back, just slap that witch one good time. Alas, she shrunk away like a punk.

Always a punk.

If Lay-Lay were there, it would've been a bloodbath. Verbally, of course. She was actually the one who convinced Neera to go without her while she was on the phone with Liam. Something about "solidifying her popularity" or whatever. Neera wished she had held her back.

Liam, who desired her trust, disappointed her the most. He basically sweet-talked her into a slaughter. The worst part was that he had the same mentality, which was why they were such good friends. He would've never given her a side glance if she didn't change. He would've seen her as a weirdo, too. A weirdo with a dead mom and constantly struck by misfortune.

Trust me, my butt.

As soon as Neera submerged herself into the tub, the tingling was more welcomed at that moment as her body transformed. It distracted her from the anger coursing through her veins. No one was around, but she didn't care if they were. They were so drunk, they wouldn't even remember whose party it was the next day. Her fuming simmered until her stomach began to flutter.

She could sense him before she could see him.

Liam looked as if he was enchanted as he shuffled towards her. When their eyes met, she felt equally beguiled. Her body felt trapped under his gaze. Not trapped. Held.

At the edge of the hot tub, he removed his clothes until he only stood in his green boxers. He climbed into the hot tub and sat in the seat next to her.

It felt strange. Intimate.

Neera expressed all her doubts, all her mistrust, in him because it looked really shady from her perspective. He actively listened with a look in his eyes that she couldn't decipher. Negativity had a hand on her back, spurring her on.

Is he mad that he got caught red-handed? What lie is he thinking next?

When she noticed the bruise forming on his left cheek, her anger started to melt away. *Did he get in a fight...for me?* His hazel eyes darkened to brown, as if he would do it again in a heartbeat.

Then he confessed, disintegrating any hurt she had hidden inside.

That was not Liam, "Mr. Popular".

That wasn't Liam, the snake-chucker.

This was Liam. The guy with a heart as big as his brain. A genius who had a habit of verbal throw-up but will research a mental health disorder to help them. A hot guy with a smile that was beautiful when genuine and hair that never remained in place for more than two minutes. A prince who was forced onto his throne, noble yet tortured.

Someone who wouldn't hurt her, but hurt for her.

When they kissed, everything was confirmed. Her feelings for him, stronger than anything she'd ever felt, infiltrated her logical brain and set up camp. He always liked her. And she always liked him.

Negativity remained in the back seat with tape over its mouth.

There's nothing you can say to stop me from telling the truth. I trust him.

Liam stared momentarily at the space her tail was after she tucked it back under the water, his body tense and his mouth slightly ajar.

She understood. He actually had a better reaction than her.

He started distancing himself to the opposite side of the tub. More space than she would like. All she could do was stare as he contemplated. The butterflies in her stomach were fusing together disgustingly and screaming in pain at his hesitation. At the possibility that she was wrong in trusting him.

After what seemed like forever, but was really like five minutes, he scanned the area. Maybe searching for others, but no one was nearby. Some people had already left, and the ones that were left drunkenly made out to R&B or smoked around a table.

Liam moved so fast that Neera barely registered that he had closed the space between them again. He cradled both sides of her face in his hands as he leaned in. Neera closed her eyes, prepared for another kiss, but he stopped just a breath away. His heart beat fast in her ears, but his eyes were stable. Determined.

His voice was low and deep. "Tail and all."

Then he kissed her. The butterflies burst through, fluttering everywhere and blinding her. She couldn't hear anything else.

Feel anything else except Liam. In their own little world. Together.

Oh no, I think I love him.

"We actually have to get out of here. Like now," Liam

tossed over his shoulder as he got out of the hot tub, Neera pretending she wasn't ogling his glistening muscles.

"Why? What happened?" Neera hoped he didn't fight Jessica. Physically, that is.

"I'll explain everything later."

He dried himself off with the towel she found in a hidden panel on the side of the tub before she got in. Then he hastily, and unfortunately, put on his jeans, tank, and unbuttoned plaid shirt. He pulled Neera up by her armpits and positioned her on her bottom, tail grazing the grass.

"Can you pass me the towel?" Neera tried to ignore his fascination as he took in her full form, her face on fire. He passed her the damp but useful cloth, and she hastily dried her body. Liam positioned himself to block the majority of her body from the rest of the party stragglers.

When the tingling returned, she quickly wrapped herself in the towel right before her body reverted back to normal. Normal and completely naked. Embarrassed at max capacity, Neera distractedly sprang off the tub edge while Liam happened to be looking back. They collided, but Liam caught her by the waist, arms wrapped around her while she fought against gravity, as if her legs were malfunctioning. His face was literally an inch from hers, and her blushing could very possibly be permanent.

"I should've known you were a mermaid," he murmured, then smirked. "Because you're too pretty to be just human."

Neera died. More out of embarrassment that something so corny could make her feel so toasty inside.

"I told YOU to get out. But you decided to have a fuck sess in my hot tub!"

Neera and Liam snapped their heads toward a shrilling witch–Jessica–holding a red cup and slightly swaying, her face beet red in anger. They jolted apart, Neera hurrying to pick up her scattered clothes.

"It's not like that. We're leaving now," Liam gritted out. Neera picked up the last of her clothes, balled up in her fists.

Right before she could flee, Jessica scoffed obnoxiously.

"I knew you were a freaky weirdo, but I never pegged you for a slut, too."

I wish Lay-Lay were here. Neera cringed at the blow, but she didn't speak. There was usually no point talking to these people, so she pulled her lips in and glared heavily.

"Shut the f-," Liam shouted but was cut off by the drink in Jessica's hand erupting and splashing all over her face. She immediately dropped the cup and rubbed her eyes in pain, screaming. The sound triggered Neera's fight-or-flight. More like "freeze". Her body trembled, and her eyes locked on Jessica writhing in pain. She reached out to help her somehow but couldn't bring herself to move, still in shock.

Grabbing her outstretched hand, Liam led her out of the yard, like Romeo and Juliet, into the night. No words were said between them. *Good.* It gave her time to process everything that happened. She chanced a glance at Liam, who stared darkly at the passing pavement.

A thought crossed her mind, a very finite one, that she refused to admit.

I hurt Jessica...and Liam thinks I'm dangerous.

Liam parked at the end of Neera's block and got out of the vehicle, giving her privacy to change back into her clothes. Which was pretty difficult because of the lack of windows. No one was outside except a nosy raccoon getting quite the show.

It was awkward the entire time, from changing to the short drive to her doorstep. Neera clutched her green heart keychain tight, the elastic material oozing out of the gaps in her fist. The air simmered instead of sparking with the usual warmth between them.

"Some party, huh?" Neera chuckled to break the tension.

"Yeah..." Liam rubbed the back of his neck, which caused Neera to tense up.

I just got a boyfriend, and he already wants to break up with me. Negativity hissed in her ear.

"Um...goodnight, Liam," Neera exited the jeep with a

wince. No quirky send-off. No funny lines. Just disappointed in herself.

"Hey, Ran."

Neera turned around and saw a tense Liam, white knuckles squeezing his steering wheel and shoulders ridged. He stared into her soul with his contradictingly soft gaze. "Your secret is always safe with me. I'm just tired tonight." He gave a hint of a smile. "Goodnight."

She half-heartedly grinned and waved as he drove away. Her heart filled with worry, but she could only trust in his words.

Trust the present, not the hypothetical future.

When she entered her house, darkness enveloped her with the exception of light emitting from her boxy telly, infomercials playing softly. Neera flipped the light switch, brightening the room, and her dad sprang up with his glasses skewed on his face.

"Neera," he blurted, then cleared his throat. "You're back early."

She tittered as he adjusted his glasses. "Yeah, it was kind of lame."

He sat back on the couch as she rounded it, standing in front of him. "I suppose that is a good enough reason to leave."

"Dad, I have something to ask you," Neera bit her lip and held herself.

He must've sensed her discomfort and patted the space next to him, which she reluctantly took. She needed to be brave, and it seemed she wasn't starting out too well. Nevertheless, she required answers to what was going on. And she needed to know if he knew this whole time.

"Ask me anything, love," her dad soothed.

Neera cleared her throat and squared her shoulders. "Did mum seem different? Did she have a secret that you two couldn't tell me?"

An unrecognizable look crossed his face.

Does he not know?

The silence stretched until he took his glasses off, wiped them on his robe, and sighed deeply. Longingly. "You've finally gone through the change, yeah?"

Neera gasped but remained silent otherwise. She never expected her father to keep secrets from her, since he always preached about transparency and trust.

Why haven't they told me about this? Why didn't they prepare me?

"I," he paused, looking at his hands. "We knew this day was going to arrive but never knew when. I knew your mum was a mermaid the moment I laid eyes on her nineteen years ago."

Neera was still shocked. "I thought you two met at a club in the 80s."

He laughed lightly, the lines in his forehead creasing. The sound seemed sad. Bittersweet.

"It was actually AFTER the club. At the beach."

Neera settled into the plush couch that her mother picked out when she was younger. To anyone else, the couch seemed raggedy and cheap, but her mum thought it was perfect. That it was full of stories and she could somehow continue filling the pages.

Her shoes off and her legs folded underneath her, Neera faced her dad.

"It was one of those days. It was my last year of graduate school, and I wanted to finally *get crazy*, as the kids say. The disco was dreadful. Bare mishap and drug use, yet somehow, awfully boring."

They both laughed.

"Well, I left my mates and headed to the beach nearby. I remember the night like it was yesterday." His face grew distant.

Neera watched him, waiting patiently.

"I was sitting on the shore with a bottle in my hand when I heard the most beautiful voice humming a melody nearby. I thought it was a hallucination until I saw..."

Neera nodded slowly. He crossed his arms and looked absently at the coffee table.

"Nerissa looked like a goddess emerging from the ocean. I almost thought I died and the ocean carried me away, until I realized it was real. She knew no English, but we connected through body language and bits of English. I practiced introducing myself to her, but she took my glasses and imitated me. When I tapped a hand over my heart and circled it, she would do the same until she understood, and it became our thing."

Her dad placed a hand over his chest, still distant. "That was when she stole my heart. It was love at first sight. I never wanted the night to end."

Neera grinned as she thought about what Liam said during prom.

"As the sun rose, we promised to meet each other at that very spot, at that exact time, every two weeks. With each visit, she gained more English, and I learned a bit about her. The last time we met at the beach, she miraculously had legs. It was so absurd, more that she sprouted legs than when she had a green tail." He chuckled. His eyes sparkled as if her mum was standing directly in front of him.

"After we had a...proper bonding," her dad's eyes grew shifty, and Neera tried not to gag at the image of her parents doing it. "She told me everything about her ability to change between land and sea whenever she wanted, yet she preferred the sea. Also, how she had water-manipulation abilities."

"Wait," Neera shook her head in disbelief. *How is this even possible? If she can control her change, why didn't she swim?* "So she wasn't afraid of water?"

Her dad chuckled and pushed his sliding glasses up his nose bridge. "No. Her control over her change became unpredictable when she became pregnant. And I suppose she didn't want to risk getting wet and exposing herself. It's quite complicated and something I can't personally explain."

All this was too much for Neera for one day. She

appreciated the honesty, but it still came too late—came from the wrong person.

"Why- why didn't she tell me?" Her voice trembled as tears pricked the back of her eyes. They were supposed to be best friends. They would tell each other everything, especially something as consequential as this.

Her dad cupped her hand, which she didn't notice was picking at a loose stitch on the couch.

"Dear, I trusted my wife," he exhaled. "And she believed it wasn't the right time. She was going to tell you. I believe that wholeheartedly."

The tears strained against her eyes, but she refused to cry. Not again.

An irrational part of her resented her mum. A secret betrayal. The fact that she had to figure out this condition by herself.

That her mother left her all alone.

"You know, love, I'm here for you. To help you through this in any way you need me to."

Neera sniffled and nodded. She wrapped her arms around her dad, the person who also could've told her sooner, half-heartedly. He would never understand her plight, an entire half of her.

I guess it's up to me to understand me.

LIAM

She's a mermaid. Not human. Not natural.

His dad would call her an abomination if he knew. Their family wasn't the "devout Catholic" type that went to Mass every week, but they still upheld their religious beliefs. One of those beliefs was that anything unnatural or not created by God should only be observed and never interacted with. An anomaly. An experiment. *Demonic.*

However, when Liam thought of Neera, she was the

furthest thing from "an abomination" he could think of. She…
she was sweet, timid, funny, and absolutely beautiful. No
monster.

Instead of sleeping, he spent the rest of the night
scrimmaging with himself, and the opposition was pretty
tough.

The opposing team was older, sturdier, and reigning
champs. They made him the person he currently was and the
person he would become when he got older and took over the
family business. The person his dad would look at with hubris.

The defense, on the other hand, was the underdogs.
New, but full of enough potential to go against the champions
and change the course of history. He knew his mom
would cheer from the bleachers for them. They challenged
everything he ever knew.

There was no way there could be a tie. Only one team
could win…

It was Sunday. Instead of the usual family breakfast, his
dad had an important project to work on, so Liam couldn't
even ask him for advice. Danny was in the yard practicing for
his soccer game, leaving his mom to prep snacks for him and
his team.

Liam was hesitant to ask his mom about it, mostly
because he didn't want to give anything away and partly
because he didn't think she'd understand. He walked up to his
mom as she packed some juice pouches into a cooler bag.

"Hey, Mom, I have something to ask you," Liam began.

His mom smirked as she paused her packing. "It must be
serious if you need permission to ask a question. What's up?"

Liam tried to gather his words to pour them out
carefully.

"Have you ever dated someone different from you?
Someone you know your dad wouldn't approve of?" Liam
leaned in.

His mom tilted her head, obviously ruminating. "I don't
think so. The only guy I've been with is your dad." Liam

deflated and prepared to turn away. "My parents absolutely hated him. They thought I was too young to settle down. That we weren't compatible."

Liam pulled out a wooden stool and planted himself there. "Why not?"

"The compatibility?" She finished packing the large bag and zipped it up. "He was very stiff, boisterous, and judgmental. Still is, I must say."

Liam shook his head lazily. "If he's all that, then why'd you stay with him?"

His mom turned her face to him, but her eyes looked past him. Far away.

"He's passionate and family-oriented. All this fame got to his head recently, but before you were born, all he could think about was children. How important having a family was. He took care of me throughout the pregnancy, and no one could pull him away from you."

"So," Liam absorbed her words, sighing. "You went against your parents' wishes, even though you two are very different but clearly in love. Did they eventually accept him?"

"Yeah, they did," she smiled. "Because as long as I was happy and never harmed, what makes the differences so bad? As long as the love is the same, nothing else matters."

With that, his mom lifted the bag's strap over her shoulder. "We're heading to Danny's game. You can join us if you want."

Liam shook his head, still processing everything. "No thanks, I have some studying to do."

His mom's smile dimmed, not reaching her eyes. Liam never went to Danny's games anymore, and he knew, deep down, that she was disappointed in him for it. Liam didn't hate his brother; he just hated the fake family dynamic they performed when they were out in public.

Besides, he had more important matters to attend to, like figuring out his life with his new aquatic girlfriend.

She leaned in closer, speaking softly. "Whoever you

choose, just know that I'm on your team."

Liam flashed her a quick smile as she kissed his cheek. Leaving her heart on the kitchen island, she headed out the sliding doors to the backyard.

He pulled out his cell and called Neera. She answered with that sultry, breathy voice of hers that he adored.

"Hey, Liam."

"Hey," he sighed, rubbing the back of his neck. "I was wondering if you wanted to come over and do some research on...mermaids? I have the house to myself for a couple of hours, so you don't have to worry about getting caught."

All Liam could hear was the electric air between them, but he was used to the silence by now.

"Just you and me?" She asked curiously.

Liam realized how suspicious it sounded for him to ask for her to come over in private, but he wanted to spend more time with her. To build up that trust he felt crumble on the ride back from the party.

Honestly, he'd been fighting himself ever since the confession. He wanted—needed—her to know that she could trust him and that she was worth fighting for. The way to accomplish that was by acclimating to her lifestyle. Her world.

"Yeah, but no pressure."

"Okay, I'll be there in a bit," she said with what Liam swore was a smile.

"Cool. It's a date."

After a quick shower, putting on a tank and some cargo shorts, and somewhat organizing his room, Liam received a text from Neera that she was at his door. He opened the door, sort of expecting Elayne to barge through, but found Neera there. Alone. And looking hot.

She wore a *very* low-cut, tight, sunflower t-shirt with a green cargo mini skirt and wedges. Her crossbody bag on her back matched her skirt. Her smile wrinkled her nose, drawing his attention to her freckles. He wished he could take a picture of her with his digital camera, but that might be a bit creepy at this stage in their relationship.

"You look hot," Liam shamelessly ogled and then cursed himself for being uncool about it.

Neera giggled. "Thanks. And you look...underdressed."

He looked down at his outfit and his old sandals. It did look like they were about to hook up. He pulled his lips in, his nerves bunching and his face heating.

I hope she doesn't take it the wrong way...but if she's up for it...

"So..." Neera smirked as she brushed past him. "Where do you keep your computer?"

Right. We're here to do research.

As much as Liam wanted to calm his hormones, he knew his next words would only rile him up more. Her palpable anticipation wasn't helping either.

"It's in my room...if you don't mind. We can just go to the library if you're not comfortable."

How the hell did I become so lame?

Neera shrugged. "I'm fine with going to your room. Lead the way."

Is siphoning coolness another one of those mermaid characteristics?

Swallowing his pride, he led her towards his room in the furnished basement. Basements weren't a thing in Cali, but his great-great-grandfather was fond of them and had one built once upon a time. From what his father told Liam, the basement was used for research, storage, or whenever his grandfather needed to bring his work home with him.

Currently, the infamous Dern basement was transformed into an angsty teen's hideaway for lifting weights, studying, and brooding sessions. Today, it was to help him and his girlfriend learn more about her new identity.

His room was large with a personal bathroom and a singular door leading to something unknown since it was always locked. Liam figured it was a storage room for stuff that couldn't fit in the garage. His "study" desk, which consisted of a desktop computer, typical office supplies, and his textbooks, was next to his bed. On the opposite side of the room were all his recreational games that were slowly collecting dust. Everything a guy would want–a fuse-ball table, a video game system with a big screen television, and even a mini fridge full of sodas and snacks–he had, but rarely used. It was his mom's idea to get items that kids liked to have "fun", yet Liam always preferred his hands on some informative texts or a pigskin ball.

"Your room is cool," Neera chimed from the other side of the room, her fingers diddling with the yellow player skewered in place. Her eyes roamed the entire room until they landed back on Liam with a hint of a smile. For a split second, he thought about playing fuse-ball or beating her in a Street Fighter match or some other silly and unsubstantial activity.

"You're free to stay if you like it so much," Liam quipped sarcastically.

Neera sauntered towards him from the other side of the room with a deadpan face. Liam was caught up by her assertiveness and backed up slightly until she stopped a few inches from his face, her eyes seizing his heart and causing his chest to tighten.

"Was that an invite to sleep over, Dern?" She smirked, eyes quickly dropping to his lips and making Liam forget the reason they were there in the first place.

There's no way she doesn't know the power she wields over me.

"Anyway," Liam cleared his throat and moved around her to the desktop monitor. Ignoring her smugness, he offered her his wooden chair before she took a seat. While looming over her from behind with his head incredibly close to hers, he shook his mouse to wake the screen, trying his hardest to focus on the task at hand. "The key to finding out info is by clicking the middle of the results pages. Never the first page for this kind of stuff."

Liam typed *mermaid* into the search bar, and the basic information about them appeared on the first page. Plenty of Yahoo Answers appeared describing their tails, gills, and how they're draped in pearls and seaweed.

Nothing mentioned anything about transformations.

There were multiple images of *The Sea Princess* and other live-action versions of mermaids, and links to blogs about the mythology of mermaids. A hundred and two pages of results. He clicked on page 51, and the results twisted into arguments on the existence of sirens and anecdotal cases of them. The images turned from happy redheads to grotesque creatures with fins, wrinkly skin, and tails. Liam sensed Neera's discomfort and quickened his scrolling.

He clicked on a link leading them to a document on "The Mythos of Sirens". His eyes scanned the information that seemed more like a smear piece than a research paper on their characteristics.

"So mermaids–sirens–have the ability to serenade sailors to jump from their ships and drown themselves...and may be able to manipulate different forms of water," Neera murmured. She leaned closer to the screen. "That's just the ones that were found. Most people that have encountered a siren were never seen again."

"If that's the case, how do they know what really happened if they never survived?"

Neera shook her head in disbelief. "I don't look like one of those...creatures, and neither did my mother. Are you sure mermaids and sirens are the same? Maybe we're looking at the wrong thing."

Liam shrugged and continued scanning the page. "It says some of them are more evolved and look as mesmerizing as their voices, so maybe the other images were just one type of siren. It also says mermaids are made-up fairytale creatures to boost capitalism and humanize them when they are actually..." He gulped, feeling like he was tiptoeing over a very thin line. "Sirens."

Neera's mouth thinned, turning her head deep in thought. Liam understood that it could be a lot to handle. It might not even be real, but the evidence was clear as day. He assumed she had a million and one questions zooming around her head about herself and her family, and he, unfortunately, couldn't help ease some of that uncertainty.

Once Liam reached the end of the document where the appendix and citation remained, a name he recognized skimmed past: Jonathan Dern.

Liam's grandfather.

The hair on the back of his neck stood tall as goosebumps cascaded down his arms. Liam shifted his eyes to Neera, who was still thinking and fidgeting with a pencil.

Liam took the opportunity to click on the article linked to Jonathan Dern.

THIS PAGE IS UNAVAILABLE

Perplexed, Liam scrolled up to the beginning of the previous article before she could glance at the screen. He made a mental note to look into it later.

It wasn't shocking that his family's work was on the internet since they were known for their research and glowing articles in various scientific magazines. What was shocking was that his Grandpop's article was deleted.

Liam faintly jumped at the sound of Neera's voice.

"Are there any known mermaids? Like any famous ones in history?"

Liam chose a results page closer to the end. Page 78. He scrolled through them until Neera yelped sharply and pointed to a link with the name *Cordelia Alannis*. He looked expectantly at her shocked face, waiting for an explanation.

"Alannis was my mother's last name," she inhaled.

Liam's eyes bulged.

He clicked the link, and it had a Renaissance painting of a woman with intelligent green eyes, long, dark and wavy hair cascading down to her hip, and a coral pink tail curled under her in a majestic pose. The top of her head donned a pearl and vine-molded crown. A closer examination of the image revealed that the woman wasn't resting on a boulder but on a throne. As regal as she was beautiful.

Liam continued reading while Neera's eyes were glued to the screen.

"Cordelia Alannis is claimed to be the direct descendant of Triton, the ruler of the seven oceans and son of Poseidon. Her birth mother's lineage is unknown, and she wasn't included in his list of known children."

"Like illegitimate?" Neera asked.

"Yeah," Liam nodded. "They don't believe she has a trident, but she has the power to manipulate the sea like her father and grandfather, and can also shape-shift into whatever she desires."

Liam was just as flabbergasted. *Triton? Where have I heard that name before?*

He looked at Neera and claimed softly, "That power is ingrained in her blood, and those abilities are passed on from generation to generation, depending on what they're mixed with."

The silence between them was wrapped in uncertainty and a whiff of belief.

So Neera is...

"A demi-god. I'm a demi-god." Her voice was laced with doubt, or denial.

She bit her bottom lip. "Can you search up my mother's name? Nerissa Alannis?"

Liam did so, and the results only brought up nothing substantial. He clicked through multiple result pages and not one mentioned her. No Myspace, no Facebook, no criminal record, nor an obituary.

That's strange.

He noticed her nose wrinkling, gears turning. No need to look too deeply into it if she already knew what happened to her mom. Liam chuckled to break the tension. "Maybe your mom was a private person and never had a reason to be on the internet. Some people are like that."

"Yeah, maybe," she muttered as she bit her lip, her chin quivering.

Liam exited the page and wrapped his arms around her. When they decided to do this, he wasn't expecting the information to be so heavy. She didn't deserve all this thrown on her, especially with her current condition. The way she held it together was admirable. Even as she sat gathered in his arms, she held his forearms not as a crutch to prop her up, but as a way to keep her grounded.

He kissed her temple and exhaled with a smirk.

"Ready to see how long it takes to turn into a mermaid?"

"Oh yeah. This sucked," she smiled.

Liam heard pattering upstairs, and his muscles tensed.

Mom's back early!

He released Neera quickly and stretched, his back sore from bending for so long. Then quietly freaked out, thinking of a way to sneak her out. Neera must've sensed his unease because she stood in front of him with her freckles overlapping each other in confusion.

"My mom's back, and she definitely can't see you in my room."

When it registered her eyes bulged, and she started pacing, matching his own pacing. "Is there another way out of here?"

Liam shook his head, messing up his hair. "The only way out is upstairs. You might have to stay over until they fall asleep."

Neera ceased her pacing. "If you want my father to come by with a SWAT team, then I need to be home before five, which is when I said I'd be home."

"And you don't have a car, so you won't be able to make it home by yourself."

Neera snapped her fingers as if a light bulb illuminated. "I can swim home." Noticing his incredulous look, she doubled down. "Look, I can swim down the shore toward my house since I don't live that far from you. When I get there, I'll change and then walk a couple of blocks inland. Just getting past your mother will be the true test."

Liam took in everything and weighed all the pros and cons. He couldn't risk them meeting her like this, but he would want them to meet in a more appropriate setting. Elayne couldn't pick her up because he wasn't supposed to bring home guests unannounced. Her plan was the only way. He just needed a way to sneak her out the back door.

He grabbed her hand and they both tip-toed up the steps with minimal noise. Liam cracked the door, peeking through the gap. His mom must've been "cooking" dinner with the aluminum catering dishes spread around the island. She wiped her hands on a kitchen towel and, thankfully, walked up the stairs. Liam turned and gave Neera a thumbs up.

They jogged as quietly as they could out the back door towards the ocean. The variety of oranges in the sky bled into the vast blue of the Pacific. Their family's boat lulled lightly against their dark-stained dock.

When they got to the end of the shoreline, Neera faced Liam, her hair flowing over her matched the waves stirring the ocean.

"I guess we'll have to finish this another time," her playful look fell and became more serious. "Thank you. For accepting me."

Liam smiled. "Don't get too sappy on me, Ran. It's a no-brainer."

Actually, it's a total 180, but she doesn't need to know that.

She took her phone and keys out of her pockets and stuffed them in her bag, securing it with a zipper. She wiggled her eyebrows. "Water-proof bag for the win."

"Mom! Liam has a girl over!" Liam could hear his brother's shrill voice from behind him, but not close. He snapped his head around and caught Danny's back running inside the house. No doubt to snitch.

Traitor.

Neera's eyes bulged, but she stepped into action. Slinging the bag over her shoulders, she ran into the water for about four seconds and then dove in. She emerged some feet away, only visible from her torso up, as if she was floating. With the way the sun hit her skin, glowing like a ball of light and mirroring the shimmering water below, she looked every bit like the "demi-goddess" that she was.

She blew him a kiss that missed his lips and planted itself on the left side of his chest. He winked at her to distract himself from her attempted murder on his heart. In a blink she was gone, leaving only a green tail shimmering briefly over the surface until the waves washed her away. Neera's parting words flashed in his mind.

"For accepting me."

Words that she could've waited to say over the cell or another day. She felt it was important to say them at that moment as if she somehow knew deep down that he was fighting against a new reality. As if challenging it was difficult. As if she wasn't worth fighting for.

Liam had spent his whole life having to uphold a facade, and it so happened that the one thing that was the sincerest was his feelings for the mermaid that defied all logic and reason.

And he didn't want to go back to that life.

In the meantime, Liam needed to uncover the reason why Grandpop Jo's article was scrubbed from the internet. He could only hope he was overthinking everything.

He really hoped.

"Liam, what are you staring at?" His mom's voice asked from behind him, taking him out of his thoughts. He didn't even bother turning around. Eyes planted on the view in front of him, the low-hanging sun caused them to squint.

"A beautiful angelfish."

UNCHARTED WATERS

Chapter 9

Neera

I can't believe I just got hit in the face by a fish!

Neera shook off the blow as she raced down the cool waters of the Pacific. It was the fastest she had ever swum in her entire life. Having a tail allowed her to move without rotating her arms much, thus saving energy and making it seem effortless.

She occasionally popped her head above the surface to find a safe enough spot to breach. The last time she scanned the surface, it was almost a mile away from Liam's place, but the rest of the neighborhood–although sparsely spaced out–had a home near the water.

So she had no choice but to keep swimming. *Just keep swimming.*

The bright side to all of this was swimming for the first time in her mermaid form since her transformation, and she had to admit that it felt exhilarating. She had swum at the beach before when she was younger, but never this far out into the ocean. Neera's tail whipped through the water like a flag on a windy day.

What was most different was, of course, being able to stay underwater for so long without having to hold her breath. Such a strange feeling for Neera. Instead of feeling that drowning pressure, the water just filtered out of her gills right below her ribcage. No more burning lungs or red eyes. Ironically, her vision happened to be at its clearest underwater.

I wonder what else I can do.

Neera broke the surface one last time and noticed she was so far down the coast that the island near Liam's house looked like a tiny, floating rock. She looked at the coastline on her right and realized that she was near Pasa Verde Park.

The palm trees were sparse yet clustered enough to cover the shoreline. Luck was on her side because no one was around, with only the leaves rustling and waves crashing against the sand.

Reluctant to leave the safety of the water, she used her elbows and forearms to army-crawl her way across the hot sand until she reached a cluster of palm trees. Ignoring her irritated elbows, she sat against the tree's slim trunk with her tail tucked under her bottom and removed her pack from her back. She unzipped the double-stitched zipper and opened it. Relieved that all her things remained dry, she called Lay-Lay with the little shame she had left from fleeing her boyfriend's place.

Elayne picked up on the second ring. "What's up, Nee-Nee?"

Neera inhaled deeply and spilled. "No time to chat, Lay-Lay. I'm literally stuck at Pasa Verde Park, and I need you to come get me," she lowered her voice and darted her eyes around. "I'm in my mermaid form, so bring a towel ASAP."

Elayne was silent for longer than Neera would prefer. "Do I even want to know how you ended up there?"

"I'll tell you later."

"Okay, I'll be there in five."

"Thanks. You're the best," Neera exhaled.

"I know." She could almost hear Elayne smirk on the

other end before the *CLICK*.

I freakin' love her.

Neera tilted her head back and watched the sky, the surface of the water reflecting a distorted version of the oranges and reds of the sky. She listened for any other movement or sounds of human fodder, which only allowed her to drink in the present.

It all started to sink in that this was her reality. Deep down, her mind began to wonder if all this was the end for her...or the beginning. Negativity snuck into the passenger seat of her mind. Despite the sublime view in front of her, its sourness haunted her peripherally.

Six minutes flat, in true Elayne fashion, the sound of an engine appeared and then died down. Neera hoped it was her best friend to the rescue. About to sneak a peek at the intruder, Neera's phone rang, and Elayne's text popped up on the screen:

ELAYNE: HERE. WAVE UR HAND.

Neera twisted her upper body, so that half of it faced behind her as she waved her right hand in that direction, hoping her friend could see her.

A warm hand grasped her outstretched one and almost startled her. She whipped her head to her best friend and at the same time, Elayne threw a white towel on her head. Releasing her hand gave Neera the freedom to rub the soft material all over her body, making sure to rid herself of even the slight dampness of her hair.

Elayne gasped as her body returned back to normal, leaving her with a wet shirt and, even worse, a bare butt. Her skirt and panties were somewhere lost at sea, maybe improving some poor dolphin's reputation.

Neera quickly stood and wrapped the large towel around her, feeling its comfort and secretly hoping no one else saw her practically naked.

"Nice trim," Elayne murmured as they walked over to

her purple buggy parked on the side of the road. A few cars passed by, probably wondering why there was a girl in a towel in the woods, yet they didn't care enough to investigate.

On the ride back to Neera's home, the alternative rock singer's voice pierced the silence as the anticipation inflated. From Elayne's curiosity of today's events to Neera's dread of retelling it.

As Neera opened her mouth to speak, her phone chimed.

LIAM: R U OK? DID U MAKE IT BACK SAFELY?

Neera grinned at his concern, her thoughts pulling her back to his arms wrapped around her after she discovered her fairytale identity wasn't as simple as it seemed. She still tried to wrap her head around everything she learned. Instead of trembling in despair, she sent a text that she was okay to Liam.

Two fingers snapped in front of Neera's face, snapping her out of some stupor since Elayne had been speaking to her the entire time.

"Earth to Neera?" Elayne sang annoyingly. "What the hell happened today?"

Neera bit her lip. Doubt crept in her rearview at the thought of telling her that her best friend was possibly a descendant of a Greek god and her kind's abilities involve "murder songs". Elayne might think of her as even more of a freak, and this time...an actual monster.

Neera exhaled slowly and ripped the bandage off. "I'm a half-god...or demi-god, or whatever."

Both of Elayne's hands gripped the steering wheel as her eyes bulged. "Shut up!" Her voice climbed. "You're a what?!"

Neera spent the rest of their trip recanting everything she learned. The entire time, Elayne was silent. Not in disgust, but in intrigue. She had the nerve to be fascinated at Neera's social descent into a carnival attraction.

Elayne licked her bottom lip. "So let me get this straight. You're a descendant of this Triton guy and freakin' Poseidon.

Mermaids aren't really lovable red-heads under the sea, but sirens that have a habit of singing sailors to death, just for the fun of it. And you think you can do the same thing or that you might have magical powers, too."

Neera scoffed. "I mean, yeah, that's pretty much it. I'm inherently a beastly murderer."

Elayne laughed, and Neera wasn't sure if it was out of disbelief or nervousness. "I've been to karaoke with you. The only thing you can murder is everyone's eardrums."

Neera snorted at her insinuation, then raised her voice. "I'm serious, Lay-Lay!"

"Ok, ok," she cooed as she tried to de-escalate the situation. After so many years, she knew when Neera's anxiety began closing in on her. They weren't best friends for nothing. It was as if a switch clicked, and she knew when to fold. Especially since the first time Neera had a panic attack during her birthday after her mum passed.

She had made consistent progress in avoiding having one, so her medication and her therapy sessions weren't as pertinent. Then on her eleventh birthday, her dad threw her a pool party at a waterpark. He invited all that was left of her friends, and then he brought out the birthday cake with *The Sea Princess* on top.

Neera couldn't remember everything, but between the "Happy Birthday" song, the clapping, and the sound of water splashing, her breathing started to shallow significantly. Her heart felt like someone was gripping it like their life depended on it. She could only imagine what she looked like because her peers started to look at her like she was...a freak.

Broken.

The only friend that stayed by her side was Lay-Lay, and that was the last thing she would remember about that day.

"You said you're the descendant of Triton, right? What if you have different powers instead of singing? Like telepathy or super strength?" Elayne clearly derailed the conversation.

Neera pondered on that for a bit.

Other abilities, huh?

Neera bit her lip. The poor thing was practically skinned at that point. "I don't know, but it's definitely possible."

As they pulled up to the brick walkway to Neera's house, Elayne parked and yanked the emergency brake. She searched Neera's gaze, then smirked.

"This is going to be so much fun."

LIAM

That was close.

Right before Liam checked on Neera, his dad pulled into the garage, leaving him no time to call her before he had to return to his room to pretend to study. He couldn't focus on the textbook in front of him as his thoughts drifted to the missing link to his grandfather's research.

Why was it missing? It wasn't like his family to hide from the public, especially when it came to their microbiological research and discoveries. His dad boasted about them the most and wouldn't miss a second to mention them.

Liam's gaze drifted to the locked door on the opposite side of the room, resting suspiciously on the multiple locks built into it.

What are they hiding?

The sound of heavy footsteps thudding down the stairs pulled Liam out of his speculations. His dad's tall and imposing frame appeared next to him from his peripheral view as he straightened his shoulders and stared at his textbook. The words were lost on him.

"Time for dinner," his dad informed.

"OK. I'm coming." Liam gave a curt nod, as usual, and closed his textbook. Before he could stand, his dad laid a hand on his shoulder, pausing his movement. Liam looked up at him.

"Since you're almost finished with high school, I think

you're ready to learn some of the 'ins and outs' of the family business."

Liam slid back into his chair, waiting in anticipation for him to continue.

His dad crossed his arms over his chest. "I received an assignment to retrieve some specimens from landmass R07, which is the island across from us."

Liam nodded his head in recognition. It was widely known in southern Cali that the island was off-limits and trespassers could get some serious jail time for even stepping foot on it. The fact that his dad had special authorization to enter it had Liam's heart racing in excitement. He had always been interested in the family business, and he devoured every little crumb his dad shared. Now, he was about to get the whole cake.

"I want you to accompany me on the assignment," he continued. "You can even invite your little friend to come with you."

Liam gulped but kept a straight face. At least, he assumed, but his dad's smug expression said otherwise.

"I don't know wh-"

"You think I don't keep up with everything that goes on in my own house, son? You know how I feel about visitors without my consent."

Liam's head fell. He'd been caught, and there was nothing he could say to get out of it. He really thought he was a step ahead. His thoughts flitted through the possible variables.

Someone must've snitched.

"You can relax, Liam," he deeply chuckled as he placed his hand back on his shoulder and leaned slightly towards him. "I was your age once. She must be pretty special for you to bring her back twice."

Liam relaxed his tense shoulders a little, still on edge at how he managed to find out. The fact that his dad wasn't punishing Liam for breaking his rules somehow kept him from fully relaxing, even with the faint smile on his strong features.

Liam nodded slowly and sighed. "I'm sorry, Dad."

He squeezed his shoulder. "It's alright, son. If she's a special person to you, I would love to meet her. Who knows? She might just fit right into our family."

Liam rubbed the back of his neck with the insinuation and glanced away from him. "You're moving too fast, Dad."

His dad chortled deeply while shaking Liam, causing Liam to laugh with him and finally relax.

Could he be right? Could she fit into his world?

After a family dinner of awkward and embarrassing conversation about Neera, Liam returned to his room and flopped onto his bed on his back. He debated whether he should invite Neera on this trip to a potentially dangerous island.

What if something were to happen to her?

However, if it were really that dangerous, his dad would've never invited him to accompany him. And bring an outsider nonetheless. The idea of his dad accepting Neera as a part of their family brought a weird feeling to his chest and even more of a reason to invite her. As long as she avoided the surrounding water and remained normal, she would fit right in.

After deciding, Liam called her number on his cell and waited for her to pick up. On the third ring, he heard Neera's soothing voice greet him. "Hey."

"Hey," Liam drew out while picking at a scab on his knee from an old scrimmage in middle school. Silence filled the air, but it was Neera's turn this time to break it.

"Um...why are you calling?"

Liam took a deep breath and just let everything out. "Uh...my dad has this work thing and wants me to join him to find some specimens on the island."

"Wow. Congrats, Dern," Neera cheered softly. "I know how much it means to you to be involved with your father's business, and now he's putting you up front and center."

"I know," Liam blushed at her excitement. "It's not just

me. He wants you to join us."

"...Really?" She hesitated. "Why?"

Liam's hand tackled his hair. "So...he may have seen us sneaking around, and he wants to meet you. But don't stress. He actually seems open to you. Just think of it as an island vacation."

The silence unnerved him. What if she took this as some love confession or, egregiously, a future marriage proposal?

Even worse, what if she rejected him?

"I've never been on an island vacation before."

Liam exhaled at her response.

"As long as I stay away from the ocean, I should be fine, right? Is it overnight?"

Liam stupidly shook his head as if she could see him. "You will definitely be fine because there will be nothing to worry about. Also, it's just for the day."

"I trust you, Dern," she said sweetly and honestly. "Let's go."

I guess Neera isn't the only one meeting a parent for the first time.

The afternoon sun beaming high in the sky, Liam and his dad watched Neera and an older man walk towards them near the boat. Neera, as usual, was a vision in her green tank top and beige, swishy skirt. Her water-resistant pack was strapped to her back and slightly bounced as she walked over to them in her flat-top sneakers.

Even if Neera never told him, he would still recognize the man next to her as a taller, dark-skinned version of her. He was lean with no hair and rocking some thick-framed glasses that hovered over his flat nose. He also looked surprisingly young, with the sprinkles of gray hair in his goatee the only indication of aging. They both have intelligent eyes and an observant demeanor.

She obviously looked like her mom also, just by her

features that contrasted her dad, but it was still uncanny. The thing that made Liam's mouth drop was his choice of apparel– which happened to match his dad.

The two dads gave each other a once-over from a few feet away, both wearing khaki shorts with extra pockets and a black polo shirt. It was like they shopped at the same "Dads-R-Us" store.

When they finally caught up to them, her dad gave a beaming smile with his hand outstretched toward his dad. "Sorry to intrude on your outing. I just couldn't resist visiting an illicit territory. I'm Garran Ran, Neera's father." His smooth and absolutely British accent greeted them like a UK detective.

Liam expected his dad to react uncomfortably to the unexpected guest, and he braced for his dad to either chastise him for the involvement or cancel the trip altogether. Liam cleared his throat and tried to add a buffer by shaking Mr. Ran's hand and introducing himself.

"I'm Liam, Neera's friend. It's a pleasure to have you here, sir."

Mr. Ran chuckled deeply. "Just friends, huh?"

His cheeks burned, definitely from the sun beating down on them. He let go and used his hand to rub the back of his neck.

Because of incoming sunburn, of course.

Instead of reacting in anger, his dad burst into a hearty laugh and gripped Mr. Ran's hand into a firm handshake.

"Completely understandable," he bellowed with his "public relations" smile plastered over his face. "I apologize for not personally asking for you both to join us. I'm Dan Dern, as you already know, Liam's father."

His dad leaned back, with his hand still in mid-handshake, and gave Mr. Ran another surveying look. "Look at this guy. I see you're a man of style."

Liam and Neera both rolled their eyes. But Liam's relief of the subject change was obvious.

Mr. Ran smirked. "My daughter said it would be too hot

for this, but it seems we look rather fit."

Neera groaned, then held her hand out to Liam's dad. "Sorry for not meeting you earlier, Mr. Dern. That was rude of me."

Liam's dad gave her outstretched hand a soft shake as he stared into her eyes. Not in an inappropriate way, but Liam couldn't help the unease he felt from it. He couldn't put his finger on it, but it was a look he hadn't seen his dad portray before.

"It's alright. We have plenty of time to catch up on each other," he smiled curtly, then glanced over at Mr. Ran. "Let's get a move on while there's still some sunlight left."

Liam's dad took their bags, and all of them boarded their 1980 red-and-white ski boat. Even with the boat's low hull, it still rocked as they got on. His dad took the captain's chair while Mr. Ran sat in the passenger seat next to him, the leather seats squeaking from their weight.

Liam and his family hadn't used their family boat in years since they rarely got together unless for a function or a publicity shoot. Yet Liam still remembered how to use one, just in case it came in handy.

"Start the motor, son," his dad commanded from the front seat, his eyes covered with shades.

Liam untied the rope from their dock, placed one foot on the stern, and pulled the cord attached to the motor. It took a couple of tries, but the vessel eventually purred to life. He returned back to his seat next to Neera near the motor and signaled his dad a thumbs up. With that, the boat jerked forward, heading in the direction of the forbidden island.

Liam had never been this far out in the ocean before, so watching the waves flow through the water was somewhat peaceful. Perfect weather, like they were meant to explore its natural beauty. He noticed his dad and Mr. Ran having a friendly exchange only by their body language, since he couldn't make out what they were saying.

Giving up on deciphering their conversation, his gaze

naturally fell on Neera, who looked reverently at the view in front of her. The breeze brushed her "half-up-half-down" curls over her shoulders that seemed more tense than they should be.

He gently tapped her knee to get her attention, and she turned her sea-green eyes on him. He gave a crooked smile, pointing to the seat under him.

"Hungry?" He half-shouted over the noise from the motor. "We packed some snacks in case it takes longer than we thought."

Technically HE stocked up their cubby underneath their seat with non-perishable snacks before they arrived. It was his mom's idea since he and his dad didn't think they would be hungry after lunch.

You can never be too prepared, she claimed.

"I'm good. Maybe later," Neera declined louder than necessary.

Mr. Ran whipped his head back, looking between Neera and Liam, making sure his daughter was okay. His eyes shifted down, and his mouth tensed. Liam followed his gaze, realizing his other hand was still on her bare knee. Horrified, Liam snatched his hand away and slid as far away as he could from her while on a 2-foot-long seat.

His dad cleared his throat loudly and shouted, "Look, everyone! We're almost there!"

This grabbed Mr. Ran's attention as he returned his eyes to the green landmass looming over them. Liam silently thanked his dad's interference, saving his ass once again.

DO NOT DISTURB

Chapter 10

Neera

I knew coming to this island was a bad idea the second my dad put on a fanny pack.

The closer they got to the forbidden island, the more caution signs emerged on the shore. About five or six bright yellow signs came into view as Mr. Dern decelerated to dock. A slight jerk of the boat indicated that they'd reached the shore.

They had officially arrived.

Neera scanned the area briefly, her eyesight not at her best without her glasses, for encroaching military soldiers or booby-traps ready to pop up from the sand and shoot them with machine guns. Or maybe she shouldn't have watched Indiana Jones before going on an expedition. She couldn't help it. She wanted to prepare for every potential scenario of trespassing on a forbidden island.

So far, it looked...boring. No native people shooting darts at them from a distance for disturbing their home or an onslaught of giant sand snakes coming from the forest.

Just the sound of the waves and an occasional plane flying thousands of feet above them.

Liam's mansion was merely a speck from there. For some reason, the mainland seemed further away. Neera stepped off the boat with her bag on her back, her sneakered feet slightly sinking in the soft sand, and watched the males spring into action.

Liam shut off the motor, picked up a thick pole and rope, and leaped out of the boat. Her dad and Mr. Dern got off the boat and started to pull it further up the shore. Liam threw the stuff on the ground and helped them turn the boat. Neera shamelessly stared at Liam's muscles tense under his white shirt as they rotated the boat to face the ocean, then glared as her sight fell on her dad's outfit choice.

She still couldn't believe he insisted on joining them when she told him about the trip.

"There is no way I'm allowing my teenage girl to go to a prohibited island with men that I don't know, and there's absolutely nothing you can say to stop me otherwise," was his exact words.

He was right. There was nothing Neera could say to change his mind, even as she stated the immense amount of awkwardness that would crush her if he met Liam so early on in their relationship. She would've even tolerated it if he didn't don a fanny pack and inadvertently "twin" with Mr. Dern, but alas, here she was.

Liam introducing himself as her *friend* was just the icing on the torture cake. She had to talk herself out of exposing herself by swimming all the way back to the mainland.

Once situated, Liam took the pole and drove it into the sand near the boat. With quick hand motions, almost professionally, he created two knots that link the boat to the pole. Mr. Dern and her dad were already at the entrance of the dense tropical forest. As the couple trudged over to them, Neera dug into her bag and handed Liam her bottle of water. He hesitantly took the bottle, swallowed a short gulp, and handed it back to Neera with a smirk.

"I'll pretend I didn't see you checking me out earlier," he accused quietly.

Neera rolled her eyes but turned her head to hide her smile. When she faced him again, she struck him with a playful glare.

"A simple 'thank you' would've been nice."

His smirk cracked as he scratched the back of his neck. "Sorry about what I said earl-."

"Hey, guys," Mr. Dern called out. "We have to head in soon."

They nodded to Mr. Dern and picked up their pace until her dad put a hand up, blocking her from joining.

"You will wait out here and be a lookout," her father asserted with a finger pointing down, staking her to the post. "Where it's safe."

"What?" Neera balked. "I'm coming along. That's the whole reason for being here."

Mr. Dern cut in. "Garran, we'll all be together, so there's nothing to worry about."

Her father cut his eyes to him. "We don't know that for sure. It'll be safer for her to be near an exit."

"Dad," she whined, annoyed by his sudden change of heart. "Please don't overreact. I'm not a little girl anymore. I can handle myself now."

"You're still MY child. My daughter," he bellowed, then took a deep breath. His anger was already diluting; he crossed his arms over his chest and glared toward the wide ocean that glared back at him.

"Mr. Ran," Liam softly chimed in. The breeze blew his already disheveled hair like a silky bird's nest. Her father still unwavering, Liam's tone strengthened. "I'll make sure nothing happens to her, sir. If it gets too troublesome, we'll return immediately."

Her father assessed Liam as if they were having some sort of nonverbal convo between them, then returned his gaze to his daughter.

Whatever private, internal discussion they had must've worked because his body had visibly relaxed. He gave her a curt nod. "Okay, Neera. Just try not to get hurt."

Neera wrapped her arms around her dad, and he

returned the gesture. After some thought, Neera understood his hesitation. He was afraid of losing her.

If only he knew she felt the exact same way.

"I hate to break up this tender moment," Mr. Dern interrupted while pointing at his watch. "We have to get moving."

Mr. Dern gave them a curt nod before leading the group into the forest. Neera and her dad released each other as all three of them followed him past the warning signs into the heart of the jungle.

The actual forest was the polar opposite of the bright beach. It was like they stepped into another dimension– a cooler, quieter, and almost sinister one. The sun that had beaten down on them earlier barely peeked through the thick canopy of the palms. Its denseness was almost suffocating at times. Walking became toilsome as they continuously weaved past hovering branches, thick bushes, and fallen tree trunks. The greenery of the foliage seemed to fold in on them like a kaleidoscope. They looked mysterious and bountiful, with different colored fruits sprouting in several areas that they passed. If they ever got stranded, at least they wouldn't starve to death.

The only thing that gave her pause was the lack of animal noises. No small creatures, or bears, or even the incessant squawking of seagulls. The further away from the shore they got, the quieter it got; to a point Neera started to think she still had water stuck in her ears. If it wasn't for everyone's labored breathing from exertion and the slaps of foliage hitting them as they passed by, she would've believed she lost her hearing.

The group continued their trek through the forest, Neera still unsure what Mr. Dern was looking for in particular. If he wanted to collect samples, they had already passed many strange-looking plants that he could've collected.

Neera wasn't annoyed, per se. Okay, maybe she was. She was sticky from sweat and whatever sap she accidentally stepped in and incredibly bored from the hike to *who-knows-where*. So bored that she focused on Liam's back as she trailed behind him. She wondered why he was the only one to wear white in an environment where it, for sure, wasn't staying that way.

However, she bit her tongue and moved forward. Only kids would complain. Not big girls like herself.

Mr. Dern halted, causing everyone else to cease their movements. Her dad, who was in the rear, moved up to stand next to him. "What is it, Dan?"

Mr. Dern stepped over a fallen tree trunk and staggered toward it in wonder. "It looks like an old-school laboratory. Fascinating."

The semi-charred "white" building blended in with the forest like it had been there for decades. The concrete, average-sized building sat in the middle of a high-fenced circle that was torn down in some parts, next to sporadically placed rusty biohazard bins. Beyond the fence, the ground had leveled with a few weeds sprouting around the building, giving them some reprieve from constantly untangling themselves from the forest's limbs. There were no windows from where they were standing, but a metal door hung off its hinges.

As much as Neera wanted to be entranced, the whole place gave her the creeps and her intuition was almost flashing a red sign to *TURN BACK*.

When they passed the threshold, it was almost like they stepped onto a dystopian movie set. Most of the furniture was gray and covered in ash, and the boxy computers left there seemed outdated. Only the sound of the floor creaking filled the air as they took in their environment. The only light they had was from the sunlight spilling from the broken door.

Neera tried not to inhale the dust floating in the air as plenty of it coated the counters, test tubes, and notepads. She couldn't resist the shivers racking her body from the sheer number of cobwebs covering everything. Rolling chairs were toppled on the floor, collecting dust and scattered as if a wild animal had ransacked the place.

Yet, not a single animal had crossed their path since they entered the forest.

Mr. Dern observed the rundown room, then removed his pack to jot something down on a notepad. Other than a few chairs toppled over and broken glass scattered on the floor, nothing looked noteworthy to Neera. Her dad used his personal flashlight to observe some of the tattered pieces of paper on the "stainless" steel counters as if he were trying to decipher their meanings despite the ash coating them.

"What exactly are we looking for, Dad?" Liam questioned his father as he tried to peek at his notes.

His father let him peep and coughed. "Well…I was hoping to procure some evidence of scientific analyses from long ago." His forehead beaded in sweat from the lack of windows. "I was unaware of how much damage was done to it. Sorry, guys. Looks like today's trip is a bust."

"A bust?" Her dad inquired with a tilted head.

Neera shook her head. "It means we wasted our time."

Mr. Dern tittered. "We can head back, grab some snacks, and relax by the shore while bonding. It's not every day you get to have a tropical vacation on a restricted island."

Neera turned to her dad and saw an indescribable expression on his face. When he noticed her staring, he switched to a content one and pushed his sliding glasses back up his nose. "Sounds splendid. As long as we leave before it gets dark."

Everyone nodded in agreement, yet Neera was still annoyed at her dad's overprotectiveness and the tension from them was obvious. They needed to have a necessary discussion about boundaries when they got home.

Mr. Dern saddled up next to her dad and threw an arm over his shoulder, squeezing it in a friendly manner as he jested. "Oh, loosen up, Garren. Enjoy the time off, huh?"

The two men exited the building first, their laughs growing faint the further away they got. Neera was about to follow Liam out until her eye caught something twinkling on the edge of a counter.

Something green...and faintly glowing.

She noticed the glowing outline underneath a charred piece of paper. This could be absolutely nothing and she was just wasting precious sunbathing time over some ancient trinket. However, the closer she got to it, the stronger the invisible force pulled her towards it. Her body practically begged her to touch it, yet her anxiety, which would usually make its grand appearance at this time, oddly remained at bay. Whatever was tugging her, even Anxiety wouldn't get close.

Removing the paper, her jaw dropped. In front of her was a small, green, quartz-shaped crystal with a gold chain attached to its end. Despite its uneven edges, the gem looked hauntingly beautiful. Unblemished and perfect, surrounded by ash and char. The light strengthened from flashing to a steady, dim glow the minute she touched the gold chain.

Neera picked up the necklace and dangled it close to her face. Despite its luminosity, she was able to peer INSIDE it. Like peering into a keyhole. She may not be as scientific as Liam, but peering into a thick gem without a reflection looking back at her seemed illogical. It felt like she was in Biology class, observing a fern leaf through a microscope. So mysterious... yet captivating.

The saturation of green and tiny shining dots swirling around each other reminded her of stars in a clear night sky. Her ears tickled at the sound of indescribable whispers. Something whirled past her line of sight, so she tried to chase it with her pupils. The entity ceased its swirling and stared directly into her eyes with its beady bright green ones, capturing her gaze and holding it hostage.

It looked like something she had seen in cartoons but more realistic. Hunter-green scales trailed down its thin body with a flowing mane of–what she could assume– pitch-black hair down its spine. Four short limbs were tipped with intimidating claws as they tucked into its body. Its long snout should've been menacing with the sword-like fangs protruding from it, but instead, Neera felt safe for some odd reason. Its regal presence produced an air of reverence and protection.

All of a sudden, the dragon's mouth opened up with a bright, white light inside. That same light spilled out of the crystal and blinded her momentarily, only noticing its presence by how warm it felt as it enveloped her entire body. It felt even hotter than it was inside the lab but with a potent energy. As quickly as it came was as quick as it left, leaving her in the semi-dark lab as if nothing happened.

Neera peered down at her other wrist and noticed Liam's tight grip on it. Her eyes lifted to his, making her heart stop with how wide his eyes were. His chiseled features were bleak, and his pale skin only made her stomach knot.

"What-," she began.

"Don't. Move," Liam murmured so low his lips barely moved.

Panic appeared and perched itself in the front seat of her mind, grabbing all the controls and forcing her to freeze. Whatever was behind her spooked the fork out of Liam, and she wasn't taking the risk.

Even as her arm ached from holding the necklace up, she avoided twitching by any means necessary.

Neera abruptly heard animalistic huffs coming from behind her, gradually intensifying the closer they got.

Don't look. Don't look. Don't look. She pleaded with herself.

If she was going to die at the hands of some bear or tiger or whatever, she was not going to look. Their whole time on this forsaken island was pure silence, *but now,* it wanted to appear and eat them?

So much for an island vaca-

An ear-splitting screech released her from her dread. A

sound she'd never heard before. This gave Liam some burst of confidence to drag her towards the exit. Neera chanced a glance at the creature in question and almost urinated on herself.

LIAM

How does a sneak peek into the family business become an island vacation?

Liam assumed his dad was really going to involve him in an actual exploration for once, but he should've known with the extended invites the real subjects were Neera and her dad. Well, mostly her dad since he hadn't said a word to Neera since their introduction. A little strange because his dad never missed a chance to talk about himself.

Annoyed at the change of plans–yet always excited to see Neera in a bikini–Liam walked out of the facility to follow their parents until he noticed Neera wasn't behind him. He returned to the lab and discovered her staring at some green necklace. The closer he got, the more Neera's inspection of the item looked...uncanny.

From a distance, she looked like she was holding up a necklace and admiring its beauty. A foot away from her, goosebumps crawled over his arms at her eyes. Their normal blue-green hue was swallowed by her blown pupils, leaving only a sliver of her eye color. Even creepier was their lack of reflection or light in them. Just pure darkness. Her lips were slightly curled up in some sort of fascination.

Whatever it was, Liam had a strange feeling in the pit of his stomach.

"I don't think we're allowed to take anything with us," he chuckled nervously but was met with silence.

Neera remained still with only her upright arm trembling. It was like nothing transpired. Whatever hold this thing had on her was freaking him out.

He heard some footsteps coming from the other side of the facility, where the door was also off its hinges, and knew Mr. Ran was returning to get Neera. Liam made a promise, and the last thing he wanted to do was get on his bad side.

"Hey, Neera," he exclaimed.

Still no answer. Just a frozen gaze.

Is she hypnotized or something?

Liam, thoroughly freaked, clasped her other wrist in an attempt to shake her, and also see if she didn't turn into a statue. He clenched his jaw at how warm she was, like touching the outside of an oven door.

Before he could shake her, a large outline emerged from the other side of the lab. He could hear clacking against the linoleum floor as it got closer. It looked nothing like their dads.

It looked nothing human.

Liam's entire body screamed in alarm as his adrenaline coursed through his body. All signs telling him to run. Fighting against his instincts, he rationed that whatever that thing was, it would be stronger and faster than the both of them and running from it would just anger it more. As much as he wanted to leave, he couldn't do it yet. Not with his girlfriend in some frozen state.

Maybe staying still will help, he thought as the creature stepped into a small fraction of light, revealing its full form.

The beast resembled a wolf but lean and humanoid. On its hind legs, it was at least eight feet tall. Thick black fur covered its entire body but was more patchy than full. Its eyes were fierce, red, and wide-open, with its pointy ears mangled. Its mouth, slightly ajar, revealed its deadly canines and sharp molars. It walked on its long, gangly limbs that were tipped with sharp claws, sniffing the air with its long and crooked snout. It looked like someone drew a wolf from memory with how deformed, ugly, and gangly it looked.

But he didn't have time to rationalize when said creature was a few feet away from them.

Liam prayed for Neera to snap out of it, but at the same

time, hoped she wouldn't completely lose it when she did.

His prayers were answered when her pupils shrunk back to normal, her temperature lowered, and she started blinking. When she started to speak, he had to cut it immediately before the beast heard them, but it was too late.

One of its deformed ears flicked toward them before it turned its head, eyes glaring ferociously. Its nails scraped against the floor as it stalked toward them. Drool dripped from its muzzle and hit the floor the same way Liam's stomach dropped. He couldn't rationalize it. There was no way he could fight that thing, and it already seemed to confirm their threat level with a growl and predatory eyes.

No matter what they did, they were prey. However, Liam would rather look death in the face than give up. Letting his instincts take over, the beast's disgusting screech sparked a fire through him to run with Neera in tow before it got a chance to lunge at them.

Not knowing where to run, where to go, and how far they could actually make it, Liam and Neera made a sharp turn and sprinted towards a hole in the fence. They sloppily crawled through the opening and sprinted through the forest without looking back. At this point, he wasn't sure if they were going towards the shore or just deeper into the abyss.

WHAM! Liam slammed into a confused Mr. Ran, almost knocking off his glasses. Mr. Ran peered behind them frantically, then returned his gaze to his daughter. "What happened?" He shouted in a panic.

Neera tried to breathe while clutching the cursed necklace that almost got them eaten to her chest. "Something…is after…us."

A few palms swayed from a distance as another blood-curdling screech rang in the air. The beast sounded like it was starving and had a variety to choose from. A dark thought finally hit him.

"Where's my dad? Have you seen him?" Liam's voice cracked.

Distractedly, Mr. Ran shook his head. "Not sure. We separated after hearing that noise, and I was on my way back."

So my dad could be anywhere on this stupid island alone? He was no Crocodile Dundy type to survive in the wild.

There's no way he'll survive by himself.

His mind twisted and turned with all the horrible situations his dad could be enduring. As the eldest son, he had to protect his family and protect their legacy.

Each thought subconsciously compelled him toward the lab. His heart and blood worked vigorously in contrast to his torpid movements. Before he could step further in the direction they came, Neera grabbed his hand and, consequently, pulled him out of his trepidation.

"It's co-coming. We got to hide," she warned with a trembling voice.

"I-I think I've seen a big fallen trunk near the shore," Mr. Ran stated shakily, yet calmer than Neera. "Let's go there, then think of a plan."

He grasped his daughter's hand and ran to the supposed hiding spot, which inadvertently tugged Liam along in some terrified version of a "Conga line" as they weaved through the forest.

Mr. Ran stopped in front of a thick-trunked tree halfway fallen over, creating a tent shape. The long branches were spread wide enough for them to seek shelter and still be hidden from the monster. *Hopefully.* They were close enough to the shore from the smell of the saltwater filling the air, thus, this tree must be the one Mr. Ran had mentioned.

They crouched as close as possible between the base of the tree and the fallen-over trunk, with their backs to the branches cloaking them with the natural colors of the forest. Facing a small opening from where they entered, with only the sound of their exasperated breathing, the peaceful silence from before had now become unnerving and daunting.

"We have to call 911 or something," Liam whispered, afraid of a single vowel leaving their semi-circle.

"No cell service," Mr. Ran responded equally as low yet labored in his breathing. He seemed to have trouble bouncing back compared to them. "Tried earlier...I can...distract it while...you run for it."

"No, you can't go," Neera whimpered as she gripped her dad's hand. Liam had never seen her so frightened, even when she was face-to-face with the monster. Eyes as wide as saucers and mouth trembling, it took everything in Liam to avoid holding her. He wished he could help her, to snatch the fear from her pretty eyes.

"Neer-"

"NO!" She protested a bit louder than Liam would like, but he understood her position. "I can't lose you. I'm sorry for everything and I promise to listen to you. Please ju-just don't go."

Liam rubbed her back, her desperation breaking his heart. Her dad was all she had, and the last thing she needed–deserved–was a chance that her whole world could be taken away from her.

"I'll do it," Liam interjected before he could stop himself. They both snapped their heads to him, but the look especially on Neera's face, sealed his resolve. "I need to find my dad anyway."

Neera chewed on her bottom lip and looked away from him and down at the stupid necklace that was still in her hands.

"No," she gritted through clenched teeth. Her trembling fingers placed the accessory around her neck, causing her confidence to visibly show as she rolled her shoulders back. She took a deep breath and declared with her chin up, "I got us into this. I have to get us out of this."

Mr. Ran's eyebrows smashed together as he hissed, "Absolutely not."

Neera stared her dad down and a chill ran down Liam at her sudden conviction. "I'm the only one that can swim back in minutes. And I'm not risking your life." She turned and looked directly into Liam's eyes, making his heart race. "Neither of you."

Is this what love feels like? Slow down, Dern.

Liam shook the notion away, dragging his gaze from her and looking at Mr. Ran with what he could only assume was the reddest face known to man. Liam nervously licked his chap lips and confessed.

You might as well mention to him that she's more than a friend to you since you might turn into monster food anyway. "Uh...this seems like a good time to mention that I'm dating your daughter, sir."

Instead of Mr. Ran offering Liam up to the beast as a sacrificial offering, he stared quizzically at the necklace. Not as entranced as Neera was earlier, but almost like he recognized it. "Where did you get that necklace?"

Liam and Neera shared a look. He was torn between keeping it a whole secret by claiming he gave it to her as a present or confessing that they STOLE the artifact and may–or may not–have conjured the beast because of it.

The look of shame plagued Neera's face, clearly about to confess, until her features twisted into pain.

Alarm bells rang inside his head as he glanced behind her and noticed the large silhouette of the creature through the branches. Before he could make a sound, her body was being dragged out from their cover, snapping sticks and branches on the way out. It all happened so fast. Mere seconds.

The same heart that was beating a hundred miles an hour stopped instantly at the sight of Neera's nail scratches embedded into the dirt.

Shock detained both of them until they heard Neera's shriek. It emboldened them to scramble out of the mangled branches and witness one of the most horrifying scenes he'd ever encountered:

His girlfriend dangling a few feet off the ground by a single arm. The beast's giant palm enveloped her entire hand as it effortlessly moved her body toward its snout. The fear in her eyes returned as the fire from the brave girl before snuffed out, and Liam felt like he plunged into ice water.

Liam noticed movement in the corner of his eye, a determined Mr. Ran preparing to attack the thing. Knowing Neera and how devastated she would be if something happened to her dad, Liam tugged Mr. Ran's bicep to hold him back. It was a subconscious act but embodied a truth that was always inside him the second she confessed her feelings for him.

He trusted her. *God, I trust her.*

Like a horror movie in real-time, they watched as the beast raised its snout around her head. It circled her head as if it was...smelling her? On its hindlegs, the imposing height was enough to scare anyone, but the sniffing gave Liam hope. He took the opportunity to silently pray for her safety or for the thing to be allergic to pretty girls.

Instantly, the beast unhinged its jaw in a blaring screech, showcasing its massive set of teeth and fangs. Even from their position, they could see spit and drool splatter onto her face. Her eyes completely shut as she braced herself–as they all braced themselves–for what was next.

Instead of a devastating scene, the monster rudely chucked her in the air like a hot potato and booked it back into the dense part of the forest before they could even react. Neera's body rolled until her back slammed against a tree.

Wasting no more time, her dad yanked his arm away from Liam and they both ran over to a conscious Neera. He checked her body for any damage, pausing at her ankle. No bones stuck out, but it was smeared in blood and purple on one side. Her back started to bruise quickly but didn't look too serious.

Her chest, on the other hand, was rising and falling way quicker than it should, and her eyes were wide and lost, staring at nothing. It must be something serious because her dad got right to it. All Liam could do was observe as Mr. Ran cradled her face in both hands, eyes locked on hers, and began taking deep breaths. A long drag of oxygen in, a long push of carbon dioxide out. Neera started to catch on, matching his breathing slowly.

"Everything is okay, dear," he assured gently despite their current situation. "Can you see my eyes? What color are they?"

"They're...brown," she wheezed, but her sight seemed to be more focused than before.

"That's right, love." He took a deep breath, then exhaled. She copied him. "What color are my glasses?"

Liam scanned the area in case the monster returned, but there was no sign of it.

"They're...black."

"Perfect. You're doing great, love."

She finally returned to them, her breathing controlled and eyes skimming the area until they fell on Liam. She looked away sharply as her face darkened a slight shade of pink.

Is she embarrassed about her panic attack?

Liam had to admit that he had never seen one in person before. Only from his research. But he found what her dad did *intriguing.* He kept a mental note of that moment in the back of his head.

Mr. Ran turned his back to her, indicating for her to get on his back. She weakly wrapped her arms around his neck and hopped on. Liam mirrored her wincing as she settled against his back. Picking her up like nothing–must be a "dad thing" – they headed to what they assumed was the shore. Liam could hear their collective sighs when they saw his boat lightly rocking.

As her dad settled Neera in the boat, Liam's heart raced as he turned to the forest.

His dad was still trapped.

Now that the rest of them were safe, Liam had to go back and save him. Just like Neera did.

"Where are you going? You can't go back!" Neera shouted from the boat.

"I'm gonna save my dad. You guys can either head back

or wait, but I'm not leaving without him," Liam shouted back. Turning swiftly, he took a few steps toward the forest until his bicep was yanked back.

"We'll get help when we get back. It's too dangerous right now," Mr. Ran dictated.

Liam glanced behind him, meeting the wrinkle creases on his forehead. "We can't tell anyone because we aren't supposed to be here. It's secret government stuff."

The grip on his arm tightened, causing Liam's already-thin patience to die out.

"As a friend, I promised to look after you. He'll survive. I know it."

Know it? As a friend? Liam internally scoffed.

You know nothing about him, so stay out of my business!

That was what he wanted to say, but out of respect, he gritted out, "I'm not leaving him here."

Annoyed, Liam ripped his arm away from him and picked up his knees to the forest edge. His heart pounded in his ears and he couldn't hear anything, only relying on determination and familial love.

A pair of lean, dark brown arms wrapped around his torso and hauled him in the opposite direction. Instinctually, Liam tried to throw him over his shoulder and gun it, but Mr. Ran was stronger than he looked. His arms corded as he struggled to put Liam in the boat. Liam struggled to break free with no luck.

His anger at an all-time high, he yelled for his dad, hoping he could hear his cries and appear out of thin air. Just show up in front of them like the ending of a fairy tale, but he didn't. Liam could feel the veins popping out of his neck, his body hot from the exertion.

His eyes stung as he was placed into the boat. Once Mr. Ran released him, Neera wrapped her arms around his neck from behind him, holding him back. Liam wanted to hate her. He wanted to call her a traitor and blame her for their problems, but as wetness hit the back of his neck, he knew she had already blamed herself.

Hating her, even at that moment, was impossible.

CHANGE OF PLANS

Chapter 11

Neera

Everything hurts, and my back and ankle aren't even the worst of it.

Neera's aching heart contrasted with the exhilarated faces of Seniors sharing their yearbooks in the halls and cafeteria. Students were smiling, teachers could barely suspend their eagerness for a second, and the whole school burst with excitement at the *torture chamber* ending in a few days.

Instead of basking in the near freedom, Neera only felt a metaphorically large storm cloud hovering directly over her head...and it was all her fault.

As soon as they reached Liam's dock yesterday, he untangled himself from her embrace and stormed into his house without a word. Without looking back. If Neera could swim back and find Mr. Dern, no matter how long it took, she would've done it with or without her dad's permission. However, the way her back throbbed and her gait gave a sad limp, it would've been impossible for her to successfully make the trip.

That meant all she could really do was ice her sore body and let the guilt fester like the scab on her ankle.

The only positive to this was her dad's lack of probing

about where she got the necklace. After he finished doting on her while she pathetically laid in bed with a mountain of ice packs on her ankle and back, he left her alone to rest.

By "rest," she meant "lay-awake-until-dawn-ruminating-all-the-possible-ways-she-had-messed-up-Liam's-life-and-hoping-Liam-wasn't-halfway-to-that-forsaken-place-to-save-his-dad-by- himself."

All because of a stupid necklace.

Well, a beautiful, enchanting, and magical necklace that felt soothing against her chest. How did such a necklace connect to some wolf-shaped creature?

Was the creature trying to protect it from getting into the wrong hands?

Neera had hours to produce several theories. Some more ridiculous the longer she stayed up.

Was the necklace the artifact Mr. Dern was looking for?

Is the island forbidden because of a botched experiment?

Does the necklace ward off evil the minute you put it on?

The last one made her think of the moment the beast had her dangling in front of its muzzle like it caught a prized trout. All she could think about was how she was going to die and how stupid she was for trying to face off against it. Her anxiety had filled to a brim, like water in a bucket, but the necklace somehow kept it from spilling. She couldn't explain it, but she felt...protected. A small part of her felt the same faith a priest had in a wooden crucifix while facing a demon.

Then the being flung her, and it almost confirmed her theory that the necklace was somehow sacred. That necklace was probably the only thing Neera had the most faith in, hence why she hadn't taken it off since.

Even when she "woke up" this morning from her two-hour nap to shower for school, the cool necklace never left her neck. Strangely, her back no longer hurt, and the only thing on her ankle was her circular birthmark. In the shower, her tail shimmered radiantly as if nothing happened. Her dad was just as shocked at her appearance but more on the *relieved* side.

Is this the necklace or one of my demi-goddess powers? If healing quickly is an ability, how come it didn't fix my crippling anxiety?

Out of all the things to heal, she would rather have a broken ankle than a lack of air in stressful situations.

I really need to get some sleep.

Neera wanted to give Liam some space, yet simultaneously wanted to check up on him. Tell him that she unlocked a new superpower before considering telling her BFF. She texted him on her ride to school, but no response.

Anxiety spiked, then settled.

It was understandable given his situation, however, she couldn't pretend that she wasn't hurt by the silent treatment. She pushed the negativity back down, hoping nothing happened and he just needed more time.

"Let me see your yearbook," Elayne interrupted Neera's thoughts from being held captive by the special bean casserole.

Neera slid her yearbook across the long cafeteria table to Elayne as Elayne did the same on the other side. From an outside perspective it probably looked cool, but it was just a regular thing with them.

Elayne flipped to an empty page–which wasn't hard to find–and seemed to concentrate with her pen positioned like she was about to write a New York best-seller. She exhaled, her bang floating up in response.

Like she didn't have a single issue in her head. No demi-goddess responsibilities. No boyfriend problems. No guilt for causing the possible demise of said boyfriend's father.

Just exams. Potential dorm roommate issues. Teen stuff.

Meanwhile, the blank page–well, the corner in the far top reserved for her–that Neera subconsciously turned to stared back at her, unable to find something to write to her best friend. Not because she didn't care about her but because there wasn't enough room in the entire book to express how great of a person she was. How much Neera secretly wanted to be like her. Then inwardly cringed at the fact that out of everything she wanted to say, she couldn't reveal what actually happened on the island.

"I wish we could switch lives," Neera murmured, then focused on her friend. "You can be the anxious, demi-goddess mermaid, and I can be the brave yet normal girl with loads of friends and a full ride to UCLA."

Elayne lifted her head and analyzed Neera's face. She was the type of person to say whatever she wanted whenever she wanted, but when it came to Neera, she was more careful with her responses.

"I'm pretty sure the world is not ready for me to have that kind of power," Elayne responded with a wry smile. "Something up with you?"

Neera absently stroked the outline of the jewel underneath her green maxi dress. As if summoned, her eyes landed on a gloomy Liam in a far corner of the cafeteria with his head down at a lunch table. He must've snuck past her because he wasn't there when they showed up for lunch, and he usually sat with her or his "friends". This time he was alone, and not even a tray of questionable food in sight.

Neera gulped, hoping it would soothe the ache in her chest.

"What if I wasn't meant to have them, either?" The back of her eyes stung. "All of this is a mistake. A girl like me shouldn't have this responsibility."

Elayne looked behind her, noticed Liam, and then returned her gaze to Neera with her eyebrows knitted together. She tapped her pen in front of Neera, causing her to tear her eyes away from Liam.

Elayne leaned forward slightly and affirmed softly, "To be honest, none of this makes sense. But that's kinda how the universe works. It has its own reasons, and we have to just hope for the best, ya know? Personally, I don't believe the universe makes mistakes."

Neera sat with that for a moment.

You don't believe the universe makes mistakes, huh? When

did Lay-Lay get so philosophical?

So everything that happened to her was all for a reason? Her mum. Her transformation. Liam's dad.

Why would the universe intentionally do these things? What's the message?

Maybe...they were trials, like Hercules. Tests she had to pass to prove that she was worthy, but it seemed that she wasn't making the right decisions. Elayne believed she was meant to be this. Chosen, even. So why couldn't Neera see it too?

Maybe...she was running from the answer instead of leaning into it. Leaning into her strength. Leaning into her legacy. The necklace felt warm against her skin.

Confidently, she took her pen and jotted down a quick message in Elayne's yearbook.

The world better watch out for a badass, inspiring genius with a good heart. She's one in a million.
XOXO
Nay-Nay

Proud of her message, Neera slid it over right before Elayne slid hers. Neera opened up her book to the first blank page and tilted her head back in laughter, the message melting her tension while filling her with hope.

In big letters, taking up the ENTIRE page:

JUST KEEP SWIMMING!
XOXO
LAY-LAY

"I'll be right back," Neera chuckled as she gathered her yearbook and tray, then strode over to Liam's table before Elayne could ask.

Sitting directly across from him, the courage that gassed her up immediately deflated in his presence. Guilt crept up her spine again. The most popular guy in school, who always had a group of people around him, was now spending his lunch by himself. He gave up his status, his friends, and his normalcy.

And she had an inkling that she was a major part of that.

Feeling the urge to wrap her arms around him, Neera held herself back for a moment and stared at his brown, disheveled curls. Even the strands on his head look tired and dull. She absent-mindedly stroked the strands, hoping– maybe–she could transfer her energy to him. Give him her protection, for once.

Liam's head popped up. A glare locked on Neera, causing her to stiffen.

Why am I nervous?

His hazel eyes were almost lifeless, encased in dark circles. His usual, lightly-tan skin appeared paler. His mouth was in a thin line and rimmed with stubble. As much as she wanted to bask in his masculine look, it was hard to ignore the pain etched all over his face.

Picking up a red grape from her tray, she held it out to him. He looked at it as if she offered him a severed toe.

"I have something really important to tell you. But I won't unless you eat something."

Liam glanced between her and the grape, then back to her with furrowed brows. "I'm not in the mood for jokes."

He sounded tense, but Neera was just thankful he felt anything other than despair.

Neera tilted her head, meeting his glare. She countered him. "No jokes. If you eat, I'll tell you how we're going to get your dad back."

His jaw ticked, but nothing else.

Neera glanced at his sports watch. Lunch was over in five minutes. She needed him to eat. She needed him to be as close to okay as possible.

She nudged the tray of food towards Liam, her soft gaze countering his piercing one.

"We're getting him back tonight. No cops. No parents.

Just you and me," Neera held the grape closer to his mouth. "With your brains and my powers, we can save him. All you have to do is trust me. Trust us."

Liam seemed to mull it over. Neera gulped down her nervousness. She didn't know when it started, but she needed his trust. She desired it. Everything counted on trust in one another, especially with their relationship, and the thought of him withholding it was something even her anxious mind didn't want to explore.

Then, like the sun peeking through dark clouds, Liam opened his mouth.

Neera visibly relaxed as she placed the fruit in his mouth, watching him chew. He picked a grape himself and held it to her mouth. She couldn't help the smile that broke out as she bit the fruit. Without a word, they continued to share the tray of food until only a few scraps were left.

Definitely late for class by the ring of the second bell, Liam motioned to her yearbook. Rolling her eyes, she handed it over, and he opened it to a blank page. He scribbled something, closed the book, and then handed it back to her.

Instead of waiting for her reaction, he got up from his seat and smirked.

"See you tonight," he gently affirmed.

Instead of following him out of the cafeteria, Neera quickly flipped to the page he wrote on. Her heart fluttered at the top corner of the page where he wrote:

Angelfish,
In a world of mermaids and monsters, it's hard to believe in anything anymore. Yet, believing in you is the easiest thing to do.
Love,
Liam

LIAM

"Dad had to go to some meeting straight from the island. That it'll be a few days, and he apologizes for not telling you."

Liam was expressionless as the lies tumbled out of his mouth. It didn't even hold a candle to the trepidation in his heart and the gears in his mind running to keep everything together. His dad would hate for his company–all his hard work–to go down the drain by him. Liam wasn't even sure if his dad was alive to worry about his potential hatred, or the very real possibility of having to take over the business...if not. The weight of responsibility felt heavy on his shoulders.

Liam rubbed the back of his neck as he tried to give his mom an equally nonchalant look. Since it wasn't strange for his dad to go on impromptu trips, he hoped she might take this one lightly.

God was on his side at that moment because his mom just shrugged as she chewed her Mediterranean salad like any other day. For a moment, her eyes landed on his as if she was studying him.

His mom gave him a quick smile and said, "When he gets back, you'll have to update me on your *little friend*, and how you two have been sneaking around the house."

Of course, he had to deal with his mom's wrath for breaking the rules, but he would rather have her angry than worried.

Liam simply nodded.

He sensed someone watching him, so he looked up and spotted Danny glaring at him. His blond bangs didn't obstruct the judgment in his blue eyes. His dad's eyes. It was like Danny was looking right through him, the mask that he perfected over the years.

Maybe Liam's worries were getting to him. How could an eleven-year-old know anything when he barely knew what puberty was?

Right?

That night, Liam tried to sneak into his dad's home office to see if there was someone he could contact to rescue him or someone he could tell about the beast running rampant on the island. Unfortunately, it was locked.

As always.

He resigned to his room, his head heavy in defeat. He spent his entire night thinking of his next move. At one point, he considered contacting Neera to let her know he forgave her. Hell, it was the monster's fault for ruining their lives and not hers.

But he didn't. Couldn't. He needed space from her.

She distracted him from what was important.

Protecting his family.

Protecting the business.

Plain and simple. The only solution a sleep-deprived guy could think of was to go rescue his dad himself. He could pretend that he was going to Nate's house but sneak onto the boat and head to the island. Then, he would bring his pocket knife and use his tackling skills only if it was necessary. If he... If he wasn't alive...then he would bring his body back or any information that was on him.

But Liam didn't want to think that way.

He'd get his dad back one way or another.

The next morning, he wore a hoodie in 90-degree weather to cover his certainly dark-rimmed eyes and disheveled hair that he couldn't care less to fix for school. He looked at his phone and noticed a few text messages from Nate asking if he wanted to go out for lunch with the gang. Liam couldn't comprehend why he still wanted to hang out with him, but he guessed that Nate would rather have him as a friend than an enemy. Liam then noticed a message from Neera:

NEERA: WANTED 2 C IF UR OK

Usually, seeing a text from Neera lit him up, but he felt so dead inside that the bulb didn't even spark. He couldn't let it spark. So he returned to Nate's text and replied:

LIAM: ZZZ IN DA CAFE. HAVE FUN.

When he entered the cafeteria, he saw Neera and Elayne sitting at a table, and his body naturally wanted to go in her direction. He was tired, and it took him the last bit of strength he could muster to lug himself to an empty table in a random corner. Everyone signing their yearbooks reminded him that he should've picked up his own, but it seemed so trivial in the end.

He took one last look at her smiling face.

At least one of us can smile.

"If you had to choose between playing football and your father's business, what would you choose?" Neera asked with a bare leg bent over him and her chest pressed against his dress shirt-covered chest. Her face was on his shoulder, smooth hair draping over his arm. Some of her prom makeup left stains, but he didn't give a crap.

"Ugh, too hard," he groaned. He totally meant the question. "Okay, the family business."

"Really?" Neera hummed, and his chest vibrated. "Okay, next question..."

Liam groaned again and wrapped his arms around her while slightly rocking her.

"Dr. Ran, I didn't ask for a therapy session," Liam stated dryly.

She literally giggled. "Listen. Which one makes you the happiest? Football or your father's business?"

"It doesn't matter what makes me happy. It's just my duty as the eldest to take over. Football...can be done in my free time."

"If you take over and no longer have time to play football, you would have to pick one or the other."

Liam was honestly stumped. The obvious answer was to give up football for the business. So easy, all he had to do was say it. Yet, he couldn't form the words.

How could Neera enter his world and completely shake it up? It was like it was some practical joke from God to give him his perfect match, but it required readjusting the trajectory of his life. All he had to do was get up and leave her, and his mind wouldn't be scrambled anymore. Everything would fall back into place.

But it would fall into place with one piece missing. And that would be so annoying…

"Hello, Earth to Liam," Neera drawled as she poked the tip of his nose. Liam grabbed her hand to stop her. She implored, "Which one would make you the happiest?"

He absentmindedly held her hand to his chest, undoubtedly feeling his rapid heartbeat, and remained silent. His other hand stroked her bare back, its smoothness unreal. He was so nervous, and not just because she was pretty, but how much the impact of her touch, her presence, had on him. It was better than he had ever dreamed it would be. He liked it…a lot.

Neera lifted her head and stared into his eyes, probably waiting for his answer; however, all he could think about was the mysterious shade of her eyes that seemed to trap anyone who looked at them, her freckles that looked like glitter sprinkled over her nose bridge, or her full lips that were soft and wonderful. She was like a Renaissance painting. He just couldn't look away, or the euphoric feelings he had would wither away.

He inwardly chuckled at her cute eyebrows as they furrowed. Then he said something he didn't mean to say out loud. He murmured as he stared at her lips.

"Neither."

Naturally, he kissed her. It deepened after her initial shock, and she melted into him. Her hand slid from under his hand and into his hair, leaving him warm and tingly all over. For some reason, it felt different this time. More realistic, like grounded in reality instead of the usual floating feeling…

Liam awakened, and his eyes squinted as they tried to

adjust to the fluorescent cafeteria lights. They then landed on Neera, who ended up sitting in front of him instead of on the other side of the cafeteria. He wanted to flee, to keep his distance from her, before she could find out about his one-man mission to save his dad and somehow stop him.

No distractions.

She tried to get him to eat, but he really wasn't in the mood. Okay, maybe his stomach was quietly growling and he could really use the nutrients. However, he didn't want to give in to her demands.

At least not until he saw the bags underneath her eyes and the stress on her face. Not pity...but empathy. She struggled just as much as him. The smile on her face from earlier wasn't happiness but a distraction from her dark thoughts.

Guilt crept up his throat from ignoring her text message, which probably made her feel worse, especially with her condition. Liam wanted to hide in his hoodie and disappear.

Then she proposed they go rescue his dad.

Together.

She was confident and secure as if it was the only option. How could someone disagree with someone like that? She was right. She was a mermaid. A badass demi-goddess. She also didn't seem hurt, especially with the injuries she endured, so she must've magically healed or something.

He completely believed she could do anything, and he was relieved that she finally had seen it in herself. She was willing to risk her safety for him, and it made Liam feel warm all over again. Like prom night. His heart raced so fast that he couldn't say anything.

The perfect teammate.

So he let her feed him. Equally, he fed his partner-in-crime. Liam mistakenly believed Neera was a distraction. That being with her made things worse.

He was completely wrong.

She was the Left Tackle to his Quarterback, or maybe

vice versa. What he knew for sure was that together, they would be victorious.

ON THE OFFENSE

Chapter 12

Liam

Sneaking past his mom after her two glasses of wine couldn't have been more bittersweet. Liam didn't have to think of an excuse to leave after dinner because his mom had already passed out with one of her romance books on her chest. She always got like this when his dad traveled for work, and deep down, Liam wasn't sure if it was to cope with his lack of company or her reprieve from being a Dern.

With the sky a deep navy blue and the full moon high in the sky, Liam threw his gym bag full of supplies in the stern of the boat, cringing at the loud thud it made on impact. He may have overpacked, but there was no such thing as being overprepared. The dingy, overused bag consisted of an emergency kit, a towel, trail mix, two flashlights, and a canteen he filled with water. Just in case.

He texted Neera to see if she was on the way, and she responded that she'd be there in a few minutes. Liam sighed, taking this time to go over the plan:

They get to the island and search the area without yelling.

They find his dad–in whatever condition–and bring him back to the boat.

They head back home and never return to that fucking

island again.

While he sat on the edge of the boat, he saw two quick flashes of light in his direction. Turning towards it, he noticed a dark Neera-shaped figure jogging over to the dock from his backyard fence that was left unlocked for her.

The closer she got, the more his ears heated. She had the same pack from their last trip slung over her shoulder, but this time, she was wearing a black tank top with black leggings. Like some sort of sexy ninja.

Focus, Liam.

He didn't get to catch a break when she ran into his arms and embraced him. Caught off-guard, he almost fell into the boat but adjusted himself in time to hug her back. Even on the brink of total exhaustion, Liam missed holding her. He could feel the hard outline of the necklace underneath her shirt, appreciating her consideration of his feelings.

Neera released him first, bringing Liam back to the present. She cleared her throat and hooked her thumb at her bag. "I brought some health bars for your dad since he'll probably be hungry."

If he's even alive to eat them.

Liam shook the dark thought away and gave her what he hoped was an appreciative smile. He pointed to his pack. "I got an emergency kit and some water."

Neera just nodded. It was still awkward between them, but there was no time for *awkward*. As much as he wanted to comfort her, he also didn't want to give her a chance to back out. He felt horrible about it, but they could fix their relationship once everything returned to normal. First, his dad. Then, his relationship.

Their entire trip to the island only consisted of water slapping against the hull and the boat's motor purring. Liam assumed Neera was as worried as him, but what if she was regretting her decision to help him?

Regretting her decision to be with him after he ignored her and didn't even hesitate to turn her down?

When he agreed to the idea immediately, even with her by his side now, he felt she would back out. He secretly hoped she'd let him fight his own battles. That it would ease some of his guilt.

A hand slipped into his and interlocked their fingers. He turned to Neera's dim face, her mouth flashing a tiny smile.

"Almost there," she murmured, barely audible enough over the motor. "You ready?"

No. Let's go back.

Let's call the cops and let them handle it.

Let's ruin the family business and start fresh.

Let's be normal people with normal lives for once.

"Yeah," he gritted out.

When they hit the same shore as last time, they sprang into action. Liam moored the boat. Neera withdrew the flashlights and turned them on, giving the area a "found-footage" feel. They both left their packs in the boat in case they had to run.

With only their flashlights and a Swiss army knife from the emergency pack, they trudged through the dense and now creepy forest as quietly as they could. Liam's heart roared in his ears. He'd never been more on edge in his life. At least when they were last there, they could sense the beast coming from the sway of the trees or a large shadow approaching.

This was a different kind of fear.

The suspense hung over his head like an anvil or a sniper, always watching and waiting to strike. Visibility was impossible, even with their flashlights and moonlight on their side. The quietness that was appreciated before now added to his perturbation and made the whole place ten times worse.

Neera gripped his hand with almost enough force to cut his circulation. He didn't let go, grateful for keeping him grounded.

I hope this thing is asleep.

As if on some sadistic cue, the sound of rustling appeared. They could either run erratically or keep their strategic pace to avoid attention. Liam gripped Neera's hand and motioned her to keep walking. Her eyes were saucers, but she listened.

Liam picked up the pace slightly when he heard more rustling and twigs snapping, praying to God that it was their doing.

What if it's your dad?

Liam halted suddenly, causing Neera to bump into him. He scanned the area with his flashlight and listened to any nearby sounds, debating if he should call out to him or not. He took the chance.

"Dad!" It was more of a hiss than a yell.

Big mistake.

The rustling became thumps, causing slight tremors in the ground.

That was definitely not his dad.

Tugging Neera along, Liam burst into a sprint as they tried–and failed–to avoid the trees in their way. Their exasperating breaths mixed with the huffs of the creature. Without looking back, the sound of its paws hitting the earth resembled a train passing by.

Liam's soul left his body when the beast screeched a few feet behind them. His ears rang from it, but he kept moving with Neera. Abandoning the search, Liam made a sharp right, attempting to make a U-turn back to the boat.

Luck was clearly not on his side because before he could register what was happening, the ground disappeared from under him. Neera squeaked as they landed in a small pool of water. Liam flailed initially in shock until Neera held him around his torso to keep him afloat.

A quick scan of their new surroundings indicated they were in some sort of underground cave. The pool of water was no bigger than a bathtub, a thick ledge forming a dome above it. Liam looked up at the smaller-sized hole they must've fallen through.

"Son!" A familiar, gritty voice whispered.

They turned to the sound, and there he was: his dad in the flesh. Tattered, dirty, with more wrinkles than usual, but alive. Liam dragged himself out of the water with the help of Neera. He hugged his father like he'd never done before. Liam pulled away just enough to assess his condition. With the exception of a few bruises and scrapes, his dad looked unharmed.

"Are you okay, Dad?" Liam inquired, maybe missing something. "How'd you end up here?"

He cleared his throat. "I'm alive," he responded with a relieved smile. "I was running from that abomination and fell down here. This pool is too deep to find a way out, and the opening is too high to reach."

Liam looked back at Neera, whose skin sparkled in the moonlight.

"Are you okay, Neera?" He tried to offer her a hand, then he retracted it, remembering her condition.

"I'm good," she responded timidly, her body only visible from her neck up.

Liam observed his dad who was watching Neera a little longer than he would like.

Does he see her tail? How did he notice?

His dad peered up at the hole above them, squinting. "How are we going to get out of here?"

Liam and Neera's eyes connected in a silent conversation.

Can I trust him? Her eyebrows lowered.

If you can trust me, you can trust him. His eyes glinted.

Neera broke contact first, her cheeks flushing as she faced his dad.

"I can swim and see how far it goes," Neera declared with a dejected expression.

His dad shook his head and countered. "No, it's not physically possible…"

His voice trailed off when he beheld her green tail shimmering over the surface as she disappeared below.

The silence unnerved Liam, and it had nothing to do with the beast above them. His eyes fell to a corner of the cave with unidentified bones scattered on the ground. He inwardly shuddered at a very human-like skull.

"So she's a..." His dad scratched his stubbled jaw, bringing his attention back to his dad.

"Mermaid," Liam sighed.

"How long have you known?"

Liam rubbed the back of his neck. Its stiffness seemed to be recurring lately. "Only recently."

A light sparked in his dad's usually cold eyes despite the darkness and his tired expression. "It must've been longer with your lack of astonishment, son. Do you know how fascinating this discovery is?"

Liam's heart pounded as he shook his head ferociously. "No, no, no. You can't tell anyone. This has to stay between us."

The potential harm that could come from revealing Neera's secret identity was alarming enough to double down on his request. The trust she put in him meant everything to him, and he couldn't jeopardize it.

His dad searched Liam's face, looking for any weakness in his resolve. "You must really care about this girl if you're willing to overlook the billions of dollars and countless accolades Dern Research would earn from this."

It was a loaded statement, dropping the bomb in Liam's lap. His dad was an intelligent man, and Liam assumed some of that intellect had rubbed off on him. Everything he stated wasn't that simple. So for his dad to question his feelings for Neera, he was questioning his loyalty to him. To their last name.

He couldn't answer that.

I don't want to.

Liam swallowed the knot in his throat. "I'm asking, Dad. That's why I'm asking you to keep this a secret."

Please.

His dad clapped a hand on Liam's shoulder. The corners of his mouth lifted quickly as he muttered,

"Okay. This stays between us."

NEERA

Darn it. Wrong side...again!

It was the third time Neera had traced her steps–strokes–to locate the shore with their boat. The first two tries led her to a rocky cliffside with a breath-taking waterfall and an empty shore.

Neera swam back to the opening and then swam in a different direction. Mr. Dern was right about how deep the pool was. The land practically floated on top of the ocean like a lily pad in a pond. Fortunately for her, her tail made swimming three times faster. Swimming also kept her mind off her scrambled thoughts.

Off her growing feelings for Liam.

She wanted to believe that going on a dangerous mission to save his dad and revealing her identity to him was solely based on guilt. In reality, and after her second try locating the shore, it was more than guilt. She cared about him more than she had ever cared for another person. Even Elayne.

It scared her...but also excited her.

The way he looked at her when she was deciding whether to reveal herself to Mr. Dern made her feel...assured. She trusted his judgment. She trusted him. She was willing to take a risk on him because he was worth it.

And that scares me.

Her head broke the surface, and with a quick scan, she saw waves sloshing into the boat's butt. *Heck yeah!*

Neera swam until the water dwindled, then army-crawled across the sand until she reached the boat. Ignoring the elbow scrapes, she forced her torso over the side of the boat and fumbled for Liam's pack in the dark. Her hands found a thick pack, and then blindly searched for a zipper. Skating across a metallic object, she unzipped the bag and retrieved a fluffy towel. Her body toppled back into the sand, quickly crawling further up the shore and away from the tide.

It only took twenty seconds of drying for her body to return back to normal. With the towel tied around her waist, she went back to the boat and untied the rope from the stick connected the boat. Once freed, Neera sprinted back into the forest like a woman on a mission. For some reason, after facing off with the creature MULTIPLE times, she wasn't as afraid of it as she initially was. If she remained careful.

Now the hard part was finding the hole...

A dim light gleamed in the distance like a beacon, her feet carrying her to it. Liam's flashlight. When she got close, the sound of footsteps caused her to pause. The hairs on her neck stood, but she didn't run. She needed to keep the creature away from them. Without thinking, she lunged for the flashlight and threw it as far as she could in a random direction.

The heavy steps quickened and faded into the distance, allowing Neera to release a long-held breath. No trees close enough to use as an anchor, she had to do something that she could only hope would work but would ultimately suck so much.

With no time to lose, she tied one end of the rope to her waist and dropped the other end down the hole. Her toes gripping the ground, she waited for them to climb up without making any noise.

Nothing happened.

Neera impatiently got closer to the hole and wiggled it. Eventually, a heavy weight pulled her down to her knees, rocks and twigs scraping against them, but she swallowed the pain by clenching her jaw. The rope continued to yank down, her palms burned as she gripped tighter and pulled harder. Thoughts of forfeiting everything bombarded her mind with just the pain alone, but a notion popped into her head before her usual anxiety took over.

I'm the great-great-granddaughter of freaking Poseidon! Act like it!

Concentrating on the hole and pocketing her pain, she fisted the rope until a dirt-covered hand gripped the edge, alleviating some of the weight. Balding, sandy-blond hair appeared, then Mr. Dern's face. He struggled to get over the edge, but when he finally did, he turned around and began pulling on the rope. Neera was grateful for the assistance.

Liam popped up faster, quickly climbing his way out of the hole. The slack in the rope caused her to fall on her butt, but there was no time to think. No time to cheer.

They had to get out of there.

Liam rushed over to offer her a hand and probably a hug, but she just grabbed it and ran toward the boat with them in tow, ignoring the scrapes of rocks on the soles of her feet. They wordlessly bolted to the shore, and a wave of relief hit her.

They did it!

I did it.

Mr. Dern caught his breath as he braced his hands on his knees.

"Let's get out of here," he huffed.

Neera and Liam nodded in unison as they jogged to the boat. Mr. Dern sat in the driver's seat. Liam grabbed the purposeless stick, threw it back into the boat, and paused. Neera turned toward the forest and saw the creature emerge on its hind legs. It let out a blood-curdling screech.

This was it. There was no way Liam and Neera could make it in the boat in time before it could lunge at them. All they could do was freeze and hope no sudden movements disturbed it.

Remember what you are. WHO you are.

The voice in her head interrupted Anxiety strangling her throat. Her necklace glowed, but she could barely register it as she focused on her instincts instead of her head. Almost like her body was moving on its own, her arms moved in the direction of the ocean, her eyes concentrating on the sea. A tingling feeling shot through her veins, like a plug connecting with an outlet. It didn't hurt or burn, but it felt...powerful.

Everything seemed to move slowly as she whipped her arms towards the creature. A stream of water followed the path of her hands and penetrated the creature's sternum. A baseball-sized hole glistened before the creature crumpled to the ground.

Neera slowly backed away from the crumpled-up creature to the boat as she stared at the weapons she had formerly known as her hands. On the trip back, Neera couldn't shake the uneasiness and nausea building up in her stomach. She was only hoping to stun the big guy, not shoot him with a freaking water bullet. Her anxiety threatened to spike.

I killed a living creature.

Mr. Dern and Liam's faces didn't mirror the disgust she felt about the cold-blooded murder as they talked about his dad's job, but she tuned them out the entire time. Her mind couldn't wrap around how she could manipulate water in her favor. How unpredictable she was...

She felt a slight burn on her knee and impulsively kicked her leg out. Peering at the cause, she noticed Liam lightly pressing a cotton ball to it. Their eyes locked, and his guilty expression kept her from spiraling.

Liam pulled his lips into his mouth.

"Sorry," he exhaled. "For bringing you into this. For everything."

When Neera didn't respond, he returned to tending to her wounds. The antiseptic licking her wounds made her suck in a breath. She covered his hand holding the cotton ball with her own, ceasing his movement.

"It was my choice," Neera declared firmly. When he returned her gaze with a blush, her face heated in return. "I couldn't live with myself if I let you go alone."

Liam's face brightened to a pale pink as his Adam's apple

bobbed.

Did I just indirectly admit that I love him? In front of his dad?

With a grin, Liam focused on her wound, tending to it as it began to cool down. His ears couldn't get any more red.

"Then thank you. I...There's no one else I would've wanted beside me."

Now it was time for Neera to blush.

Was that...

Was he going to say...

"Speaking of appreciation," Mr. Dern interjected from the front seat. "Thank you for your help and confidentiality. In return, your secret is safe with me."

Neera grinned. "Thanks, Mr. Dern. I'm just glad you're safe."

Her grin turned into a wince when Liam began treating the other knee. She snatched her knee away, and before he could question her, she leaned in and said in a lower tone, "I'll heal by tomorrow...but thanks for the help, Doc."

"Well then," Liam wrapped an arm around Neera's hip to tuck her close to his body. He used his other hand to gently, yet firmly, keep her knee in place. If she attempted to move her leg, she'd end up flashing Mr. Dern. "I'll protect you from any infections."

His smile made her want to combust into hundreds of tiny, confetti hearts.

Mr. Dern cleared his throat as he interrupted their moment. This time, his tone was more serious than the earnest one he used earlier. "Son, thank you for saving the family business. You're finally living up to the Dern name."

He grinned, but there was something off with it. Like it never reached his eyes.

OVERTIME

Chapter 13

Neera

With only two days left of school and her dad's permission, Neera spent her day at home studying for her US Government exam.

If only she could focus on the study materials instead of her new mermaid abilities.

She stared at her ceiling as she lay on her bed, completely neglecting her notes. Neera pondered everything that had transpired in the past few days and came to a few conclusions:

First, she was a mermaid that could manipulate the movement of water. That was what she absolutely knew. The connection she felt to the ocean when she struck the beast in the torso was inexplicable. It was, like, all she had to do was command it to move, and it just followed suit. That kind of power couldn't be a "one-off" thing in every heat of the moment. It had to come from within.

Or...it could come from this. Neera touched the cool jewel around her neck.

So, as soon as she came home last night, despite her body aching, she tested her abilities in her bathroom sink. After filling the sink with water, she reluctantly removed her necklace and placed it on her bed before returning to the bathroom. After a few deep breaths, she hovered her hands over the water and sent a silent command to freeze. Like a time-lapse video, the sink water frosted from translucent to opaque within a few seconds.

Neera jumped back in shock. She looked down at her hands as if it were the first time she had seen them. Returning to the sink, her heart pounded, but she remained steady as she placed her hands over the water and internally commanded it to "heat."

Nothing happened. *Was that the wrong password?*

Neera rolled her shoulders back and glared at the water like it was its fault for disobeying her.

Disobeying me? Literally, what is my life right now?

Heat. The water mocked her in its still state. She felt her ears boil.

Utterly annoyed, Neera clenched her fingers. To her surprise, the water boiled and steam rose, filling the bathroom in a vapory mist. The makeshift sauna eventually died down, and Neera was mystified to witness the sink completely empty.

She flipped her hands over and continued clenching and releasing them in bewilderment. Even without her necklace, she could naturally change the molecules of water into whatever she wanted without wasting an ounce of energy. Technically, the opposite happened. Like Neera gained MORE power from the use, like jumper cables on a car battery in a thunderstorm. Those might not even be the gamut of her abilities. Was there even a limit?

I'm a demi-goddess.

I'm powerful, self-healing, and...uncontrollable.

I'm a monster.

Negativity unceremoniously shoved itself to the front of her mind. As usual. Her body tensed at the thought, and she shook it away. Contemplating in bed like this would only backtrack all the progress she'd made, as her old therapist claimed, so she got up and went to her mum's garden in the front yard.

After grabbing a watering can from the garage and filling it with water, she sprinkled the beautiful flora. The flowing droplets dampened the earthy soil and gave the plants some reprieve from the scorching summer sun. Usually, her dad took care of the garden, but on certain days, Neera did it to keep her grounded.

Today, it brought up the memory of five-year-old Neera and her mum spending their tea time tending to her garden. Her mum would take care of her plants so delicately and full of love, like a real-life fairytale princess. She would smile at each individual plant like they had their own unspoken secret. Neera would watch her and copy her care of the flowers, but they seemed to enjoy her mum's presence a bit more.

I don't blame them. It's hard not to love her.

When Neera approached the pink and purple hydrangeas, another memory surfaced of little Neera watering them while her mum held the can for her to carry. She told Neera that she should water and care for them the way she cared for her because they were her favorite. Little Neera questioned her mum because all she did was water them.

"My little guppy..." Her smile would emit its own sunlight. "Water is healing and cleansing. It helps you grow and can humble you. Like how I water you into the beautiful Neera you are and will continue to be, I want you to do the same for these. It's as simple as that."

"I thought you hated water, mummy," Neera responded innocently.

Her mother chuckled. "I don't hate water, but I do fear it in all its beautiful and almighty nature. It's everywhere and in everything. It's merciful, and for that, I don't find it bad." Her hand tucked a stray curl behind Neera's ear.

"I don't get it," Neera shook her head in confusion, the curl bouncing back.

Her mother just smiled. "One day, you'll realize that water isn't bad or good. It's how you use it that determines it..."

Neera's heart almost jumped out of her chest at the

sound of her ringtone interrupting her thoughts. She placed the can down and answered the phone.

"Hey, Angelfish." The usual butterflies fluttered in her tummy at the sound of his nickname for her. "You think we can hang out today? Maybe check out a sparkly vampire movie?"

He wants to hang out again?

Not that Neera was complaining, even though she usually does when it comes to socializing. She didn't even hang with Elayne as much, which didn't bother her since Elayne claimed it went against Neera's introverted nature.

Instead of being annoyed, Neera was flattered by the consistency. It made her feel wanted; however, she couldn't let him see how much he affected her. Not after that embarrassing confession she made on the way back from the island. Plus, she could use the distraction.

"If I knew vampires were your thing, I totally would've worn my limited-edition fangs when I asked you to prom," Neera responded dryly.

Don't let him see you sweat.

"I just heard that this is what all the girls are into."

How cute–

"But maybe if I knew you were a biter, prom would've been–"

"Sure!" Neera's eyes widened, heat filling her cheeks. "Movie around seven?"

Smooth. Totally smooth.

She swore she could hear him smirk over the phone.

"It's a date."

A little past seven, Neera rushed down her staircase in a mint-green, V-neck skater dress with tan ankle boots. She yelled *bye* over her shoulder to her dad lounging on the couch, hoping she didn't interrupt his tennis match.

"Woah, woah, woah! Where are you going in that?" His deep voice filled the living room.

Neera surveyed her outfit, even her fringe handbag, and failed to see the issue. "I wear clothes like this all the time."

He got up from the sofa and crossed the room to stand in front of her with a serious expression on his face. He jabbed a finger at her neck.

"No. Why on Earth are you wearing THAT?"

Neera glanced at the gleaming necklace around her neck. Ever since she brought it back from the island, she'd kept it hidden underneath her clothes because of his reaction to it the day she found it. He seemed personally offended to see it, which Neera couldn't comprehend why. She forgot to hide it, but she hoped he had forgotten about it by now.

She guessed wrong. Guilt hit her chest as she wore a reminder of what was possibly one of the most traumatic moments of his life.

Instead of explaining anything, she feigned indifference by shrugging.

"It matches my outfit," her voice trembled. Her eyes shifted away from his piercing ones. "And it...I don't know... feels comforting."

"How can it *feel comforting* when it had conjured some sort of murderous creature?" His voice raised, but she didn't fear him. She just hated seeing her dad in pain and knew how much his reaction was out of fear. "We could've died! You shouldn't even have brought it back."

At this rate, he wasn't going to let her leave the house if she kept wearing it. So being the completely diplomatic person Neera was, she hesitantly unlatched the golden chain and placed the necklace on the table in the entryway. The idea of separating from the jewel squeezed her chest, but losing her dad's trust would've made her feel ten times worse.

Neera glanced everywhere except his face and huffed. "Can I go now?"

Her father raised an authoritative brow, and that was all she needed to crumble her defense. She slapped on an apologetic smile. "...Please?"

It only took one of her smiles to debilitate him. He cracked a smile, patting her head. He contently motioned her out the door, leaving part of her heart behind.

LIAM

Something's up with Neera.

Liam noticed Neera wasn't her usual self. On the car ride to the movie theater, she seemed distracted. Like she was just going through the motions. When he asked if she was okay, she just nodded and plastered on a fake smile. What was even stranger was how perceptive he already was to her for someone who had only been her boyfriend for a few days. How he wanted to make everything that upset her go away.

That, in itself, is scarier than her mood change.

But Liam couldn't help it. Of all the subjects he enjoyed studying in school, she was his favorite. He felt...lucky to be able to bask in her presence whenever he wanted. For her to look at him with a light that rivaled the sun. Even in the dark and dusty space of the cinema, she could still light up the whole room.

However, tonight, the tension she projected prickled the hairs on the back of his neck. In their seats, Neera looked straight ahead at the *"oh-so-interesting"* previews with a flat expression. Liam shifted in his seat, balancing a medium bag of popcorn on his lap.

"Did something happen between you and your dad?" Liam asked low enough for only Neera to hear.

Neera snapped out of her trance as she leaned towards him, her eyes still glued to the screen. "I didn't know your mind-reading powers came in. If you start to develop a taste for blood, you should let me know now."

Liam chortled. She was deflecting, but damn, it entertained him when she did.

You just like everything she does.

He offered her the bag of popcorn in a truce. "Wow, something must've happened for you to attack me. An innocent bystander."

An amusing smile brightened her face as she grabbed a handful of popcorn.

There's my Angelfish.

The movie began. Some pale, angsty girl had the hots for a brooding, sparkly dude while her "nice guy" friend crushed on her.

Classic love triangle.

How fun. The only things giving Liam solace were the action scenes.

Liam looked over at Neera. Her eyes were glued to the movie while his hand was in her lap, fingers interlocked with hers. Her fingers were tense despite her face being devoid of emotion. Her situation with her dad must've been on her mind. She didn't have her necklace, so maybe it had something to do with that. Maybe what happened with the beast? Maybe her dad found out what she really did last night?

All Liam knew was that he wanted to protect her. If her necklace was taken away or lost, he could be that protection for her.

He could fix it. He could be there for her the way she willingly risked her life to be with him.

The main chick and the broody vampire made out in her room in the creepiest way possible. With his new position as Neera's necklace for the night, Liam leaned in and planted his lips on her shoulder. The tension visibly eased out of her body. When he pulled away, he whispered in her ear.

"If your dad is anything like mine, all the drama will pass, and everything will be okay. Just know that I'll always be on your side."

For the first time that night, Neera locked eyes with him as he held her shimmering sea gaze. Her face softened but came to some sort of resolution as she whispered.

"I kind of hate vampires. Let's get out of here."

Liam chuckled as he watched Neera stumble through the sandy shore in her ankle boots, like a newborn deer, after refusing his help the first time her ankles buckled. He tightened his hold on her hand, afraid she might fall down if he let go.

"You know I can carry your shoes for you?" Liam offered.

Neera shoved her hair from her face as the wind blew it to one side. "I don't want to step on anything squishy or sharp."

It was dark outside. The only sources of light were the moon and a few street lamps from the boardwalk in the distance. Liam really believed a walk on the beach while looking at the stars would be as romantic as the movies claimed it to be. The movies failed to mention how light pollution, tent clusters, and litter could put a damper on the mood, especially with a stubborn mermaid by his side.

But he wanted to lift her mood and show her she was safe with him.

"You sure?" Liam asked again.

"So you can do something sappy, like a piggyback ride? I'm good."

Liam rolled his eyes. "Wait a sec."

They stopped walking, and Liam removed his shoes. His socks absorbed the sand as he knelt, holding one of Neera's smooth legs, and removed her boots before she could protest. She held onto his shoulders as he did the same to the other side. He slipped her feet into his larger shoes and tied them tight enough to secure them.

Satisfied, he stood up. Her face was bright pink, and her mouth slightly open. She looked...bashful at the action, causing Liam to ease some of the unintentional awkwardness.

"I'm lucky. This wouldn't have worked if your feet were small and dainty."

Neera's face flushed as she scoffed. Her hand fisted a handful of sand, launching it at his chest before he could dodge it. "You think that's funny, Dern?"

She grabbed another handful of sand, and now prepared, Liam ran away from her as she chased him, laughing until his belly ached. Neera got a good shot at his back, but he was able to dodge the rest of her attacks. Her feet adorably slipped a little out of the shoes, but she recovered quickly until they ran out of breath.

Neera dropped down on her butt underneath a rocky overhang between the beach and the boardwalk, further away from the shore. After retrieving Neera's shoes, Liam sat beside her while leaning back on his hands. Her shoes safely next to him, he removed his denim jacket and offered it to her. She looked at him incredulously, yet took the jacket and donned it over her shoulders after taking off her purse.

The silence was comfortable. Something Liam got used to. He took the opportunity to spend it staring at her, hoping he could make her feel better in some way. Her body wasn't as tense as it was earlier. Her face was softer, even as the wind blew her curls away from it.

"I don't think I thanked you for saving my dad." Liam stared at her until she looked back at him. "For saving us."

Her lips lifted for a second as she shrugged. "You did, but it's in the past now."

Liam didn't like her nonchalance, but he remained neutral.

"Not for me."

This was the perfect moment for him to be totally honest with her and with himself. His wall of indifference completely fell, leaving her with sincerity and a bleeding heart.

He continued. "You're literally the bravest person I've ever known. Braver than most. Braver than me. That's what I've always admired."

Neera hugged her knees to her chest, looking smaller when all he wanted was to make her feel taller. "I don't feel like it. To be honest, I think if it weren't for the necklace, I wouldn't have the courage to pull it off."

Liam shook his head. "You were brave before the necklace, Ran," his eyes turned to the sea. "You're always true to yourself, even when you feel like you're not. That's what I love about you."

The sound of the waves licking the shore was the only sound in the air. Liam swallowed his nerves at his confession, but it didn't satiate the tightness in his chest. He needed her to know how he felt. How much she meant to him. Usually the silence was welcomed, but the longer it prolonged, the more anxious he got. His pride kept his head rooted toward the low waves before him.

"You're such a passionate and caring person, even when you pretend you're not," Neera's jovial tone turned serious and soft as the night breeze. "I see the real you, Liam, and that's why I love you."

Liam snapped his head to a flushed Neera, her eyes burning any doubt he had left and her freckles staining the damage like beautiful ashes. She was like the sun. His face felt like it was on fire, but the blaze never felt better. It was like they were in their own world, their own universe. He didn't have to worry about his family's legacy or his education. It was just Liam and Neera. So simple, despite everything, and so natural.

I am falling in love with Neera Ran.

A small part of him always felt that way for Neera ever since he saved her from "drowning" eight years ago, but he was too afraid to admit it. He pushed those feelings down because they were intimidating, and concealing them was easy.

Doing what he was supposed to do was easy.

Falling in love in high school, like his parents, was unpredictable. No amount of calculating and researching could predict the perfect outcome regarding love and avoiding pain. Trying to be careful and analytical about his emotions had only led him back to his predestined point: Neera.

And for the first time in his life, he wanted to throw caution to the wind.

Liam's heartbeat slammed against his sternum as he leaned in and locked lips with her. He shouldn't have felt nervous, but he did because tonight never felt so right. This time it felt like a dream, even better than prom night, because not only did they have chemistry, they had a history in a way words couldn't explain.

Neera deepened the kiss while he claimed the cherry lip gloss from her lips. He wiped most of the sand off his hands before holding her cheek and waist without breaking the kiss. If he broke it or let go, he would start putting himself back together and following his logical brain.

When her hands clutched his shirt, like she was equally falling over the edge and desperately trying to hold on, everything started to fall into place. When she removed his t-shirt, and he lowered her to her back with his jacket cushioning her, his dream from a week ago entered the forefront of his mind.

"Are you sure you want to do this?" Liam whispered, as even the air felt precious to him. "We don't have to do anything you don't want to do."

Without hesitation, Neera pulled him down so his body hovered over her. His face was only an inch from hers, highlighting every beautiful contour. A fire–a firmness–in her gaze confirmed her feelings as she exhaled a smile.

"I've never been more ready," Neera shifted her eyes away for a split second. "Just be gentle. It's my first time."

"I won't let anything bad happen to you, Angelfish." His voice was barely a whisper as he touched his forehead to hers. Then his lips. Then his hands. Then his heart.

Whatever happens, we are destined to fall together.

SWITCHING SIDES

Chapter 14

Liam

It's past ten, and our parents are going to freak.

Neera squeezed their interlocked hands in her lap and smiled.

Totally worth it.

On the drive back to Neera's house, Liam didn't want the night to end. He prolonged it as long as he could with more conversation, but he could tell Neera was getting antsy about almost missing her curfew. Reluctantly, they cleaned themselves off, returned each other's shoes, and headed back on the road. The only time Liam enjoyed being covered in sand was put to an end.

Now he was back to the responsible Liam.

Logical Liam.

Neera tossed her head back and groaned. "I don't want to go back home."

Liam flashed her a smile. "Trust me. If I could turn my jeep around, I would. But Mr. Ran would kick my ass through my mouth."

After dropping Neera off, Liam pulled into his garage, casually exited his jeep, and headed inside through the back door. His parents were strict about many things, but a trivial thing like curfew was never one of them. Liam never had to sneak in after an all-nighter, except when he wanted to bring a guest—which was rare.

His mom must've been asleep or out because his house was dark, except for the overhead lights in the open kitchen. His dad flinched at the door slamming as he poured some whiskey into his glass, slightly spilling the brown liquid onto the kitchen island. He must've had a bad day. Nevertheless, Liam didn't want to be on the receiving end of his wrath because of it, so Liam mumbled an apology for being late and continued on his way to his bedroom door.

"You want a drink?"

His dad downed the liquor and locked eyes with him briefly before shifting them past him. Liam stared directly at him in bewilderment, searching his face for any hint of amusement.

There was none.

He was dead serious. No way would his clean-cut father offer him to underage drink, let alone drink at all, with him since they didn't have that kind of relationship.

It's definitely a trap.

Before Liam could object, his dad grabbed another short glass that happened to be next to him and poured the same whiskey into that one. He nodded his chin at the empty stool next to him for Liam to take, his face firm, and faint wrinkles exaggerated his seriousness.

Liam's entire body tensed.

After a night of freedom, he was back to his reality—the one that emphasized filial duty and obedience to his dad. That obedience he took such great pride in before felt a lot more like a leash, strangling him by his collar until he obeyed. Every tug sent a clear message:

DO NOT DISOBEY.

Spine rigid, Liam planted himself in the seat.

Like a good boy.

Awkwardness loomed over them as they sat in silence for what felt like an eternity. Liam still didn't touch his glass as he wondered if his dad noticed his internal rebellion against him rather than his usual acceptance of his place.

His dad cleared his throat and attempted to look jovial, instead looking more exhausted.

"Did you just get home?" Liam initiated to break the uncomfortable silence. "You usually come home later than this."

His dad smirked and took a long sip of his drink. "I actually got here a little before you...unless that wasn't a question." His eyes landed on him. "How was the movie? The vampire one, right?"

Is he really trying to do small talk?

Now it was Liam's turn to drink. The liquor burned his chest. He had to fight the urge not to cough. Drinking was nothing new to him, but whatever this was had him fighting for his life. While he tried to keep a straight face, his dad studied him. Always observing and analyzing.

"Kind of lame, actually," Liam answered hoarsely, the liquor drying his entire throat. He cleared his throat, choosing to omit his beach time with Neera. "Hanging out with her made it worth it."

Liam's dad finished the glass and scooted it around like a nervous tick.

No way. He can't actually be nervous?

In confirmation, his dad's eyes were glued to the glass.

"About Neera..." he began, ringing an alarm in Liam's head. "I know you and her family are trying to keep her identity a secret, but I believe that my colleagues and I can help her better understand her current state. Maybe even help reverse it."

No. Absolutely not.

He PROMISED he wouldn't mention anything. He gave Liam his word as a man and as a father, and he was willing to throw all that away for...more money? MORE accolades? This time, he really believed Liam was willing to put Neera in harm's way for the family's name. The betrayal was a slap to the face, and he couldn't make an excuse for it anymore. The tugging of the leash irritated him as he tugged back for the first time.

He glared at his dad before downing his glass of fire. "If you think I'll ever turn my girlfriend over to some scientists like she's some alien, then you don't know me at all, Dad."

His dad's hand grasped Liam's shoulder before he could retreat. The gesture that used to represent protection and strength now occurred to Liam as a reminder of his submission to him. His grip reminded him that he would always be lesser.

"Hey, hey, let's relax for a second. I'm just strongly suggesting that Neera gets the help she needs," his voice was softer now. He refilled both of their glasses with his free hand and clinked his glass against Liam's. "She doesn't know what she's capable of. What if she ends up hurting you or herself? I'm saying this because I love and care about you, Lee."

Lee? I haven't heard that nickname since freshman year.

His dad was really trying to lay it on thick. If this were a week ago, Liam would've contemplated it. Neera did claim that she was unhappy and didn't think she fit in. Maybe he could help her get some clarity; although, sending her off to a lab like a science experiment didn't feel right to him. His dad pressing him so hard about the matter didn't sit right with him.

The leash tugged taut at his defiance.

Liam shrugged the shoulder his hand was gripping to discard his dad's touch. He downed the entire glass, this time it matched the anger he had brewing inside of him. It fueled him as courage flowed through his bloodstream.

"I have cared for Neera since the fourth grade," Liam's jaw clenched at his dad's wide eyes. "Though you're my father, I'll never allow you or your science-pals to lay a hand on her." Liam stood up a bit wobbly from the liquor. His voice firm, he snarled.

"End of discussion."

His dad's friendly mask dropped into a quiet rage as his thick, light eyebrows pinched. It was a calculated rage that always kept Liam in his place, especially when he got in major trouble. The look burrowed Liam's anger under something he was afraid to admit.

Fear.

His dad took another sip as his face cooled again, leaving behind a coldness Liam had never felt before.

"Okay. The hard way it is."

NEERA

I, Neera Adenike Ran, am totally and utterly in love with Liam Dern.

The night couldn't have been any more romantic if it tried. The view, the weather, the smell of the ocean mixed with Liam's cologne, and the...love-making.

Tee-hee.

I'm such a dork.

The way he poured his heart into her took her breath away, and not just out of contentment but out of fear. They had only been dating for barely a week, and they already declared their love for each other. It sounded absolutely bonkers. To Neera, even downright illegal.

The way he looked into her eyes before he kissed her unraveled her into the mushy, sappy self she was currently. His hazel irises were swallowed by an earthy brown as if he were drowning in his emotions. She was, too. Many thoughts raced through her mind at his confession, including fear of the unknown and doubt that he could truly love her, yet one stuck out the most:

The bright eyes of the young boy who tried to save her with CPR eight years ago. The boy who pretended he didn't care about anything, only for him to dive into the restricted deep end to rescue a kid.

To rescue me.

It took Neera some time to realize it, but she finally realized she never forgot him. When she noticed him around school, her heart would always gallop. She would write it off as timidity or something unrelated to him, except it was really her feelings for him.

For Neera, it was and would always be Liam. She was no longer afraid of her feelings for him.

As quietly as possible, Neera cracked the front door open and tiptoed into the entryway. After pressing the door closed with impressive stealthiness, she hid behind a corner and peered into the living room.

Please let my dad be upstairs peacefully sleeping.

She scanned the dark room again. No dad.

With a silent celebratory fist pump, Neera made her quiet trek to the staircase.

"How was the movie, love?"

The metaphorical record scratched at the sight of her dad standing in front of the doorway to the kitchen. His striped, pajama-clad arms crossed over his chest like a drill sergeant. She should've known she would have to answer to him after going on a date for the first time that he was actually aware of.

Time to put on my big girl panties.

"Kind of lame," she shamelessly shrugged in the dark, hoping he wouldn't notice her biting the heck out of her lip.

The faint light from the kitchen traced his outline as he remained still, reflecting a bit of a glare in his glasses. He was "shrinking" her. She could feel it. The one thing she loved—and hated—about her dad was how easily he could read her. Neera's surprised he hadn't caught onto the other times she had snuck out.

He unfolded one arm to point it at their small dining table while the other hand held the elbow of the extended arm —the *Ultimate Lecture Pose.*

Shoulders slumped, she dragged her sandy boots to

the round table and plopped down in a chair, the chair leg squeaking. The lone light from the kitchen projected as much warmth as an interrogation room. Her dad disappeared into the kitchen without a word, only increasing Neera's uneasiness.

Neera hugged her shoulders and kept her head down, staring at the scratches carved into the wooden table from years of daydreaming after her mum passed. The same table that, before then, was filled with laughter and a chattery Neera who was overzealous about school, music, and fairytales. How times have changed.

After what felt like an eternity, a teal mug was placed in front of her, the sweet, rich aroma making her stomach grumble. Neera lifted her head slightly higher, seeing a cup of hot chocolate with a mountain of whipped cream, toasty nutmeg sprinkles, and two cinnamon sticks on top. Another cup was across from hers, which she assumed was her dad's.

He made his infamous hot chocolate.

"Infamous" because its milk chocolatey goodness only appeared before bad news.

So it's that bad, huh?

Neera cupped the warm mug in her hands, finally lifting her head to see him still analyzing her. She squirmed under his gaze as she prepared for his scrutiny.

Could he tell that I'm no longer a virgin just by looking at me? Do fathers come with that hidden feature?

He cleared his throat, her eyes jumping to his sincere ones.

"You know…" he began. "I was worried about you on prom night, and despite that, I completely trusted that nothing occurred. Do you know why? Because I unconditionally cherish you and trust that we have a relationship where we can talk about anything."

His dark hands, contrasting against the porcelain mug, tapped some indecipherable pattern while his eyes searched hers. Whatever he found in them propelled him to finish.

"It is only the two of us now," his tone softened and slowed. "It has been the two of us for a while now. Essentially, I need to know if you trust me, too."

Neera's trepidation subsided as she absorbed his words. It wasn't like he was wrong. Most parents, especially Elayne's father, wouldn't allow them to do half of the things her dad let her do.

And here was Neera, taking advantage of her dad's trust when he could easily be a tyrant. She thought he was overbearing when all he did was keep track of her location because, even though she lost her mum, he lost his soulmate. He continuously stepped up for her after a tragedy he was never prepared for. He desired to be the best friend that she lost.

And all Neera did was lie to him. Over and over again.

I feel like crap. The clingy guilt crept up her neck, almost suffocating her.

The least Neera could do was be honest with him since he decided to be transparent with her. He deserved, at the very least, that. Her dad was right that it was just the two of them. If her mum were here, she would've told her everything...

But she's not here.

Neera sipped her hot chocolate, the taste melting the rest of her nerves away, and sighed. Her dad remained patient. He waited quietly while sipping on his hot chocolate as his shoulders visibly relaxed. A little.

"Liam and I..." Her face instantly heated, shamelessly blaming the drink. She rushed through the rest of the confession before her brain shut down from humiliation. "We had sex tonight. I know you're probably disappointed, but we love each other. I've loved him since the fourth grade."

Her verbal throw-up made its grand appearance once again, unyielding. "And you might think it's too early or we're too young, but it felt right. There was no discomfort. I'm sorry for not telling you sooner, but I'm not sorry for what I've done. I hope you understand my decision."

Neera finished it off by gulping most of her drink, which wasn't a brilliant idea since it scolded her throat. She coughed dramatically, then cleared her throat when the worst of the damage abated. She didn't know what her dad put in this drink, but it single-handedly made her confession brave and immature at the same time.

So much for being cool and mature.

Sometime during her fit, he retreated to the kitchen and brought her a napkin since he handed her one. Neera dabbed at her mouth and cleared her throat again, her face forever warmed. Looking down at the mug, she scooted the treacherous drink away from her before it did any more damage.

Her dad's lips thinned as if he was holding back laughter, but his eyes stared at her concerningly. Maybe still discerning if she was comfortable with him asking if she was okay. After what felt like forever, he took a long sip of his hot chocolate with an unreadable expression. He gently placed the mug on the table and took a deep breath.

"Well…" He tilted his head to the side, his words stilted. "Thank you for your honesty. I'm not mad or disappointed, Neera." His voice softened again, finally done processing the information. "I'm relieved, actually."

Neera gracefully picked her jaw off the floor. Her nose crinkled in confusion. "Really? I'm not in trouble? I'm not grounded for all eternity?"

He chuckled heartily and gave a wry smile. "Oh, you're definitely in trouble for lying about watching the entire movie. Critics claim teens love shiny vamps. Therefore, only someone who has seen the whole thing would appreciate it."

Neera snorted as her dad took a sip of his drink. He must see her disbelief because his tone became serious again. "You are an adult…legally, of course. I can't stop you from making your own decisions. Doing otherwise would be, what do you Americans say, 'totally uncool'. I've learned in my many years of living that time and mistakes are our best teachers."

Fighting the urge to roll her eyes, Neera stored his last bit of advice deep in her mind. She got up and gave him a quick hug before returning to her seat. Her mug clinked against his as she responded in the most Neera way possible.

"Cool isn't exactly the word I would use to describe you, but you're the best." Her genuine smile contrasted with her sarcasm.

Her dad smiled, and then a beat passed as his smile faltered. "Were any of you wearing protection?" She could tell he was trying to be casual as he sipped his hot chocolate, but his eyes glinted with seriousness.

Her eyes bulged, and her smile dropped when the realization hit. She internally shook herself at her stupidity. She initiated the interaction, yet she didn't ensure her own safety. All she thought about were the sparks, the waves, his cologne, and his eyes.

Negativity sank its claws into her beautiful memory at the beach, tainting it by grounding reality into it. Her confidence in her maturity waned, causing her eyes to zone in on her mug.

She shook her head timidly.

Her dad inhaled, causing Neera to look up at him. He held her gaze, and she could see a few emotions pass momentarily through him: Disappointment, fear, then... reassurance. But she wasn't positive about that last one.

"Promise me that you AND Liam go to the pharmacy and purchase a contraceptive pill tomorrow. This isn't something you should use all the time, but in this circumstance, it's necessary and early enough before it actually turns into a baby. I'll even give you the money for it. Then go to the doctor and get tested." His eyes pierced hers. "The pill has to be taken no later than tomorrow, okay?"

Neera smiled half-heartedly and nodded. She was clearly not ready for a baby. If that pill would help prevent it from happening, then it was her duty to take it. Right?

But why does it feel wrong?

As an adult graduating in a few days with a dad who just told her he would always be by her side, why couldn't she be a mother? Sure, she had college or whatever, but she could do both with all the support she had. Most importantly, she would have the baby's father and his family. Her support might have been small, but it was mighty. He might get angry with her for her decision, but he would eventually understand. Her child would have a new start with a loving mother and father, never knowing pain or loss for a long, long time.

Instead of debating her dad, she held his gaze as she lied one more time.

"I promise."

PLAN B

Chapter 15

Neera

"It's officially your final day of being a Panther. The staff wishes you all a successful future and don't forget to take everything you learned here with you."

A chorus of cheers and whoops ensued after the principal's final announcement. Colorful sheets of paper were thrown about while students–now, former students–said their goodbyes and couples made out like it was their last breath.

The energy was a cacophony of emotions. For Neera, there was only relief at the fact that it would be the last time she'd be bullied in those halls.

She couldn't leave any quicker.

Across the hall, Neera spotted Elayne saying her farewells to a group Neera didn't recognize. Fellow *emos* of hers. Of course, her best friend had many friends. There was no animosity if Elayne didn't make it back to her. She would see her at any time since they were practically attending the same university.

Neera shut her empty locker and took it all in. The end of a journey. The beginning of the rest of her life. All her decisions were all up to her.

More responsibility. More accountability.

She absentmindedly touched her stomach, ready to start

her new chapter.

Directly across from Neera was a group of girls surrounding a giggling Jessica. Her bleach-blonde waves whipped around as she laughed with her friends. A sense of responsibility washed over Neera. It had been a while since she'd last spoken to her, not since the party. They happened to avoid each other until this very moment.

Not that Neera was complaining...She was still Liam's friend. As an adult, she had to put aside any *bad blood* for the sake of inner peace.

After taking a deep breath to calm her nerves, Neera turned on her wedges and stalked towards Jessica with her head held high. Jessica must've sensed her coming because her eyes were already on her, and they weren't exactly welcoming. Neera stopped just in front of her with an expression as friendly as she could muster.

"Can we talk, Jessica?" Neera asked. She held up her hands in a surrendering position. "I come in peace."

She could only assume Jessica didn't find it amusing by her blank expression. Jessica looked between her friends, seeming to send a secret message to each other to back off. Her friends regarded Neera with a threatening look before they left them alone.

"Okay. Speak," Jessica challenged.

Ignoring her rudeness, Neera brightened her smile. "This tension that we have is getting old, Jessica. We're graduating in, like, two days. So, that means we're starting new chapters in our lives. There's no point holding on when we'll literally never see each other again."

Hopefully.

Her cerulean eyes stabbed hers for a minute as if she was contemplating it. Relief flooded her as Jessica nodded her head.

"Honestly it's, like, getting annoying and old," she admitted. She glanced away for a second before returning back to Neera. "I'm willing to let everything slide and move on."

Shouldn't I be saying that since she's the one who terrorized me for years?

Neera's cheeks ached from smiling as she nodded. She held out her hand, hoping she wouldn't get left hanging and look ridiculous. "Truce?"

Jessica flung her ponytail back, clasping her hand in a weak handshake. "Truce."

They couldn't release each other fast enough.

Before Neera could walk away, Jessica grabbed the crook of her elbow, stopping her. Neera gave her a questionable look.

Jessica leaned in close, her face neutral. "I would be careful trusting Liam."

Neera's eyebrows scrunched as she moved her arm out of her grasp. "What are you talking about?"

Jessica shifted her eyes around them, then held her gaze firm. "Since we're in a truce, this is my, like, last act of kindness. Liam doesn't have any loyalties to anyone but his family. So be careful."

This was absolutely ridiculous. Why would she say that as someone who was supposedly his friend?

As if she had read her mind, Jessica huffed. "You don't have to believe me, but as his friend, I know what he's really like. He'll stab you in the back...eventually."

With that, Jessica walked away.

Her pleated skirt swished further away as she left Neera dumbfounded. A large part of her believed that Jessica was messing with her one last time because she was obviously a horrible person, but a very small part of her heeded caution.

She shouldn't even entertain it, but something kept nagging her in the pit of her stomach. It made her feel sour, but it was best to ignore it.

No negativity on my last day of school!

"Hey, Neera," Liam's smooth voice resonated from behind her. Neera turned to it, seeing the love of her life standing in his white polo and jeans. Not a wrinkle in sight. His hair was carefully slicked back on top of his head without a hair out of place. He looked...perfect.

Too perfect.

Nothing like the disheveled hottie she'd fallen in love with the past couple of days.

His backpack hung over one shoulder while his other hand rubbed the back of his neck. "Can we talk for a sec, Neera? In my car?"

Wow. No Angelfish? *Is something wrong?*

"Yeah, sure. Is something wrong?" Neera searched his face, and he looked...emotionless. Maybe he was sad about leaving? She smiled at him. A genuine one this time. Hopefully, it would cheer him up.

Instead of returning one back to her, his eyes were pained. He leaned in and kissed her, causing her toes to curl. It was like every emotion he wanted to convey was on his lips, and the only way to share them was to burn them onto her lips. He kissed her so intensely it felt like the last time.

What happened last night?

He pulled away, literally and figuratively, giving her a curt smile that didn't seem to reach his eyes. "Nothing, really. There's just something important I need to tell you."

Neera nodded her head softly, and then they walked over to his green jeep.

Without a word, he climbed into the driver's side. Despite the 90-degree summer, the energy in the car was chilly. Something was up. He just needed to hurry up and admit it so that she could finally breathe again. Negativity crept to the front of her mind, preparing to seize control.

Neera hesitated, then decided to climb into the passenger side. She waited for him to turn on the engine, so they could leave. He didn't. He just sat there, staring out the windshield into the crowded parking lot. Neera patiently waited for him to speak as she stomped down Jessica's warning from earlier.

"I would be careful trusting Liam."

Liam just sat there, thinking. Whatever was on his mind must've been emotionally taxing. Upon closer inspection of his face, she noticed dark rims under his usually bright eyes, and his hair was now slightly skewed.

Even if it were bad, Neera would always be here for him. Whatever he was going through, they would get through it together. Because he was one of the most important people in her life. Her boyfriend and the future father of her child. Where fate began and ended.

Neera held his hand that was gripping the gear shift. He briefly looked at their adjoined hands, then held her gaze. He looked so tired and in pain.

"We can't be together anymore."

It felt like Neera was sucked into a vacuum. All the strength and love that she hoped would warm up the coldness of the vehicle was immediately snuffed out like a candle. Leaving her surrounded in darkness.

All alone again…

All the air left her lungs before she could speak. Before she could process it, her vision blurred from her unshed tears. Neera held onto denial like a life raft.

Her hand tightened around his tense one, her voice wobbly. "Was it last night? Did I do something wrong? Whatever it is, we can work on it together."

She was grasping at straws. Maybe he was self-sabotaging because something happened? She couldn't give up on him.

He ripped his hand from hers and gripped the steering wheel.

"It's not that," he glanced away. "I just feel…that… we're growing apart. We're graduating and moving on to different places. I've decided to go to VTECH in the Fall for my dad. And it's, like, over 3,000 miles away. I'm sorry, but…there's nothing we can do other than break up."

A dark part of Neera wanted to laugh at his incredibility. *This isn't happening.*

He previously told her he was attending a West Coast school, so she never worried about their life outside of high school. Now it was VTECH? So was he lying the entire time?

Anger sliced through her, and she could feel the heat creeping up her neck.

"Nothing we can do?!" Neera yelled because crying was unacceptable. "We can do long distance for a semester, and then I can transfer to a university nearby. You weren't going to VTECH before. What changed? And why are you giving up on us so easily?"

Liam closed his eyes, but his fingers wrapped the steering wheel so hard that his knuckles turned white.

"Things change, and shit happens. You can't base your future on me. On a week-old relationship. This is reality, not some fairytale, Ran," he gritted out.

Neera chewed her bottom lip. It just didn't make sense. Instead of erupting, she took a deep breath and considered that maybe he got in trouble for what happened last night, and that was why he couldn't see her anymore.

But she refused to let him go. Everything he said last night couldn't be a lie.

Her face relaxed. "Listen, whatever happened last night with your parents, we can overcome it. I know you're saying all this to make it easier for me to leave." Neera tried to be reassuring, but her lip couldn't stop trembling. "Whatever it is, we can make it work-"

"We just fucking can't, okay!" Liam slapped the steering wheel, the swift beep of the horn causing both of them to flinch. "I'm trying to be nice here, Ran. We can't do long distance because it's over. We're done. Why are you holding on so tight?"

Who are you right now? Neera couldn't recognize the guy in front of her. So belligerent. His face twisted in frustration. Jessica's warning filled her head.

"Liam doesn't have any loyalties to anyone but his family."

"He'll stab you in the back...eventually."

So this was the real Liam.

This is reality. Not a fairytale. No happy endings. No

happily ever after.

Neera's eyes stung from holding back tears, but she absolutely refused to let them go. If she did, she'd feel even more stupid than she already felt. She really believed in a future with a guy she just met because he felt like her soulmate.

Her forever.

I should know more than anyone that there's no such thing as forever.

Her hand found her stomach. The usual butterflies in there lost their wings as they wriggled around like worms. She tried to hold down her vomit.

Neera trembled with her eyes closed.

"Jerk!" she hissed through clenched teeth. "You waited until after we had sex to tell me this? Did you say all those nice things because you wanted to get laid? Was any of this real?"

Neera needed answers. Now. She needed him to be truthful for the first time in his freaking life. Would it redeem him? Probably not, but she deserved it after what she was willing to do to be with him.

Liam's shoulders slumped as his Adam's apple bobbed, like he was fighting some invisible battle and was losing. His hand ran through his hair before he sighed.

"I AM a jerk, Ran. Heartless. Calculated," he revealed while looking in the distance. His eyes found hers again as he stared unwaveringly. "But having sex with you was never part of the plan. Being with you was the realest part of my life."

His hazel eyes were intense, dark with seriousness. For a moment, Neera believed him, and it relaxed her a bit.

He continued. "I can't tell you how sorry I am, and you probably won't believe me. Luckily we weren't together long enough for this to hurt that bad. We'll...we'll move on in no time."

Anger returned front and center. He was describing them as some kind of fling that got out of hand. Like her intense feelings for him were temporary. Like they could shut off like a faucet just because their story was only for a short period of time.

Since it really was over, Neera decided to pour out all of her feelings until nothing was left. Nothing but a dry husk of her usual self.

All alone.

Her eyes bored into his, with her voice devoid of emotion. "We weren't together long, so I'm *easy* enough to dump onto the streets, huh?"

He opened his mouth, but she put her hand up to stop him.

"I've liked you since I was ten. I asked you to prom. I trusted you with my darkest secrets. I gave my body to you. You were always a part of my present and my future. I even wanted to have your..." Her voice trailed off as she pursed her lips. No need to look dumber than she already looked. "If it's so easy to move on from that, then I guess I'm the only one who felt that way."

Her hand on her bag strap tightened as a tear rebelled, sliding down her cheek. She didn't even have the energy to wipe it. So tired of fighting for him and fighting for them.

If he wanted her, it was his turn to fight for her.

Her stance was only confirmed when his lips stayed shut. Since he remained silent, there was nothing left between them.

Before exiting with one foot outside of the jeep, she turned her head with the rebel tear still sticking to her warm cheek. Liam's head hung low, looking just as defeated as she was. The only difference was that he caused it.

"Thanks for being my first love, Liam," she murmured.

He winced, but she didn't dwell on it because she was already out the door.

"Hey, Lay-Lay. We need to go somewhere. Now," Neera murmured through her cell.

"Hold on. I'll meet you at the side entrance."

Elayne's purple buggy was haphazardly parked with two tires on the curb next to the building.

Classic Lay-Lay.

When she found Neera, she waved her down as Neera stalked over to her. Still disturbed by her conversation with Liam, she dropped into the leather seat cover and slammed the door behind her. Elayne's barely visible eyebrows furrowed in concern right before slapping Neera's arm because she had always been the sentimental type.

"What the hell happened to you, Nee-Nee?"

The radio began to play a song by her favorite artist in the background.

"You look so dumb right now..."

Neera squeezed her eyes shut, only making her tears fall harder.

"You're so ugly when you cry, please, just cut it out..."

Neera took a deep breath and relayed everything that happened, including what happened last night. "So, long story short, I need to buy a morning-after pill and rid myself completely of him."

"...And the award for the best liar goes to you..."

Elayne calmly nodded, but Neera could tell how angry her best friend was getting by the way her eyebrows turned into the letter *V*. She remained silent as she started the car and drove onto the road, her fingerless gloves squeaking from her harsh grip.

"That was quite a show. Very entertaining..."

Elayne glared at the innocent road as she muttered. "If I had known he was going to be an asshole, I wouldn't have pushed you to ask him out."

"But it's over now. Go on and take a bow..."

"I don't blame you," Neera sniffled.

"But it's over now."

Elayne parked in front of a local pharmacy. Without a word, they entered the place, scanning the over-the-counter shelves until they found the pill. They found it, but it was locked up, so Elayne went to flag down an employee. An elderly woman in a store uniform waddled over and unlocked the section with pursed lips. Neera could feel her judgment as heat crept up her face.

As they waited in line, Neera had her arms crossed over her chest. The shock and sadness had worn off, and now she just felt self-loathing and disgust. Her dad's words about mistakes being the best teachers plagued her mind.

If that was what growing up entailed, she'd rather cut her losses and just be with her mum.

Neera felt a pinch on her arm. She glared at Elayne as her BFF leaned over to whisper. "At least your dad was cool with everything. My parents would be fake-crying on the news about their daughter's *mysterious* death."

The only positive thing that came out of this whole situation was her growing relationship with her dad and her unconditional love for him and Elayne.

The only people in her life that really mattered.

That relaxed her a bit.

After purchasing the pill and a bottle of water, they sat in the car so Neera could ingest it. There was no time to waste, yet while reading the instructions, she hesitated to take it. For a strange reason only relating to her, taking the pill meant that they were really over. There was nothing to connect them. He would move on with his life, like everything they went through never happened…and meant nothing.

She would just have to trust that he wouldn't spill her secret. He possessed every part of her: her past, her secrets, her trust, her virginity.

Neera would have nothing left but his lies.

"Hurry up!" Elayne *oh-so-lovingly* demanded.

Neera didn't realize how long she was staring at the dissolvable object. With a huff, she placed the pill on her tongue before washing it down with a few gulps of water.

The thing tasted bitter, like her reality. How could

something change someone's life so monumentally yet be so easy?

She eyed the half-empty bottle, irrationally resenting the clear liquid that consistently ruined her life.

Elayne's nose scrunched in curiosity. "How do you feel?"

Stupid. Immature. Gross. Pathetic. Empty.

"Nothing," Neera swallowed her spit down. "Nothing at all, actually."

Suddenly, a wave of emotions over the past hour crashed into her. Neera hid her face in her hands and sobbed. The disgust from the break-up switched to devastation. Her heart ached as she cried and hiccupped. She hadn't cried like that since her mum passed, which felt ridiculous in itself.

Why do bad things always happen to me?

Why does the other shoe always drop?

When can I finally exhale?

Elayne sucked her teeth and wrapped her arms around Neera. She caressed her back while cursing Liam's bloodline and his unfortunate mother.

A rush of nausea hit Neera, the car suddenly spinning. She swiftly untangled herself from Elayne, pushed the car door open, and unloaded her entire breakfast and lunch onto the pavement.

Her best friend patted her on the back with one hand while gathering her curly hair into a makeshift ponytail. The disgusting blend of colors and chunks puddled in front of her. A perfect representation of her life.

This has to be the worst day ever.

After her puke session, Elayne dropped Neera off at her house while she planned Liam's demise with her friend's mermaid abilities, causing Neera to appreciate the universe's mercy for sparing the world with a powerless Elayne. She entered her home but was greeted with emptiness. Her dad was probably still working.

I wish Mum was here.

On her way to her room with no appetite, a high-pitched

chime came from her dad's room. She hadn't been in his room since her mum passed, so she was reluctant to enter, but the ringing started to annoy her already sensitive nerves. She had no other choice but to discover the problem.

Neera tiptoed–for no apparent reason–into his room, closed the door behind her, and then paused. It still looked exactly the same as her mum decorated it. The same king-sized bed with several frilly, pastel pillows against the headboard. The same mahogany dresser covered in animal stickers.

A large framed portrait of her mum hung over the dresser, radiantly smiling with sparkling green eyes, dark tresses, and an elegant Grecian nose. It captured her beauty perfectly.

It seemed Neera wasn't the only one who had trouble letting go. Her now sensitive heart ached at her dad's undying love for her mum. How Neera would never have a love as beautiful and pure as theirs. The longer she looked at the portrait, the more resentment and envy built up inside. It was ridiculous to feel that way, but apparently, everyone grieved differently.

Tearing her eyes away from the portrait, her eyes lowered to a music box beneath it. The same music box her mum used to play for her when she was younger. The closer Neera got, the more the ringing intensified, vibrating her insides like a tuning fork.

She carefully lifted the lid, and the same tiny, jade mermaid popped up, rotating slowly while the twinkling melody played. The ringing softened and began to harmonize with the music. Next to the mermaid was her green necklace.

Neera held the necklace up to eye level, and strangely, the ringing stopped, leaving the melody looping continuously. As before, the little dragon inside swirled around nonchalantly and peacefully. Around it was the usual bright dots that appeared to sparkle the longer she studied them.

Instead of opening its mighty jaws, it paused its dance to stare directly at Neera. Their eyes actually locked before continuing their dance without the beady eyes leaving hers. Her left ear picked up barely audible whispers that tickled the fine hairs on it, as if someone was leaning into her and speaking. Goosebumps slid down her arms at the mysterious presence. For some reason, she couldn't move her hands to swat at it even if she wanted to.

Is the dragon speaking? Its mouth was closed, but the indiscernible whispering kept going.

Unexpectedly, a stream of calmness cascaded down her body as if everything from the day didn't happen and didn't matter. Her overwhelming emotions slipped away from her and left nothing but tranquility. Neera had never felt this cool before, despite her body physically heating. It felt comforting and safe.

"Neera? Where are you, love?" Her dad's voice sounded distant. She must've lost track of time as his steps resounded.

Neera snapped out of her stupor and quickly stuffed the necklace into her side pocket while her other hand slammed the music box closed. Her wrist cramped a little from holding the necklace for so long, but she bit back the pain. She had to get out of her dad's room immediately.

Neera slipped out of his room, quietly shut the door, and stepped directly from his room to the bathroom doorway. She glanced at the top of the stairs, a bald head peaking. Taking a large step to stand in the middle of the hallway, she pretended to dry her hands on her denim skirt just as guilt hit her.

I'm mad at Liam for lying and keeping secrets, yet here I am doing the same to my dad. Hypocrite.

Neera bit back her guilt and decided to ignore his question.

"Hey, Pa! How was work?" She plastered on a smile.

"Oh, there she is!" He exclaimed happily as he cleared the stairs and wrapped her into a big hug. Neera melted into it because she could use all the strength she could get.

He leaned back, his face serious. "Have you taken the pill? Do you need me to help you through it?"

That's a big understatement.

As much as she didn't want to recant everything that transpired–minus the necklace part–and retraumatize herself, she needed to be honest with him for once. She'd also have to explain her puffy eyes and "puke-breath".

"I took it with Elayne earlier. Other than feeling nauseous, I'm feeling okay." Neera tried to give another reassuring smile. "I'll tell you the rest at dinner."

He grinned proudly and kissed her forehead. "Now that's my girl! I knew I could trust you."

Her smile dimmed slightly. *I wish you didn't...*

"Because you finished school, I'm going to order us some pizza. Anything you want," he celebrated as he opened the door to his room, entering with a huge smile on his face. He was so proud of her, and she had done nothing to deserve it.

Neera plodded to her room and fell face-first into her pillows. Removing the necklace, she slid it underneath her pillow and cried until it was time to get ready for her celebratory dinner.

LIAM

"Okay. Hard way it is."

Those words haunted Liam all night. The man that he respected the most and taught him how to be a man. The man who taught him about girls, how to shave, and how to tie the perfect Windsor knot. The man that Liam looked up to and was honored to follow in his footsteps was not the man he talked to last night. The man who was all about integrity, respect, and honor was willing to put his girlfriend in harm, and was willing to hurt his son in the process.

Maybe that was the real him.

Liam kept pushing down that theory, but like a buoy, it kept resurfacing. He wasn't ready to face that reality yet.

Maybe it's because you're rebelling against him. If you start doing what he says and are fully committed to the family business, he'll back off of Neera.

His father would only back off if Liam backed up. As much as the idea of letting Neera go cut into his chest, the idea of bringing harm to her would bleed him dry.

So he made his decision.

Liam showed up for his last day of school in a pressed polo, wrinkle-free jeans, and boat shoes. His hair was gelled and styled as perfectly as he could.

Dressed for success...or distress.

Nate clearly approved of his outfit; something about making him look like the "old Liam." If it were a few months ago, he would've taken it as a compliment. Instead, it felt degrading. All the progress he made in discovering himself and fighting against the leash was for nothing. The only person who didn't like his look was Jessica, but she wasn't exactly his biggest fan at the moment.

Liam mindlessly drifted throughout the day. Lots of students said their goodbyes, asked to be friends on social media, and wanted his signature for their yearbooks. And Liam numbly fulfilled those requests.

All of them probably had nothing to worry about once they left these halls. No responsibilities or legacies to uphold. No pressure to be absolutely perfect. If they screwed up a little bit, it was a drop in a bucket of misfortune. His was a tsunami.

They probably had no idea how fake his smiles were, but he couldn't blame them. He was practically a pro.

Naturally, when Liam spotted Neera in the hall with Jessica, his heart stopped. It didn't help that she looked breathtaking in her camouflage tank, denim mini skirt, and straw-looking belt. Her curly tresses flowed freely and beautifully, with a simple blue headband struggling to contain them. He'd been dodging her since he got there to avoid the hard conversation. It visibly pained him to walk over to her.

When she turned to face him, he wanted to back out immediately. Her eyes looked so bright and affectionate. It was obvious how much she loved him, and he wished she knew how much he loved her, too.

So he kissed her. That was the only way he could convey his true feelings. He embraced the warmth that always coursed through him when their lips met. At that moment, they were the only two people in the world.

And he wouldn't have minded staying there forever.

But he couldn't. The stress compelled his fingers to ruffle his perfectly styled hair on their way to his jeep.

In his car seat, he decided to lie his ass off. He thought using the excuse of moving would deter her, but it only exposed him more.

Neera saw right through him. She knew something happened, but not exactly how bad it was. As her hand held his own, she had no idea that the strength she supplied him was going to be used against her.

Her loyalty and sincerity clawed deeper into his chest, its shards slicing his sensitive flesh. He'd take every strike, too, like a defensive lineman. He'd keep taking the pain until nothing was left but a carcass.

Because he deserved it.

He'd cherish the memories he had with Neera so that she could shine and live a life without worries, grow up, and then become an awesome mom and wife to a guy who was stronger and more trustworthy.

Because she deserved it.

Liam tried to rein in his anger, but it continued to overflow. It would've been easier if she just slapped him in the face, but it seemed he was doing more of the metaphorical slapping by the way her face reddened, and the tears brimmed her eyelashes.

"*Jerk!*"

She was right. Liam desperately wanted to hold her to stop her trembling form. To forgive him for having such a shitty family. To forgive him for every tear he pulled out of those beautiful eyes.

Yet he didn't.

Those tears. They always hurt when he saw them, yet he caused them often. That added to the growing reasons why they weren't meant to be together.

He was a jerk. His father's son.

Defeat overwhelmed him, yet he welcomed it because it made him feel something other than desolation. In a last-ditch effort, before throwing himself off the cliff of their relationship, he had to be honest about what happened last night.

Sure, that night wasn't his first time, but it was the first time he was with someone he loved. It was special, as cliche as that sounded. It was also reckless since, for the first time ever, he forgot to use a condom.

He didn't worry about it because his original plan was to take care of her, no matter what happened or what life was going to throw at them. He was going to come to school and discuss their life plans after celebrating their last day of school. They would've had a picnic on the beach with pizza and soda, and he would've blasted music from his jeep while they chatted about the future until the sun set. A future beyond college, his adult years, and kids until they were little old people walking down the shoreline.

Whatever she decided, he was going to support her in every way because he would do anything for her. Because his life–his REAL life–started and ended the moment he kissed her on the dance floor. Just like his parents.

But plans change.

"Thanks for being my first love, Liam."

Then she was gone. Liam watched her retreating form until she disappeared. A part of him hoped she would return and kick his tires. Anything, really, to make her stay just a second longer. It never happened.

His plan worked, and the shit that accompanied it left a bitter taste in his mouth.

When he pulled out of the parking lot, he felt something

wet trickle out of the corner of his eye. Liam shook his head vigorously. Appreciation that Neera didn't witness his tears evaporated as his angst, regret, and anger boiled inside of him.

He clenched his teeth at the leash irritating his neck. His foot slammed down on the gas pedal as he tried to escape from the constricting thing. He swerved between lanes with a tight grip on the wheel as the wind whipped his hair. The one thing that he wanted for himself was gone. The one good thing that wasn't related to his father's successes.

Gone.

All because of his father's perverse obsession with success, and only caring about himself while putting others in danger or distress. The worst part was that his father had always been like this, but Liam was too blind to see it. In turn, his father created his perfect prodigy.

Liam hated him.

Muffled laughter seeped down from above. Apparently, his father invited some important guests to his home for dinner, which meant Liam, Danny, and his mom had to eat dinner in their respective bedrooms. Well, Danny was probably eating in his mom's room.

Nothing new. His family knew the drill.

Only appear when summoned.

With everything that had happened, Liam wasn't particularly acquiescent with the rules.

Instead of hunkering down in his room until the "suits" left, he took his half-finished dinner plate upstairs. To avoid interrupting, he crawled on his hand and knees, with the other hand balancing the plate, to the kitchen.

He ignored the pain from his bare knees sliding across the textured tile floor as he army-crawled behind the kitchen island, lying parallel to it. With the terracotta plate currently next to him and his arms tucked underneath him, Liam peeked into the living room from the safety of the island.

Yeah, so he looked ridiculous lying on the kitchen floor in his own house. But his instincts were screaming to not get caught. So Liam did what he was bred to do: Wait and observe.

A few of his father's guests were lounging on their sectional with glasses of what Liam would assume to be expensive whiskey. His father sat in his usual recliner with his back facing Liam. He only knew it was him because NO ONE was allowed to sit in that chair.

His own personal throne.

Like the dictator he is.

"Dan, if you are really willing to collaborate with my group, it would be pertinent for us to observe the discovery ourselves," a man, larger than his father with gray hair and a pinstripe suit, bellowed. "The entire island has been embargoed. Any evidence of suspicious activity had been officially debunked."

Liam internally shook his head.

Even his own people have no idea what's going on. Looks like his father is untrustworthy with everyone.

"Right," another man exclaimed from his seat on the far end. He thrusted his empty glass towards his father with his blue suit jacket splayed across his lap. He must've started drinking first. "Money has been tight recently in every department. You want us to use our limited resources to explore this island over a hunch and not concrete evidence?"

For some acquaintances, they didn't seem quite chummy with him, or have any knowledge of anything that occurred on the island. His father told him he had to visit that island for his "work". So, either his father lied about his reason for taking them to the island...or these people weren't his acquaintances.

Liam saw his father raise an arm to his mouth as he drained the liquid from his glass. His head disappeared, maybe from leaning on his elbows.

"I swear on my children's lives that there's a beast on that island, maybe even more. I can't guarantee it unless you send some of your men there to help investigate," he calmly responded. "My findings will be useful to you, and everything you've given will be returned tenfold. I promise you, our past mistakes won't repeat themselves."

His cool and calculative tone, which Liam always respected, now sent chills down his spine.

"Alright, Dan," the pinstripe-suit man conceded. "You seem really sincere about this, and your reputation supersedes you. That was the only reason why we entertained you in the first place. We'll provide you with a crew and allow you to lead the operation." The man narrowed his eyes at him, darkness lacing his tone.

"If we find out that you wasted government resources or if any of our men return seriously harmed, you will be taking all responsibility and will be reprimanded accordingly. Got it?"

Operation? Government resources? This was way bigger than Liam assumed.

His father was silent for a bit, maybe upset by the authoritative tone of the man in front of him. Then, his father shot his hand out.

"Crystal clear," he grunted.

The pinstripe-suit man leaned forward and shook his father's hand. It was almost like Liam was witnessing a villain council meeting...and he couldn't break it up.

The man leaned back on the couch, crossing a leg over his knee, and took a sip of his drink for the first time. "Now," he smiled eagerly. "When do we get to see this mermaid? The one you discovered recently."

Liam's body stiffened and chilled like he was transported onto an ice rink. He listened so intently that he could practically hear his father tapping repeatedly on his glass.

No. Hell no.

"Very soon," his father chuckled. Liam could practically see him grinning from his view. "Matter of fact, I will bring her to you."

Pain in his palms finally registered by his fists clenching

underneath him. He couldn't believe what he heard. Actually, he could, and that was the messed-up part.

Liam couldn't pay any more attention to their perverse intrigue with his girlfriend.

Well, ex-girlfriend.

The way his father spoke of her, like some prized seabass he caught, made him nauseous. No way Liam would allow them to get their hands on her.

"Whatcha doin'?" A tiny voice interrupted his eavesdropping.

He snapped his head to his right and saw his little brother crouching down next to him on the floor. Not exactly how Liam wanted Danny to view his role model, but he couldn't move or it would give his position away.

"Uh..." Liam whispered while he racked his brain for potential excuses. His eyes landed on his discarded plate and Danny's currently empty one next to it. He shifted his body to unleash one hand and slid the plate over to Danny. "Put mine in the dishwater for me, will you?"

Liam prayed that Danny didn't question why he couldn't do it himself or the fact that he was suspiciously lying on the kitchen floor in his boxers. If his father found out, he would be done. Overdone. His father might even force him to move back to Virginia.

His big brother privileges must have kicked in, because Danny just got up with an annoyed look and placed the dishes in the dishwasher. Liam huffed a thanks under his breath as Danny walked into their guests' line of sight. They all stopped talking and started greeting Danny.

Must be nice to be a kid...so oblivious.

While they gave him all their attention, Liam clambered into a crouching position, preparing to sprint back to his room. Taking one more peek around the island to see if the coast was clear, Liam froze. His body was basically an icicle.

His father was staring directly at him.

His expression was unreadable until he slowly pulled

his mouth into a minuscule smirk. Liam glared back. It seemed like saving Neera didn't require obedience. It required rebellion.

Fighting fire with *fire*.

Liam would do everything in his power to protect her. The second his father lays a hand on Neera, he will completely lose his son in the process.

Who knew all it took was saving Neera to hopefully sever his leash of control?

A NEW CHAPTER

Chapter 16

Neera

Neera's palms were incredibly sweaty. Properly soaked. She waited in a queue with the rest of the Senior class next to the stage as they waited to cross the platform one by one. Everyone around her was smiling and giggling. Some occasionally touched up their hair or reapplied their lip gloss.

Not a care in the world. No soul-crushing break-ups. No forced mermaid powers. No uncertainty of the near future.

Neera pushed her wire-framed glasses up her nose and wiped her sweaty palms on her blue graduation gown. She took a few steps forward.

She made sure to have glasses on this time to avoid any possibility of tripping. Clearly, she wasn't new to the spotlight, especially recently, except this attention was the one she dreaded the most: the heavy expectation that she'd leave a great mark on future generations. The misplaced pride that one of their students wouldn't be a screw-up.

How Neera would be dead-center under the scrutiny of others who see right through her and wait for her to inevitably fail. The girl who spent her school years hiding from her broken family and now, her mermaid identity. They would see the freak with no one but her dad to cheer her on.

She was up next.

"Neera Ran," her principal announced with her usual, forced smile after continuous name-calling.

Neera's heeled, olive sandals echoed across the stage while the audience held their applause. Other families never waited to applaud. Then again, she didn't have much family to break the rules.

"Yay! Go Neera!" Her best friend cheered from several feet behind her in line. Her mesh-gloved fists punched the air with each chant. Neera couldn't help her blush.

More clapping came from the center stands near the back. She glanced over, noticing her dad whooping while waving a large sign:

WAY TO GO, MY LITTLE GUPPY!

Between her dad and Lay-Lay's ambush, her face had no chance of returning to normal; yet her heart felt nothing but comfort from them. Yeah, her family was small…but their love was mighty. For Neera, their cheers just so happened to be the loudest. Her palms even felt a little less sweaty.

She smiled brightly at her principal as she received her diploma and handshakes from other teachers and the school counselor. Then, she widened the smile for her diploma picture. Neera avoided eye contact with the group of former students who received their diplomas before her. It was the only way to keep that smile on her face.

As she slid into her seat behind the other students, her phone vibrated. Neera reached underneath her gown and pulled out her phone from her denim skirt pocket. Sliding it open, she blinked twice.

LIAM: U LOOK B-U-TIFUL. CONGRATS.

Neera continued to stare at the text. A mix of feelings bubbled to the surface. It felt like a colorful painting that was vandalized with black spray paint, yet ended up being just as lovely as the original artwork. It hurt, but it was also appreciative and sweet. Maybe bittersweet. Maybe melancholy. She couldn't quite put her finger on it.

She hadn't seen or heard from Liam since their break-up, purposefully for Neera's sake. She had blocked him on social media to prevent herself from staring at his profile picture. His perfect pointed nose, his perfect square jaw, his perfect smile, and gentle eyes that always exuded kindness. Those perfect lips that always arrested her heart, captured her lips, and allowed her to have a moment to breathe.

Those same lips that stabbed her in the heart and the back.

Neera spent so much of her time crying over him, being angry with him, and in the same breath, waiting for him and hoping he was okay. It took a long 48 hours to get here.

And here? Appreciation for their time together and readiness to move on. That was the best she could do for now.

Neera placed her phone back in her pocket and focused on Elayne's turn.

"Elayne Ukiyo."

Clusters of applause sprang up from different sections of the gymnasium. No shocker. Her BFF did a curt bow in front of her principal, snatched her diploma, and threw up a "Rock-On" hand gesture. The applause peaked.

Neera stood up, applauding before she yelled, "Let's go, LAY-LAY!"

Elayne returned it with a wink.

Yes, Neera was horribly aware of all those eyes on her. Yes, she immediately plopped down in her chair to avoid combusting from embarrassment.

However, she'd undoubtedly do it again for her family.

After another long-drawn speech from the principal, the Seniors finally threw their caps in the air or switched their tassels to the other side. Neera definitely kept her cap on.

Everyone dispersed to find their respectable families. When Neera spotted her dad in the sea of people, he gathered her into a tight hug.

"Congratulations, love! I'm so proud of you." He smiled into her blow-out. His usual deep voice started to tremble. "Your…Your mum is so proud of you. I just know it."

Tears pooled in Neera's eyes. She should've known he would bring up Mum. She was prepared for it, but it still hurt.

Is she really proud of me?

Neera pulled back without letting go. "It's not the same without her here. I wish…I wish she were here." The little girl in her clung to her dad like it was her eleventh birthday all over again.

I want her to tell me she's proud in person.

Her dad pursed his lips and exhaled from his nose, his way of restraining his tears.

"Just keep her close to your heart, and it will never feel like she left in the first place."

They finally released each other, but her dad kept wiping her tears she didn't know had fallen. Neera had no idea where or what she would be without him.

Her necklace created a low hum against her chest. It was subtle yet radiated warmth. It soothed her aching heart in a way Neera couldn't explain. Its protection added a layer of stability that momentarily melted her worries away.

LIAM

Today is officially D-Day.

Ever since Liam returned to his room from his intel-gathering mission, he went straight to work on brainstorming ideas to save Neera. He drew up diagrams and numbers to see the probability of his success rate.

Plan A had a 56% success rate with a minor risk factor. Plan B had a 90% success rate but a major risk factor. It took him hours to come to a conclusion, to the point that the birds were chirping, and the sky was a grayish blue through the basement window. Crumpled-up pieces of paper were scattered all over his room, and he was genuinely shocked that his hair remained intact.

Liam decided to go with Plan A, which entailed running away with her, sending her dad to Northern Cali, and meeting up with them until he could convince the government to take action on the fam–his father's business.

It wouldn't be easy, but at least they'd be far away from the blowback. Graduation was the perfect way to keep his father distracted since, with everything he heard, he'd be too preoccupied to attend the ceremony.

Plan B was to go to the police about a kidnapping, but that would only endanger Neera if the police just so happened to be corroborating with them. He also wouldn't be able to guarantee his father wouldn't get to them first.

Both plans were sticky, but at least Plan A kept Neera as far away from the danger as possible. And he'd do whatever he could to keep her that way.

Instead of using his hands to contact Neera the next day, Liam used them to contact a few people to make sure his plan went smoothly. He used his mom's credit card to purchase some tickets since he rarely saved money for himself. He didn't steal it; technically, she lent it to him so he could host a "post-graduation party." Which he wasn't going to do. Nate was throwing a party at his place, and he was going to use that as a cover.

Liam hated lying to his mom. Honestly, she had always been his support system; however, he wasn't sure how deep she was in his father's business. For all he knew, she could be a bystander, just allowing his father to wreak havoc on innocent people. Again, he hated assuming that about his own mom, but he had to take precautions. ANYTHING could be a drawback, and he could no longer take risks.

"Liam Dern," the principal announced with elation.

Liam crossed the stage with his perfectly coiffed hair peeking from underneath his cap and a clean-shaven face. With his publicity smile, he grabbed his diploma and shook all his teachers' hands. He felt like a politician as applause, especially from the girls, echoed throughout the gym.

He felt like his father at that moment...and it grossed him out.

When he posed for the photographer, he glanced at Neera for a split second in the chairs. She didn't even look in his direction. She looked everywhere but at him. He was himself for that short second, and then he looked back at the photographer as he took the photo. Liam inwardly cursed at himself when his smile wavered.

"Neera Ran."

Liam couldn't look away if he tried. Neera looked so nervous by the shakiness in her legs and the timidness of her steps, but as Elayne and her dad cheered her on, she ironically looked more confident with every step she took. Every breath she took. Liam fought so hard to remain quiet in his seat because she deserved so much more applause. So much praise for being incredibly brave, funny, and beautiful.

Speaking of beautiful.

When she posed for her picture with her bright smile, button nose, cute freckles, and glasses, he wished he could switch places with the photographer. To be so close to her aura and not several feet away in his chair. For a split second, he would do anything for her to look upon him just once. For her to turn her smile towards him. Just once.

But she didn't.

And he didn't deserve to have it.

He wondered what life would have been if he was never a part of his family. If they met randomly because he was a new student, and they fell in love, and he gave her a corny promise ring because they were sappy teens. If she said yes, they would spend the rest of their college years just getting to know each other.

But this was reality.

He hurt her. His father planned on hurting her more. He brought pain to someone who deserved nothing but security.

Guilt wracked through him. Before he could stop himself, he texted her how beautiful she was... because she was. He was fine with her ignoring him because they'd have their time together soon.

Dan Dern actually showed up to his graduation. Liam was genuinely shocked, especially after everything that transpired. He was supposed to be at work or planning more ways to ruin Liam's life.

His mom gave him a suffocating hug and told him how proud she was. Danny gave him a high-five, and Liam was just happy that they were in a good place. His mom handed him a bouquet with a bear donning a cap and gown that said *2008 GRAD!* The green carnations reminded Liam of Neera, but he shook the image away as quickly as it came.

A strong hand clasped Liam's shoulder as he held out his other hand.

"Congrats, bud," his father expressed with a fake smile on his face. Liam stared at his floating hand for a second too long, then eventually took it. Both of their grips increasingly tightened until Dan finally released it without his smile faltering. "I'm really proud of you, Liam. I've never doubted your potential."

Liam nodded because he knew it was just a bunch of crap. Also, a small part of him believed it was one last plea deal to get him on his side.

It wasn't working.

He continued. "Your intelligence, grit, and, most importantly, your loyalty to your family will continue to take you far in life."

Something about the way he uttered those last words made Liam feel uneasy.

Is that a threat, Dern?

Liam pursed his lips to avoid causing a scene. There were still plenty of students and parents around them. He dropped his shoulder, causing Dan's hand to fall from it.

"I'll see you tomorrow morning, after my graduation

party tonight," Liam reminded his mom.

In Liam's peripheral vision, Dan dropped his publicity mask and shook his head.

"You absolutely can't have a graduation party. We're supposed to have a celebratory family dinner at home tonight. There will be plenty of other times you can party. Just not tonight," his father commanded.

Liam clenched his jaw. He knew exactly what Dan was doing. "There will be other times to have dinner at home."

Dan's scowl deepened as his neck flushed beneath his dress shirt collar.

"I think you're starting to forget that since you live under my roof, you have to follow my rules," he threatened. Liam was sure he wasn't talking about the graduation party. "Don't let this graduation get to your head, son."

They were face-to-face now. Liam scowled back, his ears heated in protest.

So this is what fighting fire with fire *means?*

His father was still tugging on that leash, and Liam had to admit he was doing a decent job at it. He put up a good argument on the basis of him being his parental figure and landlord of the house. What he didn't know was that Liam was a legal adult, so the man was pulling on a limp leash.

Liam's mom cleared her throat, breaking the silent tension. "Dan, I'm actually watching Andy's baby girl tonight." She placed a hand on her husband's clenched one. "Why don't you let him have some fun with his friends?"

Dan, pinker now, sighed and gazed at his wife. His kryptonite, it seemed. Deep down, Liam understood the feeling. After what felt like forever, he finally made a decision.

"Fine. But you have to be home by twelve," his tone darkened. "It's dangerous out there nowadays."

His mom innocently smiled and winked at Liam. She might not be fully aware of what was going on, but he was forever grateful to her for it. Liam wanted to call Dan out but decided to bottle it up instead. He nodded again while chewing the inside of his cheek.

"Thanks, *Dad*," he muttered.

On their way out of the gymnasium, Danny talked about how excited he was for middle school, but Liam's brain was racing. He only had one shot at warning Neera about everything. It didn't help that she was ignoring him–rightfully so–and he wouldn't be able to get within a foot of her without help.

He pulled out his cell and prayed that this person cared enough to answer his call. He called, but it went straight to voicemail. As expected. So he tried texting and mentally pleaded for a response.

LIAM: CAN U MEET ME IN SENIOR WING? V IMPORTANT.

He waited for a couple of minutes, holding his breath the whole time. His phone vibrated.

ELAYNE: Y DO U STILL HV MY #?

Liam exhaled. All he needed was an inch.

LIAM: PLS? NEE IS IN DANGER. PLS?

The response came too quickly. He was almost afraid to open it. It had to be a rejection. A simple *NO* or *GTFO*. Hope deflated until he opened his phone and saw the text.

ELAYNE: SEE U IN 2.

ONLY 4 MINUTES TO SAVE THE WORLD

Chapter 17

Neera

"I'm out of time, and all I got is four minutes...come on."

Elayne bobbed her head to the funky, pop beat as she laid two outfits on Neera's bed for Nate's graduation party. How did she get the hook-up in the first place? Neera had no clue, but she wasn't surprised at what her best friend was capable of.

Honestly, after a stressful week, Neera wanted to spend the evening with her dad, watching scary movies–because that was the only way she could watch them–and drinking his mind-blowing hot chocolate. Elayne, for some inexplicable reason, wanted her to go with her to Nate's party. Apparently, Neera just HAD to be there to party as a Senior for the last time.

To be fair, everything was going to change from being high school students to college freshmen. More opportunities...and more responsibilities. Neera hadn't even truly figured out what she wanted to do. Her goal was to graduate with a degree in Psych and a minor in Family Therapy, like her dad. That meant mad studying and no time to actually enjoy life.

So yes, what harm could one little party do?

She also couldn't admit that Liam potentially being there made her kind of...sort of want to make him jealous.

Neera stared at the eerily similar outfits and scrunched her nose. "Is this a costume party? Are we going as Tia and Tamera again?"

Elayne rolled her eyes. "They're not that similar. Plus, I want us to look like a team for our last high school party. Just like sixth grade."

Neera chuckled at the memory of them in middle school wearing matching corduroy skirts and rock band t-shirts. Elayne had said she wanted to "look like twins", but really, Neera knew it was just her way of showing her solidarity and support after her mum's death. A sympathy card and flowers simply weren't Lay-Lay's style.

Neera eyed the outfits with skepticism. One consisted of a camouflage mini-skirt, a brown sleeveless V-neck top, a tan belt, and gladiator flats. The other one had camouflage shorts, a brown camisole, and combat boots. She assumed that was Elayne's choice.

"Time is waiting...we only got 4 minutes to save the world."

Neera grabbed the first one and went to her bathroom to change. Not that Elayne had never seen her naked. It was more for dramatic effect.

When she emerged from the bathroom, Elayne was already dressed in her outfit, minus the shoes. She must've liked what she saw because her eyes lit up, but for some reason, her smile wasn't as bright as usual. Neera almost questioned her about it until Elayne whisked her in front of the mirror, gazing at each other through the mirror.

"The guys are gonna be all over us tonight," Elayne remarked with her eyes glued to their outfits. Her camisole hugged her slender frame, yet she added a wide tan belt around her middle for extra support. Her voice flowed with humor. "Your chest looks great in this top. How are we supposed to pass as twins if you look like that?"

Neera's cheeks heated but covered it by laughing. "If you

keep giving me googly eyes, then I'm going to change."

As she shifted to leave, Elayne clutched her hand, bringing her back to the mirror.

"We have to finish your look," Elayne giggled. She flat ironed Neera's hair and added a pink lip gloss to her lips. No other make-up for some reason. Elayne also went without her eyeliner for the first time in years.

Neera attempted to curl her stubbornly straight hair but gave up and just tied a brown bandana to her head. Elayne requested the same lip gloss, which almost knocked Neera out because she hated pink.

I guess she's really trying to sell this twin gimmick, Neera chuckled internally.

She reached for her glasses on her dresser, but Elayne halted her movements.

Neera raised an eyebrow. "No glasses? How else will they tell us apart?"

Elayne shook her head with a smile that didn't reach her eyes. Again, strange.

She took a deep breath as she eyed Neera through the mirror, placing her hands on both of her shoulders.

"Wear them when you come back," she asserted. Her tone lifted. "Now, let's hurry up and get there before all the booze is gone."

Instead of questioning her BFF, Neera smiled and finished getting ready. To finish Neera's look, she slipped her necklace that she usually kept under her pillow into her skirt's back pocket.

Speaking of strange, Neera's surprised her dad hadn't discovered the necklace missing yet, or if he did, he hadn't mentioned it to her. She chalked it up to her dad's inexplicable trust in his teenage daughter. The trust she deeply felt she didn't deserve after her constant fibbing.

After a bunch of mirror pictures, they headed downstairs to say goodbye to her dad as he waved "cheers" from the couch–where he'd probably remain until Neera returned home–and drove in Elayne's car to Nate's party to have the time of their lives.

The beeping of a police car siren blared from Nate's backyard.

"Okay, lil' mama had a swag like mine..."

"I love this song," Elayne sang as they entered his backyard.

They both entered from the front door, then the kitchen, then out the sliding glass doors to his extravagant backyard. If they thought Liam's place was huge, they clearly weren't cultured enough because Nate's yard looked like a park. Maybe because Liam had a literal beach in his backyard, it didn't seem as big.

Here I am, thinking of Liam again.

The land had a huge in-ground pool in the center of the yard with lights inside that illuminated the water in multiple colors. What Neera would give to be able to swim in it.

There was a DJ on the other side of the pool blasting music through ginormous speakers, a foldable table with beer-pong already set up, another table with snacks and hors d'oeuvres, neon lights strung up gave everything a Vegas-look, a small basketball court off to the side where people were already playing, and a bunch of people dancing and mingling.

Elayne carted Neera towards the snack table and started going in on the mini sandwiches. Neera eyed her suspiciously. Elayne didn't eat like that unless she was extra stressed out.

Matter of fact, she was acting strange the entire time. Just bobbing her head and stuffing mini-dogs down her throat. Neera couldn't ignore it any longer.

She ceased her friend's feeding frenzy with a firm grip on her hand. "Are you okay, Lay-Lay? You've been acting weird all night."

Elayne dropped her mini-dog on the table and gave her a half-smile.

"Yeah, yeah," she replied dismissively. She shook her head. "I forgot to eat dinner."

"Hmm," Neera hummed, knowing she wasn't going to get a real answer any time soon.

"Hey, you guys," Nate greeted as he popped up in front of them, interrupting Neera's interrogation. "Thanks for coming." He eyed both of them.

Neera gave him a once-over before responding. "Yeah, your party is dope."

He smiled at her with bright, straight teeth that could be in a toothpaste commercial. He ran a careful hand over his sharp waves, then pointed a finger between Neera and Elayne. "Do you twins want a drink?"

Before Elayne could respond, Neera spoke up in a voice she hoped was seductive. "Yeah, we would love some."

That earned Neera a glare from Elayne, but she could thank her later. She needed to cool down, and Neera's nerves were already bunching. Nate snapped his fingers and got to work at making some concoction that looked as blue as punch but smelled nothing like punch.

He handed them their cups, and one for himself. He held it out to them as if waiting for a toast, and Neera bumped hers to him while Elayne hesitated. She eventually bumped her cup, and they all lifted their cups to drink. The "punch" was stronger than the one at prom, and the blue color was just a facade of its sweetness. Neera glanced at Elayne, who barely lifted her cup.

Huh, weird.

The entire time, Nate stared into Neera's eyes like a shark, just waiting for his chance to bite. Neera coughed at the drink's bitterness–yes, definitely the drink–and smiled at him.

"It's good," she lied. He grinned.

"You can get the recipe later once everyone else leaves tonight," he implied with a cheeky smile.

Neera bet that smile got him anything he wanted. For some reason, it did nothing for her, so she just fake smiled.

She kind of couldn't believe that her ex's friend was hitting on her. The same person who hadn't had one conversation with her in the four years they'd attended school together. Now he suddenly wanted to be alone with her?

He leaned on the table and took another sip of his drink, eyes still on Neera.

"I mean, I assumed you and Liam weren't a thing since you both showed up separately," he inquired. "Or am I wrong?"

Liam. He's here already?

Neera fought the natural urge to seek him out like his eyes were a lighthouse in the dark sea. She giggled, which was obviously fake since it sounded harsher than she intended.

"No, you're not wrong," she disclosed. She took a longer swig of the blue potion. The fire scorching her throat encouraged her. "We're over."

Elayne scoffed.

She wasn't acting much like a twin.

Nate ignored it and smiled at Neera like he'd hit the jackpot. Elayne eyed them and grabbed Nate's free hand, breaking their eye contact. He raised his eyebrows as if he just noticed she was still standing there.

Elayne put on her own flirtatious smile and started pulling Nate towards her. "Let's go talk by the pool. I wanna show you something."

She is so not cock-blocking right now!

Neera bumped her friend's shoulder as she pulled him towards the pool. The entire time, Elayne hadn't said a word to him, and now that he was making moves, she wanted to step all over Neera to get to him. This whole night was not as fun as Neera thought it would be.

She should've stayed at home and watched a paranormal movie.

As they headed to the pool–because Nate couldn't decline such a promising proposal–she watched them before freezing when Liam stood in front of her.

Her heart picked up speed, threatening to take her to her

mum. At least if that happened, she wouldn't have to face him like this.

So many emotions popped up as his hand surfed through his brown waves. He didn't look like his usual self– well, by usual self, she meant the "Perfect Liam"-facade he had been sporting whenever they were at school. His hair was free of gel, and the soft waves on top were disheveled, a few strands hanging over his forehead. He wore all-black: black t-shirt, black hoodie, black jeans, and even black hiking boots.

Is he trying to leave a low profile? All that black in the Summer is literally a suicide mission.

Still, he was as handsome as she had last seen him. Even more, because the guy in front of her was the Liam from the beach. She had to resist. He absolutely couldn't walk back into her life after everything he said. He couldn't just send a sweet text to her and expect her to just fall at his feet. It didn't work like that. She didn't work like that.

Not anymore.

So she went the annoyed route. He couldn't know how he affected her.

Neera finished the rest of her drink, then slammed the cup on the table and screwed her face into an irritated one.

Yeah, that should do the trick.

"What do you want?" Neera demanded.

Liam glanced between her and the empty cup, eyes dancing with amusement. He half-smiled and held a hand out to her. "I wanna dance with you...Can we dance?"

Neera blinked at him.

What kind of game is he trying to play here? He really has some nerve coming up to me and asking me to dance. Does he think I'm bloody stupid?

She took a deep breath to calm her nerves, holding her hand to the necklace she placed around her neck before they got out of the car. Her mind blared alarms at his request, telling her to reject him and move on. It was the safest thing to do. The only way to protect her heart. Yet, with her hand clutching the necklace, rejecting him felt impossible. It felt like she was being nudged towards him because deep down in her heart, she knew she didn't hate him and that she would do anything for him.

Ugh, I hate being sappy.

His hand remained floating, his hazel gaze seeking hers out. The smile was gone, leaving sincerity on his face.

She cleared her throat and took his hand. He held it tight and led her to the basketball court, which was adjacent to the wooden fence. It was secluded since most of the players had moved on to other activities and left them to be alone. The music softened the further they retreated. The neon lights danced off their skin, giving them a romantic glow.

The music changed to a slower, more passionate one.

"Tell me how I'm supposed to breathe with no air..."

LIAM

Liam watched Corey do a keg stand while a group of people crowded the scene, cheering him on. Usually, he would've joined them in the festivities, but he had more important things on his mind.

Tonight was the night. Everything has to go according to plan.

His father's threat left him uneasy the rest of the day as he prepared and made sure his plans went well. The only thing left was to make sure Neera showed up to the party.

He peered at the entrance and still didn't see Neera. Hopefully everything he said to Elayne had reassured Neera's safety and trust in him.

When he spoke with Elayne in the hall, she wasn't exactly welcoming to him. That was until he spilled his father's possible plans. She slowly started to process the situation, allowing him to explain her part. He could tell she wasn't convinced entirely, but she was willing to do it to protect her. And it wasn't going to be easy for her.

That was why Liam would be forever grateful.

Liam had been at the party for an hour, and there was still no sign of her. He took a sip of his orange juice, wishing it was vodka. A tall girl with long, straight strawberry-blonde hair and red lipstick sauntered up to Liam and asked him to dance. He politely shook his head in refusal, but she was persistent.

"Oh, come on, Liam. It's just a dance," she started closing the space between them before slowly caressing his bicep. "You're single, and I'm not seeing anyone..."

Liam forgot how fast word spread that he was single, even though he told no one. He could only assume some random person saw what happened and blabbed.

"I'm really not in the dancing mood," he dismissed. He pulled his arm out of her grip and put his hoodie on that he kept around his waist. It was hot as hell in his all-black, but he had to stay hidden.

Her head tilted in disbelief, yet she wisely backed down. Liam appreciated the surrender as she strutted away. If that happened a month ago, she would be cute enough to dance with, and he would've. He would've gotten her number, and they would've hooked up afterward.

But that wasn't him now. His heart belonged to someone else.

He turned back to the sliding door entrance and froze. At the snack table, Elayne and Neera were chatting and smiling with Nate. His hand tightened around the plastic cup, pushing the juice up to the surface. They were wearing similar clothes, just as he planned. Elayne really pulled through. Now all he had to do was ignore his friend's trifling antics and somehow get some alone time with Neera.

He imagined different ways to get her alone. It was difficult because she probably wanted to slap him more than be alone with him. He finally decided to just be himself and went to her as humbly as possible. The hairs on his neck spiked at the potential confrontation.

Then she giggled at Nate, giving him some sort of googly eyes. That only meant one thing: Nate's "macking" was leaving her putty in his hands.

His chest ached.

Sure, it was technically okay for her to hook up with Nate because they weren't together. She was single and could possibly mingle. However, Liam had come to discover that he was actually a selfish dude. He would rather cut off his own limb than find out Neera hooked up with Nate-fuckin'-Fields.

Determined, he downed the rest of his drink and stalked over to the *happy* group. Elayne spotted him first with wide eyes because she was facing his general direction and then smiled at Nate. Like the total "wing-man" she was, she pulled Nate with her to the pool, leaving Neera alone and probably annoyed. She looked after their retreat, then froze as soon as she locked eyes with Liam.

Wow, she looked incredible.

He wanted to spend the night in reverence for her beauty, but he had a mission to accomplish. She, on the other hand, was slightly irked at his presence. However, something else crossed her face that he couldn't comprehend.

Focus, Liam.

Before he could say something, she downed her drink and slammed it on the table. Her face looked intimidating yet cute. He couldn't hold back his smile, because it was impossible. He decided to ask her to dance to calm her, and hopefully, the physical contact would remind her of old times.

Please don't say no.

It felt like forever before she finally conceded. He finally released a breath he didn't know he was holding. That was all he needed. Just a little crack. He could jimmy his way in after that. He hoped his desperation didn't show, but he had a feeling it did. He'd never been so nervous.

Calmly, Liam led Neera towards a secluded part of the yard. One near the exit so they could sneak away. The music miraculously slowed to a more passionate one, which made the moment feel more natural. More like the first time they danced together.

"...losing you is like living in a world with no air."

Liam clutched one of her hands in his sweaty palm and placed his other hand on her lower back. Hesitantly, she placed her other hand on his shoulder as they fell into a natural sway. His steps unsure, he ignored the faint embarrassment creeping up his cheeks and looked up at her unreadable face. When her eyes finally landed on his, he gave her a faint smile.

"Am I doing this right?" Liam coyly asked.

A look of amusement passed over Neera's face before she cut her eyes to everything else but him.

"Close enough," she mumbled.

Her body was close but not close enough. He could still feel her tension, but he continued to smile and wait. Liam definitely didn't have all the time in the world to dance and pretend that time had stopped.

However, making every second with her precious was his main priority. Earning her trust was the most delicate task, and he couldn't move forward without it.

"When my world revolves around you, it's so hard for me to breathe..."

Her hands began to relax, allowing him to take a second to pull her closer, closing the gap between them. He expected Neera to freeze or reject him, but she followed along with his irregular steps.

Her head on his shoulder, she melted into his touch while heating his entire body.

Liam tried to hide his smile as they swayed into the next song, saying everything they felt by saying absolutely nothing.

"Say what you need to say...Say what you need to say..."

He swallowed the lump in his throat and prepared to unleash his spiel he'd been practicing to persuade her.

"Neera-"

"I missed you so much," Neera confessed as her voice

broke.

Liam peered at her face on his shoulder, now facing his, and her eyes closed.

She took a deep breath and continued. "I hate how much I love you in such a short time. I hate how I haven't forgotten you at all. I hate that despite everything you said, I still want to dance with you. I still want to be with you...and it sucks."

He let his grin widen as he took in her freckles that were bolder from her blush-laden face, her glossy bottom lip that disappeared into her mouth, and her thick eyebrows bunched in the middle of her head.

Liam knew how much strength it took for her to reveal that. Something he always admired about her. Her authenticity and strength. A queen worth fighting for, and she didn't even know it.

He placed both of his hands on her waist while she wrapped both arms around his neck. She lifted her head, and they were practically nose-to-nose. Her sea-green eyes penetrated his earthy ones. His mind was lost at sea. Drowning.

Hopelessly hers.

He hoped she couldn't feel his heart racing as he prepared to make his own confession. He dragged his eyes from hers and stared at her lips.

"There hasn't been a time we've been together or apart that I haven't felt the same as you. The only difference is there's no hate. I don't regret any moment I had with you," Liam slid his thumb back and forth over her waist tenderly. "The only regret I had was hurting you when I wasn't brave enough to hold on to you."

She just stared at him, patiently waiting for him to finish. He laid his forehead against hers and whispered. "But I'm braver now because of you. Brave enough to apologize..." He licked his bottom lip. "Brave enough to run away with you by my side."

Neera's eyebrows shot up as she processed what he said.

She stopped swaying and searched his face for answers. He could only imagine her mind swimming with options. Her anxiety was probably dragging her down, keeping her from seeing his heart holding out a hand for her to latch onto.

She loves me and trusts me...so I need to do the same.

So Liam waited for her response. He didn't pressure her to decide.

"Why?" Neera inquired, her face skeptical.

"I can't explain everything right now, and I know it sounds suspicious. All I can say right now is that everything I do is because I love you and want to protect you. Do you trust me, Angelfish?"

Liam half-expected her to push him away or pry more of his reasons, but using her nickname seemed to soften her up. Surprisingly, she leaned forward and planted her lips on his closed ones. When his millisecond of shock faded, he opened his mouth to her.

They fell into a deep kiss, making him disoriented. Unbothered by the alcohol, he deepened it by wrapping his arms around Neera so there wasn't even a sliver of air between them. She caressed the back of his head with her hands, causing him to lose himself in something as natural as breathing.

He missed this...He missed *her*.

Neera broke the kiss and touched her forehead to his. "Will we come back?"

Liam's mouth lifted into a grin. That was all he needed.

He almost forgot he was at a party with others. He almost forgot that they were running away because of his narcissistic father and not because they were just two troubled teens in love. That this wasn't Romeo and Juliet. This was a rescue mission.

His expression hardened at the fact, his smile faltering.

Before he could respond, he heard Nate yelling from the DJ booth.

"Yo, the cops are here! Everyone, get the hell out now!"

Teens scrambled, and the music scratched to a halt. Red-and-blue lights illuminated the sky around Nate's mansion. To anyone else, this could've been a noise complaint from a cranky, old neighbor who wanted to ruin a night of fun.

However, Liam knew better.

Let the real games begin, Dad.

THE FINAL LAP

Chapter 18

Neera

Uniformed men stormed the party. A bit more dramatic than necessary as they shoved scrambling teenagers out of the way. The DJ ferociously packed his equipment; some teens unnecessarily heaved themselves over the wooden fence, and some ran past the sliding doors to escape potential capture.

It was chaotic...yet strange. Well, not the police arriving, but their uniforms. Instead of the usual blue-and-gray collared shirt and pleated pants, they donned all black from head to toe. Black t-shirts, black bulletproof vests, black trousers, and black combat boots. The only things that weren't black were the gold badges on their waists and their transparent face shields. They looked like they were about to capture a terrorist instead of a bunch of underage drinkers.

Something stranger. They seemed to be letting most of the suspects go. They would stop one of them, briefly inspect them, and then let them run away.

What is going on?

Neera scanned the area for Elayne, which shouldn't be hard since they dressed alike and saw her sprinting towards Neera and Liam. Liam's hand tensed in her hand. As she headed towards them, Neera was about to yell her name before Elayne slapped a forefinger to her lips. Neera, utterly confused, glanced back at Liam, who was tugging her to the gate opening.

"We gotta go now," Liam commanded as he pulled her arm.

Neera held her ground until Elayne saddled up next to them. She chanced a glance over her shoulder as they exited the yard and noticed one of the cops pointing in their direction and speaking into his shoulder.

She saw Liam's green jeep, but they ended up passing it and heading to Elayne's purple buggy. Neera was lost at this point, especially as Liam gently pushed Neera into the back seat and then got in afterward, with Elayne quickly getting into the driver's seat. The two shared a look as Elayne started the car, speeding off towards the driveway.

Around them, Neera noticed three black SUVs scattered across the large front yard, one of them blocking Liam's vehicle from behind. Most of the other cars were gone, some still barreling down Nate's winding driveway to freedom.

Liam leaned forward, his head right next to Elayne's headrest, and started spewing directions. He pointed diagonally to an exit that Neera didn't recognize. Elayne's car screeched as she made a U-turn towards it. In the opposite direction of home. Instead of looking afraid, they look coordinated, like they knew this was going to happen.

Practiced it.

Red-and-blue lights suffocated the car, highlighting everyone's stoic faces. She could hear Liam whispering something to Elayne about how she "needs to concentrate" and to "not worry about them". Neera could see her BFF's eyebrow's furrow underneath her bangs. She was distressed but also focused.

Neera looked behind her and saw two of the SUVs from the party behind them. Not too close, especially with the way Elayne was ripping down the highway.

Aren't they being a bit excessive?

Technically, they were at a party with underage drinkers

and just so happened to be speeding down the highway, but that should just warrant a ticket and not a stupid blockade.

Sense slapped her in the face. Her anxiety spiked as she gripped her necklace with a death grip, hoping it would keep her panic attack at bay. A brief look at her friends' firm faces showed she was the only one freaking out.

The cops weren't chasing them because of a stupid party or for speeding over the limit.

The cops weren't coming to arrest them for drinking and driving.

They stormed the party for *her*.

"What the bloody hell is going on?" Neera barked as her anxiety escalated. She could feel it climbing up her throat, threatening to strangle her. Her chest moved feverishly as she struggled to breathe. She closed her eyes and imagined her dad's words whenever she had a panic attack.

What's your name? Neera Adenike Ran.

What do you see? A freeway.

What color is the sky? Dark blue.

Everything will be okay. Say it: Everything will be okay.

Neera heard Liam's voice calmly mutter more directions to Elayne. She opened her eyes and saw his tender ones on hers. His face crumpled in...pity?

She hated that look, but she waited for his answer.

"I know this is a crazy situation right now, but long story short: A small government subdivision knows about the island, and more importantly, they know about you." He looked past her at the tumultuous yet steadily decreasing blend of lights chasing them. His shoulders relaxed the smallest bit. "We're going to try to get out of here with my uncle's speedboat. Elayne will be the bait while we make our escape."

No. No, no, no, no!

How did the government find out about my secret? Did they say something? Did he say something? That's why he knew what would happen. Then why is he trying to help? To try to soothe his guilt? And now he's trying to bring my best friend down with him?

Neera trembled as she took in the situation, her heart betraying her expressionless face.

So the party, the outfits, pulling Nate away? That was all part of the plan. That was why they looked alike, so they would think they were chasing Neera instead of Elayne. Neera knew Elayne didn't drink it because she needed to drive. She also stuffed herself, thinking she was just nervous, but it was also because she was going to be caught and held by the police.

Everything started to fall into place.

If she weren't so concerned for her best friend, she would've been impressed by the solid strategy. Neera grabbed her friend's shoulder, trying to snap her out of such ridiculousness.

"Lay-Lay, please," Neera whined, her voice cracking. "I can't let you get caught in my mess. There's no way."

"Now, Nee-Nee, I can't let you have all the fun," Elayne smirked in the rearview mirror. "Besides, your rich ex-boyfriend gave me some cash for bail or whatever. I left it in my mom's purse, just in case. I'll be fine."

The sound of pebbles and sand was the only thing that could be heard as the car slowly entered a small empty lot. With no light but the crescent moon hovering above them, Neera could barely make out their location.

All she could see was a small wooden shack with a variety of boats and rafts behind it. The biggest boat looked medium-sized, so they definitely weren't at the usual luxury yacht rental. The smell of the ocean wafted into the car, granting Neera a sense of familiarity in an insane situation.

Elayne shut off her headlights and kept her foot on the brake, not fully parking. She was prepared to drive off immediately, like a literal getaway driver. Turning around in her seat, she stared at Neera with the most serious look she'd ever seen on her childhood friend. Her "Soul-Sister".

"Don't worry about me. I'll be waiting for you when you get back," Elayne claimed confidently. Neera's eyes stung as she kept her tears at bay. Elayne reassuringly smiled. "Just focus on staying safe. And remember, you're way stronger than you think."

Neera gawked at her best friend. The person who always had her back, whether it was from bullying or loneliness. Elayne had always been the fire-cracker in Neera's life. To everyone else, she was fiery and dangerous, but to Neera, she had always been that spark protecting her from the darkness.

It was subtle at first, but as she stared at her, Neera realized that all of this wasn't spontaneous. It was long-awaited.

"We gotta go," Liam insisted firmly, then turned to Elayne. "Thanks again."

Elayne nodded and pulled a handle to pop the trunk. Liam quickly got out and headed to the back of the car. Neera, reluctant to leave, ignored whatever Liam was doing to hug Elayne from behind.

If only she held on long enough, somehow, all this would go away.

Neera turned to the sound of the back door opening as Liam cocked his head outside. She sighed, pried her fingers from Elayne, and exited the car. She tried hard not to resent Liam, who was just trying to save her, but a small part of her was still hurt. Then, she had to put all her trust in him and be dragged away while her family remained in danger.

In danger because of HIS dad.

He's turning my world upside down.

Neera walked past Liam, avoiding his outstretched hand, and went straight to Elayne's window. From her peripheral, she noticed a split second of Liam frowning. When Liam reappeared at her side, Elayne flashed him a crooked smile.

"Take care of my sister, okay?" Elayne quipped before dead-panning. "Or you'll have an ex-con to deal with when you get back."

"Of course. Stay safe," Liam vowed quickly.

He must be in a hurry.

Elayne took the hint, winking at Neera and reversing out of the lot. Her tires screeched as she swerved towards the lot entrance, turned on her headlights, and barreled down the road.

Neera bit her lip as sirens resounded in the distance, her heart breaking with every whoop. It took all her strength not to crumble to the ground as she forced herself to stand and brace herself for whatever came next.

For Lay-Lay.

LIAM

Liam clutched the handles on his emergency bag as he watched Neera wrap herself in her arms and stare at the ground, wishing he could replace her arms with his. Wishing he could take her emotional pain away.

But he had to focus on the plan. One misstep and all of it would be for nothing.

Liam tore his eyes away from her and ran to Uncle Pete's speedboat. He threw the bag into the metal compartment to keep it from getting wet. He found the key already in the ignition, as he requested, and prepared to undock the boat.

When he begged his uncle to lend him his speedboat, of course, the man was skeptical. Liam had to convince him to keep it a secret from Dan, too, which actually wasn't as difficult since his father was, in Pete's words, "a total prick". All Liam had to do in return was keep it clean and refill it before he brought it back.

Neera finally joined him, sitting stiffly at the stern while Liam checked on the motor. Her worried face stared in the direction of the fading sirens that were probably tailing Elayne, her fingers gripping her necklace tight.

He could only imagine how anxious she was, with everything that happened with her mom and now, the uncertainty of her friend and her dad's well-being. It was probably eating her up inside.

Focus, Liam.

"Hey. Can you turn the engine on while I start the motor?" Liam suggested, hoping the task would pull her out of her stupor.

She rotated her head at him, the slight breeze causing her hair to caress her face. She finally acknowledged his request with a stiff nod and headed to the steering wheel. When she turned her wrist, he yanked the cord to rev the motor.

No sound. She looked back at him and tried again, Liam pulling it again.

No start.

You got to be fuckin' kiddin' me!

Liam stemmed his racing heart. He did not take the boat NOT working into account. The boat was their Trojan horse. Sure, the boat was a little old, but it had always been efficient, and he made sure to fill it with gas yesterday. There shouldn't be a reason for this boat to stall.

God, PLEASE let this work.

"It's not working," Neera mumbled lifelessly.

Liam's blood boiled, but not in anger. In determination. He had something to prove. Promises to keep.

This boat WILL move! He took a deep breath.

"Keep turning," Liam demanded. She frowned yet returned to turning the key.

Liam rubbed the engine and pleaded with the hunk of junk. "Please start. Please start."

He yanked again. Still nothing.

He ran a shaky hand through his hair, yanking with all the pent-up anger he built inside. He tried two more times, and with the grace of God, it purred to life.

He fell to his knees in relief.

We lost too much time already.

He sprinted to the wheel, causing Neera to step back

from it. She seemed tense around him, and he couldn't blame her. He'd make it up to her later when she was safe and sound. He'd tell her everything he always wanted to admit to her. To pour his whole heart into her.

He put it in drive, and the forsaken boat sped off into the deep blue ocean.

His uncle might have exaggerated the "speed" part. Instead of ripping through the calm water, the thing kind of... cruised. Liam was hoping they would be riding waves like in a spy movie, escaping the bad guys and flipping over currents. On the contrary, they moseyed along the coast at medium velocity, extending the silence between them.

"If you're hungry," Liam blurted, trying to break some of the tension. "I packed some protein bars and jerky in the metal bin over there." He nodded his head swiftly at the compartment behind them. "There's also a blanket if you get cold."

After a minute of silence, he glanced at Neera. Her usually full lips were in a thin line as the wind whipped through her straight hair. If it was any other day, he would've basked in the calm waves and the serenity of her face.

Except he knew she was probably feeling all sorts of emotions, and one of those was most likely anger towards him.

He could definitely tell she was visibly cold and tired by the goosebumps scoring over his skin, and he was wearing a hoodie. Since they were in the ocean, the temperature had dropped exponentially. It'd only get worse as they travel further North.

Liam scanned the ocean in front of them for any potential hazards before he tried to tug Neera closer to him with his free hand. She planted her feet, refusing his warmth.

A part–a large part–of him was wounded by the constant rejection, despite his understanding of her reasons. She would rather freeze than deal with him.

He wanted to go back to the Neera from the party, who melted into him as he confessed his feelings. Better yet, the Neera he sat with on the beach as they mutually shared their love with each other. He didn't want to lose her, so he did something unlike him.

Liam snatched his hands from the wheel like a hot plate. The boat started to sway, causing Neera to spring in front of the wheel, holding it with her eyes bulging and her mouth falling open.

"What's your problem?" She basically shrieked as she used her hands to steady the boat. Liam simpered before moving to stand behind her, trapping her between the steering wheel and himself. He still kept an inch of space for Jesus between them because he was a gentleman. His hands held her arms to keep her in place.

"Can you hold on tight really quick?" Liam jested. Not waiting for an answer, he removed his hoodie and laid it over her shoulders. She was still tense, but he swore she relaxed a little.

Liam returned his hands to the wheel, on top of hers. Subtly, he guided her hands to steady the boat, avoiding tiny waves that occasionally appeared. The tension visibly left her body as she concentrated on steering. His arms trembled from the wind cutting through them, but he held it in to not ruin Neera's one moment of comfort.

She was not a half-bad driver, either.

"Where are we going?" She inquired after some time.

"We're docking in Venice Beach," he disclosed. He chose it because Venice was halfway to their destination, and they needed a coastal city. Also, if they happen to be tracking them, adding more locations in route would confuse them further.

"That's over eighty miles away from home."

"I know. We just need to hide out for a couple of days until I can figure out a way to get to Napa–"

"Napa? As in Napa Valley?" Neera interjected, her voice climbing octaves. She started shaking her head, and Liam started getting nervous. "That's too far, Liam. What about my dad?"

"He'll be fine, Angel. I told him about everything, and he's supposed to meet us over there so that it wouldn't raise suspicions."

Telling her dad everything was one of the hardest parts of this whole plan. Telling him that his daughter was in danger made him complicit, but when he told him it was because of Dan, Mr. Ran was quiet. Not just regular quiet, like his gears were turning but he refused to show it on his face.

Like father, like daughter.

He ended up accepting the plan and the train tickets to Napa Valley for that night, but he treated Liam coldly, like a stranger and not his daughter's boyfriend.

"I'll do anything for my daughter." Mr. Ran's vow burned in the back of Liam's head. Now that he thought about it, it sounded more like a threat.

"We'll have to ditch our phones soon," Liam continued, focusing on the plan at hand. He directed his face to Neera, so he could see her expression. "Do you know Elayne and Mr. Ran's numbers by heart?"

This was very important since it was the only way they could keep in touch. If she didn't, then they would have to keep their phones and risk being tracked.

"Of course," she claimed, her expression serious.

Liam exhaled in relief.

"Good."

He reached into his pocket and pulled out his cell. Then, he reached into the back pocket of Neera's skirt and removed her phone, holding both in his right hand. He backed away and turned to the back of the boat. With a grunt, he launched them as far as he could at the empty ocean. The devices plunged to their deaths as the boat left a trail of bubbles behind them.

Neera gave a choked yelp. Liam turned around to see she had seen the whole scene unfold. Her bottom lip disappeared into her mouth, and he just knew the plump flesh was about to go through it. Her eyebrows crinkled in pain, but that was for her safety.

"Were you always an evil genius, or did this just happen recently?" Neera sighed in defeat. Liam grinned at the jab, finally seeing a spark of his old girlfriend return.

Liam returned to his position behind her but decided to wrap his arms around her instead. It was less than two hours since they danced together, but he missed her touch. Their closeness.

Leaning his head on her shoulder, inhaling her beachy scent, he chortled. "Have always been one. Did you think I got into the Ivy Leagues just because I'm a rich kid?"

Her body vibrated as if silently laughing. He could hear the amusement in her voice.

"Yeah, duh."

The crescent moon still loomed high above them, so they were making good progress. He noticed the docks for Venice Beach up ahead, hoping to find space for their speed boat in the clusters of yachts and medium-sized boats.

With pure luck, he found a decent size spot to dock. They might receive a ticket when they return to the boat to leave, but that wasn't important. It was the weekend, so they were likely not to pay attention to extra boats.

Liam switched places with Neera and steered the boat to the empty spot in between two medium-sized yachts. When the boat crested the dock, he turned the key and then rushed to the motor to turn it off. Neera stood dumbfoundedly with his hoodie, watching Liam run around to dock the boat.

After mooring it to the dock, Liam sighed in exhaustion. Now that they were at their location, all his adrenaline finally deflated, and exhaustion slammed into him like an unforgiving wave. His eyes drooped, tempting him to drop down and sleep right on the tail...

Until he turned to his nervous love, trying to reassure her with a smile. He couldn't drop until she and her dad were safe. He had to keep going.

Focus, Liam.

He steeled his spine and, with one foot on the dock and the other on the tail of the boat, jutted his arms out in feigning spectacle. His eyes crinkled in forced exuberance.

"This is our stop, Angelfish. Welcome to Venice!"

TIME OUT

Chapter 19

Neera

I've never been to Venice Beach before.

Neera hadn't been much of a traveler, except that one time she went to Sutton to visit her dad's family. She was barely old enough to remember, but from what she did remember, it was nice...more urban, and very cold.

Ugh, it was so dreary.

Not something she was into, in particular, and the sea was cold, dark, and harsh. However, the few people who held her as a toddler seemed friendly. That was the last time they went to England, and she hadn't left Pasa Verde since.

Neera took in her surroundings. It was still dark, but there were more lights placed around the area, allowing Neera to take in the beautiful yachts lining the pier. The white vessels reflected off the water like stars in the sky. When she peered up, the actual stars weren't as visible as the ones in her town, but the bright moon gave her some solace and tranquility despite her overactive nerves.

Low buildings lined the coast, not as many as in her hometown. Her nose scrunched at the amount of litter on the ground near such beautiful water. It definitely depreciated the magic of the place.

I guess all cities are the same.

Her eyes landed on Liam, her heart picking up pace when she realized he was already staring at her.

He smiled. "Are you hungry?"

The last time he asked her that, she honestly wanted to push him off the boat. It wasn't like she didn't appreciate his help in this rescue mission. She just felt all these emotions, her mind scrambling to find some stability in this situation while trying to keep the negative thoughts at bay. Her panic was crawling up her throat, threatening to drown her, so she focused on the open waters instead of Liam's constant chatter.

Then he tricked her into driving the stinking boat that was carrying her away from her family. From her life. She was tempted to turn the thing around so she could go back to normal.

Then, as he held her and kept her steady, she remembered there was no normal life anymore. She was on the run. Her friend would be in jail, and her dad would be somewhere hundreds of miles away.

All because of Liam...because of Liam trying to protect her and her family. He even made sure Elayne had a way out.

He broke up with her...to protect her from his dad. The one person he valued the most in the world. He went against him...for Neera. She found it harder and harder to excuse his behavior as anything else but love. Her frosty interior began to melt for him, confirming why she fell for her hero in the first place.

Neera nodded lazily, all the energy almost drained from her. Liam hastily opened the metal compartment, digging for something. He paused, probably finding what he was looking for, and fished out two protein bars with two water bottles in his other hand.

Only the best for his Angelfish.

He set them on the "deck" and then returned to the compartment to pull out a folded gray wool blanket. He unfolded it and laid it flat, making sure to spread it evenly to cover most of the deck. Neera had to back into the wheel to allow an even cover.

Once satisfied, he sprawled onto the blanket. With the "refreshments" in the center, Liam laid sideways on his side with his feet facing the tail and propped himself on an elbow. He patted the empty space next to him, supposedly for Neera to join him.

While she sat with her legs crossed next to him, he handed her a protein bar he must've opened when she wasn't looking. Thankful, she bit into the gritty thing. The chocolate sprinkled on top of it was so not enough to mask the taste of cardboard, but she smiled anyway. The added calories gave her some energy that she didn't realize she needed.

They munched in silent content for a few minutes as they finished their meal. Neera didn't know what to say, so she spent the time enjoying the present. Not thinking about what was next or why they were there. Not thinking about anything else but the slight rocking of the boat, the unexpected softness of the blanket, the calming breeze caressing her skin, and Liam's lovely face.

They discarded their trash in the nearest bin next to the dock and returned to the blanket, laying on their backs as they gazed at the moon and three stars. Liam's hand was right next to hers, hovering and longing to hold it. Neera didn't understand his apprehension but then remembered how she had been treating him since they left the party.

Back to reality.

"What's the plan?" Neera inquired with a sigh.

"I don't know. Sleep out here for a couple of days."

Neera snapped her head in his direction with wide eyes. She was not sleeping outside. It did not matter what the situation was. She would NEVER lay out in the open air without mosquito repellent and indoor plumbing.

He turned to her and bit back a grin. "I'm kiddin–"

Neera cut him off with a half-hearted elbow jab to his ribcage. He winced overdramatically and feigned discomfort as they both laughed. A laugh she hadn't had in a while. The interaction wasn't that funny, but for some reason, it ripped a toe-curling belly laugh from Neera.

Liam held her hand and interlocked their fingers, finally finding the courage to hold her. He began to calm down and lazily continued. "We'll find a nearby hotel or motel for the night, get some real food, and then explore Venice Beach before heading out. We might have to catch a ride with a stranger. Is that okay?"

The way he kept asking for her consent and reassuring her was new since he kind of just took charge and led her everywhere. This, however, was better. It made her feel all fuzzy and warm inside.

She nodded her head. "I trust you."

And she meant it.

He graced her with a lazy grin that tugged on her heartstrings. He clearly cherished every time she told him those words.

They spent a few more minutes "star-gazing" and hand-holding before folding up the blanket and placing it back in the metal compartment. Liam made sure everything of Neera's was in the metal compartment, including her house key with the green heart attached to it, and latched the box close. Neera reached for the boat keys, but Liam stopped her.

"Keep them there so we don't lose them. I doubt anyone would want this old speedboat anyways," he claimed.

Neera, who didn't want to get in the way of his plans, simply nodded.

They left the dock and headed into town in search of the nearest motel. Surely a touristy town like this would provide them with some shelter. Neera didn't care where as long as it had a clean bed.

A few blocks away from the boating dock, they stumbled upon a gaudy motel with chipped flamingo pink paint coating the cement exterior and dollar-store neon lights strung about the entire building. A big, black sign stood tall in front of the vicinity, framed in neon-pink lights, that read "Venice Inn".

Ironically, no animal print in sight.

The parking lot was barren, with the exception of three vehicles, which Neera found as a plus. It was no skyrise building, expectantly, with only two floors and room doors on the outside. In case they needed to make a quick and dramatic escape.

As they strode down the sidewalk leading to the main entrance, Liam held Neera's hand and stopped walking, halting her in the process. He looked across the street and pointed to a red and white fast-food restaurant, his face just a bit brighter.

"Let's grab some burgers, bring them here, and then get some sleep. What do you think?" He asked lazily.

Neera's stomach growled in approval, hoping he didn't hear it.

"Sounds good."

They crossed the street and entered the establishment. The first thing that hit Neera was the smell of burgers grilling and fry grease, her mouth instantly salivating. She hadn't had a decent meal since lunch, and her dinner was small because she thought she would eat at the party.

Nevertheless, she was ready to grub.

The red and white interior provided Neera with a sense of familiarity and comfort. The place was packed with late-night partygoers who wanted to end the night with a greasy meal.

Neera sighed as she imagined her and Elayne ordering some burgers and laughing about how ridiculous Nate's party was. Trying to hold her sadness back, she focused on the menu on the wall in front of them.

She glanced at Liam, whose head was constantly swiveling like a service dog surveying their surroundings. Now that they were in proper lighting, she noticed that he was sporting large bags under his eyes, and his hair was a mess of loose curls. He looked like he hadn't slept in days. Guilt bubbled in her chest.

He had been constantly working hard to protect her,

even in this moment, and she had no idea how much all this had been taking a toll on him. She reached out and held his hand, tightening it, hoping she could convey how much she appreciated and supported him.

It's the two of us against the world.

After ordering two protein-style burgers–no buns, wrapped in lettuce–they immediately left after they received their food. Liam asked for a room for the night, which the aggressive front desk lady *happily* obliged, but he had to pay up-front for it.

Throughout the entire exchange, she eyed both of them with suspecting eyes and an unyielding amount of cigarette smoke. Neera tried to plaster on a fake smile to soothe the lady's suspicions, hoping the lady didn't call the police about a two, teenage runaways.

Then again, this place looked seedy enough for her to look the other way.

They received their singular key and headed back outside to go up the metal stairs scaling the motel. They entered the RM 222, and Liam flipped on the light to display a typical motel room, like the shady one prostitutes used in some movies Neera had no business stumbling upon.

There was a queen-sized bed in the middle of the room with one of those dirty walls directly behind it. The bed looked clean from Neera's perspective, but the ugly comforter and lopsided frame showed that the bed had some stories to share.

It consisted of the typical motel stuff: a chunky telly on the other side of the bed, a wooden desk in the corner, and a wooden nightstand next to the bed with a lamp, phone, and remote control.

Not exactly The Ritz, but at least she could rest her head. It had been hours of her plateauing stress, and she was hitting her wall.

Neera shuffled over to the bed while Liam scanned the room like a madman. She dropped onto it, dust puffing into the air and causing her to cough. Liam rushed to her side with their bag of food still in his hand and patted her back.

"Are you-" He started his own coughing fit. Their journey just began and they were already getting taken out by bed dust.

Neera jumped up and headed to the bathroom with her hand over her mouth. Turning on the light, the rusty bathroom came into view. She tried her best to ignore the cockroaches scattering underneath the bathroom cabinet and washed her hands.

Looking into the smudgy mirror, she took a careful breath, finally able to once she left the bed. From what she could see, her hair was frizzy and starting to change into her natural loose curls. She groaned in annoyance.

Hands thoroughly washed, Neera went back to the bed and Liam, who was staring out of the closed blinds, went inside. He shut the door, leaving Neera with the disgusting comforter. She scrunched her nose as she tossed the thing on the floor.

At least the sheets are white.

Neera spied an alarm clock on the other nightstand and turned on the radio. They needed something to cheer them up after a rough night. She might as well set the mood. Changing the stations, she landed on melodic violins and rhythmic thumping as the music filled the room.

"Be my mirror, my sword, my shield...my missionaries in a foreign field."

Liam reappeared from the bathroom with a lazy grin Neera knew was fake, and they ate their food without a word. They were both exhausted, but Liam definitely took the trophy.

He languidly ate his burger with an expressionless face. She wished she could see inside his head for once. He seemed to keep his cards close to his chest, and that was saying something since Neera was not the most open person.

Neera volunteered to throw away their trash in the waste bin at the far end of the room. When she got back, Liam was already laying on his stomach with his arms folded under his ear and his eyes closed. He looked so peaceful. Guilt finally overflowed in her chest as tears pricked the corners of her eyes.

Trying not to wake him, she carefully laid on her back next to him. So close to his face but leaving a foot of space between them. She took in his sleeping form and let the guilt flow.

An alluring voice resounded around the room as the radio played another song.

"You cut me open, and I...keep bleeding, bleeding love..."

The last two days they've been separated, Neera only thought horrible things about him. She cursed him, along with Elayne, when they first broke up and resented him when he came up with this plan to save her. The first night without him, she went to Elayne's house and ate a bunch of ice cream until she threw up the next morning. She repeatedly threw the green, squishy heart to the wall to see if it would crumble the same way he crushed her heart.

She couldn't even swim the pain away because she was afraid of turning.

In only two days, with how fast they were moving and how fast she fell for him, it felt like weeks of being separated. She had never felt like that with anyone, like someone sent him to her, and she had to hold onto him. If she didn't, he would slip right through her fingers and lose the very thing that person trusted her with.

The one thing connecting her to them. *To her.*

"I don't care what they say, I'm in love with you..."

Neera swallowed the emotions in her throat as a tear fell. She studied the popcorn ceiling and took deep breaths.

I love Liam. Always have.

This plan only solidified his place in her heart, like an astronaut stabbing the moon with a flag pole.

"Are you hurt?" A deep, groggy voice asked next to her.

Neera turned her head to Liam, his eyes so bowed they looked closed.

She swallowed again, trying to get herself together. She

quickly swiped her eyes with the sleeve on Liam's hoodie.

"I was just...just thinking about how you did all of this by yourself," she stammered, hoping the praise would distract him from her crying. She chuckled. "All this for 'little ole me'? You're more impressive than I thought."

He made a noise between a scoff and a snort. "You still think I'm just some rich kid, huh?" He tsked with a hint of a smile. "After all we've been through?"

Neera scoffed because she knew he was joking. "And you thought I was nerdy."

He shrugged his shoulders as if to say *touché.*

"I did all this to save you, of course, but I also did it to save myself," he confessed while his eyes never left Neera. "I needed to get away from him before...before I turned into him. Someone who would do anything to get ahead and care about nothing but his career, or status."

Neera's eyebrows scrunched in confusion. "I thought that's what you wanted? To protect your family and inherit the business."

Liam pondered a bit, his glassy eyes glancing around him in thought. They settled on Neera again, looking resigned. "Deep down, I never wanted to be like that. It just made sense. It was easy. Thanks to you...I was able to start fighting back and see that it was possible to be...anything else."

Neera took a minute to absorb everything. She even thought about their previous conversations to see if she missed anything. He seemed so...sure of himself. Well-put-together, smart, driven. The things she loved about him. To her, he always seemed faultless until their break-up.

Now that she really thought about it, he did seem reserved at first. Restrained. Like he was holding back something important. But he also seemed to become more relaxed in her presence. He laughed more and held her more than expected.

Although she loved his goal-oriented side, she loved his messy hair and corny jokes more. She loved his caring side, he always subconsciously helped people and took up for those more unfortunate. He probably didn't even know it.

Neera noticed.

He just needed the confidence to recognize his nuance and depth.

Neera decided to reveal how she felt about herself since he was being honest with her.

"At least you know your own potential. I still don't even know what I want to do with my life," she chewed on her bottom lip. "I'm not smart like you, and the only thing I've ever enjoyed was swimming, but as you can see, I can't even do that. So I decided to be a therapist like my dad."

They both remained quiet as their confessions marinated. Neera looked at Liam again, and his eyes were closed. Did he even hear her? She had no idea, but she wasn't angry.

She swiped another tear.

"You were never meant to fit in a square space when you're clearly a triangle," she murmured the truth. He was more than he believed, and she hoped all the brilliance he possessed found its rightful place in the world.

"And you're greater and more capable than you think," Liam mumbled, sleep dragging him deeper. "You were never meant to fit in a space in the first place."

Before Neera could quip about that sounding like a fat joke, his breathing evened out into a slight snore. Neera's heart swelled at his admission. She stroked his messy hair until the movement eventually lulled her into a deep sleep.

LIAM

Water sloshed against the shore, taking sand from underneath his sneakers and dragging the crystal particles into the deep blue ocean. The occasional squawk of a seagull sounded from afar. Other than that, he could only hear the waves...and Neera giggling next to his ear as he gave her a piggy-back ride along the shore.

The night they proclaimed their love for each other.

The night he would never forget.

The night Liam believed Neera was who he wanted to be with for the rest of his life. That nothing would tear him from her.

The moon guided their path down the beach as the breeze caressed their skin. He had goosebumps, but not just from Neera wearing his denim jacket and stealing his warmth. It was from the words she whispered in his ear.

Some things were innocent, like admitting her love for him. Other things were...

He looked over his shoulder at her blushing face. The freckles over her button nose replaced the stars in the galaxy. He was lost, but not really lost. He was content.

He returned her smile with as much love as he felt, but it wasn't enough. The weight of her arms around his neck provided comfort as strands of her curls tickled the side of his face.

Nothing could be more perfect.

Suddenly, the ground disappeared from under them. The world flashed past him, like a movie frame fast-forwarding to another scene. His mind barely caught up with the transition when everything finally settled.

He stood in the small cave within the island they were previously trapped in. Darkness surrounded him, aside from the moon peering down the hole at the top of it, shining a sliver of light into the small pool of water in front of him.

Something is missing.

There was no weight on his back, yet a tightness encompassed his neck. He reached up, touching his neck, and felt a leather collar around it with a metal loop in the back.

Liam started to panic, his breaths shallow and his heart rate skyrocketing.

"Neera!" *He called out to the darkness. No answer.*

He tried again.

"Don't you know when you call out to the dark, it answers

back," a deep, familiar chuckle echoed around him. Liam's muscles tensed, his adrenaline spiking.

"Where's Neera?" Liam gritted out. "What did you do to her?"

Liam couldn't pinpoint where the sound came from. It seemed to resound from every direction like it was in his head.

Like his own personal Hell.

"I didn't do anything yet," his father's voice laughed. "Besides, you're the one who brought her to me. Aren't we on the same side?"

Liam was tired of his voice. "If you touch Neera, I swear–"

"You swear what?!" His father's voice boomed. "What do you think you can do to me? Do you think you can abandon our family? Abandon me?"

"I'm nothing like you," Liam growled.

His father laughed harshly. "No, but you want to be. You're just the weaker version. Worthless, pathetic, and treacherous."

Liam tried to ignore the sting in his chest as his insults punctured his heart like needles.

Who cares what he thinks? He's just trying to get under my skin.

As if he read his mind, Dan's voice uttered a low growl. "To disgrace your whole bloodline for an experiment that you end up putting in danger anyway is idiotic. Even for you."

Liam covered his ears. Anything to block out his incessant verbal jabs.

This is all a dream. A nightmare. He can't hurt me or Neera.

A muffled scream shook his core. He removed his hands from his ears. Neera's raspy screams emanated from the pool, but he couldn't see anything in it.

"Leave her alone!" He yelled to the darkness and the still water in front of him. Her cries sounded wet like she was choking on liquid. His body was in full-on fight mode, ready to tear his father to pieces.

"Liam, please help me," she gasped. "He's hurting me."

His fingers tangled in his hair as he swiveled around, looking for something, anything to help. His knees gave out at her screams as he internally curled into himself.

He felt...helpless.

"Please stop," Liam weakly croaked.

Dan's chuckle grated his skin. "That's better. Know your place."

Liam clenched his jaw in protest, head down as her cries faded away. He would do anything to take her pain away.

"Here's some fatherly advice, son. If you want to be a strong man, you have to know when to sacrifice."

Liam's nails dug into his palms. He couldn't remember the last time his father had ever sacrificed anything for him or his family. Dan only commanded, and people followed his will. The person Liam looked up to the most would never have to sacrifice because he always got what he wanted. He never truly fought for anything, not even the love of his children.

A clinking *sound appeared from behind him as if a lock clicked in place. The collar around his neck tightened, and as much as Liam wanted to fear it, he was too accustomed to it that he barely noticed.*

"Now, let's try this again," his father's voice darkly distorted. Neera's screams in agony filled the small space. This time louder. Closer.

Liam's fists twitched as he stared at the pool of water before him, her cries now rippling the water. He felt powerless. He wanted to fight back, to do something, but he exhausted all his options.

I'm not capable of protecting anyone.

"I didn't name you Liam for nothing," a voice chimed from within. It sounded a lot like his mom, causing his eyes to water. If someone should lecture him about sacrifices, it should definitely be his mom.

His mom might've been an enabler, however, she gave up her whole life to be with his father. She had him when she was young and never went back to school to do what she wanted. Her life had been for her children. She had always been a housewife and stay-

at-home parent.

Apparently, she named Liam, despite Dan's wishes to make him a junior, because it was her one act of rebellion. His name was important to her and she always wanted her first son to have it. That, in itself, was a sacrifice.

His mom was a fighter.

Since half of his genes came from her, that would make him a fighter, too.

Liam's heart pumped with newfound strength as his body tensed for battle.

"A strong man...knows how to sacrifice," Liam uttered aloud, mainly to himself.

He shuffled to get up, but whatever was attached to the stupid collar pulled him back down, practically strangling him. It yanked back, but Liam held his neck still. It was a mystery that his neck didn't break. His eyes bulged, his face flushing from the pressure. His arms flailed as he fought against the sinister force, refusing to be dragged into its dark depths.

He was escaping something older, stronger, and formidable.

"Know your place!" Dan demanded again over Neera's screams.

Liam squeezed his fingers into the centimeter gap between his neck and the collar, allowing him a second of reprieve. With one knee up and the other scraping against the ground, he stretched his neck forward.

"Go...to...Hell," Liam strained out.

With a grunt, he lunged and dove into the small pool that he knew wouldn't save Neera. He knew it would undoubtedly kill him.

But at least he would be free.

Sunlight spilled into the room from the slits in the blinds. Liam dragged his forearm over his eyes to block out the annoying brightness.

He felt like he was up for hours. The nightmare came at the one time he actually needed sleep. His body shivered at the memory.

Of the guilt, the torture, and the idea of his father being

that evil. There was no reason for that dream to be that metal...
unless it was a message.

I'm never eating fast food before bed again.

Too tired to look deeper into it, he begrudgingly raised
his arm off his face and into the air as he peered at his sports
watch.

11:18 am. *Shit.*

Liam hauled his body into a sitting position, stretching
his arms up high. He overslept. He was only supposed to nap
for three hours, so he could prepare for tomorrow's trip: fill up
the gas tank, buy disguises, and grab train tickets to Napa. It
was fine that he was a little behind as long as he completed
everything off his to-do list.

Besides, the extra time was for him and Neera to spend
time together without the pressure of having to skip town. He
just had to cut down on their free time.

While scratching his jaw stubble, he glanced at the other
side of the bed, expecting to see Neera, but only an empty space
greeted him back. His scratching hand ceased.

Slightly alarming, but she could be in the bathroom. He
got up and pushed open the already-ajar door.

Nothing.

Now completely alarmed, his hands ran through his
waves as he tried not to full-blown panic. He paced the room,
his thoughts growing darker with each second that she was
gone. She could be in trouble, and he would have no way of
contacting her.

*What if Dan snuck in and grabbed her without him
noticing?*

*What if the chain-smoking employee was in on it? Or ratted
them out?*

How did he find where they were staying?

I can hear his deep voice snickering in my head.

Liam gripped the back of his neck as he shook his head.
The sound of the door unlocking pulled him out of his spiral.
He stopped abruptly near the door, ready to defend himself.

His curly-haired girlfriend nonchalantly entered the room, cradling two Pop-Tart packages, a bottle of orange juice, and an energy drink in her arms.

He sprang on her, gripping her shoulders while giving her a once-over. Once he established it was really Neera; he pulled her into his embrace as a relieving sigh escaped his lips.

She's here. She's okay.

He peeled himself away from their awkward hug.

"I thought..." His mutter trailed off when the worry subsided, leaving him annoyed. "You should've told me where you were going."

Neera rolled her eyes. *Rolled them!*

Stomping over to the bed, she tossed her stash onto it, the items slightly bouncing. She sharply turned to him with her arms crossed over her chest.

"You were knocked out," her tone very much irked. "I thought I could help you, at least, by getting breakfast. I had ten dollars crumpled in my pocket."

His admiration was quickly snuffed out by his worry, his hand still glued to the back of his neck. He needed her to see that their whole situation was serious and they couldn't afford to split up.

"Still, Angel. You should've left a note or something," his voice subconsciously rose. "We're on the run. Anything could've happened!"

Neera gave him an incredulous look and scoffed.

Scoffed!

She stomped over to her side of the bed, picked up a napkin, and tossed it on the bed. Liam watched it listlessly fall on the sheet before grabbing it. He flipped it over; something scribbled on it.

BRB. GRABBING US SOME GRUB DOWNSTAIRS!
LOVE, N

Liam's ears overheated. He ran a hand over his face

and cringed. He was being ridiculous, acting like her dad. Reluctantly lifting his eyes to hers, Neera smirked while shaking her head.

"Forget what I said last night. You're definitely a square."

Still embarrassed yet relieved there were no hard feelings, Liam picked up his pillow and gently tossed it at her chest.

"It's not my fault your writing is trash," he laughed.

Her mouth dropped. Then she chucked the pillow back at his head, a little rougher than he would like. She giggled at the way his head fell back.

"Shut up and enjoy the lovely breakfast I prepared for you."

They both ate their breakfast, making fun of each other's messy appearances. When they finished, Neera went to take a shower while Liam waited for her to finish.

Like a good Christian boy.

He refrained from telling her about his dream and how much it unnerved him, even though he wished he could share it and see if she also experienced something similar.

His mind away from a naked Neera, he thought about their next steps. Mr. Ran should be in Napa Valley at this time, so he needed to contact him to make sure he was okay. This brought him back to his father.

Liam had recently been two steps ahead of his father, and the man wasn't some average man. Instead of bringing Liam comfort in his capabilities, it only made him more paranoid. He was just waiting for the other shoe to drop. A large part of him didn't think his plan should be going this smoothly. Not because of his intellect but because of how much his father knew him.

He finished the last of his energy drink, the false boost giving him enough confidence to get through the day. Neera reappeared, her natural sea-breeze scent mixed with the generic soap permeated the room. Liam diverted his eyes from her towel-clad and slightly moist body while heading straight to the bathroom without looking back.

Liam emerged from his much-needed shower to find—unfortunately—a fully dressed Neera. She was lying down on the bed with her legs bent over the edge, facing up at the ceiling with her arms crossed under her chest. Her puzzled face turned to Liam, her eyes sweeping his towel-clad waist and dripping hair before jerking her head back to the ceiling. Her face rose-tinted, and her lips pouty; he attempted to ignore her while he stood on the opposite side and got dressed.

He tied his hoodie sleeves around his waist before laying in the opposite direction as her, his face inches from hers.

"We should probably call your dad's phone and update him so he's not worried," Liam suggested. He stared at her lips subconsciously. Before she could question how, Liam added. "We can use a store phone or a pay phone if we find a quarter."

Neera nodded, returning her gaze to the ceiling. Her face seemed distant despite them being only six inches away from each other. Mentioning her dad left her teary-eyed, but he didn't confront her about it.

They left the motel room. Liam returned the key to the coughing woman, who snatched her key and dismissively looked the other way, which was fine. He'd trade customer service skills for confidentiality any day.

Strolling down the boardwalk, the couple took in the scenery. Summer in Venice Beach was not only extremely sunny but overwhelmingly crowded. This only worsened Liam's paranoia. He was constantly on the lookout for any suspicious-looking people, which was ironic because out of all the vibrantly clothed tourists, he was the only one sporting all black.

Sure his father wasn't the president or some hot-shot politician, but he was wealthy with connections and pretty famous. After the dream he had, it wouldn't be astute to underestimate him.

Liam couldn't even enjoy himself, but the look of fascination on her face made it a little more bearable. As they walked the boardwalk, she would point to a random sculpture or artwork spray-painted across a wall or skate park ramp. Her face would light up as she stopped frequently at different plaques or looked through street viewfinders. To be honest, they could be in Antarctica, and he would still enjoy himself as long as he got to bask in her smile.

They stopped in front of a tourist stand packed with Venice Beach merchandise that most people would see when on vacation: T-shirts, tote bags, magnets, and other touristy junk. It seemed like the perfect place to pick up some disguises.

As his eyes roamed the cluttered stand, he spotted Neera tracing her fingers over the letters across a cap. The white *I LOVE VENICE BEACH* letters contrasted the green and blue tie-dye swirling pattern, giving it a fun and earthy look. Unfortunately, Neera would stick out like a sore thumb.

Liam checked out the row of sunglasses, picking up two neon green sunglasses–to hide in plain sight, obviously. He circled to the front of the stand where a balding man was finishing another transaction, never taking his eyes off Neera. When it was Liam's turn, he greeted him while holding up the two sunglasses.

"I'll take these two sunglasses," he muttered. While the man calculated the price, Liam glanced at a smiling Neera trying on the hat in the tiny mirror installed into the side of the stand. He pointed to the hat on her head. "And that too."

The man glanced back, grinned, and told him the price for everything. *Thirty-eight dollars!*

Liam clenched his fists, ready to deck the scammer in the face, but took a deep breath. With pursed lips, he shoved a fifty-dollar bill in his hand. The greedy bastard smiled and gave Liam his change back.

"You two make a wonderful couple," the scammer cheesed.

He was lucky they were in hiding, or else he would've stolen the plastic items.

With the glasses in his hand, Liam strolled over to an

unsuspecting Neera posing in the mirror. Just as she lifted the hat off her head with a pout, he placed it back on her head, turning it sideways so the brim faced her left side.

"It looks good on you," Liam pushed a few stray curls away from her face. "You should keep it."

Neera stuck her tongue out teasingly. "It's okay. We don't have much money anyway. Maybe next time." She took the hat off again.

Liam held in his laugh while, once again, taking the cap and placing it back on top of her voluminous curls. This time, with the brim facing backward.

She giggled, and his chest swelled.

"It's yours. I bought it," he reassured. He placed one of the pairs of sunglasses gently over her eyes, making sure the ends didn't get trapped in her hair. Putting the other pair on himself, Liam posed in front of her with his chin in the cleft between his thumb and pointer finger. "How do I look?"

She snorted, and the sound was forever embedded in his mind. Neera shook her head yet looped her arm in his. The gesture warmed him more than the mid-afternoon sun.

"Like my partner-in-crime," she chuckled.

Liam couldn't help the smile beaming across his face, one that was so big and genuine that his cheeks heated instead of ached.

This is what true happiness is, huh?

He cleared his throat to keep down his excitement. They had to focus. His stomach growled because it just so happened to be the perfect time for it to do so. Scanning the crowded boardwalk and line of restaurants, his eyes landed on another brightly-colored, possibly inconspicuous, pizza joint. They couldn't go wrong with pizza.

He smiled down at Neera and jutted his head behind him towards the building.

"You want a slice, Bonnie?"

She sighed, almost in relief, and nodded.

"That breakfast was a bit disappointing." She raised her

hands innocently. "I have to admit, not my best."

He wrapped his arm around her shoulders, pulling her into his side. "At least you finally admitted it."

Liam loved how she could always calm his nerves with her easy-going personality. Most girls he knew would be a blubbering mess if they were in her position, and that would only further unnerve him.

Not Neera.

She had no idea how her presence grounded him and simultaneously comforted him like an emergency blanket. The whole time Liam had been spending every ounce of his energy protecting her, Neera was saving him from self-destruction.

An emergency raft to his sinking ship.

"You'll have plenty of chances to redeem yourself for that subpar meal," he wryly smiled.

Her laugh tickled his eardrums. She unwrapped his arm from around her shoulders and gripped his hand, interlocking the fingers. Neera pulled him towards the glass doors of the pizza joint, completely unaware of the electricity sparking through her touch.

"Enough talk, Ramsay. Lunch is on you. Plus, I'm craving some water."

TREACHEROUS SEAS

Chapter 20

Neera

Being with Liam helped me forget all my troubles. Well, almost.

Neera had almost forgotten what it felt like to be a normal girl until she spent time exploring Venice Beach with Liam. The place was not as urban as she thought it would be, which she was grateful for.

Small, colorful shops lined the boardwalk. Crowds of people gathered around beautiful murals, skate parks, and fascinating sculptures. It was like Pasa Verde, except with more exciting things to do. Before she even knew it, she was a full-blown tourist and wanted to explore every inch of the sunny place. And she wouldn't have wanted to do it with anyone else but Liam.

Instead of a scary undercover mission, it felt more like a vacation. Liam did most of the work and looked out for her the entire time. The extra layer of surveillance allowed Neera to relax and be herself. Secretly, she was into feeling like the president's daughter with her very own bodyguard.

At first, having to rely on him for everything made her feel guilty, dependent, and fragile, but the more he asked for her permission and kept her in the loop, the more it felt like they were on a getaway. Just them.

They were a team.

Every minute with him made her appreciate him more, and that a future with him didn't sound too bad. Her cheeks heated at the thought of a family with him.

Shaking the hasty idea away, they strolled hand-in-hand into the establishment. Typically Neera wouldn't eat much, preferring a gallon of water instead, but the additional stress from her predicament left her starved. The tarts and orange juice burned immediately through her metabolism, leaving her craving some cheesy goodness and, well, a bottle of water.

The smell of garlic and parmesan cheese immediately caressed her nostrils, her mouth instantly watering. The pizza pies lined up in front of them looked delicious. Luckily for them, the place was nearly empty, with a few patrons seated near the large windows. Neera would've been suspicious of them if they didn't seem so uninterested in their arrival, despite her and Liam looking like a pair of stoners.

If Liam wasn't worried, then Neera wouldn't be.

Neera pointed to a delectable, thin-crusted cheese pie on an elevated tray. One slice was like three dollars! Way too much, especially after the purchases Liam made earlier. As much as her heart soared at his attentive and compassionate heart, Neera knew they were low on funds by the way his jaw clenched at the price tags.

They had more important things to worry about if they were planning on staying longer and definitely not splurging on "couple" items–no matter how cute he was in them.

Neera looked back at Liam with a grin. "Let's share a slice. I'm not that hungry."

Liam's eyebrows shot up.

"But I'm so thirsty, I'll need at least two bottles of water," Neera added.

Still puzzled, he asked, "Are you sure you don't want your own slice?"

I would eat the entire pie right now if I could, but water is only a dollar.

She gave him a tight smile. "Yeah. If you want, you can have some of my water since I'm feeling quite generous."

Liam scrunched his straight nose, yet his grin was wide as he nodded. "Deal."

He told the middle-aged man, with a hairnet over a full head of black hair and a welcoming face, behind the counter their order: one cheese slice and two bottles of water. The man rang them up as he wiped his bushy brow with his wrist, his stare a little longer than Neera liked.

Maybe some of Liam's paranoia is starting to rub off on me.

While they waited for their pizza, they headed to an empty booth with their waters, a booth far away from the other seated patrons. Liam briefly left and returned with their large slice of pizza, definitely bigger than the one she pointed at earlier, but she was not going to complain.

After they removed their shades and right as she was about to dive in, Liam closed his eyes and bowed his head. Neera halted.

Should I do the same thing? Would it matter?

Neera and her family were never religious; thus, praying was foreign to her. But clearly, it was important to Liam, so she copied him. It wasn't like it would do more harm than good, and she needed all the help she could get.

Her hand held one of his outstretched ones across the booth. His palm was warm in hers. Then she held onto her necklace with the other, as she knew no one else to ask for protection. The jewel had been the only thing to give her inner strength, instant relief from her panic attacks, and kept her sane from the insanity of her life.

When Neera opened her eyes, Liam's soft gaze was already on her. She felt tingly from her head to her toes–not in a "creepy stalker" way, but a favorite "hot cocoa" way.

She hastily downed a bottle of water, hoping the coolness would flush out her heated cheeks. Liam smirked and crudely split the slice, digging into his portion. Neera followed suit, enjoying the present with him.

After choking down her slice and giving her crust to Liam, who appreciated the extra calories, they both used the bathroom in tandem. When Neera emerged, he held her hand, and they walked back to the cash register. The man didn't greet them at first as he restocked napkins in a tiny holder. Only when Liam cleared his throat the man lifted his head to acknowledge them.

"Hello again, sir," Liam greeted professionally. "If it's not too much trouble, can we use your phone to call our parents? I lost mine, and hers died."

"No phones, huh," the man's voice dripped with an Italian accent as he wiped his brow with his wrist. "Sounds, uh, unlucky."

Liam chuckled like a millionaire. "I guess so. I promise we will be quick, sir. Just want to let them know we're okay."

The man peered between them. Neera decided to nod pleadingly to add to the effect. However, Liam's confident request might've countered her begging stance.

"Sure," the man acquiesced, pointing to the gray landline in the corner behind the counter. "Press one first."

They rounded the long counter and stood in front of the phone. Liam shot her a *go-ahead* look.

All she had to do was call her dad, let him know of her wellbeing, and they could move on. Seeing the phone, the thing that had the time displayed, brought her back to reality again.

To the reason they were there in the first place.

With a trembling hand, Neera picked up the phone. Her heart raced with every button she pressed, her nerves coiling more than the phone cord. As much as she cared about her dad's wellbeing, she couldn't help the anxiety crawling up her spine. She barely noticed Liam's hand gripping hers, his touch grounding her.

She squeezed his hand back as the phone rang. And rang. And rang.

The ringing abruptly cut, replaced with silence on the

other end.

"Dad?" Neera implored.

No answer.

Her heart never lost speed.

Why isn't he speaking? Is he okay?

Instead of hearing a velvety British-accented voice, she heard a familiar, gruff American one.

"Hello, Neera. I would appreciate it if you put my son on the phone."

Neera swallowed the lump in her throat.

Mr. Dern.

Why does he have my dad's phone?

"Mist-mist–" Neera stammered, still in shock.

"Yes. It's me, Neera." His voice made her stomach churn. "I need to tell my son that he's doing a fine job keeping you company until I come to get you. He knows how important you are for our business, so I asked him to keep this discreet."

Liam was standing in front of her with his shades off, eyes full of concern. She refused to look him in the eye.

Mr. Dern is lying. There's no way. I refuse to believe he would do something like that.

"How..." her voice trailed off, losing its confidence.

"How?" Mr. Dern interjected. "How did I know? Or how did I get Garran's phone?"

Neera released Liam's hand and bit her lip, waiting for him to speak.

"My son is pretty smart. He kept you away from your father, leaving him vulnerable enough for us to...*keep* him from leaving. If you want him to be safe, I suggest you come back to the island. That's the only way you can ensure his safety."

Neera was properly irate. His calm and arrogant demeanor only roiled her stomach in disgust. She flicked her eyes between Liam and the phone. Whether this was all part of his dad's plan or not, his dad had intentionally hurt hers and was threatening her through the phone.

Her mind racked through the past fifteen hours, looking for any signs of betrayal or underhandedness. He had always been attentive to her...but what if that was to keep her complacent while they moved to the next step of their diabolical plan?

Was her dad even on his way to Napa Valley?

I don't know what to believe.

"What about me?" Neera emphasized. Her eyelids burned from holding back tears.

"If you're safe? I can't guarantee that, per se," he responded as if she asked him about bloody brunch. "Your father, however, depends on how quickly you get here. Now... give my son the phone."

Neera ripped the phone from her ear, ready to slam it into the receiver, but halted. She shoved the phone into Liam's chest, unable to look him in the eye. When he grabbed the phone with a confused look, she stood behind him with her arms wrapped around her body.

Why is it that every time I put my trust in him, I regret it? Every time!

Neera didn't even hear their conversation as her mind raced. Her adrenaline pumped through her veins, compelling her to get away from him. To save her dad on her own.

She had to do it herself, because that was the only person strong enough to take Mr. Dern down.

Liam was holding her back the entire time for whatever reason. It all trickled down to his lack of trust in her. He was too close to his dad. He basically idolized him for most of his life, and suddenly, he just flipped a switch to resenting him. It did not make sense to Neera.

She had to handle this situation on her own.

While Liam was facing away from her, Neera booked it out the door. Her breathing was erratic, her steps unsure as she tried to retrace her steps to the dock. The song from their break-up corrupted her brain as she headed to the motel.

"So you put on quite a show...really had me going."

The memories of the hotel flooded her head: their silent contentment, a shirtless Liam, their late-night confessions. Instead of swelling her heart, it sat in her stomach like coal. No flame of passion or burning love, just a cold lump of regret.

I have to save my dad.

She ripped her eyes from the memories and ran a few more blocks towards the dock that was now alive with people. Some people gawked at her, probably because she looked mad in her neon shades and gladiator shoes. Thoroughly upset, she wrenched the shades off and tossed them in a waste bin.

Neera remembered his speedboat was parked between two medium-sized boats, but that could've changed. She stalked down the dock, looking for a smallish, rusty speedboat with a black stripe down the middle.

After what felt like forever, she found it in between a medium-sized boat and a larger one. The space was tight, but there was enough room to squeeze out of the space. She carefully stepped into the boat, trying not to rock it.

The breeze flowed past her raw nerves as she turned the key that was still in the ignition. Going to the motor, she yanked the cord immediately after. Nothing happened. She ran back to the ignition and turned it again, then sprinted back to the motor, yanking it with all her might.

Still nothing.

Her hope was dwindling with every attempt. She should've known it wasn't going to be so easy with how it acted the night they left.

What if it died? What if she was stuck?

Panic took over as her breaths shallowed and her heart raced. She paced the boat, clutching her necklace. Slowly, her mind defogged, and she straightened her spine, ready to try again. She had to try.

She took one more deep breath and got ready to turn the key, putting all her faith in it.

"Hey!" A masculine voice called from behind her.

Neera's eyes bulged.

Instead of every muscle in her body telling her to high-tail it out of there, she turned her body towards the sound and saw Liam's heavily breathing body. His glasses were gone, and his hair was sticking up in all directions. His hoodie was nowhere to be found. With his shirt askew, he looked like a fugitive.

They stared at each other in a wordless conversation. Neera could see the regret in his face, the hurt and the helplessness. She saw his vulnerability, all that he was, at that moment.

It doesn't change what he's done to me and my family.

He broke eye contact and began untying the boat from the dock. He tossed the rope into the boat, landing with a *thud*. Still crouched, he held onto the motor cord and gazed back at her. Neera took the hint and turned the key, her eyes never leaving his.

He yanked hard...and the engine purred. *How convenient.*

He slowly rose, then placed his hands in his pockets, watching the boat inch away from the pier. Neera was afraid to move a muscle. Afraid to tear her eyes from him.

Her heart ached at his betrayal, but it also ached at his solemn and exhausted face. She continued to drift away from him as if the air itself was separating them and reminding her of her duty.

His usually bright hazel eyes, which reminded her of a forest on a sunny day, were currently darker and flooded with tears that never fell.

"I'm sorry I couldn't protect you and your family," Liam quavered. "Be careful, Angelfish. Hopefully, we'll meet again in another life."

Emotions piled onto Neera, weighing her down and keeping her frozen.

Why does he have to confuse me so much? Why does it feel like I'm tearing a piece of myself when we separate?

Neera ripped her gaze away from him and focused on the

water in front of her. It was difficult to see without her glasses and the tears blurring her vision, but she still managed to find the accelerator that she had witnessed Liam use.

She sped off in the direction they came, hopefully following the coast would prevent her from getting stranded at sea. The island should be the only landmass directly across from the mainland.

The boat eased down the coast as the early evening sun beamed down on her, completely unaware of her world falling apart. The sky was quite clear and crisp, oblivious to the storm raging within her. The wind whipped through her hair, knocking her cap off her head.

A teeny part of her wanted to turn back, to run back into Liam's arms, but the logical part of her knew the only arms she should run into were her dad's.

LIAM

"Mist-Mist," Neera stammered next to Liam, then immediately pursed her lips.

Liam watched her eyebrows hike up like she was receiving devastating news, and this caused his mind to race.

Did something happen to Mr. Ran? All he had to do was go to the train station, catch the train, and meet up with them in the nearest hotel. There shouldn't be an issue.

Unless...his father is more ruthless than he calculated.

All Liam could do was watch Neera's breathing shallow and her lips thin in disgust. Her hand that he held to strengthen her went limp as the seconds ticked on. He wished he could read her eyes and see what was torturing her.

Suddenly, she ripped her hand from his grasp and clenched her fist as if his mere touch burned.

This alarmed him.

Whoever was on the other end was definitely not her dad. The longer she remained on the phone, the more Liam had to fight the urge to snatch the phone from her and demand the person on the other end to *fuck off.*

Neera practically shoved the phone at him with thin lips. Gratefully ready to curse out whoever was on the other end, Liam grabbed the phone, and she immediately stood behind him, like being in his line of sight pained her.

Something is totally wrong.

Liam, upset from her retraction, gritted into the phone.

"I know this isn't Mr. Ran, so who the fuck–"

"You should watch your mouth, son," Dan's gritty voice spat into his ear. "Let's not waste time. Hand over the girl, or I'll have to deal with Garran myself."

Liam's mouth thinned as his neck burned in pure rage.

Honestly, Liam wasn't surprised that Dan found him since every time he had an ounce of happiness, Dan was always right around the corner to destroy it. Liam was more upset at Dan resorting to violence against Mr. Ran to get his point across, supposedly someone who was a friend to him.

Was Mr. Ran really a friend? Did Dan even have friends?

Nevertheless, Liam was fed up. All the respect he had for the man was out of the window, and he would curse him out more if it didn't possibly lead to harming Mr. Ran.

Liam took a deep breath to calm his rage. If he kept him on the phone, the more likely Mr. Ran could get help or escape.

"How did you find him?" Liam inquired, trying to sound nonchalant.

Dan chuckled darkly, the sound grating Liam's ears. "I'll tell you all about it when you BOTH come to the island."

Wait. Mr. Ran should already be in Napa. Is he bluffing?

Liam quirked an eyebrow. "Why would we go back when we're almost in Napa."

Liam tried to throw him off his location, hopefully, to goat him into a confession.

"I know you're in Venice, son. Don't play coy."

Liam swallowed the lump in his throat as his eyes lifted to the large windows of the pizza spot, scanning the clusters of tourists roaming the boardwalk. He was confident that they weren't being watched and made sure that no one knew where they were headed.

Every one of his fears emerged one by one as he realized Mr. Ran had never made it out of Pasa Verde. Dan forced the information out of Mr. Ran, somehow, since he was the only one to know their plan because it was the only way for Mr. Ran to corroborate with him. Dan got a hold of his phone and waited for the opportunity of Neera's call. He knew she would be frazzled, but he didn't know about the trust they'd built with each other over the last fifteen hours.

Liam's gears whirred. Maybe he could risk using his mom's card to book a flight to Washington. That way, they could find a cabin to stay in until they could get the police involved. He ran a shaky hand through his hair in frustration.

As if Dan could read his thoughts, he rasped rapidly. "You may be thinking of leaving the state, but you don't want a missing person's report on you both. Then you'll have to deal with not just me chasing you." His voice lowered. "Who knows how long Mr. Ran will last until then? The choice is yours, Lee."

Before Liam could curse his grandmother, he noticed Dan's voice was rushed, as if his impatience had worsened. He dropped his mask. If Dan was losing his cool, that meant he was either bluffing or he was being pressured, too.

He didn't have the upper hand Liam thought he had.

Liam rolled his shoulders and declared. "I'd rather take my chances with the cops than you."

Dan was silent for a minute, unnerving Liam in the process. In a cool tone, one that ran a shiver down Liam's spine, he disclosed, "I don't know if your little *girlfriend* will approve. She already thinks you set everything up. You intentionally separated her from her father and confirmed your location."

He shook his head. *No.*

Liam snapped from the insinuation. *She would never believe that.*

"Don't you fucking dare put this shit on me!" He barked

into the phone, surely disturbing the nice employee.

"No, don't you *fucking dare*," Dan sneered, revealing his true self. The man he feared the most.

Arrogant prick.

"You tried so hard to come into your own and run away from the inevitable, but you ended up being just like–"

Liam slammed the phone on the receiver, tempted to rip it from its plug and toss it across the restaurant. The place felt smaller. More cramped. Reality slapped him in the face at the realization that he wasn't smarter or clever than his father. Dan was more ruthless, and he, unfortunately, was correct about Liam running from his future.

But he had Neera. Neera would keep him afloat.

After spending time with each other, Liam was sure of their trusting relationship. They were a team. Unstoppable together. Even if Dan lied about this being all Liam's idea, he knew Neera wouldn't believe such a lie, especially from a notorious liar like his father.

All they had to do was cut this trip short and catch a flight to Washington, where she would be safe, and Liam could find a way to get the police to look into his father's business. Maybe he could convince his mom to do a wellness check on Mr. Ran.

Liam spun around to reassure her of the new plan.

She was gone. *Gone!*

Alarm bells rang in his head. *Where did she go?*

Then, realization slammed into him like a defensive lineman.

She left. She's headed back to save her dad. She actually believed him.

He thought back to her conversation on the phone. The way Neera looked disgusted and yanked her hand away from his hand. She actually believed Liam would put her in harm's way, and she was devastated. She was hurt. Betrayed...by something that wasn't even true.

Not wasting any more time and avoiding the aching

disappointment that threatened to consume him, Liam bolted to the docks. His body felt lighter as his hoodie fell from his strides. He tossed the shades that hindered his focus onto the ground, tossing the feelings embedded inside with them. His anger with his father fueled him to keep moving, or else he would drop.

He had to meet her. He had to tell her that he was lying and that he had been protecting her. That there was another way to help her dad.

As Liam passed several awaiting boats at the docks, he spotted Neera with puffy eyes trying to start his uncle's boat. The look on her face was...heartbreaking.

That's the face of someone who'd been utterly betrayed and had enough.

Liam desperately wanted to run to her and pull her from the boat. To tell her how much she meant to him and that he would never do anything to harm her.

But he couldn't help her. Her dad was in danger because of him. She had to be on the run because of him. He wasn't even sure if his mom was neutral enough to confide in her to help them. His father was too cunning. He was always a step ahead of Liam, no matter what he did.

Liam should've never underestimated him. His steps slowed.

"No, but you want to be...You're just the weaker version. Worthless, pathetic, and treacherous." His father's voice echoed in his mind from the nightmare.

He was right. Liam should've stayed away from Neera the day she asked him out. He should've never asked her to dance. He should've left her alone. Then she wouldn't have such pain on her face.

It's all your fault for trying to be more than what you're supposed to be.

Liam decided to let Neera go in his heart. He couldn't hold onto her. He couldn't be a Dern and love Neera at the same time. It was an impossible play. He could, however, defend her from his father doing any more damage.

"If you want to be a strong man, you have to know when to sacrifice."

Liam clenched his fists in his pockets as he watched Neera speed off, increasing their distance, with not so much as a goodbye. He didn't blame her. Pretty sure his father told her all kinds of bullshit about him. It was actually wise of her to leave by herself, as much as he hated to admit it. He wouldn't put it past Dan to send some secret retrieval squad to capture them and bring them there before sunset.

In the meantime, Liam needed another way to get to that island. Fast.

He swept the crowded dock for a solution. There was a rental shack a few feet down, but he definitely couldn't afford to rent anything with the card he was now sure was frozen.

Next to the empty space that his boat occupied was a rowboat with oars splayed lazily inside. Probably an emergency raft. It will take him forever to get there with that.

He sighed heavily with a hand rummaging through his hair, losing hope by the second. Taking a chance, Liam turned to some people on the other end and started heading to them. They were climbing aboard, so he picked up the pace, nearly sprinting.

The closer he got, the more he was able to make out their features. One of them was a middle-aged, severely tanned man with an exaggerated captain's hat. Clearly, the driver. The couple climbing aboard looked older. The man's gray hair glowed in the sun and wisped in the breeze. His brown designer shoes matched his navy blue and white linen outfit. The older woman had a decent jet-black dye job, with make-up covering her sun-kissed skin. The couple looked retired, ready to sail around the world and feed grapes to each other.

Right up my alley. Liam was used to schmoozing up to rich folks.

Skidding to a stop in front of the boat, Liam quickly fixed his hair and adjusted his shirt. He cleared his throat.

"Hello, there!" He plastered on his winning smile. "Can I speak with you for a moment?"

Everyone on the boat turned in his direction with suspicious looks, except for the driver, who was preoccupied with the boat's controls. Liam, used to the attention, straightened his shoulders. His voice became sturdier and confident.

"If you're heading South, I was wondering if you could drop me off at the island near Pasa Verde? My boat was stolen, and I have no way of getting back. I'm in a bit of a hurry."

They paused for a minute and stared at each other, probably having their own silent conversation. Liam couldn't blame them for not assisting him since he was a stranger, and in his all-black, he didn't exactly scream, "I'm totally here for a leisure sail." He didn't have time to be understanding since he had so little of it to rescue Neera.

His smile widened in, hopefully, sincerity.

The man regarded Liam and uttered dismissively, "We're headed North. Sorry, kid."

Liam's smile faltered as he strategized another idea, but with how dejected he was currently from the past ten minutes, his hopes sank hard into the sea. This was his only way of getting there in time. His last shot. He analyzed the couple, hoping to find anything that could pull on their heartstrings.

His eyes lingered on their wedding bands and then glanced at the woman's disappointed face. He decided to give them a half-truth and play up the sympathy.

"Please? I'm not much of a beggar, but I really need your help," Liam scrunched up his face in agony and softened his tone. "I was going to propose to my girlfriend over there. Her family and friends are waiting for me. You see, we've been dating for a while, and I don't want to disappoint her father."

Of course, most of this was a lie. Well, maybe the proposal date. He had previously planned to make her his wife one day, as crazy as that sounded.

You already blew up that chance.

He pushed the negativity out and performed a fake sob. "I don't even have my phone because it was onboard."

The wife's face scrunched in pity as she frowned at her husband.

"Look, Harold," she whined. "He's trying to surprise his love. He even looks to be the same age as you were."

Harold, Liam presumed, considered his wife's plea. He seemed to be mulling it over. Coming to some sort of conclusion, he gave her the tiniest smile on the planet. She grabbed his bicep and gave him what Liam knew very well as "the eyes" as she continued. "We have all day to go to Napa."

Liam choked down the irony, waiting for Harold's answer in anticipation. His heart beat feverishly, but he tried his hardest not to show it, hoping the couple didn't see right through his lie. He also hoped the man wouldn't ask to see the non-existent ring.

He silently pleaded to God for mercy. He'd even take pity. Pride wasn't available at the moment and hadn't been for a while.

Harold gave a thoughtful grunt, surveying Liam one more time before motioning him on board with the flick of a wrist. Liam thanked him continuously until Harold walked over to the driver, probably informing him of the change in plans.

The driver looked annoyed, shooting Liam death glares, but since his guests were paying, he conceded. His wife smiled genuinely at her husband, a wrinkled hand rubbing his back.

Liam stepped on board and sat adjacent to the couple, who sat near the stern. The boat exuded wealth with a lounging area near the center of the boat, the deck had near-perfect wooden planks, and the helm sat high near the front.

Once everyone was seated, the boat slowly swayed from the dock, the propellers picking up speed once they were far enough away. Each slap of the propellers cutting through the water matched the beating of Liam's heart. Instead of the win soothing his nerves, he only became more anxious the closer they got to his destination.

Neera could be there by now, or even worse, stranded in the middle of the ocean. He wasn't able to fill up the tank because he was supposed to do it on the last day of their stay, but now, Neera will only have less than half of a tank to make it back. That was if she didn't get lost on the way there.

His guilt swallowed him whole.

It's all your fault.

His knee bounced uncontrollably as he tried to focus on the view of the magnificent horizon. The sky blending into the ocean. The beauty of it used to give Liam solace, but after all the drama that'd unfolded the past few weeks, moving back to the East Coast didn't seem like such a bad idea.

A wrinkled yet strong hand touched his right shoulder, and Liam instinctively tensed. Coming out of it, Liam snapped his head in that direction. Harold offered him a barely-there smile.

"You nervous, son?" He asked with a hint of amusement in his tone.

It took Liam a second to realize what he was referring to. Then his eyes widened in recollection.

Oh yeah, my proposal plans.

Liam nodded his head, lifting his lips into a shy grin.

"So what's the story?" Harold dropped his hand, looking expectantly at Liam. "She's got to be something special if you're going through all this trouble."

She sure is.

"Um..." Liam licked his bottom lip in thought. Of course, they would want more answers. This wasn't some random act of charity. This couple actually thought they were the fairy godparents in some dramatic love story. Of course, he had to stroke their egos.

Instead of spewing some fake story about them being star-crossed lovers, he provided them with a half-truth.

"We met in the fourth grade...she was my first real crush. The way she swam in gym class, so carefree yet swift, it stole my heart away."

Liam did have a little crush on her back then. Ever since the day they met, he had kept an eye on her occasionally, still unsure of his feelings back then. He rarely saw her in classes but would sneak away from his football scrimmages to watch her swim in the empty pool after school. He never told anyone about it because it made him look like a creep.

Liam glanced from Harold to his wife, who offered an encouraging smile, so he continued pouring his heart out.

"I knew I loved her since then, but my family...didn't approve of dating at a young age, so I never admitted my feelings until this year. Technically, she asked me first since it turned out she liked me all this time, too. We've been dating for only a little while, but I feel like..."

Liam's chest pinched and tightened as his feelings slammed against his chest in tandem with the waves hitting the hull. His voice softened. "Like we've been unknowingly together since forever, ya know?"

And...I ended up doing a star-crossed lover *story anyway.*

From walking past each other in the halls to borrowing pencils once in a while, their paths have always crossed.

For Liam, the feelings were like...tinnitus. At first, he felt it loud and constantly but didn't do anything about it. He couldn't, because he had more important priorities. Then, as time went by, the feelings dulled, and he barely noticed, especially with his unpredictable moving schedule. It became almost non-existent until recently. The ringing was constant and now that he heard it again, he could never ignore it.

It was always there.

Harold nodded his head, patting his back while his wife covered her heart with both of her hands, giving him a heartfelt sigh. She used Harold's hand as leverage as she carefully maneuvered around them to sit in the seat on Liam's left side.

Liam could feel the love and support pouring from these complete strangers, more than his parents had ever shown him. They weren't egotistical, pompous fakes that he was used to. They genuinely wanted to help him for nothing else in return.

He basked in their warmth and comfort. Just for a bit.

"My Harold was only seventeen when he asked me to marry him," his wife laughed. "And my parents absolutely hated him for it."

She glanced at her husband and smiled teasingly.

"Eileen was someone I couldn't pass up. I had to take the chance despite the many obstacles we faced." Harold smiled back at his wife. An actual smile this time. "It's been over forty-eight years since, and I don't regret a damn thing."

Liam just smiled, taking in their story. It was romantic and kind of...optimistic. They remained together despite all odds. Sometimes love beat logic, and love could overcome anything.

Hopefully it can do the same for me.

Continuing their interrogation, Eileen inquired, "Does your family approve of everything now? Yes, you're still young, but both of you are no longer children."

Liam pondered on how to answer that. He decided to be honest.

"Unfortunately, they don't. They don't like that she's... *different*."

He really emphasized the last word to stir them towards a cultural difference instead of an *interspecies difference*. Eileen seemed to catch on quicker than Harold, her mouth flattening into a straight line as she nodded.

Harold removed his hand from Liam's back and rubbed his chin in thought. He locked eyes with his wife pensively before sighing.

"If your love is true and you both are strong enough to face all the crap it'll throw at you, like the possibility of losing touch with your family..." Harold shrugged one of his shoulders. "Then you shouldn't let anything get in your way. Not even blood."

Liam sighed, looking across the boat at the swaying ocean. More clouds filled the sky as they floated along the coast.

Am I able to give up everything, including my family... for her?

Honestly, he wasn't sure since all he knew how to be was a Dern. He had plenty of reasons not to be with her. Hell, he even decided to let her go just now, but something about Harold and Eileen told him to hold on just a bit longer. That it was possible to overcome their pain and their differences, and maybe go on a sail to Napa Valley in forty years.

At the end of every scenario without Neera, it all led to misery. There was no timeline where he could live comfortably without her because the ringing would incessantly ring in the back of his head for the rest of his life.

So Liam decided, now and there, he would hold onto her. He would convince her to be with him. He would save her, and they would go to college in the same state. They'd graduate and hold up signs at each other's graduations while cheering the loudest for one another. They'd find a modest apartment with two pet plants. Maybe he'd ask her how she felt about dogs.

Then live happily ever after.

All you have to do is figure out the stuff in between.

Eileen interrupted his contemplation by squeezing his hand. She gazed endearingly into his eyes, her blue ones matching the darkening sky above them.

"Now...don't think about anything else and marry that girl."

Liam smiled wide for the first time. She searched his eyes for any doubt, prying and picking until she was satisfied with what she found.

"And if your family still gives up on you, I'll write down my number. Even though we just met, you'll always have a place with us." Then she smiled warmly with perfect teeth.

Liam looked between Harold and Eileen as his chest finally relaxed. He got on the boat to save his girlfriend but ended up figuring out his entire future.

Funny.

THE BIGGEST CATCH

Chapter 21

Neera

How did my life get so messed up?

In times like these, Neera would be gliding through a pool while drowning all of her troubles. The water would be her therapist, her companion, her lifesaver. She could float for hours, escaping the pain of her world.

When did the one thing that kept her heart afloat make her feel like sinking?

Neera started to resent everyone in her life. Elayne for keeping Liam's plan a secret and encouraging her to trust Liam. Liam, obviously, for setting her up and ripping her heart out after she recently patched it up. Her dad for keeping the plan a secret and hiding her mum's true identity. Especially her mum for passing on this *trait* and leaving her alone to deal with it.

A trait? More like a bloody curse.

It was like everyone was constantly conspiring against her, never trusting her to make her own decisions. As much as they claimed they didn't pity her, it felt pretty much like they did.

Her tears eventually flew away with the wind, leaving her hollow.

Neera shook her head as she cut through the waves,

keeping the negativity from dragging her down. At least she was able to drive in the right direction. Her dad never allowed her to drive because of her mum, so despite being in the water, the feeling was just as freeing.

She was no sea captain, but it didn't require much eyesight to locate the small green island surrounded by nothing but ocean. An intrusive thought snuck to the front of her mind.

Liam might have been leading me into a trap when he helped me escape. I may be heading into a dozen secret operatives...and Dad may already be dead.

Neera bit her bottom lip to restrain the notion. With the solemn expression on his face, there was no way he knew what happened to her dad. Now that she thought about it, his expression wasn't guilt...but utter disappointment.

Deep down, Neera probably knew that. She was so caught up in her shock and fear of her dad's safety that she didn't consider him being...insecure.

She still didn't believe he would choose anyone else before his family, but she knew he was not heinous enough to actively hurt her. Good thing she went alone, so she had time to think. If he had come with her, she would've been an emotional mess.

When the boat trekked a little over half a mile away from the forbidden island, Neera pushed the accelerator up, halting the boat as the motor continued to run behind her. She turned off the noisy thing, so she could think of a plan to enter the island inconspicuously.

The shoreline was barely visible because of her sight, so she could only speculate that there were many guards watching the perimeter, waiting for her arrival. If they noticed she came alone, she wouldn't have the upper hand.

She knew for sure that there was only one building for them to occupy, and it was the dingy lab. All she needed to do was get onto the island without reaching the shore...

That's it!

Neera stood on the very edge of the boat, her weight causing it to tilt, but it still kept her balanced. She clutched the jewel on her chest, asking for protection. Instead of the usual tranquility that ensued, courage and strength coursed through her veins. Her grip tightened on it as she took two deep breaths. On the third breath with her leg lifted high, she stepped over the edge, dropping into the water below.

The water enveloped her like a cool sheet on a summer day. It felt like home or her mum's garden. With only a few seconds to enjoy the normalcy of swimming, she began to feel her body change.

The two legs treading under her fused into a singular, scale-covered tail. Her camouflage skirt stretched as it adjusted around the intruding tail. Her brown top remained as her chest underneath grew green scales. Her hair hovered around her like a silk crown. Cuts sliced her rib cage before they turned into gills.

Instead of murkiness, her vision sharpened and illuminated everything around her. A few fish and a shark passed by her without paying her any mind as she gaped at the beautiful flora of the sea.

As much as she wanted to enjoy the scenery, she had to find her dad. She instinctively whipped her tail as fast as she could towards the secret exit. Her arms formed a triangle overhead as she sliced through the water like a hot knife through butter. Since her vision was currently near perfect, she made sure to avoid any sea creatures or coral that were in her way. An area a shade lighter than the rest of the ocean appeared a few feet in front of her, so she swam towards it, separating her arms to float upwards.

Neera broke through the surface with a large gasp. She looked around, still adjusting to the surface world as her eyes returned to their usual blur. The cave was much more lit than the last time she was there. Good thing she could see better because of it.

Bad thing: she could see SEVERAL bones scattered along

the edges, some of them still looking a bit ripe. The stench of the decomposing bodies seemed worse.

The beast must be at it again. She shuddered at the memory of it.

Gripping the edge of the pool, Neera clenched her jaw as she dragged herself out with her elbows. Sitting parallel to the edge, making sure to avoid any bones, her hands hovered over her tail as she squeezed them while bringing her hands up her body. Steam enveloped her as her body began to return to normal. She wiggled her bare toes, regretting not taking off her shoes before transforming.

Getting up and wiping the dirt off her clothes, she squinted up at the thirteen-foot hole above.

How the heck am I going to get out?

Neera paced the small space as her gears spun. She scanned the area for something to aid her escape. Maybe she could disgustingly tie the human remains together and make a foul-smelling rope to *disgracefully* pull herself out.

She grimaced at the idea. *I'd rather take my chances with the guards.*

She clutched her necklace and bit her lip in thought. Then, an idea sparked. Something that she hadn't tried yet, but was surely capable of doing. It just took a little faith and a bit more science.

Neera listened out for any footsteps or sounds, maybe growls. It was quiet, only the sound of rustling leaves. She studied the pool of blue water for a moment, connecting to it. She lifted her arms towards it with her palms facing forward. Like a magnet, the middle of the pool protruded upwards at the same height as her hands.

Ignoring the *epic-ness*, Neera focused on her connection with the liquid and commanded it upwards at the same time that she slid her arms up. The water continued its ascension until it met the exit.

A quick inspection showed it was blocking the hole entirely, so she lowered her arms until the water was about two feet away from it. Then while focusing on the molecules, she silently commanded the liquid to solidify. The water froze from the top to the pool below, turning the blue pool into a crystal sculpture with jagged edges circling it.

A bit overwhelmed, Neera dropped her arms to her knees and breathed. It required more thinking and energy than when she shot that water missile at the beast a few days ago.

Impressed with her abilities, she grabbed ahold of the jagged edges of the column carefully as she climbed the structure, like a rock climber. Mindful of every step, every crevice, ensuring she didn't slip. There was absolutely nothing she could do about the cold, so she just gritted her teeth through the discomfort. When she placed her toes on the last step, which was more sloped, her foot slipped. The tiniest yelp escaped her mouth before she froze.

Please let me be alone.

Nothing happened. No footsteps, no rustling leaves.

Exhaling, she slid to the top and crouched, her body shivering. The sun was lower, haloing most of the area.

Extremely quiet, Neera stood up and placed shaky hands in front of her on the edge of the hole. Her head popped up like a gopher. Not a soul was in sight; the area looked deserted.

She pulled herself out and dragged her body across the dirt until her feet were above ground. Standing up, she peered down at her dirty clothes and shrugged.

Way to go, Lay-Lay, for picking brown and camouflage. You're a literal genius.

Then her heart plummeted as she remembered her BFF and what she might have gone through.

I have no time to break.

Her toes mushed into the dirt as she stalked toward what she hoped was the laboratory. If she found it, her dad would be there, and she could rescue him. Now that she knew how to freeze water, she wondered what else she could freeze.

The palms on the trees swayed with the wind, and

fortunately for Neera, the sun was still out. The forest was still eerily tranquil, despite its quietness. She looked left, right, even behind her, for a rusty box of a building.

What if I'm lost?

The faint sound of a branch snapping had her stomach in her butt. Her back immediately flattened against a thick palm tree with her heart literally jumping out of her chest. The guards were probably onto the sculpture she made and knew she had arrived. Neera cursed herself for not getting rid of it. She didn't even consider what she was going to do if she ran into them. Failing at dodgeball during gym class didn't exactly make her a master fighter.

The snapping continued, steadily increasing, and then suddenly stopped.

I'm so dead.

She had two options: Wait it out and fight once they revealed themselves.

Or run for her life.

Neera took the biggest breath of her forking life and on her exhale, sprinted down a path with the least number of trees. When it came to swimming, she would have no doubts about escape; however, on land, she was basically a baby deer.

But she was tenacious, and right now, she needed to get to the lab at all costs.

Heavy steps intensified behind her, far heavier than any she had heard before, but she didn't look back. Couldn't.

It took everything within her to stay the course, lungs burning and legs aching. She figured if she kept running into the green abyss, she would eventually stumble upon the heart of it.

Strangely, there was no yelling or chiding. Just loud huffing and the sound of her own heartbeat pumping through her eardrums. Hot air pressed against her neck, making the hairs stand up. Whoever it was stayed hot on her trail, not letting up for a second. Fear threatened to drag her down, but she had to keep moving.

Neera pumped her legs faster and faster, despite the ache in her calves and ignoring the possibility of barreling right into a trap. *Fight-or-flight* had taken over, with her only conscious decision being to run faster and avoid hitting a tree.

THUD. Neera heard a grunt right behind her before the Earth gave an ominous tremor.

Should I keep running?

Before she could figure out what happened, a sharp point pricked the side of her neck. Other than the prick, it felt like nothing happened.

Neera skidded to a stop to inspect the intrusion. Her fingers skimmed over a metal cylinder, about the size of a pen, in the crook of her neck. The angle didn't allow her to see what it was, but the object had a soft material on the end, like a feather-like tail. Fear washed over her like a cold plunge.

I've been caught.

Before she could rip it out, her arms grew heavy to the point that she couldn't physically lift them. Because gravity clearly had some animosity towards her, her legs followed suit, crumbling on themselves as her knees scraped against the dirt.

Her body was shutting down.

If she could feel fear, she would, but any and all sensations were dissipating like the wisps of a dandelion in a short breeze.

Finally chancing a look behind her, instead of cowering in obscurity, she wanted to look her captor in the face before she slipped into the dark unknown. Her eyes glossed over as her mouth drooped open, and not just from the nerve failure reaching her face.

It wasn't a guard or Mr. Dern.

Her vision faded as her body collapsed, the side of her face colliding with the soft ground. Her mind tried to process what she was seeing before the world around her ceased.

There on the ground, with several darts in its body, was the monstrous beast.

LIAM

Hang in there, Angelfish. I'm almost there.

Despite the older couple's genuineness and comfort, Liam's heart raced with worry. He had no idea what he was walking into.

What if Neera is strapped to some cold, metal table with creepy masked scientists experimenting on her? Or her dad is beaten on the ground and held captive?

Liam shuttered at the notion.

He was adamant that he knew his father. He really thought he knew him. Not just in a *spiritual father-son* energy. When Liam was a child, he studied the man. He used to look up to him like he was the smartest man in the universe, and he was lucky enough to have him as his father. Not even Einstein could measure up to him.

He never knew Dan would turn out to be Dr. Frankenstein instead.

The fact that Liam shared the same last name as Dan disgusted him to his core. That man had made conniving and apathy seem normal to Liam and Danny, molding his sons into crueler versions of him. The cynical parts of him. *Crueler* because Dan would mold the lumpy imperfections of his humanity, like his morals, to create two cold and flat clones of himself.

His actual experiments.

What if he succeeded in doing so?

"Up ahead," the captain exclaimed from the helm, interrupting Liam's reflection and Eileen's story-telling about how they met.

She explained how Harold was a young Catholic boy when they first met. Eileen, a young and timid Jewish girl, was fascinated by his passion for sailing. Back then, her parents weren't the only ones skeptical about them dating, especially since it was right after WWII and the Civil Rights era. That explained why she was so understanding of his half-truth.

Liam stood up and held onto the back of the console, peering at what the captain alluded to. The sight of his uncle's empty speedboat immediately alarmed him.

Where is Neera?

He slapped the back of the console, signaling the captain's attention. "Sir, this is my boat!"

The boat he was currently on slowed as it saddled next to the abandoned one. A million questions popped up in his head.

Did it run out of fuel? Did she swim to the shore by herself? Did they see her coming and decided to grab her in the middle of the ocean?

Liam balanced on the beam and glanced back at the island a mile away. The shore had a couple of boats, but they seemed abandoned. The coast was clear.

Liam turned back to the concerned faces of his new companions and smiled reassuringly. "Looks like my stop is here. I'll bring my boat to shore."

Harold's bushy eyebrows smashed together. "You sure about that, kid? If it ran out of fuel, we can strap it to the port and bring it to shore for you."

Liam shook his head vehemently. "No, I think it'll be fine."

He didn't have time for that whole process. He'd have to take the risk and hope the hunk of junk makes it a little bit of distance away.

Harold still looked unsure, yet grunted his approval anyway.

Just as Liam was about to step onto his boat, which was close enough to their boat to cross, Eileen slipped a piece of paper into his hand. With closer inspection, he noticed a phone number scribbled on it. His eyes widened as she gave an embarrassed smile.

"Oh, well...we shared our whole life story with you and forgot to get your name."

Liam smiled timidly as he thought for a second.

"Liam," he affirmed. "Only Liam."

Eileen's smile smoothed into a gentler one as she patted Liam's arm.

"Well, *Liam*," she emphasized his name. "I wish we had more time to witness your proposal. I know it will be wonderful. Good luck!"

Harold nodded in agreement with a semblance of a smile, his tone stern.

"Don't forget our number, son."

Son. Harold tried to act indifferent, but Liam could see right through his tough persona. He kind of liked it.

Liam shared one last smile and nodded to Harold and Eileen before leaping onto his boat, crouching to minimize the rocking. Their boat carefully executed a U-turn and jetted off in the direction they came. Eileen waved one last time from a distance.

He didn't expect this wholesome experience from the couple when he first interacted with them, and he hated to admit that he was going to miss them. That was the first time in years that he felt like a kid, even when he was explaining his fake proposal. He felt like an actual son and not a means to an end or a body to inherit an empire.

Liam stuffed the scrap paper into his front pocket, turned the key that was still in the ignition and rushed to the motor, almost slipping on a blue and green hat. There was no time to unpack why it was left there.

He shook off his scaling anxiety, then yanked the motor cord a bunch of times.

Nothing happened. *Of course.*

He stomped over to the key, twisted it, and ran to the cord to yank it again in silence. His anger increased with every failed pull. So much that it almost swallowed him whole.

He couldn't break. If he let it get to him, he'd lose his fucking mind.

Jaw clenched, he calmly walked over to the wheel. Liam

squeezed the key with an iron grip and paused with one hand on the steering wheel. He resorted to bribing. If it behaved well to him, he'd feed it all the luscious fuel it desired.

He ran to the motor and gripped the cord.

"Please," he muttered.

The thing sprung to life. Without wasting another second, he ran to the accelerator and slammed it down, quickly closing the distance between him and that hell of an island.

Pushing a branch out of his face, Liam stealthily trudged the vast greenery to the lab. At least he thought it was the lab. He had been to that lab way more than he'd prefer the last two weeks, so it wasn't like he could get lost...

Didn't I just pass that palm tree?

The sun hung lower in the sky, and Liam would appreciate saving the love of his life before nightfall, but he couldn't exactly track his steps. He also had to look out for guards that might be lurking in the bushes.

All he could do was trust his gut.

Keeping his footsteps light and his head on a swivel, Liam picked up the pace. As he plunged deeper into the foreboding forest, an uneasy feeling crept up on him.

It's eerily quiet for a place full of armed guards and scared hostages.

Not one scream for mercy.

Breathing harder than intended, he tried maneuvering around trees until something caught his eye. A dilapidated wooden sign about a foot off the ground, covered in vines and mud read:

RESTRICTED ACCESS.
AUTHORIZED PERSONNEL ONLY.

Liam had never seen that sign before. To be fair, most of his time spent there was while running in terror. Maybe there was another entrance into the lab, and they'd only been through the rear entrance. Then that would mean Dan knew about the lab the entire time, and he made sure to lead them through the back to avoid suspicions.

A headache started to form. All the stress was getting to him. Bad.

He refocused his brain on the task at hand. Spiraling would happen later.

About thirty feet from the trunk he hid behind was the busted laboratory that he remembered; however, the doors looked new and reinforced. At least two huge bolt locks molded to the outside doors–which looked large enough to transport a car inside. He spotted two security cameras on top of the roof–one pointing towards the forest and the other pointing at the entrance. He could only assume there were more at the other entrance.

With their probing, blinking red lights, there was no way he could get in there without being detected. The only plus side of all this was that Dan must've only prepared the other side of the building for his rescue attempt. It also explained the lack of guards or people.

Liam almost chuckled at the unintentional dupe.

Guess there's a downside to thinking you know everything.

Liam still had no plan. Trying to penetrate a bolt-locked door with his bare hands already seemed impossible, but to do it without getting caught was hopeless. He even considered burning the damn thing down, but if Neera and Mr. Ran were right behind it, he couldn't risk it. He had to do something, though. He was basically a sitting duck otherwise.

Taking a chance, Liam sprinted to the side of the building, right behind the camera facing the door. He took a few breaths and scanned the area, but he was still alone. He stalked along with his back plastered to the building. Halfway down, he spotted a small rectangular window that was way too small for a person to fit through. It looked difficult to peer through with all the dust and smudge on it.

He slid his back down the wall and leaned his head

towards the window to get a closer look...until the sound of leaves crushing and steady footfalls closed in on him.

Oh shit!

He shuffled back to his feet and booked it to the entrance he came from. His heart pounded faster as adrenaline coursed through his veins. The sun was disappearing, the sky painted in oranges and purples. They were going to be surrounded by night soon. So, Liam decided to head back to the forest to hide out. With the shadows on his side, he could wait there and figure out a more solid plan.

Before he could step a foot out of the clearing, everything went dark...

He was still conscious, so he wasn't hit on the head. His fingers clawed at something rough over his head. The more he scrambled, the tighter the cloth tightened around his neck, challenging every breath he took.

His hands scraped across beefy hands, gripping the end of the bag as he felt a stocky body pressed behind him. Like a trout on a hook, he was caught. That didn't mean he should stop fighting.

Liam kept slapping, flailing, and grabbing at anything he could since screaming was futile. At some point, his body was lifted up, and he took the opportunity to kick at anything and everything.

More hands surrounded him, grabbing his limbs and trying to subdue him, but it was pointless. He was losing air. The pain from his windpipe crushing felt endless, weakening him further. His head pounded, but he somehow felt lighter as the adrenaline disappeared, and his head started to feel like a balloon.

Liam couldn't even discern if he was conscious or not.

"Hey, son," a familiar gritty voice sounded beyond the bag. It also sounded far away, like Liam was floating above the ground and away from the torture.

He only knew the owner of the voice because of how it made his blood run cold. He never knew that voice could enact so much disgust. So much hatred.

So much disappointment.

Liam's body went limp, only comprehending a little bit before his world completely darkened. Dan's slimy voice drawled before Liam's hearing faded away.

"We were waiting for you. Now we can begin."

DR. FRANKENSTEIN

Chapter 22

Neera

Being tranquilized actually wasn't the worst part. The excruciating headache that ensued after regaining consciousness took the cake. On top of that, she couldn't move! She almost wished it was poisonous so that it would take the pain away.

Refusing to open her eyes, Neera channeled her other senses. Her sense of touch? Still pending. She could smell aged metals, cleaning solutions like the ones in hospitals, and a strong whiff of urine.

Her hopes ballooned, thinking it was all just a dream and she was waking up in a hospital after bumping her head. Help arrived, and they were able to handle the situation. Her dad and Liam were waiting by her hospital bed on the edge of their seats, hoping for Neera's eyes to flutter open.

That would be too perfect. Too lucky.

What brought her back to reality was the coppery smell of blood nearby and a thick forest musk in the air. Footsteps scattered about while someone gave orders before the sounds disappeared, but she still refused to open her eyes. Her fear kept them shut tight, hoping that if she kept her eyes shut long enough, they would stay forever closed.

Then images of her dad appeared. The reason she was

there in the first place.

I have to keep fighting.

Using all the courage she could possibly muster, Neera slowly opened her eyes. Blinding fluorescent lights attacked her retinas. They beamed overhead, even though she was sure they didn't work the last time she was here. Matter of fact, most of the lab looked completely renovated. She lifted her head–grateful for the ounce of movement available–and chanced a look at the room.

The walls of the lab were still crusty and rundown, but all the equipment looked different. A blank standing monitor stood over her left side with a small steel tray next to it. It lacked the ashen tables and the windows from last time, with the exception of a tiny window at the very top of the wall that looked more like a vent than anything.

On the opposite wall from the window was a thick metal panel that hung from the ceiling, like a floating box. Aside from a leather strap hanging from its bottom, there was nothing else on the strange square. The space seemed tinier and lacked doors, only deflating her hopes for escape.

How did I get inside?

Neera noticed a tall and muscular man on her right, lying on a silver table with his wrists, ankles, torso, and neck leather-bound to the chains welded to the table. He looked like her dad's age, but life had surely aged him. Crow's feet hugged his closed eyes. His salt-and-pepper beard, which matched his matted shoulder-length hair, reached his collarbone and contrasted against his severely tan skin. She was surprised he wasn't peeling but figured he had naturally tan skin.

He was also mostly naked, with the exception of a dirty beige sheet over his lower half.

Neera couldn't tell if the man was alive or dead since he was covered head to toe with scratches, gashes, and bruises. It looked like he was dragged across the forest to reside there. She only sighed in relief when she glimpsed his chest rising and falling slowly.

Hoping her body wasn't in a similar state, she gasped as her eyes trailed down her body. Her wrists and torso were similarly bound to a metal table. Her legs, however, were free. Not that it benefited her at the moment.

Vomit rose up her throat at her blackened camo skirt. The wretched urine smell was coming from her.

I shouldn't have opened my eyes.

As though it couldn't possibly get any worse, her dad wasn't even there–the whole bloody reason she risked her life in the first place! She fell immediately into Liam's dad's trap, and she had never felt more helpless.

As anxiety and negativity moved permanently into her brain, she instinctively reached for her necklace. She couldn't even lift a finger, like a pathetic loser.

Wait a second.

She looked down her nose at her chest.

Where's my necklace?!

That was the last straw to break her. A whimper spilled out as her head flopped down in defeat. Her last bit of lifeline had been snipped, leaving her with nothing but barren despair.

The last time Neera had felt so low, so hollow, was the year after her mum died. 364 days after her birthday, her life was a rollercoaster of panic attacks, depression, anger, and resentment. They weren't ideal, but at least she felt *something*.

After the water park incident, Neera had woken up barren. Empty of even her worst feelings. Her heart knew that every emotion would never be answered, that no matter what she did or felt, her mum was never coming back.

So she stopped…feeling, that was.

If there was a level under hopelessness, that was where she resided. Such a dark void, a deep trench, that took months to climb out of. A place she swore she would never fall into again.

And Neera was currently standing too close to the edge.

Her fight was no more than a tiny glint.

"You were meant to have this power."

Ha, what a joke.

Whatever these perverted scientists wanted to do with her, Neera didn't give a crap anymore. Her mind began to match the numbness of her body. She even planned what she would leave behind for everyone. Lay-Lay would keep her scandalous diary and all her clothes and accessories. Her dad–who she hoped was still alive–would keep her awards, diploma, and whatever money he put in her life insurance.

And Liam...would keep her CD player and her heart. Especially her green heart keychain that meant everything to her. Even though they left on a bad note, she knew deep down that he was a good person, no matter how much he believed he was not. The last thing she wanted was for him to blame himself for the rest of his life.

Look at me, still caring about him in my final moments...

"You." A deep, hoarse voice sounded from next to her. "I know you."

Neera's eyes snapped open, and she forced her head to the previously unconscious man next to her. His deep brown eyes pierced hers in...recognition?

All Neera could do was blink. She had no idea who that man was. Hopefully, he could explain further, but he seemed to be waiting for some response. She swallowed the lump in her dry throat.

"Sorry, sir, but how do you know me?" She asked warily. He could be mad.

Oddly, he seemed quite...comfortable. He didn't seem distraught about his current situation and was more interested in their interaction like they were old schoolmates running into each other at a coffee shop.

Maybe he's drugged too.

His lips curled into a crooked smile that looked...off, causing the hairs on the back of her neck stand.

"I can recognize those green eyes anywhere," the man cackled as he tried to raise his arms but failed against the restraints. He grunted in frustration, then switched to a grateful smile. He asked with a slight Latin American accent, "How are you doing? You're darker than I had last seen you, Nerissa."

Her eyes nearly bulged out of her head at the mention of her mum's name. He thought she was her mum.

Wait.

How would he know Mum? He wouldn't have seen her for over eight years, so how come he didn't know she was gone? Is he related to her?

The man was clearly unhinged but luckily unable to free himself, so she wasn't in any more danger than her current situation. She humored the man who looked like he'd been through heck and back anyway.

"How do you know my mother?" Neera asked with mild curiosity, using an American term so he wouldn't be confused.

His mouth pursed. The man tilted his head a little, looking genuinely puzzled. "Mother? You're not Nerissa? Where's Nerissa?"

"She died a long time ago from a car crash," Neera sighed, picking at old wounds. "Nerissa hasn't been with us for over eight years."

Still puzzled, his eyes shifted like he was shuffling through his brain. Neera overheard him faintly mumble to himself. "There are no cars on this island. How could she die in a car crash?"

Neera's eyebrows twitched.

She was done humoring him. He couldn't possibly be talking about her mum. In a way, she felt bad for him. He must have gone through something and was confusing that person with her mum.

Neera sighed again. "I'm sorry, you must have gotten the wrong–"

"No!" The man roared. His whole face changed from calm curiosity to distress. Lines crinkled across his forehead. "They finally got her!"

His eyes cut to hers, dripping in anger. "I know exactly

what I'm talking about."

Neera pursed her lips shut. Her dad mentioned to her once, when he would share stories about some of his patients, that when dealing with an "unwell" person, it was best to shut up and let them chat.

"Was your mother the granddaughter of Triton?" He implored less loudly than before. "Long black hair and green eyes? Beautiful beyond comparison?"

There could be hundreds of women like that, but...there was only one granddaughter of Triton that she knew, and that was her mum. Pieces were coming together, but Neera was unsure of the mysterious image. She was now intrigued.

"How do you know her?" Neera urged.

The man started to relax and smiled as if he was waiting for her confirmation.

"I knew it!" He exclaimed, then winked. "My brain isn't as bad as I thought."

He cleared his throat and shook his head like he was clearing his thoughts and preparing to answer. It reminded Neera of a dog after bumping into something.

"We met here. Actually, in this spot. We were both captured and tested on. Me first obviously. I thought we would escape together." He rolled his eyes up. "I guess not."

This man is absolutely mad!

Neera couldn't believe a word he choppily said. Still, she hung onto his every word.

"I couldn't tell how long we were locked up," he explained more energetically. "The entire time we talked. She told me all about you. So much. I almost felt like you were my daughter." He paused, dramatically so, and searched her eyes for something. When she apparently didn't give him what he wanted, he asked, "You're probably wondering why I'm here, aren't you?"

Oh, I'm wondering more than that. Neera nodded.

"I'm the beast that haunts these grounds, as they say." The man gave a sloppy smirk. Pride mixed with sorrow. "Sorry for almost killing you and your friends. Well, not the older man. I should've killed him when I had the chance. I thought I was helping you–well, your mother–escape. Sorry for any damage to you."

He had the nerve to lower his head in shame. If Neera hadn't been paralyzed and strapped to a metal table of doom, she would've probably fainted.

This "man" was telling the truth. Had to. Which meant everything she knew was a lie. Everything she knew about the *infamous* beast was a lie.

There were so many questions and not enough answers. Besides, she had no chance of making it off the island, so she should, at least, learn the truth. Even if the truth was coming from a half-naked, unstable jungle man.

Neera took a deep breath. "What kind of...creature are you?"

He cocked his head at her question as if he wasn't expecting her to ask. "I'm a werewolf. Well..." He licked his lips nervously. That was the first time he had looked self-conscious since they interacted. "Through all the tests, I turned into something almost completely different. Your mother remembered me as one. All the poking, prodding, and dissecting. All the random injections. All the *experiments*," he spat out the last word like a curse. "It all turned into this."

He motioned his restrained hands to his body, which shockingly had more dirt than blood. The blood looked more like brown paint. He must've healed extremely fast.

Why are they doing all of this?

Neera blinked. All the physical and mental torture he endured turned him into an uncontrollable monster.

As if he heard her question, he gritted out, "They used mythical creatures like us to find our weaknesses. Exploit us. Once someone finds your weakness, they can control you. Fortunately for me, it only made me stronger and more resistant. This silver table is supposed to burn my flesh, but it doesn't feel hotter than a spa stone."

His eyes peered up at a wall beyond her legs thoughtfully, his demeanor sorrowful. "I used to be a linguist professor, you know? I had a wife and two kids, Olivia and Edwin. But I had to die to protect them. It's the only way to keep them from getting hurt. From them. From me. My mind is mush most of the time because of what happened. So in a way...I did die."

Neera's eyes burned in anguish. They made him into the very thing they wanted to avoid, tearing his family away from him and ruining his life and sanity...*FOR WHAT?* To exploit him? To make some sort of superhuman army? Is that why the government was involved and covering up everything?

Then a dark realization hit her.

"Are you saying my mother." She closed her eyes. "My mother was tortured too? That she..."

"She never admitted that she had a child or a husband around the monsters," he interrupted quickly. "No matter how much they pried. She wanted to protect you from all of this. She had to die for you. I only hoped she was able to escape like I did. I guess not."

The tears Neera wanted to hold back fell effortlessly. Just two or three drops.

Her mum was in pain. She endured it all so that Neera could live a normal teenage life. The resentment she felt for years for her mum's death melted away like an ice-covered lake on a warm spring day.

Replaced with yearning, sorrow, and a whole lot of anger.

Where was my dad when all this happened? Why couldn't he protect her? Did he even know?

Neera wished she could hold her mum. Tell her how much she loved her. Tell her that she didn't deserve Neera's anger and resentment. Her mum sacrificed her life for her family. For Neera...and Neera was just lying about, ready to give up in vain.

For the longest, she believed things happened because

life sucked sometimes. She thought her mum's accident was just one of those things people couldn't control. Sometimes, people had to just roll with it and heal with time. It turned out that what happened to her mum was malicious and planned.

They murdered her...*They murdered my mum!*

Neera's heart combusted in pure and utter rage. Its fiery passion couldn't blaze any hotter. She no longer had a reason to lay there and take it. No more rolling with the punches. No more laying low.

It was time to get up and fight.

Her will to live skyrocketed to the top of her to-do list, right under the desire to burn everything to the bloody ground.

For Nerissa.

The man stared at her, unaware of her inner turmoil and newfound desire for destruction. Neera opened her eyes with a determined glare.

"Let's get the hell out of here."

LIAM

"Did you really think I would harm Garran just to get you two over here?"

Dan tutted, then shook his head as he sat on a stool in front of Liam, who was tied up in ropes from wrists to ankles and flanked by two muscle-headed men.

The shabby lab Liam was used to seeing had some sort of upgrade. Everything looked clean and pristine. The dusty test tubes were stuffed into a corner, leaving the tables and counters with modern equipment. The lights were fully functional, emitting a low hum that caused Liam's body hair to stand.

Only the crustiness of the walls was familiar. A decent paint job must have been too much of an expense. A bulletproof-vested guard blocked the exit, while two younger men in white lab coats on the other side typed nonchalantly on a computer and prepped syringes for whatever nefarious reasons. With the number of adults occupying the room, it made the space feel smaller.

Liam returned his attention to the man he used to call his dad. To the man whose voice now made his skin crawl. The icy blue-eyed man with tough hands and an even tougher voice was a stranger to Liam. He wasn't the same person who used to take Liam and Danny to the museums and parks. He wasn't the same man who taught Liam how to drive and shave or cheered on all his scientific fair competitions.

Or maybe THAT version of him was the stranger, and this man was his real dad.

Liam glared at him.

"It's not like you're incapable," Liam countered. "Where is he, Dan?"

Dan raised an eyebrow, his arms crossing over his chest.

"Dan? You mean dad, *son*," his tone lowered. "Remember who raised you."

"Know your place." The evil voice echoed in his head, causing Liam to lose it.

Oh, he remembered who raised him. He could never forget it, and would have to live with the consequences of his actions for the rest of his life. Liam could only hope that one day in the future, he'd have a moment of not thinking about Dan or his family's *legacy*.

Currently, he'd rather burn than stay in his place.

Itching for release, Liam squirmed as he struggled against his ties, the rope probably bruising his skin. His nails were nonexistent, and the sheer amount of knots intertwined together only caused more irritation in his struggle. He took a break, glaring back at Dan as he gritted out through clenched teeth.

"Where is Mr. Ran and Neera?"

The man had the nerve to look at Liam like HE was the crazy one. Dan twisted his face in frustration and raised his voice. "Are they all you care about? How dare you turn your back on me?"

Liam stared him down as Dan continued. "I tried raising you to be rational and logical. Cunning and intelligent. To be the greatest scientist of your generation. Now look at you..." He thrust his arms at Liam like a failed experiment. Like the family disappointment.

Liam sneered.

"I swear your mother made you soft–"

"Leave MY mom out of this," Liam blurted, his mouth scowling.

They matched glares as tension filled the room. The man really thought he was trying to help him like he was trying to talk down an unstable person. Like Dan was a priest performing an exorcism on Liam. His narcissism actually preceded him. His cold contempt only enraged Liam more.

Dan just kept talking. "Everything that I've done and will continue to do is for you and this family." Liam stared at the exit for an escape plan. They were both blocked off. "You don't understand now because you're young and naive, but these creatures–"

"People." Liam cut his eyes at Dan.

"–aren't reliable and very unpredictable. All they can comprehend is survival. They can't think critically like us." Dan scooted his stool closer to Liam so they were directly in front of each other. He clapped a hand on his shoulder and squeezed, this time dangerously close to his neck. He leaned in.

"Do you truly think if the roles were reversed, she would fight this hard for you? Think about it. We turn her into the DOD and they'll compensate us for our troubles. We'll be set for life this time."

Liam's eye twitched as he stared at Dan. His argument wasn't even sound because the same person Dan claimed had no conscience or morality was the same person who risked her life to save him. Neera had just met him, yet she put in her blood, sweat, and tears to pull him AND Liam out of the cave. Specifically because of how much Dan meant to Liam. She didn't owe him anything, especially since they just met, yet she had shown more bravery and nobility than the man sitting in front of him had ever done in his privileged life.

And here he was, still trying to "save" his son. He wanted to be the fucking *hero* in this story. Saving his son meant saving the business and, in turn, saving his image. All roads led to Dan. The way he was trying to dress up his selfishness as heroism had to be a world record.

After all, Dan didn't even see them as people and would do anything dehumanizing to them as long as it benefitted him. Maybe just for the hell of it. It made Liam sick to his stomach. The way Dan played with EVERYONE'S lives like chess pieces. There was no saving someone as entitled as him.

Fight fire with fire.

Dan could honestly choke, but he decided to play into Dan's ego to give him one last chance. Any love he had for Dan was quickly fleeting.

Liam relaxed his shoulders and gazed into Dan's eyes, searching for an ounce of humanity.

"I never needed anything more than I already have… Dad," Liam swallowed and softened his tone. "It's not too late. If you want to move, we can move anywhere else in the world. I don't care about the money if it means losing the people I care about. Please…Dad? Please let them go. If you want me to leave her alone, I will. We can pretend like none of this happened. Let's go back to normal."

Dan's face softened from its usual harshness as he ruminated. Liam had to wait, despite his wrists aching from the ties and his feet going numb.

That was the true test. The last test of Dan's humanity. If he passed, Liam might even look the other way. He wouldn't be an active son in his life, but the man wouldn't be dead to him.

The hand on Liam's shoulder slid off as Dan's face blanked. He sighed heavily.

"There's no getting to you, son. You're too far gone." He

slowly shook his head. "You'll just have to see for yourself."

Liam's heart plummeted.

I can say the same for you, Dad.

IF I COULD ESCAPE...

Chapter 23

Neera

"If we're going to do this, you have to do some things you don't want to do. Without hesitation. Without question. Agreed?"

Neera gave a curt nod, despite her heart feeling like it was about to explode.

"Yes."

After officially deciding to escape together, Mateo–the name the man introduced himself as–explained how he escaped the first time. No one had entered the room since they had woken up, so it was a good time to compare strategies. For Neera, however, it was a chance to learn what really happened to her mum over eight years ago.

The truth, for once.

The lab was much less complex then. Instead of shiny trays and monitors, there was only one rusty metal table in the center of the room with a faint overhead light. Next to the table were tools and sharp instruments. Outdated but useful.

Since the room was crowded with more scientists than "subjects", they had to bring them in one at a time and interchange them between experiments.

The room Neera and Mateo currently occupied was where

the torture happened. Hence, it was underground and only offered fresh air through the incredibly small window. The room upstairs was the holding room for the "subjects".

The room upstairs was riddled with different scents of pain, agony, defecation, and blood. It was unbearable for Mateo to even breathe at times with his heightened sense of smell. He had only seen two others who were taken downstairs, and when they came back up, there was no life behind their eyes. Mateo dreaded being the next victim, only seeing the aftermath.

Both of the victims, a woman who smelled like a forest and a kid who smelled like a meadow, were wheeled back up the stairs in black body bags. The stench singed his nose hairs, yet the faces of the captors were indifferent.

One day, a beautiful woman with long, dark hair was carried into the holding room in a towel. Unlike Mateo, who was shackled to the wall in silver chains that scorched his flesh and inhibited him from morphing into his true form, the woman was wrapped in rope from hands to feet. They even positioned a heat lamp in front of her so she'd be constantly dry.

Apparently, they didn't want to take any chances.

When she awakened, she was cool under pressure, but he could still smell a bit of fear from her. Instead of trembling like him, she gazed at Mateo and started to sing some sort of lullaby to him. Strangely, her calm demeanor started to calm his nerves. She introduced herself as Nerissa. She claimed she was a mermaid. Triton's granddaughter, a direct descendant of Poseidon. He didn't believe her at first, but the powerful smell of magic and the ocean was hard to deny. He struck up a conversation with her.

Despite their unfortunate situation, Nerissa felt his pain and hopelessness, then countered it with heartfelt lullabies. Apparently, the ones she would sing to Neera.

She talked non-stop about Neera with so much admiration. When no one else was around, of course. How it was her birthday and she had to give her something special, and because she couldn't make it, she would stay alive for her daughter and husband. When the captors were near, she would remain silent for hours. It allowed

Mateo an escape and helped him conjure the strength to live.

When it was time for him to be brought down, he was detached from the wall, but a silver chain remained around his neck like a collar. They unlocked the padlock on the ground, and the floor opened to metal stairs that led them to the malignant room.

In there, that was where the unspeakable things occurred. No matter how intensely Mateo pleaded how much he wanted to see his family, they dismissed him like a lab rat, squeaking nonsense.

Mateo admitted that he regretted mentioning his family, as he assumed something happened to them from their lack of a search effort.

He was left a shell of himself after days of "tests". The heavy use of silver and mysterious chemicals they injected into him only enabled him to build a tolerance to them. The agony from the incessant torture was compartmentalized into a small chest in his mind, threatening to burst into pieces every now and then. It was the only way he could survive.

His usual painful and involuntary change became more controllable, which as a result, turned his majestic wolf form into some freakish, humanoid version. As time went on, none of their tools could penetrate his flesh, and when something did, the effects lasted shorter than a minute.

The things they used to try and break Mateo only made him stronger. Nerissa was a big part of his resistance. He could survive for her, so they could leave on their own two feet and not in a black bag. When pain arose, he would subconsciously disassociate, opening and locking the chest, and then everything became virtually painless.

That wasn't the case for his friend.

The captors told her something about her husband, but Mateo couldn't remember. Maybe they found out about her family. He just knew that ever since then, she would return from "testing" more and more hollow. The beautiful Nerissa, with eyes that lit up an ocean, was slowly losing it. Honestly, they both were. They *forgot about time. They forgot about basic needs.*

They had forgotten to escape.

On the day Mateo could never forget, Nerissa was dragged back to her spot with her tail deformed. Scaly and pink but chipped in some places. It was split completely down the middle, like a horrid combination of a tail and legs. If it was painful, her face didn't display it. Her head was shaved, and her melodically soft voice became raspy and croaking. He could only imagine what she endured.

Either with determination or resignation, Nerissa lifted her limp wrists towards a green crystal necklace on the table. She repeatedly sang for him to give it to her daughter when he escaped because "today was Neera's birthday". She rocked back and forth in what Mateo assumed was excitement. She insisted she must give her daughter something special.

That sparked the bulb in his head, reminding him that he was a prisoner and deserved freedom.

They both deserved it.

Mateo wanted her to desire freedom too, but she said she couldn't change her tail back into legs. That sobered her as she claimed she was useless. Mateo begged her to fight back and that he would carry her all the way to safety. Nerissa just shook her head and affirmed that her family couldn't see her in her current state.

She must've noticed him hesitating and strategizing on a plan to save them both because she finally reassured him that she would escape herself. Her way.

He reluctantly agreed.

Only one White Coat sat in the room, too preoccupied with paperwork. Everyone else was either guarding the entrance or downstairs. Nerissa only had a rope tied around her wrists because they either underestimated her powers or damaged her so tremendously that she was no longer a threat.

Nerissa scooted herself closer to Mateo with her bottom, then stopped when she sat directly next to him, close enough to touch elbows. She spat in her hands–which, with her lack of energy, was more drool–and slid her wet hands over the metal chain around his neck that connected him to the wall. Coated in her saliva, she squeezed her eyes shut and concentrated. The metal started to turn orange and warped into thin, oblong shapes.

They were weakening.

As if she used all the energy she had left, she opened her hooded eyes and flopped against the wall with a heavy sigh. She gave him a weak, half-smile.

"Now go get them."

He never forgot her last words.

All the dormant anger, frustration, and pain coursed through his body, enveloping him into something unrecognizable. The chest in his mind, overstuffed with agony, burst open. He was ready to rain Hell on those bastards.

His legs elongated and thickened with dark brown fur and dense muscle. His limbs elongated as sharp claws protruded out of his fingertips. His head sprouted with fur and morphed into a wolf, except with a human skull and snipped ears. Bright red eyes glowed and burned with fury. He had changed so many times in his life that the total recomposition of his bones no longer hurt.

The complete monster they feared.

Before the White Coat could react, Mateo had already broken through his chains and pounced on her. Her screams filled the lab, warning everyone of the monster that broke loose. They either attempted to control the situation or made a break for it, which was the smarter option.

Mateo tore through the lab, his thoughts scrambled, making it difficult to control himself. Any time he noticed movement, he attacked anything in white or black. As they scattered like mice towards the shore, all Mateo's one-track mind could think was to stop them from leaving by any means necessary. Whenever he caught one, he shredded them like paper, the smell of fear fueling him and the metallic smell of blood no longer sickening.

He was like a dog with a pack full of squirrels. Some fell down a hole leading to a small pool of water where he had just left them.

He continued his warpath all the way to the white shore.

Only a few managed to leave. Unfortunately, it was the one he wanted to punish the most. The one that destroyed their humanity and extinguished any light in his friend...

Friend? Nerissa!

Suddenly he remembered the promise he made to Nerissa, the thought already fleeting. Mateo raced back to the dilapidated and burning laboratory. It looked ransacked. The doors were falling off the hinges.

Nerissa was missing.

He ran around and searched both rooms for his friend, but her body was gone. Mateo didn't remember much, but he did remember the only thing left of hers was her necklace on the table. Ashamed and grief-stricken, he circled the building with no sign of her. Her words passed through his mind.

"I'll escape myself. My way."

He stopped running in the middle of the dense forest and let his agony out through a cry, his screech penetrating the cloudy sky...

A loud sob ripped through Neera's throat. All her pain and sorrow tearing her apart. Her regret for resenting her mum, for blaming herself for thinking she caused her mum's death, and for hitting Mateo with her water missile. How her mum suffered so horribly, and yet, she still thought of Neera in her last moments...It was too much for Neera to bear.

A hero. A martyr. A mother.

The necklace...was Mum's!

Why didn't I recognize it?

Her mum wanted to give a piece of herself to Neera, and Neera ended up finding it anyway. Her mum poured her faith into getting this to her, and it worked. And Neera didn't even have it on her.

Her head shook in despair as tears coated her cheeks and the silver table. The immense sadness burned with each streak as hopelessness and anger wrapped their dangerous claws around her neck. Neera coughed, unable to breathe, but the coughs ended up turning into more sobs. She was tempted to let darkness consume her, so she could meet her mum face-to-face again.

To tell her how sorry she was.

Neera needed to destroy those bloody bastards, and according to the first escape, it required freeing Mateo to do so. She had to put her panic aside and be strong for Mateo and her mum. It was up to her to end it.

For now, she let the overdue grief take over.

Mateo stared at her in silent understanding. He gave her an awkward half-hearted smile. "I would cry with you, but it usually sounds like nails on a chalkboard."

It took Neera time to process what he meant through her crying. Then it hit her, causing her to sob harder. The first time she encountered the beast–well, Mateo–and screeched, then they ran away from him and left the island. He wasn't yelling some sort of territorial war cry.

He was crying because he thought he saw Nerissa again.

LIAM

A portly man in a lab coat and round glasses leaned down and whispered something in Dan's ear, interrupting Liam and Dan's "heart-to-heart" conversation. Liam couldn't decipher the message, but whatever it was gained him a devilish smile from Dan.

"It looks like we're ready to start," he goaded Liam, his eyes reflecting an evil glint. "If you want to join in on the fun, it's not too late."

"Screw you, Dan," Liam chewed out.

Dan, unfazed, turned to the other man and scoffed. "So mouthy. Teenagers, right?"

The man shook his head in agreement as they walked downstairs, going underground. The panel remained open with the latch hanging loosely.

Were they trying to taunt Liam with potential escape? Or his failure of being so close to saving Neera and Mr. Ran, knowing they were right underneath him the entire time? For her screams to consume his last bit of composure until he broke into tiny, insignificant pieces?

Liam struggled against his ties for what felt like minutes. He despised feeling helpless. He despised giving up. Mainly, he despised his *father*. However, a small part of him believed Dan's evilness would always be a part of Liam, and he was just fighting against the inevitable.

He stamped down the notion when loud, raspy cackling gradually increased from the opening. The creaking of metal wheels joined in. Liam noticed Dan and the same scientist from earlier drag a table with a man, strapped from head to toe in leather ties and silver chains, up the stairs, purposely bumping into every step on the way up.

They rolled him until his body was horizontally stationed in front of Liam like they were presenting a science project in front of a judge. He looked to be Dan's age but had more muscle. His wild hair splayed out as much as his long beard. The man looked like he didn't believe in grooming...or baths.

Oh yeah, and he's fucking naked.

With only a sheet covering his genitals and upper thigh, the only other things covering his body were his scars and dried blood, which exposed a horrendous past.

Ignoring Liam's presence, the man continued to ridicule Dan. Liam knew it was getting to Dan because he looked utterly furious. Jaw tightened, and fists clenched, his cold contempt melted into controlled fury. Liam had never seen him so offended in his life.

Now, he was curious.

"When I chased you guys down the first time, I thought you were him," the man jeered. "You look just like that fucker."

Liam's eyes shifted between the two men. There was a

story here, a history behind the fire. Curiosity winning over safety, Liam boldly inquired, "What are you talking about?"

The man snapped his head to Liam, just realizing he was also in the room. He looked between him and Dan, a sloppy smile appearing on his face and his shoulders shaking in silent laughter.

"*Aye Dios Mios*, he didn't tell you? How rich! I get to witness THREE generations of mad scientists?"

The sarcasm was thick.

"Don't listen to him, Liam. He's mentally unstable," Dan growled, almost scaring Liam with how angry he was.

"Hey, the bastard looks just like him," the mystery man continued jovially, totally immune to the smoke pouring out of Dan's ears. "His *daddy* was the one who did this to me, and I guess it was time to pass the torch. How's the bastard, anyway? Did he die in his own shit?"

Dan's icy blue eyes darkened into ocean trenches, almost black. He raised his fist and struck the man in his cheek. The man's head had barely moved a muscle. Then Dan wrapped his hands around the man's neck, on top of the leather strap already placed over his neck. Liam flinched, his own throat feeling the pressure.

The man, on the other hand, just kept *laughing*! He cackled like he was Dan's boogeyman hiding in his dark closet. Like his personal demon, ready to torment him for eternity. He laughed like a possessed man, and the way Dan's face turned beet-red and his knuckles whitened, Dan wasn't too far behind.

Liam didn't want to witness some random man die in front of him, so he broke the tension.

"So Grandpa Jo was hurting people, too? Why would you follow his footsteps?"

Dan pried his hands away, the laughing man wheezing. He turned to Liam, but the acid never left his eyes. He cleared his throat while straightening his lab coat.

"Your grandfather was a brilliant man. He built this facility to discover the secrets of these monsters that hide in plain sight. In case they ever use their abilities against us, which they already have." He cut his eyes at the man. "Then we'll be ready to defend the country. The government understands and helps with funding, but they would rather clean up than get their hands dirty. It's my duty to continue the legacy, son."

All this information was overwhelming, rocking Liam off his already skewed axis. That truth was worse than a nightmare. Everything he ever knew was a lie. The reason he was into microbiology and the house conveniently built across from a "forbidden" island.

All the sticky parts started to fuse into a crap pile in his brain, all leading to one conclusion: His family lineage wasn't full of brilliant scientists. It was full of murderers. His family killed many people.

People like Neera.

And his *father* wanted to pass the blood-covered torch to *Liam.*

Liam could say so many things, but all he could muster was a sigh. Either that or projectile vomit. How could he be with Neera? How could he have the audacity to look her in the face without her looking back at a monster-in-training? Did she even know?

"You even sound like him, too," the man harassed, his eyes roaming over Dan. "A splitting image. You must be so proud."

The man stretched his neck to look at Liam. "Except he's a lot dumber than his daddy."

Dan threw another punch at the restrained man, this time in the gut. That only made him cackle even louder, his chest heaving like he told the funniest joke on the planet. Dan raised his fist again but pulled back at the last second and bent down so he was at eye level with the laughing man.

"I should cut your head off right now," Dan grumbled through clenched teeth. "Just like Nerissa."

Why does that name sound familiar?

For the first time since the man appeared, he went quiet. His lips were slightly puckered in a pout. Just as Dan was about to rise, the man projected a gob of saliva and blood into his face, his glare burning a hole into Dan's spit-covered face.

"Do it."

Dan rose, wiping his face with the sleeve of his lab coat. His face and neck bright red and jaw clenched, he turned his attention back to Liam. His cold mask was back on his face despite the anger rolling off him in waves.

"This is why we do the work that we do," he affirmed flatly.

With that, Dan walked towards the stairs that the other scientist must have closed before returning. Liam started to panic.

"Yo-you're not going to leave me alone with him?" Liam glanced at the scowling man. Liam might have been on his side and hated everything his family represented, but the man didn't know that. All he saw was another Dern. He couldn't take his chances with him.

"You wanted to make friends with them so much, here's your chance," Dan coldly replied. "You can handle it yourself."

Dan lifted the panel and disappeared downstairs, shutting the panel behind him.

With no other scientists around, Liam tried to untie some of the knots to no avail. The whole time, he could see in his peripheral vision the man watching him.

"Are you here to betray Neera? Griminess seems to be a trait in your family," the man stated matter-of-factly.

He's not exactly wrong.

But how did he know he was here for Neera? How did he even know Neera?

The man noticed his confusion and responded. "I heard you two talking earlier."

Liam bristled at the random man who thought he knew him.

"I'm nothing like him," Liam huffed.

His crusty face feigned fear, then sniggered, "Sure." When Liam didn't respond, his tone harshened. "I made a promise to a dear friend of mine to watch over Neera, so I need to confirm if you're a friend or a problem."

A million questions flooded his head. The first and most prominent one: *How the hell does he know my ex-girlfriend?*

He seemed like an ally if he was willing to protect her, and he didn't have much time to go into a deep dive into their complicated relationship.

Liam's cheeks heated as he stared at the panel on the ground, wondering how he was going to save her. He sighed longingly. "I wouldn't...She's the love of my life."

He returned his gaze to the man, who was analyzing his face. Liam's face remained sincere, too tired to don his mask.

"I believe you," the man divulged, his eyes narrowing. "But, I need to know this. How much do you love Neera?"

Liam shifted again at his invasion. He didn't think that in the span of twenty-four hours, his feelings for Neera would be challenged by two old men. He'd rather they discussed how they were going to escape or how they could save Neera.

Liam opened his mouth and then closed it. He somehow couldn't form words.

The man must've taken his silence as uncertainty because he smirked and asked a question he was even less prepared for.

"How much do you hate your father?"

CRUEL TIES

Chapter 24

Neera

"Pretend you're paralyzed by any means necessary. Until I come back," Mateo whispered to Neera right before a group of White Coats stormed their quarters.

Right behind a round White Coat, Liam's dad descended the stairs like a supervillain. He looked at her briefly before landing on Mateo, and his impassive face turned dark. Mateo shared a similar expression like they were arch-enemies.

Neera felt...dismissed. Like they didn't just hang out a week ago. Total strangers. Just something to be used later. His presence crushed her heart and, at the same time, turned her stomach. She knew Liam's dad was a part of her capture and probably sponsored her case, but she didn't know he was going to be hands-on, practically leading the charge.

The lying twat. She could bet her life savings that her dad wasn't there either.

Good. He won't witness the total devastation she and Mateo will rain on them.

"You look much younger than I remembered," Mateo drawled, smiling cruelly.

Mr. Dern glared in irritation. "You don't know me, but I absolutely know you."

Mateo contemplated briefly, then queried, "Aren't you

Jonathan?"

"You know that's my father, Mateo."

Mateo whistled in feigned astonishment. "Wow, I thought you looked familiar. Who knew pieces of shit could reproduce?"

Mateo cackled as Neera's mouth dropped open.

My role model.

Mr. Dern's face flushed, radiating heat off him. He motioned to the fat White Coat, and they started rolling Mateo out not too gently. In between his cackling, Mateo shouted a reminder for Neera.

"Don't forget what I said!"

Suddenly alone with a bunch of bustling White Coats, Neera swallowed her anxiety down. She had to. The feeling in her limbs returned, but her fear weakened her. At a time when she needed to be at her strongest. Even as three more White Coats descended upon her, she had to remember the plan.

Mateo was the "muscle," and Neera was the "stealth," the secret weapon. Both were strong, but the plan required her to be *mentally* strong. If they knew that the paralyzing drug wore off, they would immediately inject her again, rendering her useless.

One young White Coat stuck a needle into her inner elbow, then connected it to an IV bag hanging from a stand. Luckily for her, her arms were the last to regain feeling, and it barely hurt. He flitted his attention between Neera and the monitor next to her. Another White Coat was inspecting some tools on a tray. Some of them looked scarier than she expected. A few of them resembled syringes filled with mysterious fluids.

Another White Coat, older than the rest of them, started tapping on her limbs, possibly checking for movement. Neera closed her eyes and concentrated on not moving, trying her hardest to control her reflexes. It was extremely hard, but she promised.

Hurry up, Mateo!

She thought the tapping was over until the older White Coat asked, "Ms. Ran, can you feel this?"

Bracing herself at his warning, he pulled out a small pin. The tip gleamed before he plunged it into her big toe. The sharp pain climbed up her foot, and she desperately wanted to kick him in his pretentious face. Or scream. Or cry.

Instead, she bit the inside of her cheek until the metallic taste of blood flowed into her mouth. Tears ebbed her eyelids and stung the back of her eyes, but with all her might she held them back, refusing to show him any weakness.

Neera blinked once.

He stared intently at her, looking for a specific reaction. He turned to the White Coat monitoring her vitals and whispered something in his ear that Neera couldn't make out. The one at the monitor smiled faintly before returning to the monitor. They must know she was faking from the rapid beating of the monitor, tattling on her anxious heart. The White Coat inspecting the instruments sniffed the air and looked pointedly at Neera.

"That smell is getting worse. Can someone change it?" He scoffed.

Neera's eyes widened in terror, and according to the accelerated beeping on the monitor, her heart raced. The last thing she wanted was for any of those weirdos to touch her. She had to find a way out of this without messing up the plan, but she doubted there were any words to say to convince them otherwise. They barely even acknowledged her as a person.

"There should be a duffel in the corner with a gown," the older White Coat suggested while pointing to a black bag under the metal panel exit. He looked at his colleague and affirmed, "I'll do it."

When he glanced back at Neera, she swore her soul left her body. She was officially in "freak-out" mode. She sniffled and shook her head incessantly to keep her body from trembling. The anxiety crept up her throat, and her body flushed from the effort. She began to plead.

"No, please," Neera begged. "There has to be a woman or something. Don't."

The older White Coat shook his head nonchalantly like her voice didn't matter. As if it was insignificant in the grand scheme of things.

"Don't worry, I won't do anything inappropriate," he tried to reassure her. "You're just a subject to me. Besides, you won't feel a thing. The faster we get this done, the faster we can all go home."

Her stomach flopped. *Just a subject?*

Meaning her body no longer belonged to her. She couldn't trust him or his words, especially the part about everyone going home. As he pulled out some shears, she squeezed her eyes shut and kept the plan playing on repeat.

Don't move. Not yet.

Even if they left the island alive, Neera didn't believe she'd ever overcome such a blatant violation. Ever.

Their cold eyes. The wandering hands.

Then her mum entered her mind. She could barely get through this for a few minutes, so she could only imagine what her poor mum endured. If it was worse than this, then she understood her mum losing her mind or not wanting her family to see her.

Neera squeezed her eyes shut and bit her tongue, pressing down so hard that her tongue grew numb. Hands unstrapped her wrists to slip them into some thin material. In that split second, Neera thought about fighting back. All she had to do was attack...but she couldn't. By the time she attempted anything, they would have her restrained or worse.

They were bigger. Cunning. And she was outnumbered.

So she remained faithful to the plan, no matter how much her skin crawled.

During the dressing, Neera couldn't help eavesdropping on their conversation while waves of goosebumps skated across her skin.

"That new presidential candidate is planning on pulling

the funding for our work. Can you believe it? Who does he think he is? He's too young and inexperienced to comprehend the importance of this program," a voice huffed. She recognized it as the older White Coat.

"Exactly. That's why he's not getting my vote. If he gets elected, these monsters will run us into hiding again," another voice grumbled. "And if we lose funding, how am I supposed to take my annual summer vacation to Hawaii?"

The older White Coat grunted in agreement as a cold cloth wiped down Neera's lower half. The sensation made her want to vomit, but she pushed it back down her throat and kept listening.

Please hurry, Mateo!

There was a pause, a weird silence in the air.

Then, as if nothing happened, the older White Coat boasted.

"We're not as ignorant as we were before. We know the mermaid uses her hands to activate her elemental manipulation, and that bastard upstairs is basically indestructible and insane. We just have to keep him talking and away from the little one. If a problem arises and all else fails..." He paused, then lowered his tone. "I heard fire is very effective."

Neera swallowed the huge lump in her throat. They were intentionally keeping Mateo away from her, so they couldn't reenact what her mum did.

How are we going to get out now?

Their plan counted on them being in the same place at the same time. He was supposed to upset them so badly that he was brought back, and in the brief moment of passing, she spits on the leather binding on his wrist to freeze it. He frees himself, frees her, and they take them down together.

Mateo would have to find a way to free himself. Hopefully, they didn't destroy Neera's legs or fragile sanity before then.

The sound of metal shutting hit her ears. A familiar

voice filled the cold room.

"I'm so sorry we had to meet again like this, Neera," Mr. Dern tried to convey solemnly, but it only scratched her eardrums. "I honestly had no idea that you were Nerissa's daughter. You have to understand that this whole operation is bigger than both of us. Nothing personal."

Neera opened her eyes, immediately looking down at her body now donned in a thin gray gown that ended mid-thigh. Internally cringing, she looked at the person who single-handedly ruined her life. He gazed into her eyes and gave her a smile that almost conveyed sympathy but ended up more pitiful, like staring at a puppy with only three legs. Speaking of legs, Neera very much desired to kick him in the face with them.

He rounded the table, so he could stand closer to her face. He opened his mouth as if to speak, hesitated, and then closed it. He turned to the White Coat managing the instruments of terror, and the White Coat nodded. Mr. Dern nodded in return, then turned his icy gaze back on Neera.

Her blood ran cold. Literally, it felt like ice chips flowing through her veins. She clenched her jaw, trying not to move. Their invasive stares pressed down on her like a weight. Her jaw almost snapped with pressure, and she was sure there was enough blood in her mouth from her cheek to leave a scar.

The older White Coat started scribbling on a notepad, the others were looking at the monitor, and Mr. Dern continued to stare at her.

He cleared his throat.

"My father, Jonathan, was a brilliant scientist with many awards and accolades for bioengineering and experimentation to advance the human race. He used traits from other creatures that increased their survival to see if humans could adopt them, eventually evolving to decrease our mortality rates, especially after the Vietnam War, and now with the war in the Middle East. To everyone else, he's a genius and a hero. To me, he's like a god. Many people look up to him and believe in his mission, especially our precious government."

Another cold stream of liquid entered her veins, but it quickly turned lukewarm. The tingling surged through her legs, ready to transform into its scaly alternative. Yet, they remained the same.

Weird...

Mr. Dern did a quick scan of her body, then kept TALKING.

"My father was lucky to have caught that beast." He looked pointedly at the metal panel, clearly indicating Mateo. "He would sit at the dinner table and tell us all about his progress."

I don't care about your mad family and bloodthirsty stories!

Neera wanted to scream. His voice must've been part of the torture; listening to him drone on and on to convince her that all the torture he conducted was a *learning experience*.

"Then, one day, he was out doing his usual Friday fishing by a ravine. He saw the most beautiful creature he had ever seen, coming up for air in the water..."

Beepbeepbeepbeepbeepbeep.

The monitor matched her heart as she sensed where his story was going. At that point, it'd probably give out. And Neera wouldn't mind.

Don't. Say. It.

"He called the team to plan a capture before she was able to get back to her van. His initial plan didn't include harming her in any way...if she came willingly. She wasn't human, so they had to use excessive force. Other than that, he still took it easy on her. You can say the old man had some attraction to her. Who could blame him? Every man has his own vices," Liam's father chuckled.

The way those White Coats casually listened and the way Mr. Dern tried to lighten the mood made Neera's blood boil. The way they tore her mum away from her, broke her down until she wasted away, and thought it was perfectly normal was a slap to her face. People like her didn't matter. People like her were nothing but objects to be toyed with.

Neera's control cracked further with every admission lashing her in the face, and all that oozed out was pure, unadulterated anger. She didn't know if it was the liquids they were injecting her or the trauma weighing down on her psyche, but her morality and diplomacy were slowly dissipating.

These White Coats...These HUMANS think they can do whatever they want to us because they're less than. Inferior to US. So inferior that they fear US to the point of hatred and would rather destroy US and our normal lives instead of...I don't know... fucking asking!

The next round of mysterious liquid entering her system wasn't gentle. It burned as it coursed through her blood like each molecule was a razor, followed by a stream of lemon juice. She'd never felt such pain in her entire life.

That...was the last straw.

Between the tingling intensifying in her legs, their cold, assessing eyes prying into her soul, and her fight to stay still, Neera officially broke. Her facial features twisted in frustration and agony. She was tired of people deciding her fate.

Fuck the plan! Fuck them! Fuck everything!

I'm in control of my own bloody body! I belong to me!

"Shut the fuck up!" Neera roared. The razors coursing through her lessened in pain as they matched the fire burning within.

LIAM

"What do you need me to do?" Liam demanded. The man's questions were loaded, almost impossible to answer in a few words. He didn't have time to tell his life story.

The man searched Liam's eyes like dark obsidian with a hint of silver in them. The man's trust was as thin as an ice chip, but honestly, Liam was more skeptical of him. Who was to say he wouldn't kill him after enacting his revenge? What if he…ripped people apart? Could Liam really stand by and watch Dan die at the hands of him?

Liam cleared his throat.

"Do you promise not to hurt me?" He squeaked, unsure why puberty decided to interrupt his brave persona.

The man smirked devilishly. "I can't do that."

He's definitely serious.

His mom used to tell him never to make a deal with the devil, but Liam's options were extremely limited, and the consequences were infinite. Not many in his favor. There was no time to weigh them since his angelfish could possibly be dissected at any second. The idea made him sick to his stomach. The guilt ate him from the inside out. She was in her predicament because of his family, and only someone in his family could stop it.

"A real man knows how to sacrifice…"

Liam squared his shoulders and nodded to the intimidating man in front of him.

"What do you need me to do?" His voice was deeper, more resigned to his fate.

The man, finally satisfied with his answer, responded in a low voice, "Scoot your chair closer to me with your back facing me. I'll rip your ties with my teeth."

He can't be serious. The ropes were about an inch thick.

Liam scooted his chair closer to him as quickly as possible, stopping a few times when the legs caught onto a dent in the floor. Every time the chair squeaked, he would pause and scan for a guard to tackle him to the ground.

When he reached the man's eager face, he reluctantly gave him his back with his ropes grazing his mouth. Liam felt the ties tug and scratch his skin, waiting for the man to work his way through them.

Something sharp pierced the center of his right wrist. Liam bit back a yelp and thinned his lips. In seconds, the sweet release of the binds hitting the ground happened. Liam focused on quickly untying the rest of the binds at his ankles and torso.

Officially free, Liam rose from his chair and backed three feet away from the menace. He faced the man, yet the man looked unfazed by Liam's very possible betrayal. With the amount of adrenaline coursing through him, he had enough power to run into the lab, save Neera, and escape with everyone left behind.

More importantly, no one else would die.

Maybe the man, but he was unpredictable and a stranger. He would most likely betray Liam if he freed him anyway. It was the safest option for the greater good.

What made Liam uncomfortable was the man's calmness, like he had the upper hand underneath all those binds. Liam turned towards the stairs.

"Before you decide to leave me here, you might need me to fix that for you."

He pointedly glanced at Liam's right wrist. Liam looked down and saw two crescent bite marks, blood still sitting on top of his skin.

His eyes grew wide.

"A werewolf's bite comes with some nasty side effects," the man hummed. His teeth were stained pink as he smiled, making him look even more menacing.

Liam knew nothing about mythical creatures outside of the research he had done on mermaids. He was more of a "scientifically proven"-kind of guy. However, the look on the man's horrid face could indicate that whatever he did was diabolical.

Is it poisonous? Will I possibly...turn into whatever the hell he is?

That cunning little...

Instead of waiting to find out, he defeatedly approached the man and started to unbuckle the leather straps around his arms and wrists. With those free, the deviant made quick work of ridding the rest of them. It was a good enough time to hit the stairs while he was preoccupied.

"Shut the fuck up!"

Liam heard Neera's voice from downstairs and simultaneously spotted in his peripheral vision a green light on a table in a far corner of the lab. So bright, it was almost blinding. Despite the imminent danger Liam was basically knee-deep in, he was practically compelled to bolt toward the light.

Neera's necklace.

He grabbed the jewel, but it singed his palm immediately. While looking at his sizzling palm, before he could even register the pain, his palm returned to its original state. Just a little pink.

What the hell is going on?

His eyes shifted between his hand and the demonic necklace.

"Looks like that's my cue," the man announced as his large hand unbuckled the last of his bindings around his neck. He leapt off the table and landed on his feet with his profile facing Liam and his back facing the staircase door. He stretched, his muscles contorting unnaturally, and snapped his head to Liam. His eyes shone a bright red. If Liam were a lesser man, he would've defecated his pants.

"You might want to run," the man growled animalistically.

Time to go.

Liam snatched the gold chain of the necklace, which only tingled his hand, and shoved it into his pocket. Not even chancing a glance at Mateo, he headed for the metal panel. He unlatched the hook and lifted the door, unfolding the metal stairs underneath. As he descended the staircase, he paused at the blood-boiling scene unfolding in front of him.

Nothing could've prepared him for what he was witnessing.

Neera was in some sort of hospital gown that she clearly

wasn't wearing before, surrounded by lab-coated men holding her down. Her face was in complete distress, beet-red under her light brown complexion, with tears streaming down her face. Her torso wriggled around while her legs flailed, but almost unnaturally, like she was treading water instead of kicking.

Multiple syringes on a small tray were shattered. One of the scientists had blood running down his face while Dan had his arms locked around the injured man, trying to keep him from attacking Neera.

Liam, dumb-struck, stalked towards Neera, ready to punch every one of those bastards for laying a hand on her. When she noticed him, her face returned to its original color, yet she still struggled against the scientists' grasp. A mixture of relief and anger spread across her face.

"Liam," Neera cried, breaking the last shard of his heart into pieces and flooding his body with rage.

"How did you get out?" Dan grumbled, still holding back his injured colleague.

Liam ignored him and gripped the arm of the scientist trying to hold down her legs. Although the man was taller than him, Liam had the element of surprise on him by sending his fist flying into his jaw. The man almost flew across the room. Liam's knuckles hurt on impact, but the pain disappeared instantly. He wasn't the only one shocked by his strength, as even Dan's mouth hung open.

Then the men turned their attention to Liam, their new target.

Hands held him back around his arms and neck while Neera was just shrieking at that point. Dan lost control of the injured man, who grabbed one of the broken needles with the intention to stab Neera, and all innocent Neera could do was squirm in her binds. Liam's anger quickly flashed to fear as he shoved some people off, trying to get to her.

Everything was moving so fast, yet so slow at the same time.

The enraged man raised his arm menacingly, ready to bring it down on her precious face. Liam's fears escalated as no matter how much he fought to get to her, to save her, he wasn't fast enough.

Wasn't strong enough...

A head-splitting, blood-curdling screech roared from behind Liam, ringing his eardrums and deafening him for a few seconds.

Everything and everyone froze.

Time stood still before all of them, including Liam, turned towards the noise as shock and fear consumed their faces. Well...everyone's faces aside from Neera.

Neera's terrified face morphed into a wicked smile.

SNAPPED

Chapter 25

Neera

Beepbeepbeepbeepbeepbeepbeepbeep...

As a White Coat attempted to inject Neera with yet another substance, all her fury and pain collected in her clenched fists, her knuckles turning white from the tension.

Don't touch me! Don't touch me! Don't touch me!

A small burst of glass exploded from the small tray, its tiny shards shooting out sporadically. Then another burst. Then another.

A few vials were next to explode, tiny sparkles glittering like deadly snowflakes around the room. Everything happened so fast that Neera could barely keep track.

What's happening?

One last blast, however, ended up ripping a yelp from the White Coat who was about to inject her. He clutched his face in agony, his white-gloved hands stained with blood. Before Neera could register that she'd caused the explosions, the White Coats were on her.

Get off of me! Get off of me!

More of her control had shredded. Like threads of a rope, leaving her more unraveled than ever before. She felt like the main character in a horror movie that was about to meet her end by the villain.

Or maybe the villain about to meet her rightful demise.

How could something so evil happen to someone who didn't deserve it? Neera's humanity mixed with her morals as she questioned her loose grip on reality and her own identity. Those White Coats were backed by the government and by other humans who felt that her existence was immoral. No one was there to save her, so did that mean that was her fate?

Her mortal and her immortal sides fought over the last thread of her mind.

One White Coat tried to calm her through thinned lips, while another held down her wrists, making her resist more. *Cold hands.*

Another White Coat attempted to grab her legs, but she wiggled them in the air to avoid his hold.

Please, not my legs! Images of her mum's distorted legs interchanged with the present.

Don't touch my legs!

Neera spotted the White Coat with the blood-covered face trying to reach for her throat before Mr. Dern wrapped his arms around him, holding him back. Shards of glass were embedded into his cheeks and one of his eyes, his whole eye red and leaking down his face. He looked like the mad one as he hurled every obscenity on the planet at her.

As if I'm the problem!

While all the chaos occurred, her panic attack sat on her chest, keeping her breathing shallow. The walls were closing in on her. She didn't even have her dad or the necklace to pull her out of it. Hopelessness collided with pain, and anger collided with anxiety until they all swirled together like a tornado, knocking down walls and destroying the Neera she used to be.

She'd snapped.

Hazel eyes appeared in the hazy madness that she never thought she would see again at the bottom of the stairs. It had to be a mirage or something. Her mind was completely mush, so she wasn't too shocked at her imagination.

Or maybe he wasn't a part of her imagination, but he

was some sort of angel ready to take her away from that horrid place, the one Liam had told her about when they spoke in the hotel room. He told her how there were guardian angels who stepped in during harrowing times to save people. How they were beautiful and strong, and some would take on the image of someone they knew to make them comfortable.

He absolutely looked like one. Liam descended the stairs with a regal air to him, like the past few days were a vacation. He looked refreshed and strong, a certain glow to his already slightly tan skin and brawnier arms. The only indication of struggle was his disheveled hair and dirty clothes.

Unreal, a knight ready to save his damsel in distress.

"Liam," Neera cried to the warm-eyed angel, her breathing returning to normal.

Her mind twisted, the angel image warping into something abhorrent.

What if this is a trick? The final boss in my personal torture to hit the final nail on my coffin?

Her skepticism ceased when Mr. Dern looked totally livid at his son's presence and Liam's impressive punch to the White Coat's face. That distracted Mr. Dern enough for the bleeding White Coat to break free from him and scramble towards the needle tray. He fisted one in his hand and readied himself to strike Neera's face. The needle gleamed underneath the fluorescent lights as it descended.

Neera couldn't move. They were holding her down, and the straps were holding her down, leaving no options for escape. There was no water around to manipulate and stop the White Coat. The sinking feeling of dread hit Neera in a way that wasn't as shocking compared to everything she'd been through.

She hoped for a miracle, for her angel to save her as her life flashed before her eyes, and everything seemed to slow down.

It wasn't much. She remembered her mum, dad, and her dancing together in the kitchen. Elayne and Neera meeting for the first time in art class. Her mum's funeral without a body to bury or cremate. Dancing with Liam at Prom. Drinking hot cocoa with her dad. Walking across the graduation stage. Spending time in Venice Beach...

Then a sound that used to make her heart stop shrouded the room in terror and tension. Everyone froze...except Neera, who felt relief wash over her.

Mateo, in his beast form, stood at the top of the stairs in all his glory. His large torso was half-bent, and his head grazed the ceiling just so his towering build could fit. He had always looked beastly to Neera, but after hearing his story, he looked majestic.

The burning sensation in her blood was replaced with the heat of vengeance and justice that she was more than delighted to serve. Revenge consumed her mind as her non-human side took over.

That mortal side was holding her back anyway.

It was time to take back control. Time for those bastards to feel their pain. The irony made her laugh inside.

Oh, you wanted monsters? We'll show you monsters.

She smiled so hard her cheeks hurt.

Mateo let out another screech. His massive paw-hand slammed into the bleeding White Coat's head, sending him across the room with, no doubt, a broken neck. The White Coat holding her wrists immediately clambered around the room, trying to find a way around the Great *Beast*.

The fear they exuded only fueled Neera's delusions. They looked like roaches, running around or hiding in different corners, trying to escape the giant shoe that was Mateo.

You can run, but you can't hide!

Laughter escaped her mouth uncontrollably, the cackle maniacal and pure madness. Neera basked in the mayhem unfolding before her.

Mr. Dern somehow made it up the stairs while Mateo was preoccupied ripping the arms off a White Coat.

Coward.

Neera expected Liam to follow his father. She expected them both to run away, far away from whatever she had become. No longer his "Angelfish" but a mad shark that couldn't differentiate between fish and humans.

Instead, Liam dashed to Neera's side and hastily untied her restraints.

He untied her wrists quickly but carefully. Then her torso. The entire time, Neera searched his face. Peering through her fog of anger and vengeance, she tried to make sense of his behavior.

Why is he still here?

His usually full lips were thin in effort. His thick brown eyebrows furrowed as his earthy eyes continuously flitted between Mateo and her binds. She searched for any sign of disgust or betrayal.

The new Neera saw a guy, fearful of the monster he was about to unleash, and hate for the monster who ruined his entire life.

Good.

She snuffed out the old Neera, who saw worry, pity, and disappointment etched into his face. Every pitiful look in his eyes, more and more, shrunk the old Neera that kept reaching her tiny, pathetic arms out for him to save her. That was too much to bear, so she embraced her new self.

The monster in her. The *goddess* in her.

Where there were no expectations, no heartbreak, and absolutely no pity.

LIAM

In the whirlwind of disaster storming around him, the only thing that kept Liam's feet rooted to the floor was the person strapped to an examination table, laughing maniacally at all the gore. Even the blood droplets occasionally splattering over them led to her laughing harder. His only reason he could never live a normal life again.

Any rational guy would run for the hills at the sight in front of him, especially since the stairs were cleared. Liam noticed Dan sneaking up the stairs while everyone scattered, making a clean escape. He looked briefly at Liam in an unspoken language, beckoning him to follow him up the stairs.

Who knew the man still cared about me?

All Liam had to do was follow him up the stairs, and they could leave the island and never look back. He could put the whole lab behind him, go off to college all the way across the country, and start a new life. Without Dern Research. Without Neera.

Is that possible?

Liam darted to his cackling girlfriend and freed her from her restraints. While untying the one around her torso, she went suspiciously silent with watchful eyes. The switch made his heart race more than it already was, but he focused on freeing her.

The beast behind him was busy tearing someone's limbs off from behind, red spraying everywhere and turning their already high-stakes situation into a full-blown horror movie experience.

When Liam finally freed her, he wrapped an arm around her back and another arm under her knees to lift her out of danger. He knew she was in pain, and it would be much faster if they could make a break for it with her in his arms. Startlingly, Neera pushed Liam away, creating distance as her face twisted in anger.

"LET ME GO!" Neera yelled in his face, her voice an octave higher than her usual pitch.

Taken aback by her reaction and the ringing in his ears, he shook his head and the disorientation with it. Unfortunately, that gave Neera time to crudely rip her IV needle out, hop off the table, and make a break for the stairs. The shards of glass under her bare feet didn't even phase her. Liam headed in her direction until the monster blocked his path and swiped its claws at him.

So much for alliances.

Liam ducked, then hurled his body over the table. Another swipe by the thing caused Liam to drop into a crouch, leaving an opening between the table and the beast. He scurried past the beast on all fours and ran up the stairs in his normal gait.

Being back in the lab explained why no guards assisted them downstairs, despite the noise and screams of terror. Liam almost emptied his stomach at the sight of blood streaks on every surface of the room. Huge, black-uniformed men were laid around the room, most with their body parts on the opposite side of the room. The stench of copper and death invaded Liam's nostrils so intensely that he had to pinch his nose. He could hear the room downstairs was deathly quiet, with only the sound of heavy footsteps pattering about.

The whole scene almost brought Liam to his knees.

The pocket encasing the necklace grew hotter. It felt like a leather car seat parked on a hot day. That brought his slipping mind back to Neera. He couldn't break. He had to find her.

Focus, Liam.

Liam ran out of the building, avoiding the fallen bodies that were near the exit. That monster was definitely a force to be reckoned with, and the fact that Liam was able to survive its clutches only reminded him of what the man mentioned about bites and wolves. If that thing was a "wolf", then Liam was not looking forward to becoming anything like it.

The beast better keep its promise to help cure whatever infected me.

Guilt hammered down on his conscience at even more fallen bodies littered outside of the building. The beast must've torn through the entire vicinity within a span of a minute.

And it was all Liam's fault.

He selfishly released the monster and was the reason it wreaked havoc. All for Liam to be tricked into becoming a "wolf" anyway. Stamping down the guilt before it dragged him under, he sprinted down a clear path.

Night was apparent as the crescent moon shone on the forest, illuminating the usually dark area. Its eerie quietness was still present, yet immediately cut by the annoying chirps of crickets.

Along the path, Liam could smell what he could only describe as ocean and lilies. It was pleasant but different from the other smells amongst him.

Was the forest always this...musky?

He looked down and spotted small footprints on the path, dark brown and spaced out. He followed them until they faded away into the dense trees. Liam peered left and right, only the same amount of foliage surrounding him. Nothing but swaying palms and shadows.

He couldn't afford to get lost again, so he paused and took in his surroundings. The same scent of ocean and lilies pulled his head to his right side. Even some of the plants were spread apart in that direction as though someone recently walked through them.

Liam trusted his gut and forged down that path, shoving branches and vines out of the way. The scent strengthened, beckoning him to quicken his steps. The warmth of the necklace in his pocket suddenly cooled significantly.

At the same time, Liam could faintly hear muffled screams and talking. His mind thought the worst, already preparing him for a battle he wasn't really positive he'd win.

"All of you...are pathetic and weak." An ominous voice uttered coldly.

He broke through a clearing, which happened to be the very shore he arrived on. With the ocean and lilies scent at its peak, Liam found Neera on his left with her arms out, glowering at Dan. On his right was a wrecked boat and Dan, his body coiled in water like a mouse in the clutches of a snake. His face was beet-red, almost purple, and enveloped in water as Neera attempted to drown his father.

ALL FALLS DOWN

Chapter 26

Neera

Who pays for the sins of a father? How does one decide who lives, even when the sins weren't personally done to you?

In the end, someone had to pay the price.

Neera's feet ached for so long that her soles numbed. Her fingers cramped from her fists as she pumped her arms. The air felt cool on her legs, but none of those things deterred her.

The forest was dark. So dark. She could barely see where she was going. Although many plants and trees tried to stop her along the way, as if fate itself was keeping her at bay, Neera stubbornly trudged past without a second glance. With the quietness of the veiled forest, all she could hear was the sound of her feet slapping against the Earth.

Her initial plan was to get the bloody hell off the island and find her dad, who she assumed was definitely in Pasa Verde. Once she found him, she would return to the island with him to retrieve Mateo. There was no way she was going to leave him after everything he'd endured. Hopefully, he would be able to transition back into civilized society, not easily, but she was going to help him every step of the way.

However, seeing Mr. Dern running to safety sparked something in her.

Neera couldn't see a future with him getting away with the crimes his family committed. What he STILL committed.

So with determination behind the wheel, she followed the scent of the sea until she hit the shoreline. Liam's father was at the front of the boat, trying to start the engine at a frantic pace and completely oblivious to Neera's presence.

Neera took the opportunity to motion her arms towards the sea. She immediately connected with it, her power only growing as fast as her hatred. Yanking her arms in the direction of the boat, a medium-sized wave crashed into the vessel. The bow cut most of the force, but it lifted and rocked the boat, causing him to fall flat on his butt.

Mr. Dern frantically looked around as he scrambled to his feet. His cold eyes locked with Neera, his glare filled with anger and a little fear.

Fear.

Neera basked in it, sending a larger wave in his direction. It blew back the boat into pieces. Its parts scattered along the shore, with Mr. Dern lying haphazardly in the sand.

He sat upright while trembling. Eyes that were so arrogant before now bulged in terror. The beast in Neera chugged it all down, and yet...still not satisfied. She thrived in his humility. His mortality...

I really sound like a monster.

"Get away from me, you freak of nature!" He cried as he scooted away from her, the blondish hair on his head skewed. He looked smaller than usual.

Very...pathetic.

"Don't even think about harming me if you know what's good for you!"

Oh, he still has the nerve to threaten me right now?

Neera smirked at his worthless attempts, causing the human to scoot further up the shore. Her footsteps matched with every scoot he made, avoiding the tide skating across the shoreline. Her voice took on a grim and lower tone, unrecognizable to her.

"How do you know what's good for me?" Neera tilted her head at his audacity.

Didn't he know that with a simple flick of her wrist, he could drown where he sat?

No one would know. It would all be over.

"Mon-monsters like you need our help. Y'all-you can't be out in society. You're too dangerous," he stammered as he chided, a voice like nails on a chalkboard. "In the grand scheme of things, what we do is crucial and for the greater good. My father was right. He–"

Waves smacked into each other with such a great force that it finally silenced him.

"HE WAS," Neera hoarsely roared, her mind tired of being quiet. It was his turn to listen for once. She lowered her tone, slithering back into its dark depths. "A murderer with a fucking god complex."

The irony. This human doesn't even know what he is in the presence of!

"He destroyed homes. Families. Lives. He did it for decades and never got caught. He was a monster. And I hope he's burning in some Hell as he rightfully should!"

Neera didn't sound like herself and was aware of it. Since her mum's death, she had practiced restraint and control. Her dad taught her that if she ever felt her emotions take over, all she had to do was talk to him. To let him carry her burden. Her pain. Though he meant well, it never allowed Neera to truly process her grief. She couldn't put that darkness on him, so she kept it tucked inside like a shaken bottle.

All her true feelings, unshed emotions, and unadulterated power were packed inside. Learning about her mum's true death had only re-traumatized her. Any progress she made was gone, only shaking up the bottle further until it finally exploded. The grief and pain transformed into unyielding power.

She wasn't sure if it was part of her Poseidon lineage, that desire for power, but it personally felt magnificent coursing through her veins.

The human opened his mouth, then snapped it shut. His face was red and his lips were practically nonexistent as he scooted to his right, next to a metal box. He dove inside the lunchbox-sized container and whipped out a small, black L-shaped object. It was too dark to identify what it was, but she could only assume it wasn't harmless.

Neera shot her arms to the sea and thrust them towards him. A thick, anaconda-like stream of water jutted out and coiled around his feet. He screamed as it winded up his body and stopped at his shoulders. During the struggle, the object ended up falling out of his hands and landing a few feet away. *Good.*

He eyed the coiled stream with a pale complexion, his mouth gaping open. Gone was the arrogant scientist. The evil mastermind prodigy.

Ha. Now you know how it feels to be played with. Tormented.

Capturing him was too easy. So easy...it kind of bored her. The fact that that human and his father spent years capturing and murdering people like Neera could be stopped so easily only enraged her more.

Those humans envied their abilities, their fast-healing process and their strength, SO MUCH because they could never be like them. They were and always would be weak. Undeserving.

Capturing a Dern just didn't feel like enough. Neera still felt...unsatisfied.

"You and your father are pathetic and weak," Neera rebuked coldly. An image of her mum tucking her in bed burned her eyelids. The last night she had seen her. They took a mother from her daughter. Her chest clenched as her–once huge–heart shriveled into a black lump of coal inside. "*All* of you...are pathetic and weak."

So many people–humans–have let her down, hurt her, and made her suffer over the last eight years. Her dad for keeping the truth away from her, all of her potential away from her. For not investigating her mum's death. For not protecting her to the very end. The girls at school bullied her and spread idiotic rumors about her.

Liam...just his existence as the offspring to a long line of bastards. How could she trust someone like that ever again? The guy feared her. She knew it. They all did.

Even Elayne.

She didn't need them. She'd take care of her mum's killers. All by herself.

So you can be proud of me, Mum.

Neera circled her hand, coiling the stream of water around his entire head. His face flushed as he struggled to breathe. Unfortunately, he was smart enough to inhale beforehand. The human wiggled like a worm in the sand, so helplessly.

Aw.

Neera's mind splintered. Her head tilted again in contemplation.

Should I boil this shrimp or just let him drown?

Her fingers were cramped in their curled position. The tiniest bit of morality struggling to keep her fingers from turning into a fist.

"Hey, Angelfish."

Neera heard HIS voice from her right side. The voice, although slightly deeper than usual, was calm in spite of the dire predicament at hand. "What about Elayne? Your dad? Me? Are we also weak and pathetic?"

She could feel Liam's presence next to her, but she refused to give him attention. When she didn't respond, he urged softly, "You're not this person, Neera. You're better than him and the rest of these assholes. Don't let them drag you down with them."

How did Liam always calm the storm raging inside her? Only fate could tell. His voice was cool, ocean water colliding with fresh flowing lava. Her resistance to his words, to his attempt at resurfacing her humanity, faltered as her craving for destruction waned.

Neera felt the human's heartbeat through her connection with the stream wrapped around him. The erratic beats haunted her from within. So fast that it was on the verge of giving out, reminding her of her purpose.

What Neera really wanted. The darkness in her craved it.

Yet…a small, nagging part of her was disgusted by the idea.

The stream unraveled to his shoulders. He sucked in air so fast, like a fish out of water, that blood dripped from his nose. Instead of being grateful for her mercy, the insolent human tried to slither over to the black object he previously dropped.

Neera scoffed. *Typical.*

The worm pleaded helplessly at his son as he ungracefully wiggled his body across the sand. Unkempt and wild, a few drops of blood dripped from his nose.

"Don't you see what kind of monster that is, son? I told you that you will see their true intentions. They're ruthless beasts!"

There was no getting through to him. Neera felt foolish for believing otherwise. For letting Liam get inside her head. For all she knew, Liam had always been on his father's side. At the end of the day, he would always choose his family while hers was torn apart.

He would return to a large home with a whole family to share it while Neera had her world blown to pieces? He could always come back from it…but Neera couldn't. Life would never be the same for her. There were no do-overs for Neera Ran.

How come the worm gets to go home to his wife and kids while Dad goes home to an empty house?

How does that seem fair?

"Someone has to pay," Neera prompted, her voice husky and distorted.

Why do these HUMANS think they can decide who lives and who dies?!

The sky darkened, the moonlight no longer visible as massive waves circled around the island. The vicious waves encased them like an animated fortress, falling and climbing as they created a barrier around the entire island. The dark blue waves were gnarly and hungry, just waiting for Neera's command to attack.

Tremors wracked the area, ready to submerge the island. Liam's speedboat was behind her on the shore, but still intact. It all looked like a scene out of an apocalyptic movie, but Neera didn't feel scared or hopeless.

She felt numb.

"Shut up, old man!" Liam yelled, but his head never turned away from her. Neera reluctantly glanced at Liam. He looked tense, but if he was afraid, it didn't show. His eyes softened with his tone, keeping all his attention on Neera.

"That man has no one in his life that would do what we have done for you. His payback is a life of loneliness and failure."

From her peripheral vision, the outline of the worm wiggled as it inched to the black object on the ground. His head bobbed about as if trying to use his mouth to grab it.

It still thinks it can outsmart me.

Neera glared at him and slowly closed her rigid fingers. His heartbeat thumped in her ears as he stiffened in pain. His screams of agony pushed her over the edge and brought her back to her purpose.

I decide who lives and who dies!

The tremors increased as the island teetered and tottered. Liam had his arms out to stabilize himself as the waves surpassed the height of all the trees. Darkness slowly eclipsed them, leaving only a sliver of light.

The island was going down. It would submerge and become part of the ocean, truly forgotten and lost, sacrificing the souls on it.

I'll end it all. Everything.

Her chest clenched only for a second, but it pulled her out of the haze. Her mind cleared momentarily, like peering through a screen door, as her mind finally made out a clear image.

Liam. Why didn't he run away when he had the chance? Being here is a sudden death for him, so why stay? Also, what about Mateo?

Without her eyes leaving the worm, Neera raised her left arm to the wall of waves. The falling water created a curtain, splitting into a calm path. A way out. He didn't have much time before her clarity blurred again, and the beast inside of her was ready to retake control.

"Go," Neera gritted out. "Get out of here."

Her mind fogged again.

Mateo and I can't go back to society. We're monsters, like the rest of them here. He said he died that night. There's nothing left to save. Liam hasn't taken any lives, so he should live. That's justice.

The rest of us...the world would be better without us...

"No," Liam simply stated.

No? As if his life wasn't on the brink of being snuffed out.

"I gave up everything for you, got bitten to save you, and was held hostage with a bag over my head." He took a careful step towards Neera. "Elayne and your dad changed their entire lives for you. To protect you. Because that's what PEOPLE that love you do."

Her mind flipped through everything that happened the past few days, like an old film. Like when her life flashed before her eyes, but focusing on...her family. Her dad was ready to protect her by going to Napa Valley, or almost going to, without hesitation. Elayne, a person who had always had her back, was willing to sit in a jail cell for her. Their strength, loyalty, and bravery weren't even a consideration compared to their priority to protect Neera.

The fog of her mind lessened.

And Liam?

His black clothes were covered in dirt and blood, and his hair was a nest of loose curls on top of his head. The preppy and perfect A-student looked more like a criminal. He threw his entire future away and still chose to remain by her side in the face of death.

For Neera.

Her mum was probably rolling in her grave at Neera's short-sightedness. The woman was a full-fledged goddess and mermaid, probably more powerful than Neera could ever be. She could've easily destroyed the world, yet despite all the torture she endured, she spent her last moments saving it and her family. No matter how the world treated her.

There was a strength in control. And a certain power in forgiveness.

Everything started to hurt.

Her body. Her head. Her heart.

Because that's what people do when they love you...right?

LIAM

I thought I completely lost her.

When Liam laid his eyes on Neera, she looked otherworldly. Nothing like the girl he loved. Yet...he couldn't resist being inexplicably drawn to her.

Her blood-spattered gown almost matched her skin. Hands so painfully curled that her knuckles were consistently white. Her bare feet were black with dirt and blood-covered soles about half an inch thick. He could only imagine how painful it felt but considered she might've been numb to them.

The most unsettling part was her eyes. Their usual sea-green color drowned in pools of darkness. Compared to her mermaid form, he had never been more mesmerized.

So bewitched. So raw.

If the physical manifestation of anguish was a person, it would be Neera. That fictional girl who got covered in pig's blood at prom would be a close second.

But Liam wasn't afraid. Even as she currently boiled his father alive, he wasn't afraid of her. The man kind of deserved it. Neera, on the other hand, didn't need to lose herself in the name of vengeance. She wasn't a violent person, by any means, and Liam will prevent her from falling off that cliff with the rest of them.

He knew she wasn't the real Neera. Deep down, it was her suppressed grief bubbling to the surface, swallowing her in loneliness.

And Liam would not allow her to believe she was for another second.

The world around Liam trembled. California was no stranger to earthquakes, but there was something about that one that seemed terminal. The tree branches shook in fear, and the wall of waves menacingly paced around them, ready to take them down at any second.

It felt...final.

The wall separated like a curtain, leaving a path out of the murder fortress. Right next to it was his uncle's boat. All Liam had to do was turn it around and push it into the sea.

To freedom.

Away from Neera.

She had every intention to throw herself off the cliff while sparing Liam. Even in the murkiness of her mind, she considered his well-being. His safety. His future. She imagined him living a regular life without her.

Strangely, the likelihood of that happening had never crossed Liam's mind.

I'm different from them, Angelfish.

"*No.*" And he meant it.

He didn't know how many times he had to convince her that he had given up everything for her. Because there wasn't going to be a future without her. Liam, two weeks ago, would find it all unbelievable and extreme. He wouldn't have to think twice to save his father and leave the "creatures" behind.

But that Liam clearly hadn't lived for once in his fucking life. The new Liam would cringe at that sheltered and arrogant Liam who saw the world in black-and-white instead of the many shades and hues of gray.

So the true Liam stood his ground, despite the impending doom. For once in his life, he was standing up for something. Not just something. *Someone.*

Someone he would save or drown trying.

"I said go, Liam," Neera croaked. "Go now!" The hand in the air trembled as if it would drop at any second.

Resigned to his fate, Liam told her *no*, again. He could see the shock on her face. Then, as if she didn't notice, a lone tear slid down her cheek. Her gaze unfocused for a second before hardening again, her cold eyes remaining on Dan.

Hard and cold?

Liam all but remembered the necklace in his pocket. Avoiding any sudden movements, Liam stepped behind her, out of her line of sight. The second he stepped away from her, the tremors intensified, and the waves grew taller with the curtain to the calm waters still accessible. Her ocean and lilies scent turned saltier.

She thinks I'm leaving.

Liam dug into his pocket, retrieving the sleek gem. It glowed softly in his hand as if it didn't almost melt his palm moments ago. He took the ends of the chain and lifted his arms over her head, laying the jewel across her chest and clasping the ends together.

Right where it belongs.

Once safely placed around her neck, Liam wrapped his arms around her torso with his chin tucked in the crook of her neck. Her skin was so cold and clammy, her body tense in his arms.

He held on with all his might, preparing himself for the world to collapse. He wasn't going to give her another reason to hate the world. If she had to go out, she would leave with an inkling of warmth in her heart. So he closed his eyes, ready for the end, and whispered.

"Didn't you know, Angel? I have a thing for saving you from drowning."

All the tension left her body as it racked with sobs. Her sobs became cries that tore at his heart but were necessary. So he held her while she let it out, having a couple of his own tears slip out.

There's my girl.

Her crying became wails as the island ceased its shaking. The ominous waves rolled backward, receding back into the ocean and shrinking into small waves. The waves passed slowly and less forcefully until they gently flowed. The moonlight returned to its glory in the night sky, a beacon of hope in what would have been a thick gloom.

The high tide blanketed the shore, skating across their feet. Within seconds, Neera's body sagged as her legs morphed into a scaly tail. Her gown still flowing on top, she continued to cry with fat tears streaking her face. The exhaustion of the past few days finally slammed into Liam as his knees buckled, collapsing onto the sand.

That was fine with him.

As long as his Neera remained safely in his arms until her sobs ceased.

TOUCHDOWN

Chapter 27

Neera

"Didn't you know, Angel? I have a thing for saving you from drowning."

Neera wiped her face with the inside collar of her gown. Liam, still holding her, rested his head on her shoulder as his thumbs absentmindedly caressed her upper arms. She could stay in his arms forever.

He's so warm.

Everything went back to normal, with steady ground and clear skies, although she was vaguely aware of causing the chaos in the first place. The screen that separated her from reality had completely peeled away, leaving her vulnerable under the moonlight and every part of her body aching. She still couldn't believe what she did.

Neera gazed at her tail, a trait she hadn't seen in a while. It still looked exquisite, with the exception of caked blood and dirt on the fins.

As if Liam could read her mind–which wouldn't be shocking if he did–he shifted from behind her, causing Neera to lean back on her hands. Her body was already chilly from his absence as he crawled to the end of her tail and sat directly across from her. Neera's heart fluttered as he carefully yet firmly brushed the mess off.

No words were shared between them, but the gesture demonstrated how much he loved her. She still wondered if she even deserved it after what she almost did.

Neera winced when he plucked a glass shard out. He paused, gauging her reaction with apprehension etched on his face. Although the pain pulsed, she flashed him a small smile to indicate she was okay. He continued gently plucking and brushing her tail.

"So…" Neera broke the peaceful silence, chewing on her bottom lip. "How are we getting out of here?"

A thoughtful look crossed his exhausted face, brushing the last of the dirt off. The natural movement of the waves calmed her heart, and the moonlight captured the handsomeness of Liam's face. The slight breeze blew brown hair strands over his forehead so ethereally.

Despite his tiredness, he'd never looked sturdier and more poised. Not like a mask, but exuding genuine strength. The bit of stubble on his chin shifted as his full lips moved into a pondering pout. If her fingers weren't in so much pain right now, she would've reached out and held his face reverently.

"I think I know someone that can help," he drew out vaguely, breaking Neera out of her absurd thoughts.

Liam got up and staggered over to his breached boat. He assessed the vessel before stopping when he got to the other side. He crouched down slowly, staring at something, then shook his head with a smirk.

What's wrong?

After grabbing an object from the metal compartment and stuffing it in his pocket, Liam walked over to the boat wreckage and scanned the ground as if searching for something. He paused, then headed directly to the box the man retrieved the black object from. The memory of the thing caused her to shiver.

He rummaged inside it until he retrieved a thick, gray block with a thin rod on top. Retrieving a crumpled paper from his pocket, he started jabbing it several times before holding the end with the stick to his ear.

Oh, it's a phone! Wait, how is there a working phone?

Maybe it was for emergencies. From where she was seated, it looked like the world's first cell phone. Hopefully, it actually worked.

"Hey Harold," Liam greeted into the device. "It's me, Liam. From earlier."

Harold?

"I know it's last minute, but is there any way you can give us a lift back to the mainland? My boat was completely trashed by a wave."

Neera watched him pace with a hand rubbing the back of his neck. He stopped, his eyebrows furrowed.

"I didn't mean to interrupt your trip, sir...Really? I totally owe you one." A smile broke out on his face as his voice climbed in excitement, inadvertently calming Neera's nerves. "We'll be waiting where you dropped me off earlier. Tell Eileen 'Thanks', too. See you soon!"

Liam tried to hide his excitement as he jogged back to Neera, but she could tell how relieved he was by the way his eyes illuminated.

"Our ride is on the way. Maybe an hour."

Relieved herself, Neera smiled at his enthusiasm.

A loud screech erupted from the forest, interrupting their tender moment.

That immediately woke up the man on the beach. Confused, disheveled, and without his bindings, he rose to a seated position. He swiveled around, looking for the origin of the noise, knowing his fate once the noise caught up to him.

Neera turned her head and stared at the dense forest, patiently waiting for Mateo's arrival. Liam, on the other hand, looked tense and conflicted. He kept glancing between the forest and the man in suspense.

She understood his internal turmoil. Even though the man was inherently a monster, he had been Liam's father all his life. It would be difficult to watch him get shredded into pieces. Neera could hear the gears whirling in his head, but on the outside, Liam remained as still as a statue, witnessing everything unfolding.

A black blur barreled out of the foliage. All Neera could hear was Mateo's loud snorts and heavy footsteps advancing towards the man. He screamed in terror as he clambered to the edge of the water, but not quick enough. Mateo caught up to him faster than she could blink, seizing the man's calf with his massive paw-hand.

Mateo chucked the man in the air like he weighed less than a sack of potatoes, landing closer to the forest's edge with a satisfying *thud*. As much fun as that was for Neera, she was aware of Liam's discomfort and started feeling ashamed. Right before Mateo could rip into the man, Neera called out to him.

Piercing red eyes stood out against the darkness with his teeth bared, showcasing his impressive sharp rows of fangs. Drool mixed with blood dripped in anticipation. To anyone else, he would look like a blood-thirsty beast and would probably soil their pants. However, for Neera, she knew his pain and desire for revenge.

She was there.

His pupils shrunk as he noticed Liam. He began running towards them at full force. Liam braced himself, ready to defend them against an eight-foot beast.

Aw. She gave him props for his confidence.

Neera quickly threw her arms to the ocean, connecting with it, and then flung them in Mateo's direction. A thick stream of water with a flat end slammed into his right temple, knocking him out cold. She cringed apologetically.

He'll be fine...I think.

Liam glanced between her and Mateo, his body visibly relaxed.

"I'm so glad you're on my side," he claimed dryly.

Neera snorted.

They patiently waited for their rescue team to arrive in peaceful silence. The man eventually pushed himself up and limped into the forest without a word, clearly distraught but too battered to run in panic.

No one could convince Neera that he didn't deserve any bit of it. If the man had felt an inkling of remorse for his and his father's actions, she might have felt bad for him. She would've seen a man who blindly followed his father's footsteps, not realizing the damage he actually brought to others.

But he didn't. He felt *honored*...so Neera felt satisfaction in his demise.

"What do you want to do about your dad?" Neera asked Liam.

Liam's jaw clenched as he pondered.

It was awkward, but she felt like it should be his decision. Neera and Mateo acted impulsively, not even considering how Liam was treated. He deserved some revenge for being lied to his entire life. For the man trying to turn him, and probably his little brother, into monsters like him.

Whether it was lethal or he wanted him to rot in jail for the rest of his life, Neera would respect his decision.

"He can find his own way back," Liam admitted solemnly. "He needs to reflect on himself for a bit. Then we'll handle him later."

Neera waited for more, but that was it.

She nodded in agreement before her eyes landed on Mateo. He was now in his human form. Unfortunately, he was more naked, but fortunately, he was lying on his stomach. Sprawled out like a homicide victim. At least that was what she momentarily thought until she saw his back rising and falling with steady breaths. With his hair covering his face, he looked to be in the middle of a much-deserved nap.

"What do you want to do about him?" Neera looked back at Liam as he jabbed a thumb towards Mateo.

"We're taking him with us," Neera answered frankly. "I promised."

Liam pursed his lips as his eyebrow furrowed. He was

holding something back. Neera stared at him intently. Liam opened his mouth, closed it, then sighed heavily.

"There's something I need to tell you since you're back to normal..."

Neera tried focusing on Liam's words until her attention was held by a medium-sized boat approaching them. Its lights brightened the dark waters like a floating angel. Relief hit her, finally letting her guard down. Before it fell all the way down, she pointed to the incoming boat.

Liam must've stopped speaking at some point because he turned around, his shoulders visibly relaxing and his head tilting back in relief.

Neera remembered her mermaid form and tapped him on the shoulder. Using their usual silent communication, she pointed to the tail with wide eyes. Realization hit and his eyes similarly widened. His eyes scanned the shore for a dry place to leave her, but the entire shore was still covered in a thin layer of water.

"Pick me up!" Neera hissed.

Liam tucked his arms under her and stood up, lifting her up as if she weighed nothing. Not that she was complaining, but he used to put a bit more effort into carrying her. Maybe it was adrenaline? She didn't have time to speculate.

Neera dried her tail within seconds, turning the scales back into her legs while Liam yelled to get their attention. Her face heated from having to be held, his strong arms clutching her close to his hard chest and his forest scent teasing her nostrils.

What am I doing? Now is not the time to be turned on!

As the boat reached the shore, an elegant older woman with black hair waved at them. The older man with gray hair next to her was scanning the area, probably wondering what the heck was going on. Their boat looked big enough to carry everyone, which relieved Neera. There was a younger man, with a tan cap and short black curls peeking out the sides, at the wheel who must have been the driver. How they were able to find a driver so late left Neera stumped.

Liam trudged through the shallow water to the back of the boat, where the rescue crew occupied.

"Well, look at the happy couple," the woman smiled, then cringed at Neera's gown. Hopefully, it could pass off as ketchup. "The water's not that deep, dear. You don't have to carry her."

Neera's face somehow heated exponentially more.

"Uh…" Liam glanced down at Neera and then back at the woman. "She has a fear of water."

Neera bit her lip to keep from laughing but ended up coughing as she played along. Liam placed her on the deck and didn't let go until her feet were planted.

"That's terrible," the woman cooed sympathetically. "Especially living on the coast."

Before Neera could come up with an explanation, the man inquired, "Is that man over there alright?" He pointed to an unconscious Mateo.

Neera and Liam exchanged looks, his sort of countering hers.

"N-no, actually," Neera stammered, then cleared her throat. "He's a…"

She looked to Liam for help and didn't miss his little eye roll.

"Drunk," he scoffed. He tilted his hand up to gesture drinking. "He partied a little too hard…and sort of ruined the night."

Liam chuckled nervously, then Neera laughed not-so-quietly, making it more awkward than it already was. The old man just smirked, shaking his head like they triggered some nostalgic memory.

"Be careful, Harold," the woman warned while overseeing Harold stepping off the boat. Liam and Harold made their way over to a knocked-out Mateo. Even in the dark, Neera managed to see Harold hesitantly nudging Mateo's shoulder. Mateo rolled onto his back but didn't move after that.

She noticed Liam nudging Mateo's foot with his hands in his pockets, but still nothing. When their nudging didn't work, Liam straight-up slapped him across the face!

Hard.

What was that all about?

Well, it worked. Mateo shot up like a geyser. His glare on Liam was so intense that she could see the fire from the boat. He then looked at Harold and all his anger dissipated, replacing it with an awkward smile, which made sense. He probably had not had a proper human interaction in almost a decade, and aside from Liam, Harold's a non-threatening stranger.

The two of them helped Mateo up and assisted him over to the boat. As they approached, the woman and Neera proceeded to turn their backs on them to avoid "eye contact". The boat swayed from movement, and other than a few grunts, it quietened.

"Okay, he's decent now," Harold announced amusingly.

Eileen made a hand gesture to the driver, who nodded curtly and started backing away from the shore as they prepared to leave. Neera turned back around to see Mateo sitting on the deck lazily, with his arms spread over the sides and a pink cardigan wrapped around his waist. Harold and the woman, whom she assumed was his wife, sat in the seats facing Mateo. Harold had his arm over her shoulders to keep her warm.

If only she had a sweater or something.

Neera and Liam sat in the seats adjacent to the couple, with Neera sitting next to a lounging Mateo. As much as she wanted to judge Mateo, her outfit choice wasn't any fairer. Her gown was short as the cold ocean air blew through it. Luckily it was dark enough for the blood splatters to resemble dirt stains.

"Well," the woman began, hopefully not to question their predicament. "Since this young man hasn't introduced us yet. I'm Eileen." She put a wrinkled hand to her chest. "And this is my lovely husband, Harold." She put another hand on the older man's arm.

She gave Neera a friendly smile, obviously waiting for a reply. Neera's cheeks heated as she shoved her nerves down. *Okay, time for small talk.*

"I'm Neera," she greeted, then pointed at Mateo. "And this is my uncle, Mateo."

Mateo flashed a toothy grin at the couple, his two fangs unmistakably wolfish. He dropped his amusement when he faced Neera, sincerity and relief in his dark eyes.

"I'm glad you're okay."

Neera's eyes softened. "I'm glad you're okay, too."

Mateo sniffed, diverting his eyes to the front of the boat as if showing his soft side was a crime. However, she knew deep down he was just a big teddy bear.

"So, how was the proposal?" Eileen blurted excitedly.

Neera blinked once. Twice. "Proposal?"

Her eyes found Liam, whose eyes were glued to the deck, and his hand permanently fused into the back of his neck.

Harold spoke up. "This young man right here." He reached across and gave Liam's shoulder an encouraging shake. "He was so desperate to find a boat to get here. He couldn't stop talking about how much he wanted to see you and how much he loved you. We hoped he made it. Regardless of his age, he was adamant about how much you are worth it."

With each admission from the couple, Neera's shock grew, and Liam's face flushed harder. Neera shook her head in disbelief.

Why would he tell them that he wants to marry me?

That was the most ridiculous, yet most romantic declaration of love she had ever received. She had to bite her lip to keep from laughing, full-on guffawing, to avoid further embarrassment. Maybe he said it to get to the island in time, but he could've said anything else to hitch a ride. A wedding? A funeral? Medical emergency? Why would he pretend to ask for her hand in marriage?

There's no way he actually wants to marry me. Right?

"I wasn't able to do it," Liam disclosed to the couple.

"With all the drama that happened and half of the party didn't even show up...I guess I'll have to try another time." He lowered his head as if dejected, but Neera could sense it was all an act. "But the cat's out the bag now..."

Harold grunted in embarrassment, then recovered with a frustration only an old man could pull off. "Well, ask her now!"

Eileen slapped his arm.

Liam's eyes turned into saucer beams. Mateo, on the other hand, had the biggest grin on his face as everyone waited in anticipation. Liam glanced at everyone until his eyes landed on hers. It felt like hours had passed as they stared at each other. The breeze caressed the brown hair on top of his head, causing him to repeatedly run a hand through it.

Finally, Liam squared his shoulders with hers. He turned his body so he was completely facing Neera, his knees slightly brushing against hers.

Don't.

He placed a hand over her hand, fisted on her thigh. She could feel his fingers trembling.

Don't you forking dare, Liam.

He cleared his throat, slightly squinting eyes searching hers. "You, uh, want to get married?"

Neera could feel everyone's burning gazes on her. Now it was her turn to feel the pressure. She hoped he wouldn't ask to avoid the second-hand embarrassment, but of course, he decided to drag her down with him.

Not this time, Liam.

"No," she responded as casually as she could.

Sorry, not sorry.

After the initial gasps and the twitching of Liam's eyelid ceased, she added, "Maybe we can talk about it during Senior year."

Despite the awkwardness from the rejection, Liam exhaled in relief while everyone else looked disappointed. Well, everyone except Mateo, who practically cackled.

Mateo kissed his teeth and shook his head as everyone stared at him. He turned to Liam with a cheeky grin.

"Aren't you supposed to ask me for my blessing?"

LIAM

I fucking hate this guy.

As if the pressure couldn't get any worse, the lunatic had to open his obnoxious mouth. Liam wished he could deck him in the face, but he swallowed his anger, and glared a hole in it instead.

Neera, who was adorably unaware of their beef, looked between them curiously. Then her face lightened in realization.

"I forgot to introduce you both." She held her hands up between them. "Mateo, this is Liam, my boyfriend. And I guess...my, maybe, future fiancé."

"Oh, Liam," Mateo annoyingly drawled in mock surprise. He held his hand out to Liam as if Liam wasn't itching to slap the smirk off his face. "Nice to FINALLY meet you."

Liam glared impossibly harder at him, not even attempting to hide his contempt. He reached his right hand out and grasped his hand. Before he could pull away, Mateo gripped his hand firmly, halting his movements. Mateo's black eyes lowered to the inside of his wrist with intensity while the rest of his face held a mask of amusement.

"Looks like it healed quite nicely," he spoke lowly enough for only their ears.

Liam immediately snatched his hand back. Everyone's confused eyes landed on Liam. He tried his hardest not to attack the bastard but convinced himself that he was the only person who could help cure him.

So Liam clenched his hands, rerouting his anger to his palms instead. Only the sound of water slapping against the hull filled the air.

Thankfully, Harold knew how to cut tension. He laughed and jokingly wagged his finger at Mateo. "Oh, come now. He sure deserves that blessing after all that he's done for you. Maybe you should focus on holding your liquor."

Neera snorted, then covered her mouth. Eileen slapped Harold's thigh. Liam pulled his lips in to stifle his laughter but still worried Mateo might go berserk on his new friend.

Mateo laughed loud enough to wake up the entire West Coast.

"Never," was all he managed to say, which earned a laugh out of everyone else. Whether he meant the blessing or the allegations of alcohol abuse, it left a scowl on Liam's face.

This fucking guy...

Harold, on the other hand, heartily laughed with the biggest grin Liam had ever seen on the man since they met.

"I like his style," Harold eventually uttered to Liam before turning his attention back to Mateo. "Let me know if you ever want to go fishing."

Liam's jaw dropped.

How anyone could enjoy the company of that jerk was beyond his comprehension. If only they knew the type of person Mateo really was, maybe they wouldn't befriend him, or Neera wouldn't be so quick to claim him as her "uncle". She'd been through enough already, so he didn't plan on telling her... yet.

The rest of their journey to the beach on Liam's property was filled with merry conversations between the two men. Liam decided to tune out everything they said and focused on Neera. Eileen switched seats with Liam, so she could massage Neera's stiff and discolored fingers. Her wrinkled hands massaged over Neera's frigid ones in circular motions while she whispered something he could barely hear over the waves. Something about knowing what it was like to be young and in love and following her heart. Or maybe something about courage.

Liam expected Neera to be uncomfortable with her

closeness, but she seemed to gradually warm up to her. Neera's smiles grew just a little wider in Eileen's comfort. Maybe it was Eileen's maternal energy that Neera hadn't experienced in a while, but the interaction made his heart swell. He never knew how much the upturn of her lips or the bunching of her freckles could affect him.

Honestly, Liam was unaware of how strong his feelings were for Neera until she stood before him, ready to end everything and everyone. At that moment, a tunnel vision began and ended with her. As if fate redirected itself so that their lives were intertwined. A new beginning...and if she succeeded in drowning them, a new and certain end.

Even when she stood there in her otherworldly aura and dark, stormy eyes, he felt her reaching out to him. For help, for protection, for air. The urge to protect her took precedence. The second she returned to him, she never looked more beautiful. No angst or pain. Just a carefree Angelfish. He wanted to kiss her so badly.

Even on their rescue trip back to Pasa Verde.

Neera tucked a loose curl behind her ear before locking eyes with Liam. Her lips lifted into a heart-stopping smile, her eyes slightly squinted.

Liam held his breath.

To be completely honest, he wouldn't be opposed to marrying her if she said yes. He kind of wanted her to, as crazy as that sounded, hence why he was so nervous to ask her in the first place. His desire to forever be with her was frightening, yet felt right.

But he could wait. Since he decided his life would end with her by his side, there was no rush.

"Are you sure you don't want to stay for some food and supplies? It's pretty late. My mom could whip up something real quick," Liam insisted.

Once they reached the shore next to Liam's house,

Liam jumped onto the dock and held out a hand to Neera. She blushingly took his hand and stepped onto the dock. Liam noticed Mateo step off the boat, staggering in the knee-deep water to the sandy edge, still wrapped in Eileen's sweater. Instead of running for the hills as Liam hoped, Mateo remained in that spot as he said his farewells to the couple.

"As much as we appreciate that, we have to get home. Spencer has to get home to his little girl." Eileen put an arm around her husband.

With the trio sharing looks with one another, Eileen turned around and motioned towards the helm. A young man, probably in his late twenties, with a blue polo, cargo shorts, and a tan cap, walked onto the deck and stood next to the couple. He had a dark scruff on his chin and black curls sprouting from under his cap. His brown eyes were bright as he waved at them with a smile. When Liam first appeared on their boat, they definitely had a different driver. Someone older and none too friendly.

The guy moved his hands around while mouthing something, which suddenly hit Liam that he was hearing impaired.

"This is our son, Spencer," Eileen introduced while using sign language. "Only family can help out at the last minute like this, but we really have to get going. We promised we would get him home before dawn."

"It's nice to meet you and thank you for your help. Sorry for the trouble," Mateo said while signing.

Liam and Neera's eyes widened. Mateo turned to them and shrugged with a smirk. He continued speaking and signing. "What? Just because I lost my mind doesn't mean I forgot how to communicate."

Liam blinked at him.

Harold reminded them to stay in touch. Eileen bent down and Neera leaned forward as they shared a farewell hug. She whispered for her to call her if she ever needed some motherly advice.

Mateo looked down at his waist and started fiddling with the knot in the sleeves. "Let me give this back to you–"

"No!" The couple yelled in unison.

He halted his movements, smiled, and then bowed his head in, what Liam thought was impossible for him, gratitude.

Spencer headed back to the helm and prepared to leave. As the propellers kicked up the water and the vessel drifted from the dock, Eileen and Harold waved at them for the hundredth time.

Liam didn't feel that dejected from their departure. He knew that wouldn't be the last time they saw each other. Besides, they were practically invited to their hypothetical wedding.

Once the shock from the eventful day dissipated, he'd need someone to talk to about everything that transpired. Someone he could trust.

Liam held Neera's cold hand as she gazed at him.

Were her hands always this cold?

He smiled back, jabbing a thumb behind him at his mansion. The looming home seemed bigger than he was used to.

"Let's go inside and get some food. I'm starving."

He wasn't lying. His stomach felt like it'd been twisted and knotted. The urge to fill it was almost all too consuming.

Neera nodded in agreement and they walked off the dock onto the sandy shore. She stopped and turned to Mateo, who was staring at his mansion with an unreadable expression.

"Let's get you some actual clothes," she giggled and held out her other hand to him.

Liam rolled his eyes at the impromptu invite but was too mentally exhausted to argue. He could put up with him for the night, as long as he knew that if he tried to hurt his mom and Danny, he'd personally and delightfully end his life.

Simple as that.

Mateo smirked as if he could read Liam's mind, then held

her hand as they made their way to the backyard.

Even in the darkness, something seemed a little off with the house. Sure, it was a little after one in the morning, and his mom and Danny would be sleeping at this hour.

But it was quiet. Too quiet.

A rubber band right before it snapped. A chill of unease crept up his spine and settled at the base of his neck as if the energy was telling him to stay alert.

Liam rubbed the back of his neck with his free hand. In his peripheral vision, he noticed Mateo's tense shoulders as he surveyed the area.

Liam also scanned the property, but nothing seemed out of place. His mom's car was parked off to the side of the house, as usual, when she came home late. The lights at the front door continued to light up the area. No detectable property damage, aside from the bent gutter on the roof from a dare his sophomore year. The uneasiness was still present.

Wait. Why is the kitchen light on? And the living room light?

Maybe his mom was waiting for Liam to return. Sometimes when he couldn't make curfew, his mom would leave the foyer lights on until Liam showed up, and then ground him for a few days.

But the lights in the foyer were off...

Adrenaline immediately spiked. He released Neera's hand and stalked faster towards the sliding doors.

"What's going–" Neera asked before Mateo shushed her.

So he can feel it too? It wasn't just in Liam's head.

The two followed behind him while Liam lifted a medium-sized rock up next to the outdoor mat, revealing a shiny spare key. He picked it up while ignoring the burning sensation and, as quietly as he could, unlocked the door. He only cracked the door open, but the door always had a knack for squeaking. The squeak sounded like a shrill against the silent background of the night.

"Liam! Liam, don't come in here!" His mom's distressed cry rang in his ears.

Jumping into action, Liam shoved the door the rest of the way and...saw nothing. He tossed the key on a counter while scoping out the kitchen and ignoring the sound of the glass splintering. He sprinted around the wall that separated the dining room from the living room as Mateo and Neera puttered behind him.

"Mom, are you–" was all Liam could say as he skidded to a stop in the living room. He raised his hands and placed them behind his head, trying to remain as calm as physically possible despite the scene in front of him. The air was knocked out of him as his mind whirled, keeping his breathing shallow.

What the hell is going on?

Neera and Mateo also skidded to a halt next to him. Neera let out a choked sound in her throat, her eyes as wide as saucers.

"Dad! What are you doing?!"

SINS OF A FATHER

Chapter 28

Neera

This has to be a dream...or a messed-up nightmare.

Maybe she completely lost her mind and never stepped foot off the island. That was the only reasonable explanation for the scene right in front of her eyes.

Neera dug her nails into her palm, pain radiating in their presence.

Oh, this is real. This is bloody real!

In the center of Liam's living room was her–supposedly non-violent–dad shakingly aiming a handgun at a kneeling woman on the floor. Her hands nervously kneaded her jean-clad thighs while rocking back and forth. Other than trepidation, she had no physical injuries. The woman, however, looked familiar with hooded brown eyes and a pointed nose similar to Liam...

Wait, this is Liam's mum!

It's unfortunate they have to meet like this.

Her dad looked like a shell of his former self. His thick-framed glasses perched halfway off his nose. His hoodie and cargo pants were disheveled and dirty like he'd been in a scuffle outside. His eyes, which usually held compassion and warmth, were wild and encased in dark circles. The man looked nothing like her dad.

Neera had never seen her dad in that much grief and angst, even the day her mum died. That day, he hid away in his room for hours, then reappeared the same compassionate man she'd always known. It seemed Neera wasn't the only one to crack under the pressure.

Although her heart broke at his current state, she was still relieved that he was alive.

"My little guppy," her dad sighed as his eyes landed on her, yet his gun remained on Mrs. Dern. "I thought they hurt you. I thought–I thought they..." He choked on a sob as tears welled in his dark brown eyes.

Neera pressed her right hand over her heart, hoping the pressure would keep it from crumbling.

"No, I'm fine. Everything's fine. You don't have to do any of this, Dad," she soothed.

To be honest, she knew she didn't look fine at all, and she could only imagine how he was taking in her state. If only he knew that they had taken care of everything on the island, so he didn't have to take matters into his own hands. She still had so many questions to ask, like where he retrieved a gun, but de-escalation seemed like the best decision at that moment.

The sob cut short before he raised his weapon next to her. Distrusting eyes landed on Mateo as he demanded, "Who is he, and why is he naked?"

Neera forgot all about Mateo. After Liam strode towards his house, leaving Neera behind, Mateo continued holding her hand and stalked protectively in front of her. She immediately dropped his hand when she came upon the scene before her.

Mateo looked calmly at her dad as if a deadly weapon wasn't pointed at his chest. His nonchalant demeanor contrasted with the curiosity in his eyes.

"Apparently, Neera's uncle," Mateo shrugged. "I guess that makes you my brother-in-law."

A vein appeared on her dad's temple, his patience waning. Afraid of her dad doing something he would regret, Neera interrupted.

"Mateo was experimented on when Mum was captured, too. He tried to save her, but..." Neera bit her lip. What if her dad didn't know what happened? She almost opened another can of worms. "But he's a friend. He's a good person."

Her dad assessed Mateo for a moment, then lowered his gun...back to Liam's mum. Mrs. Dern closed her eyes, either praying for mercy or accepting her fate, but he didn't pull the trigger. His eyes hardened before they returned to Mateo.

"Thank you for helping my wife and daughter. But you understand why I have to do this, yeah?"

Mateo scratched the side of his head and shrugged. "It won't affect me in any way."

He strutted over to a recliner next to the sectional and plopped down, casually draping an ankle over his knee. As much as Neera should be shocked by his actions, she'd seen him curse out Liam's father and rip apart literal humans. A hostage situation shouldn't make a dent in his psyche.

Liam, however, radiated anger as he stiffly lowered his hands to his sides, balling them into tight fists. Their deep-seated animosity was still a mystery to her, but now was not the time to explore it. She needed to distract her dad from pulling the trigger.

"Dad," Neera swallowed. "Why haven't you told me what happened to Mum when she died?"

Her dad blinked, clearly taken aback by the change in conversation. That question had been bugging her for years, so she was going to selfishly lay it on the table. Hopefully, he took the bait.

His arm lowered stiffly, yet his finger remained on the trigger.

"Because," her dad sighed. "I had no idea what really happened. I only knew that there was not enough evidence to deem it as a car accident."

Neera waited patiently for him to finish. To finally get his side. To understand why he didn't fight harder for the love of his life.

He cleared his throat. "That day, I received a call from the police station claiming Nerissa died on impact. It was plausible in my shocked mind because the car...her car...they revealed to me was totaled and burned. When I insisted on viewing her body, they insisted that it was cremated. Without my permission."

He squeezed his last sentence through clenched teeth.

"It didn't make sense. I made some calls and asked people in the area, begging if they saw anything or if they could reopen her case. They refused; therefore, I've done my own digging. One week later, I received a call from an unknown number threatening me that if I kept investigating her death..."

Her dad suddenly raised his arm again towards Mrs. Dern with hard eyes on Liam. Neera turned to see Liam in a crouch as if he was preparing to strike. Neera shuffled over to Liam and laid a hand on his stiff back to *stand down*. Liam remained tense with his eyes locked on her dad, yet he dropped a knee and waited.

Her dad continued. "If I kept investigating her death, the government was going to hurt you." He brought his eyes to Neera, worried lines etched into his forehead. Tears welled in Neera's eyes, but she couldn't break.

She needed to hear everything.

"At first, I wasn't afraid. I wanted to call their bluff. However, a truck crashed into my parked car while you were at school. Totaling it. No cameras. No evidence, so I couldn't do anything. The next day...it was replaced with a new and exact model. Like it never happened. Registration was forged, and keys were on the welcome mat."

A chill ran down Neera's spine. *Ruthless humans.*

"They were watching us...most importantly, you. Thus, your life, your safety, was my utmost priority. He wanted me to know that we were at his bloody mercy. So I focused on you... and I had to leave my wife behind." A tear snuck past as his octave rose. "It *killed* me every day, but I had to move on."

Her dad tore his eyes from hers, glaring between Liam and his mum. His voice deepened.

"It's quite interesting that the day I met Dan was the last time I spoke to him. He never called or answered my calls. Then his *precious* son suddenly tells me how he's planned to nick my Neera and how I should *trust him* with her. Or how I didn't hear from him until he cornered me yesterday for my phone. His men roughed me up pretty good for it. It all reminded me of the dodgy bastard who threatened me years ago. I'm a smart man. I can put two things together."

Neera's anger spiked when he mentioned Mr. Dern's guards hurting her dad. They deserved every bit of their gruesome fates.

Tearful eyes scorched Neera's soul as her dad shouted, "How come this family can tear mine apart?! Why can he keep his wife when he destroyed mine? Now I'm standing here like a madman while he gets to live his life? Instead of sitting on my hands like a waste man, I finally get to return the favor."

Tears finally slipped down Neera's cheeks at his confession.

Is this what I looked like earlier?

She could see his pain, felt it unwind him until he was nothing but pure misery. The inhuman part of her believed he was absolutely justified for the way he felt, and he had every right to serve his own bout of justice. He had to sit in his anguish for almost a decade because he chose something more important than the truth, justice, or revenge.

His daughter.

That was probably what her mum would've wanted. Neera's heart ached from ever blaming him for backing down, for treating him like a coward. Her dad, just like her mum, was the epitome of strength and patience. Strength shouldn't be categorized as how well someone could dole out destruction. It should be finding the patience, mercy, and restraint to not take the easy way out.

Neera heard sniffling before Mrs. Dern blurted out, "I'm

so, so sorry!"

Her face blotchy and tear-streaked, she finally opened her sorrowful eyes and stared directly into her dad's hate-filled ones.

"We really had no idea, yet we benefited from them. Didn't even question what was really happening or the lives being destroyed. Plea-please, forgive us."

His mum lowered her head in submission. Neera assumed she said that to earn sympathy with her dad, but she released a shaky breath and continued. "I'm aware there's nothing we can give to replace what you've lost, so...So I'll accept whatever decision you make."

Neera's eyes bulged; impressed by her humility.

She doesn't deserve this.

"Mom, no!" Liam shouted before rushing to his mum's side. He knelt in front of her, his back protectively facing her as he glared up at her dad.

Neera's heart banged against her chest. She loved both of them, and she was beginning to love his mum, too. She couldn't let anything happen.

Neera glanced at Mateo for assistance, but he was too busy casually watching everything unfold. She'd have to step in to keep it from escalating, but she was definitely not faster than a bullet if he were to fire it.

But she could try.

She could use her powers for good. For once.

Her dad glowered at the gun as he revealed softly. "Dan told me he would do worse to you than his father did to Nerissa. When I never received a call from Liam...I didn't have anything left to live for..." He sniffed. "I would get my revenge...then I would get to finally see my wife again."

"You don't have to, Pa. I'm right here," Neera cried while tapping the mess that formerly resembled her heart three times. The mere mention of his willingness to exit this world so easily because of her absence stole the air out of her lungs.

If I had never left that island...How could I be so stupid?

Neera circled her fist over her heart while gulping down mouthfuls of air that seemed scarcer than earlier. She shuffled closer to him and rasped. "I'm right here, ok? We... can see Mum another time. She needs us here. Right now, I need you here with me. Please?"

Closing the distance between them, Neera wrapped her arms around his neck from the side. Her tears blurring her world, she noticed his arm languidly dropped. He placed the gun on the floor before wrapping his arms around her.

Her world wasn't destroyed. It was right there.

A warmth heated between them. She noticed her necklace was glowing, its warmth like a blanket. A flame melting the last bit of frost.

Sensing movement next to her, she turned her head to Mrs. Dern standing next to them. She looked down at her hands while shuffling on her feet until hesitantly wrapping her arms around both of them. Although it was tense and awkward at first, they eventually accepted her hug. Neera could smell Liam as his arms wrapped around her and his mum.

Will a group hug solve everything? Not even close.

Yet it was a confirmation. A display that they were all victims, and although still in pain, they remained stronger despite it. At that particular moment, everything was okay, which was much appreciated after the night she had.

A slow clap erupted from a few feet away. They all looked over at Mateo, still sitting in the chair like the monstrosity of a night was a performance.

"How sweet," her uncle drawled sarcastically. "Are we still getting food?"

Her dad, Mrs. Dern, and Liam gaped at his insensitivity, except Neera, who just burst out laughing.

Typical Mateo. Forever my favorite–and only–uncle.

Mrs. Dern sniffled and then started to nervously giggle, melting the last bit of tension in the air. They released each other, except Mrs. Dern, who took Neera's hands in hers and gently squeezed. Now that Neera had a better view of her, she was actually quite pretty and younger than she expected. Her long, dark lashes lowered before raising them to gaze at Neera's face, apology etched in her face.

"Neera, I," she breathed. "I'm sorry for the pain we've caused you..."

"Mrs. Dern, I understand," Neera interjected.

There was nothing they could do about the past. An apology wasn't necessary, especially from someone who not only benefited from it but also was a victim of it.

She was almost shot in the face, for goodness' sake, and she's apologizing to ME!

Mrs. Dern tilted her lips into a hint of a smile, subconsciously showcasing the small beauty mark next to her mouth. "You can call me Lana. It's actually a pleasure to finally meet the girl my son is head-over-heels for."

Lana winked before letting go and strutting over to a still-seated and extremely hungry Mateo. Wiping a hand on her thigh, she confidently stretched that hand out towards him.

I guess it's never too late to be a great host.

"Um...well, this is an awkward first meeting, but I'm Liam's mom, Lana. I'm also truly sorry for what my father-in-law and Dan have done to you. If there's any way we can repay you, we will."

Mateo cut his eyes to Liam and then returned them to Lana. He gently grasped her hand and held it to his face before quickly pressing his lips to her knuckles.

"Pleasure to meet you, *Lana*," Mateo drew out her name as if he already knew it and just wanted to commit it to memory. He gazed into her eyes as pink filled her cheeks. "Also, please don't worry about reparations. I already got what I needed."

In a flash, Liam was at his mum's side. He looped an arm in hers, breaking their contact. "Let's grab some leftovers, Mom. I'm starving."

Before she could respond, he led her into the kitchen. Liam opened up shelves and pulled out stacks of terracotta plates while Lana removed large Tupperware from the fridge. Neera's stomach growled at the sight, reminding her that she hadn't eaten since that half slice of pizza.

"*Mom?*" Mateo scoffed with just Neera and her dad in the living room, yet loud enough for Liam and Lana to hear. "She must be his adoptive mother. She's way too pretty to be his *mama.*"

"Hey, stop bullying my boyfriend," Neera jokingly chided.

Mateo shrugged. "What do you think uncles are for?"

Neera shook her head.

Maybe I should have called him a family friend *instead.*

Her dad left her side and lumbered towards Mateo. Adjusting his glasses on his face, he cleared his throat before holding out his hand to him. Mateo straightened in his seat, the air shifting into something more earnest.

"Again, I absolutely cannot thank you enough for saving my world." Her dad looked over his shoulder at Neera, his smile sincere, before looking back at Mateo. "If you have any family to contact, it would be my honor to assist you in your search. It's the least I can do. If she hasn't told you before, I'm Garran."

That's the gentle dad I know and love.

Mateo stood this time, almost towering over her dad, which was rare because her dad was pretty tall himself. He grasped his hand and shook it heartily. Right before he let go, Mateo's face turned solemn, all his half-heartedness gone.

"No, I'm-" Mateo coughed into his fist. "I'm sorry about Nerissa. She-she saved me. She's a true gem. Your daughter seems to favor her a lot." Garran's eyes crinkled as he pulled her uncle into a side hug. Mateo raised his arms as his body visibly stiffened, but then gripped her dad's shoulder and pulled him in closer.

He probably couldn't recall the last time he was treated like a human being. It was kind of bittersweet.

When Mateo broke the hug, he sniffed before clearing his throat, his mask of indifference making its grand reappearance. "Besides, I no longer have family to contact anymore."

Neera headed over to them, looping an arm around her dad's already bent one.

"Well, now you do," she punctuated with a curt nod. "Me, my dad, Liam–"

"Never gonna happen," Liam chimed in from the kitchen island.

Mateo ignored him and reached out, messing up the nest of curls on her head.

"Thanks, *sobrinita*." He grinned.

"Ah-hem," Lana interrupted their tender moment, smiling like a restaurant host. "I hope we can put this behind us, for now, and have a peace-making dinner. My other son, Danny, is at a friend's house, so feel free to stay as long as you need."

Her eyes traveled up Mateo's body, from his dirty feet to the nest of salt and pepper on his face. "I'm going to grab some clothes for you."

As they headed to the kitchen island, Mateo leaned towards her dad and smirked. "She definitely wants me."

Neera snorted.

"Over my dead body," Liam scowled.

THE DEEP END

Epilogue

Neera

"Don't forget our study sess later for the Psych exam," Elayne sang as she and Neera crossed the grassy quad.

Despite the autumn season in L.A., the sky was clear as the palm trees swayed with the breeze. The villa-style architecture contrasted with the academic atmosphere as exam season unfolded before the holidays. The quad was full of students scattered about, enjoying the pleasant day while studying or relaxing with friends.

Neera shifted her books to her side, using her other hand to push her sliding wire-framed glasses up her nose. She smiled at her best friend in the entire world, then imitated her cheery tone.

"By *study sess*, you mean staring at a textbook for thirty minutes before watching *True Blood*."

"Exactly," Elayne winked as she threw an arm over Neera's shoulders, her fingerless-gloved hands squeezing her shoulder. "It's supe important, so don't be late."

Neera rolled her eyes. "Okay. I'll meet you at the dorm later."

Elayne nodded, then ogled at a shirtless, short-haired jock running in the opposite direction. Elayne looked back at Neera, wiggling her eyebrows. Neera laughed, already aware of Lay-Lay's new target. Without a word, Elayne spun on her combat-booted feet and retreated in his direction, waving lazily at Neera in departure.

Some things never change.

Five months had passed since Neera became a mermaid, and her world turned completely upside-down. Those months were spent trying to put the pieces of her life together while simultaneously finding space for all the extra ones.

With the help of a therapist and her newly prescribed anxiety meds, of course.

A twinge of hurt still appeared when she thought about what happened to her mum, but it wasn't as consuming as before. Her mum died, sacrificed herself for her and her dad, and that was a heavy burden to bear. The only way to move forward was to think of all the positives that came from her sacrifice.

Her mum died...but she never left. A piece of her was around Neera's neck when she spent her holidays with her dad and *Tio*–Mateo insisted she referred to him as such–and whenever she transformed. Consequently, her death caused her tiny bud of a family to bloom vibrantly.

Slowly but surely, her life would be back on track again. She decided to major in Psychology to follow in her dad's footsteps. He, of course, was all for it. Learning about what was going on inside her and how to cope was a big part of it, but there were times when she believed she wasn't *normal* enough to become a therapist herself. Like she didn't fit in at times, then she remembered to stay in the present. She'd cross her career path when she got to it. Although the fact that Neera was miles away from home put a dent in his enthusiasm, making sure to call him every day gave him some solace.

Well...both of them.

Since Elayne was attending the same university, Neera begged anyone she needed to for them to room together. It sealed the deal when she explained that Elayne was her "Emotional Support Friend" for "medical reasons" or whatever, and she needed to be by her side. Elayne didn't complain. That was kind of what BFFs did.

Neera owed her so much. When they finally reunited after the "island incident", they collided in a bittersweet tangle of hugs, tears, snot, and apologies. Elayne revealed that she was in the holding cell for hours until her parents showed up and reprimanded the police for making a mistake. All she could do in the cell was hope Neera wasn't probed or chopped up into pieces. Her words.

Speaking of the "island incident", Liam had been a bit... clingy since they had returned. He insisted he attend her university, but Neera wanted him to follow his own dreams for once. To make his own choices and do the things he always wanted to do. Not for her nor his father.

After a few choice words and arguments–and making up–he decided to join Donald Harvey University, a small, more in-land campus that happened to be an hour away from her. He was fine with it because his choices, his dreams, still led to Neera. His words.

Everything was almost perfect.

"Coming through!"

A group of guys in ROTC uniforms jogged past her from behind, one accidentally bumping her shoulder.

Before she could think, Neera had already shrunk into herself, clutching her books to her chest and crouching onto the balls of her feet. Her breathing constricted as the air around her thinned. Her heart hammered against her chest.

Alarms blared in her head, her mind back in the lab. The needles. The bloody screams. The cold, cold hands holding her down. The torture. Fire scorching her veins...

Don't touch me!

Don't touch me!

Don't touch me!

Neera clutched the jewel on her chest like a lifeline. Its warmth smoothed each of her mangled nerves. She inhaled, then exhaled slowly. Her eyelids flitted open, still unsure of closing them, and she glanced around.

I'm on campus. We escaped. No one is after me.

Okay…so everything isn't exactly perfect.

She *might* have a teeny-tiny bit of PTSD from the whole debacle, but she was working on it. No one had to know unless it worsened. So, she had the occasional night terror or trouble being in large crowds.

Humans.

Neera shook her head before standing back up, running her trembling hands down her pleated skirt.

Nothing she couldn't overcome…in due time.

The sun sat on the horizon, highlighting the palm trees under it. Excited as always at that time of day, Neera quickened her pace to the indoor rec pool on the other side of campus. No one really used it besides old people and children, learning how to swim and such.

But on weekdays, an hour before they close up, she managed to convince the instructors to let her swim for an hour, which involved her insistence on confronting her *water phobia* in privacy.

Taking in the empty pool, an alluring mix of oranges reflected off the pool ripples from the floor-length windows while the smell of chlorine tickled her nose. Most people hated the smell, but to Neera, it smelled like memories.

She placed her textbooks on the bottom bleachers before removing her glasses, then stripped into her green bikini– fully aware that she would have to collect the bottoms once she finished. One day she would be brave enough to dive in without them.

Just not that day.

Her feet slapped against the tile before stopping at the edge of the deep end. The anticipation right before a dive felt like a thousand tingles down her spine. It never got old. That was what made it so exciting.

What made her feel alive.

Taking a deep breath, Neera raised her arms over her

head in a triangular shape, bent her knees, and plunged into the cool water below. Uprighting herself, she watched her light brown, treading legs fuse together into a sparkling green tail. The scales were covered by her bikini top while her not-so-lucky bottoms slowly drifted to the bottom of the pool. Right before hitting the concrete, she scooped up the flimsy material and placed it on the pool's edge.

The chlorine felt gritty every time she filtered water past her gills and not as refreshing as the ocean; nevertheless, it felt comforting. The cool water glided off her as she lapped the perimeter of the deep end, remaining underwater.

Neera spent her time swirling and tumbling, swimming becoming effortless every time her body was submerged. It was easier than walking around on campus. Instead of being surrounded by strangers out in the open, she would be protected by a barrier between the surface and the water below. The pressure was like a hug as she willed her body to lie on its rough bed.

Instead of reflecting on her life, she just basked in her surroundings. Life was always a whirlwind, but there, she didn't have to worry about that. She could just be in the moment and...breathe. The flash of light from her necklace brought memories of her mum to the surface.

Only briefly.

Her grief came in small waves. When they showed up, they were no longer a tsunami of pain and anger. They were more of a high tide at its worst, wading slowly in and then wading slowly out. Instead of trying to hide further up the shore, Neera dug her toes in the sand, patiently waiting for it to recede.

Because it was okay and necessary.

The water near the pool's edge bubbled with movement. Neera's body tensed as her mouth gaped open.

Someone is here! No one is supposed to be here! Literally, no one is EVER here at this time!

Neera remained still as a statue, hoping the stranger

would eventually leave, but nope. They didn't. A small shadow lingered at the edge of the pool. The intruder stopped kicking their feet, then dipped a hand in, waving at her.

Actually *waving!*

Okay, so whoever it was knew Neera was there, and that she couldn't run. Adrenaline raced through her veins.

I can't run...but I can fight.

If it resorted to violence, she could knock them out with a water stream.

Neera flexed her fingers, affirming her decision. Her body shot upwards, ready to face them head-on and hopefully drag them down with her. When her head broke the surface, she was greeted by a beaming, slightly-tan face.

"Hey, Angelfish," Liam smirked, his unusually sharp canine gleaming. "You might want to start locking the door if this is a regular thing."

LIAM

Extremely satisfied by her shock, Liam watched her face revert back to its usual, cute look. When she first broke the surface like a fairytale princess with a murderous vendetta, he had to bite back his laughter.

He smiled effortlessly at the thought while the ache from not being near her finally subsided.

"What are you doing here?" Neera questioned, scanning the area behind him. "And how'd you even get in here?"

Liam pouted and dramatically clutched his left pec. "Why am I getting the feeling you're not happy to see me?" *Not even one smile!* "You're supposed to attack me with kisses, not questions."

A splash of water struck his face with a sniper's accuracy. His hands shot up in surrender as a chuckle bubbled in his chest.

"Okay, okay," Liam conceded as Neera lifted her arms,

preparing for another attack. He wiped his eyes on his soaked sweater. "I knew you couldn't stay away from the water, and this place happens to be the farthest from campus. I tried to surprise you earlier but was met with annoyed, old people."

Neera giggled. "But what are you doing here *now*? I don't remember us having plans tonight."

Liam's eyes fell on her smile, her plump lips capturing his attention. He leaned forward on his hands, bracing the rolled-up denim on his knees.

"That's kind of how surprises work." He smiled, which earned him another unwarranted splash.

Liam leaned back and wiped a palm down his face, expecting another attack. Instead, Neera's hands braced against his knees as she hoisted herself up on straight arms, face-to-face with him.

With no time to think–technically, there was plenty of time, but he lost most of it staring into her eyes–Neera brushed her lips over his.

"I missed you, too." Her voice, a whisper over his lips.

Liam held her elbows while deepening the kiss. Their kisses after *The Incident* were much different than before. Before, their lips met in naivety and uncertainty. Now, they held passion and promises. The good kind. As if every kiss could be their last, so he had to savor every single one of them.

Is it passion? Obsession? Love? All of the above?

All Liam knew was that the past five months have been nothing but eventful. He didn't care, though, as long as he was able to spend them with Neera. Despite her vehement demand to attend a different university from him. Some fluff about wanting him to "follow his dreams," or whatever, while knowing damn well that his dreams involved her.

They compromised, and he decided to attend DHU. It was no Ivy League college, with its small campus and lack of prestige programs, but it was only an hour away from UCLA with a decent biology program. Liam wasn't exactly into microbiology and genetics since everything that transpired, but he was still interested in science and research, so biology was generic enough to pursue other specialties in the near future. When he finally knew exactly what he wanted to do with his degree.

Well, he technically lost interest in microbiology and genetics the minute his family received the call confirming Dan's death.

No one took the news lightly, especially Danny. His little brother was unknowingly released from his father's hold on him, which caused him to lash out at Liam for not protecting him. Maybe when he grew up, he'd see that his death would lead to their freedom, as messed up as that sounded. Then again, Liam wasn't exactly faring any better from it. He just had more distractions to keep him from sinking.

Their worlds were flipped upside down while Liam knew the inevitable. Might've even caused it. Over time, the remorse just kept piling on his shoulders...until he spent less and less time with his family. Every weekend turned into every month, and sometimes even that wasn't secure.

Luckily the government didn't retaliate for *The Incident*. They called his family out of the blue, trying to intimidate them, except Liam now knew how they rolled. He countered them, claiming that if they tried to take them out, the scientific community would get very suspicious and appreciate uncovering a good conspiracy. Also, they have a practically indestructible–and unbearably annoying–force of nature constantly on standby at his home.

Long story short: They wouldn't spill if the government stayed still. A stalemate.

Speaking of Mateo...Liam still hadn't told Neera about the repercussions of that bite. When he almost admitted it on the island, he felt she wasn't in the right headspace with the way her eyes were dazed. Then time went on. Funeral, school, and family drama made Liam put it off until the next time.

Which never came.

Then, one night, while Liam was in bed, his body

suddenly itched all over. Something or things were crawling underneath his skin. When he checked, nothing was visibly there, yet the incessant itching didn't stop. He took a shower, practically scrubbing his skin raw, but it only worsened.

Then in an explosion of blinding pain...he could only remember bits and pieces.

He remembered water spraying him, then a bright, full moon and a deep howl penetrating the night air. It all seemed like a dream at first if he hadn't woken up in the middle of a forest, naked and covered in blood from a deer carcass next to him. No one witnessed it and called the police...at least he hoped.

That went on every full moon, but the itching would appear whenever Liam was furious or overwhelmed. He felt completely different. So out-of-control. He had to avoid activities that might cause his change, like hanging out at home and, unfortunately, football scrimmages. Although, he could handle tossing a ball around with acquaintances once in a while.

There were positives like his body was more muscular yet agile, his vision was sharper than ever, and his hearing was so precise that he could hear footsteps from a mile away and a person's heartbeat if they were up close.

The worst part was the almost-rabid craving for meat. He had never been a vegetarian in any form, but if he didn't eat rare-temperature meat for every meal, he would lose it. The craving only curbed the day after hunting, which he barely remembered. Maybe there were other ways to stave the change, but he'd rather pierce his ears than ask Mateo for help.

Liam had controlled his secret for as long as he could, so he was in no rush to tell Neera. Besides, if she found out, not only would she blame herself, but she'd force him to ask for Mateo's help. She'd be upset for keeping a big secret from her, but she'd forgive him once he explained his reasons.

Eventually.

Now, Liam would enjoy his time with his girlfriend. The

only thing in his life that made sense while the world spun around them.

Neera broke the kiss and glided back into the water with a smile capable of stealing any guy's heart. Fortunately, he happened to be her target. An amber hand reached out to him.

"Come to my world," her voice smoothly beckoned, like a siren leading a sailor to his impending death. However, Liam was prepared to fall and was nowhere near afraid. "I've got you, Darling."

Liam immediately cut his eyes away from hers at the mention of her nickname for him, his cheeks burning. Ever since he flustered the first time she called him that, she liked to sprinkle it occasionally whenever she really desired something. He had to admit, it worked every time.

It also beat being called *Dern*.

Officially ruining his nonchalance, Liam gazed back at Neera and noticed her smirking.

Oh, she definitely knows what she's doing.

Maintaining eye contact, he removed his sweater and tossed it to the side. Neera dropped her hand and backed up, making room for him. Still in his rolled-up jeans, he slid into the pool water, dipping his head in to adjust to the cold temperature. While treading in place, Neera swam around him like a shark circling her prey but more gracefully.

Her head popped up a few inches from his face so stealthily he briefly tensed. She cupped his face with both hands, staring into his soul with her sea-green eyes. Her freckles peppered over her nose and under her eyes resembled small footprints across a smooth shore. He wanted to kiss each one of those footprints.

"I will never let you drown," Neera whispered a promise.

Liam placed his hands on her waist, skimming the area where her skin hardened into scales. "I don't doubt it."

Not for a second.

She smiled again, then grabbed his hands from her waist. She took a deep breath, causing Liam to follow suit, and pulled him further down. The pressure built as they descended, his eardrums popping. Liam's eyes burned from the chlorine as he kept them open.

He refused to miss a thing.

When his bare feet flattened at the bottom of the pool, his lungs were on fire. His body wanted to freak out, but he reigned it in, trusting his love floating in front of him. Neera eyed him suspiciously, waiting for something.

His heart raced as his body went into alarm. Lungs burning, his veins constricted in his limbs as his mouth threatened to gape open. He tried to distract himself by staring at Neera. Her hair floated behind her as her eyes began to close in concentration. Her necklace glowed dimly before brightening.

Then her eyes fluttered open...the irises glowing dimly.

That was new.

Neera floated closer to him before cupping his face and planting her mouth over his, blocking the water from entering his mouth. Instinctively, Liam wrapped his arms around her waist and pulled her flush against him.

Air–actual oxygen–entered into his lungs from their kiss!

He couldn't even think of any scientific reasoning for it before his body felt heavy, as if gravity was turned back on.

Neera's body started sliding down, but Liam pulled her back up and tightened his hold on her waist, her hair no longer floating but hanging heavily. He peeled his eyes away from her and examined the area.

They were still in the pool but inside some sort of air barrier. A bubble, maybe. The water was actively being repelled away from them in a dome formation.

The pocket of air she provided in their kiss waned as he reached his breathing limit, some of the trapped carbon dioxide slipping out. He stopped himself from inhaling a little longer. Neera broke the kiss, causing Liam to clamp his mouth shut, preserving as much air as he could.

"Breathe, Darling," she mouthed.

The old Liam would've retreated, swimming as fast as he could to the surface to obnoxiously inhale gulps of fresh air. The logical side of him would never take a breath at the bottom of a pool.

Except...when was the last time the world made sense? When has following the rules of life benefited him?

So Liam closed his eyes, inhaling glorious air.

TO BE CONTINUED...

AFTERWORD

Want to know more about what happens to Liam and Neera's story? Want to hear more about our beloved Mateo's life before the island? Want to discover the origins and beginnings of the two families?

Look out for Sunken Secrets, the second book in The Fated Tails series, coming soon in 2025.

If you want any more information on the Fated Tails series, or more content on our favorite characters, feel free to follow me on Instagram, Pinterest, and Facebook.

ACKNOWLEDGEMENT

Since I am a self-published author, I'll keep this short and cute.

If it wasn't for the love and unyielding support of my family–Ilene, Qiana, and Don–I wouldn't be here today. For providing me the space, time, and continuous opportunities to be my true self and follow my true passions. I wouldn't have the courage to write or be anything more than I believed I could be. They may be small, but they're mighty.

I want to thank all my best friends who have shown me that family can be as diverse as an ocean, and that it doesn't have to be linked by blood.

Lastly–and most importantly–I want to thank the people taking time out of their day to read my book. For giving a first-time, self-published author a chance. I am forever grateful for you all, and will never forget your enthusiasm for diverse stories. I hope you continue to ride my emotional rollercoaster of a series with me.

ABOUT THE AUTHOR

Stephanie Gidron

Stephanie Gidron is a Black, debuting author from Arlington, Virginia with a huge dream of becoming a best-selling author. Spending most of her life watching Korean dramas, learning multiple languages, and dabbling in a variety of art mediums have contributed to her love of emotional rollercoasters disguised as diverse "Romantasies", and anything related to the human condition. The more meaningful the story, the better.

As a person living with anxiety and depression, she writes stories depicting characters with mental health issues or have suffered from severe trauma because they deserve love, too. They shouldn't be hidden from society or have to wait to receive it, they're deserving of love the way they are.

www.ingramcontent.com/pod-product-compliance
Lightning Source LLC
Chambersburg PA
CBHW030545260626
47157CB00006B/2192